THE MAGICIAN AND THE MECHANICAL DOLL

TALES OF A VERNIAN YOUTH

VOLUME 1

Editing by Julie C. Gilbert

Cover illustration by Florian Garbay

Interior illustrations and design by Gaius J. Augustus, PhD

Published by JourneyWorx

More information at gaiusjaugustus.com

THE MAGICIAN AND THE MECHANICAL DOLL

TALES OF A VERNIAN YOUTH

Volume 1

GAIUS J. AUGUSTUS

TABLE OF CONTENTS

DEDICATION

To you, without whom this book—a combination of sometimes random words printed with ink on random bits of paper and glued together in, hopefully, a non-random order—would not exist.

ABOUT THIS SERIES

Octavian, a promising graduate student of magic, is about to have his dreams shattered. As he activates his magical robot, Replika, the duo finds themselves thrust into an alternate reality of stuck doors and steam-powered tech. Little did Octavian know that his enigmatic research advisor, Teacher, held the technology to traverse alternate realities! Octavian and Replika embark on a quest to uncover Teacher's hidden secrets and find their way back home.

Join Replika and Octavian as they journey through immersive universes that will make you laugh out loud. Amidst their adventures, they encounter a vibrant cast of characters and stumble upon more than their fair share of other people's problems. Will they ever find their way back home, or will they remain trapped forever in this web of realities?

The Tales of a Vernian Youth Series beckons you into a multiverse brimming with enchantment and absurdity. With diverse characters that infuse a refreshing twist into the narrative and a writing style reminiscent of the great Douglas Adams, this series promises laughter, adventure, and more stuck doors than you can shake a wand at.

Get ready for a whimsical, magic-filled adventure that transports our travelers to both fantastical and eerily familiar destinations. Think Terry Pratchett with a dash of scientific curiosity and Ben Aaronovitch minus the police. This thrilling concoction will keep you turning pages long into the night.

Are you ready to traverse the boundaries of reality? Don't miss out on this epic adventure!

INTRODUCTION

Thank you for embarking on this magical journey full of twists, turns, and stuck doors. I hope you enjoy this heartfelt tale punctuated by humorous asides. I started on the first draft of the ToVY Series in 2014. It's gone through many iterations to get to where it is today—including a shift in genre—but I'm very proud to present the first in this series of adventures.

Please note that, at the end of this book, you'll find the Compendium, where many terms are defined and explained.

Many characters in this work use gender-neutral pronouns. Here is a guide to the usage of a selection of common pronouns.

FEMALE	MALE	GENDER NEUTRAL
She	He	They/Ze/Xe/It
Her	Him	Their/Zir/Xir/It
Hers	His	Theirs/Zirs/Xirs/Its

Examples:
He/She/They/Ze/Xe/It went to the store.
I want to talk to him/her/them/zir/xir/it.
This book is his/hers/theirs/zirs/xirs/its.

CONTENT NOTES

This story contains direct or indirect mentions of the following themes. Please ensure you have a care plan in place if any of these items may trigger you. Note that these may contain spoilers. This list may not be comprehensive.

Death (on and off page), abandonment, verbal abuse, vertigo, being pursued, enclosed spaces, guns (including a shooting), violent attack, hoarding, theft, drowning, kidnapping/capture, held at knife point, large fire, gender dysphoria.

1

TALES OF A VERNIAN YOUTH SERIES

THE *Magician* AND THE MECHANICAL DOLL

1

THE MAGICIAN GRAD STUDENT

The average graduate student isn't excitable. Bring up the latest weather, sports event, or culinary experience, and they may even nod off from overwork and underpay. Of course, if the topic of conversation is their latest research project, the newest magical proof in their field, or starting a bakery, a graduate student's attention will be piqued, but they are sure to have opinions that are more adept at keeping them awake than the triple espresso latte they pick up before each work day.

Octavian wasn't a typical PhD student, though he was as overworked and underpaid as any other. He didn't drink coffee, and starting a bakery sounded like one of the most tedious career paths he could imagine. These were good enough reasons not to commiserate with his peers but weren't the reasons his peers avoided commiserating with him. He not only was under the tutelage of an Exalted Grand Magician known for being reclusive, ornery, and bad at sharing. Additionally, Octavian's course of study was taboo.

This unorthodox course of study was what led Octavian to arrive on the campus of the National University of Magic far earlier than any sane person should. The meeting time had been set by his academic advisor, one of the most dislikable people he'd met since beginning his PhD program at NUM. And he'd met his fair share of dislikable people here.

The NUM campus was nestled in the western mountainside overlooking O'er, the capital city of the large island nation of Ledina, and the Bay of Levashka. In the bay below, tour guides bobbed up and down on boats, enjoying the breeze on what was, for them, a normal Friday morning. Sunbeams peeked from behind the mountains to the east, where the sun was rising with no sense of urgency. A dozen tour boats waited in the open water, each controlled by a magic marble with computing power one might categorize as overkill. The tour boats held hundreds of tourists, who couldn't care less about the everyday marble computers within their boats. Instead, they held cameras at the ready with increasing anticipation as the sun crept upward inch by inch. Despite the sun's sluggish ascension, the hundreds of onlookers were waiting on it, their gazes locked on a single white, silver-capped obelisk.

Stretching higher into the sky than any other building in the city, the structure was home to the International Council of Exalted Magicians. Only the most powerful Magicians were granted the title of Exalted Grand, and only those with the title could be part of the council. This exclusivity was great for ensuring the integrity of the science of magic as well as procuring the best seats at any sporting event, theater show, or cafe. And the secrecy of ICEM was ideal for a myriad of reasons, including keeping the tourism business booming in cities around the world, apparently.

Obelisk onlookers weren't shy about trading hypotheses regarding the mystery of what lay within its walls. Many guesses included deep occult secrets, private illicit rituals, and dark conspiracies, while others assumed there were private pools, badminton courts, and ample meditation.

Neither of these was true. In fact, many Exalted Grand Magicians had harsh feelings against the dark side of the occult as well as badminton.

Finally, the sun emerged from behind the mountain peaks, figuratively smiling upon the silver cap of the obelisk. Meanwhile, the tourists in their boats literally smiled in the exaggerated way that tourists often do. Unknown to the sightseers—though not to the tour guides, who were quite knowledgeable about their city—the sun's rays also reflected off of the obelisk, back toward the mountains, through the National University of Magic's historic archway, and into a large circular plaza.

Stone Plaza, as it was called, was not so much made of stone as it was made of millions of gemstones. A two-hundred-foot-wide masterpiece of design and craftsmanship, each shard of noctralite was laid at a precise angle such that, after charging in the sun's light, it luminesced at the intended intensity.

The university seal sat at the center, and the gemstones that made up the university's initials glowed even in the daylight. It was quite a remarkable display, which was tainted by its proximity to one of the most unremarkable and frustrating buildings on the campus: the administration building. This, unfortunately, was Octavian's destination.

The intrepid graduate student sighed as he walked around the edge of the plaza, glancing at the explanatory sign nearby. Although he had never read it—and today was not the day that was going to change—he correctly assumed it listed facts about the university's connection with the International Council of Exalted Magicians.

After glancing back to be sure his bag was still floating beside him, he started up the ramp to the administration building. His bag bobbed up and down as it followed, oblivious to his angst. Even the fresh coat of paint on the administration building's trim didn't soothe the uneasiness in his stomach.

Once inside, Octavian started up the large, circular rampway that wound up and around an atrium that stretched to the third floor. Portraits of Exalted Grand Magicians lined the walls, each a former student of this National University of Magic campus. Octavian read each of the plaques below as he passed, scoffing at the words "Exalted Grand Magician," which sat before every single name.

He followed the signs up the rampway, down hallways, and through doorways until he reached the office of Grand Magician Kastra. A "Do Not Disturb" message glowed just in front of it, and beyond the message, Octavian could sense a low-level trap keeping the door locked. That message was meant for him, so he resigned himself to waiting.

Casual seating areas scattered throughout the hall, as if to warn visitors they were going to waste precious moments of their lives waiting there. With a heaving sigh, he sat down, The chair was even more firm than it looked, and not in a good way.

Along the walls hung frames with portraits of each year's doctoral graduates. On one side, the people of the feminine discipline stared across the hall at the graduates of the masculine discipline, who stared right back.

It was a total misnomer to call the disciplines "feminine" and "masculine" as there was nothing masculine or feminine about magic. When the study of magic was in its infancy, the not-so-grand magicians sought to organize magic. At the time, Grand Magician Ostara Patel noted in an often-quoted paper that magic could be categorized into a finite set of research areas. He divided these areas into two disciplines based on wild, speculative, anecdotal, and overall bad evidence.

Magicians who happened to be women weren't allowed to be designated Grand Magicians at that time. Years later, some forgotten magician who was much grander than Ostara Patel awarded the title to Chioma Obiakaraije. On that day, she became the first woman to be named Grand Magician and the most powerful Grand Magician of her time. Grand Magician Patel's blunder was not taught in schools, though the later reorganization of subdisciplines by Grand Obiakaraije had become a standard part of every magic curriculum.

Octavian, still being stared at by NUM graduate portraits, rolled his eyes at all of their smiles as he contemplated whether he would make it to graduation.

The seat remained awkward—maybe even worse the longer he sat in it. He leaned forward, then laid his head back against the wall, then crossed his legs. None of it comforted him. He tried to ignore the frames along the walls, instead focusing on what he would say when that door opened. Someday.

He may have been about to die from boredom and anxiety when a loud click preceded the creak of the door. Octavian rushed to his feet, almost tripping over his floating bag as he tried to keep eye contact with his academic advisor. The effort to do so was enough to knock the wind from him, and he missed the opportunity to say hello.

Grand Magician Kastra was not a man of few words, but he knew how to hone his words into sharp edges. Octavian had only met with him twice before today, once for his initial course suggestions and then again for a progress review at the end of his first year.

It was distracting enough that the man had a pointed nose that looked like it could cut butter, but his taste in clothes was, to put it kindly, dated. To put it unkindly, his clothes were gaudy, in poor taste, and ugly. The flashy outfit made Octavian quite embarrassed to even be in a room alone with the man, and he was suddenly glad that the office was in a seldom visited hallway of one of the most avoided buildings on campus.

When Octavian managed to pull his attention back to Kastra's words, they gave him no better feelings toward the man.

Those ill feelings meant that, while most of Octavian's cohort was getting course suggestions from their academic advisors, he had chosen to fumble along on his own. That limited approach had brought him here, where he was obligated to contact the Grand Magician for assistance. Despite the need for advising, he already regretted reaching out.

"Your message said that you need assistance choosing classes for next semester," the Grand Magician said.

Grand Kastra stepped back into his office and gestured toward a wooden chair with ornate carvings decorating every exposed inch.

"Yes, Grand Kastra," Octavian responded as he eased into the chair. It creaked, and fear shot through him. Had he broken it? The many layers of lacquer and dozens of hand-carved reliefs probably made the chair priceless. And if there was one chair that Octavian did not want to break, it was this one. Somehow, this seemed like the most inappropriate and yet most likely time for it to happen.

As soon as the two magicians were seated on opposite sides of the desk—both in unbroken chairs, thankfully—the door closed with a gentle click. Octavian sensed the trap on the door activate, locking it. Swallowing the lump in his throat, he forced himself to sit up straight, though his fidgeting hands betrayed his anxiety.

"I was hoping to get recommendations from you based on my unique professional goals," he said.

Grand Kastra sat back in his chair. He held up his hand, and the small marble sitting on his desk glowed. The dark red marble was a typical computer, though it sat on a decorative stand tuned to Grand Kastra's unique aesthetic.

An interface appeared above it, floating in the air and glowing faintly. Although the contents were obscured from where Octavian sat, he knew what Grand Kastra was doing: looking for ammunition to add to the judgment he had already made.

"Your unique professional goals, yes." Grand Kastra's tone bordered on mocking, though he kept a stern expression. "I was reviewing your records."

Octavian gripped the arms of the chair to keep his hands still, but his tense posture was no less revealing of his emotion.

"You're still in the Exalted Grand Magician's tutelage, correct?" Kastra asked as he controlled his marble with gestures.

The Exalted Grand Magician that Kastra mentioned was Octavian's research advisor, who was responsible for the PhD student's research and training. Grand Kastra, as his academic advisor, was responsible for helping him craft an academic plan of study. Though the Grand Magician was strict and curt, Octavian knew he'd face this same disheartening conversation no matter who he was assigned as academic advisor.

"Yes, that's right," Octavian replied. "And the Exalted Grand has approved all of my coursework so far. So I just need help with—"

"Octavian, I'm concerned," Grand Kastra interrupted as he stopped scrolling, probably devoting an entire inner monologue to his triumph in finding the ammunition he needed.

The man's sharp nose turned back to Octavian. Trying to distract himself from wondering how many times the man had stabbed someone with it, Octavian made eye contact and immediately regretted the decision.

Grand Kastra's irises were mostly gold, with a small rim of brown remaining at the edge. The eye color change from natural to unnatural was a clear indicator of his Grand Magician expertise, but Octavian also wondered if it was possible for the eye color change to be a measure of his haughtiness.

That wasn't a thing, but it gave him a thought to escape to for a moment.

He knew what was coming because it seemed to be what everyone in the magic community focused on. Not his talent or his persistence, but his course of study. The only comfort he could bring himself was to bite the inside of his cheek and clench his jaw, which wasn't all that comforting.

"I recall you attended a small university for your undergraduate degree," Kastra continued. "It's quite unorthodox that your school allowed you to double major in both Life Science Magic and Magical Engineering. But that kind of indecisiveness cannot continue."

And there it was.

This wasn't the first time a professor expressed their concern about his choice in disciplines, or, to be more accurate, his lack of choice between the two. Life Science Magic was in the masculine discipline while Engineering & Technology was a feminine subdiscipline.

Octavian opened his mouth to recite the response he had practiced in the hallway.

"Grand—"

Kastra's hand dropped down onto the desk, sounding a firm thud with a clear meaning. That small but loud gesture asserted with great clarity that nothing the graduate student said would be heard.

"One does not try to be an expert in both disciplines, Octavian. You either study in the masculine discipline or you study in the feminine discipline, not both. Your graduate transcript makes it obvious that you are continuing on a path unbecoming of a magician trained at NUM. And I cannot believe your mentor, a member of the International Council of Exalted Magicians, would approve such a reckless and offensive academic plan.

"My understanding based on your first-year statement of study was that your . . . unique undergraduate career was somewhat inspired by your gender transition."

This was why Octavian hadn't visited the Grand Magician to share his second- or third-year statements of study. His words would be taken out of context as long as he chose to ignore discipline boundaries.

Kastra continued as Octavian concentrated on not rolling his eyes.

"I applaud your ability to challenge your limits and complete your double major at the undergraduate level. However, I cannot advise you on any further graduate coursework until you get past this roadblock and choose a discipline."

Grand Kastra stood, the door traps unlocked, and the following click and creak told Octavian it was time to leave.

His body felt heavier with each step toward the building's back exit. Tears welled up, but he wiped them away before they could reach his cheeks. Every portrait he passed in the halls seemed to stare down at him with proud arrogance.

As soon as he was outside, he let out a frustrated scream before looking around to make sure no one was watching. Not that he had a reputation to worry about, but it just seemed like the thing to do.

A glow emanated from around his neck. He pulled out Notebook, the glowing marble computer that hung from his chain necklace. Bursts of light relayed a message from his research advisor.

"From: Teacher

Message: You're late."

Octavian's face reddened. He screamed again, this time kicking his bag as hard as he could. Unaffected by his effort, the bag bobbed up and down until it was back at his side. He took a few deep breaths before tapping the marble to send a response.

"Reply," Octavian said. The marble's green glow pulsed on and off as it waited for his response. "Be there in five."

2

The Mechanical Doll

The School of Biomedical Sciences Building sat to the east of Stone Plaza. Clad in bright white stone with gold detailing, it stood in stark contrast to the building where he worked, the original lab building which was tucked behind. Octavian lovingly referred to it in his mind as well-worn, but it was quite obvious that the building was in a state of disrepair. The brick exterior was cracking, and vines that once were charming now blocked the side entrance.

As Octavian pushed the vines aside to reach the door, he had to swipe his hand across the old lock three times before it recognized his magic essence. If he was in the mood, he might have laughed at how the lock's dim glowing computer marble was twice as large as the one he kept around his neck. But today, he just heaved his shoulder against the unlocked door to try to get it unstuck in one push. It took throwing his body against it twice and a groan of annoyance to do the trick.

As he exited the stairwell into the hallway on the third floor, he was met with less than kind words from his mentor, known to all only as Teacher.

"Seven minutes."

Octavian pushed his hand through his short, white hair and bit the inside of his cheek. He wasn't in the mood to bicker today.

"I'm sorry, Teacher. My meeting with Grand Kastra started late. I'll do my best to—"

"You're late because you met with that sleazy old bastard?" scoffed his mentor.

Bickering would be unavoidable, it seemed.

"You haven't had time to help me choose my courses for next semester since the Replika project is almost complete, so—"

"If you got yourself here on time once in a while, she would be done," Teacher interrupted again.

It was the usual complaint, well-founded by Octavian's typical two- or three-minute tardiness.

"And Kastra doesn't understand the first thing about your academic plan," Teacher continued.

"He refused to help me," Octavian explained.

"You shouldn't need his help."

Teacher furrowed his brow, his deep wrinkles squeezing together to accentuate his distaste. He shook his head and waved his hand as if willing the conversation away. "Nevermind," the old magician stated. "It doesn't matter anyway."

"Nevermind? But my academic plan—"

"Doesn't matter. Did you not hear me?"

How many times did he have to be interrupted today? Octavian huffed. Of course it didn't matter to Teacher. He was just a lowly, underpaid, underappreciated graduate student. He spun on his heels and stomped from the hall into the break room, where he threw his bag into the cabinet he used as a locker.

In blatant disobedience, the bag decelerated to keep itself from hitting the back wall, then bobbed downward until it sat just so on the shelf below it. Octavian snatched his work clothes from the top shelf.

"I'll join you in the lab as soon as I change," he called.

Teacher didn't respond and was gone when Octavian returned to the hallway.

In the bathroom across the hall, Octavian pulled on his worn brown pants, lightweight white shirt, and soft leather vest. He checked the loops and pockets. With a quick spell, he tightened the thread on a loosened loop. After fastening his steel-toed boots, he made his way toward the active lab at the far end of the hall.

His footsteps echoed around the empty hallway. At some point before Octavian joined, more than fifty researchers had worked in Teacher's laboratory group. Many of those researchers went on to win their own prestigious awards. They were never shy to mention their association with Teacher in public forums. After all, to be mentored by an Exalted Grand Magician was a huge honor.

But those researchers grew adept at avoiding speaking about Teacher's demeanor. This came as no surprise to anyone who knew Teacher, especially his university colleagues and his sole overworked graduate student. The halls that once bustled with activity were now empty. The only sounds were those from Octavian's boots making their way down the hall.

Octavian stepped into a small, glass-walled room at the lab's entrance. A panel sat next to the door, and he pressed a button to activate the contaminant scanner. As he waited, Teacher leafed through a hand-written notebook. Teacher usually preferred to review his notes in the early hours of the morning, before Octavian arrived, so Octavian was quite surprised to see Teacher busying himself, flipping through pages, and making last minute scribbles.

Once the scan was complete—with no contaminants found—Octavian collected his tools for work. Teacher was pacing while he grumbled at his notebook, so Octavian took a few moments to calm himself.

During the first moment, he took several deep breaths.

For the next, he noted the smell of machinery lubricants and reveled in the smell of old clutter.

And then he ruined the moment by remembering the meeting he had come from. Oh, well. It was worth a try.

Teacher still seemed lost in thought, leaving Octavian with time to look around the room. He'd done so on many occasions, but it was better than retreating into his thoughts.

The only window in the room was long and horizontal, as if designed to sit above the built-in, wooden cabinets that sat underneath. At a particular time in the early morning, light peeked in through tree branches and vines. Despite how much Octavian liked the natural light, Teacher often threatened to cover it up, complaining that windows didn't belong on the south sides of buildings.

The National University of Magic had once debuted an international campus in the Middle East. The architecture firm chosen for the project had no experience on design for that climate, and it later became obvious that they overlooked many important points in such a design.

The most famous—and deadly—example was in the choice to face the entire south side of the building with windows. It was rumored that during the first class held there, every student left with a serious sunburn and several were taken to the hospital for heatstroke.

It's rare for rumors to be less serious than the real story.

In this case, the architecture of the building contributed to the deaths of construction crew members before a student ever stepped foot inside. A lawsuit ensued after the first, and it wasn't until the fourth that an agreement was reached to redesign the structure under the supervision of a new, local architecture firm.

After the first semester, during which several popular ghost chasing shows featured the building, the campus was shut down. Apparently, most students weren't keen on taking classes at a haunted campus.

The discipline that this campus was meant to focus on? Engineering & Technology, specifically architecture.

Octavian had never heard the story of the cursed middle east campus, and he thought a bit of natural light in the lab was very nice.

He turned his attention to the old, wooden, glass-front cabinets that sat underneath the window. Among the lab notebooks, random mechanical parts, and books on magical theory was one item that always caught his eye.

It was an old computer, but unlike the small marbles used for modern magic, this computer would fill his palm. He'd never had the chance to get a good look at it since Teacher kept the cabinets locked, but it was unique enough to always catch his eye.

It was round but ornately decorated. The bottom half was coated in gold plating with flourishes of vines and flowers that wound around like ivy. Three branches of these vines reached up over the top half where they came together around . . . something. Octavian thought it was a crystal, but it was facing away from him, so he couldn't be sure.

Between the vines was the distinctive quality of the computer's design. The computer hanging on the chain around Octavian's neck, like every computer Octavian had ever seen, was translucent but solid. But within the three branches of flowers and vines tarnished from time, the computer in the cabinet appeared to have a hollow interior. Peering from afar and squinting as hard as he could, Octavian thought he almost, maybe, possibly saw some color inside.

With a deep sigh, he returned to his workstation and pulled his personal computer marble, Notebook, from under his shirt. He tapped it to bring up its visual interface and reviewed the previous days' notes.

He couldn't help but glance up every so often to check on his mentor. Teacher was a very old, very strict, and very private man. He was a member of the International Council of Exalted Magicians—one of only two from the university, twenty from the country, and one of just a hundred in the world.

He had developed a slew of magic therapeutics for several diseases. His work on permanent prostheses had won him many accolades and continued funding. This success earned him enough laboratory space to fill the entire top floor of the building, even though it now seemed lifeless and neglected. Instruments and machinery gathered dust day after day, even as other faculty members requested access.

No one was clear why Teacher wouldn't share his space. Some claimed he didn't learn the value of sharing as a young boy, while others claimed he was trying to hide a secret research project. One of these was very close to the truth.

Octavian scrolled through the schematics of his thesis. The Replika project was a marvel of robotics that would change the way biomedical treatments were performed. Replika's capabilities were far more advanced than any robotic system before, and it was the first to have a fully integrated magic-based operating system.

Teacher was rather aloof and never one to share too many details. However, Octavian's own work notes of Replika's innovative systems convinced him that their work would make leaps and bounds for prostheses quality, drug delivery, and regenerative medicine. As Octavian reviewed the systems that he would be testing today, he couldn't help but smile at its ingenuity.

Replika rested on an adjustable table that sat at a forty-five degree angle to the ground. Although Teacher called Replika a "mechanical doll," he had designed it—that is, he had designed "her" to be lifelike in aesthetics as well as in demeanor.

Her dark brown skin was indistinguishable in texture from his own golden tan. The tight black curls that cascaded from her scalp were soft and full of body. Octavian once joked that her hair was more real than his own white, thick locks, which he styled short and tidy.

Teacher had been less than amused.

The one hint that Replika was artificial was a pair of large purple eyes, a color that Teacher must have special ordered or custom-crafted. Despite standing out, the eyes didn't detract from her realism. Had Octavian not known this was a robot, even her eyes wouldn't have been enough to convince him. It was the kind of craftsmanship only possible from an Exalted Grand Magician.

Teacher's fashion sense was another story.

Replika wore a dress more suited for a child than a medical device. Though it was a simple design, it poofed out at the shoulders, and the skirt was lifted into a round shape by a petticoat. Octavian was no fashionista, but he didn't see people around campus dressing like this. He couldn't imagine why Teacher thought it was appropriate.

When Octavian reached the part of his notes discussing Replika's behavioral algorithms, he skipped to the section covering the order to activate each startup element several times.

Of particular importance was when to activate her personality matrix. Replika had a full and enriched personality, as far as Octavian could tell from the cursory review he was allowed. Her complex personality matrix had fascinated him ever since he got his first look at her a few years prior, and Teacher's offhand remarks inferred a feminine demeanor.

However, despite the gendered personality and fashion, her actual body was androgynous. Octavian never asked Teacher why he made this choice, and Teacher never brought it up.

In fact, Teacher avoided talking about gender altogether. When Octavian had built up the courage to discuss his own gender transition with Teacher, the old man had refused to hear it, going so far as to leave the room without a word. He even locked himself in the office he used as a bedroom for the rest of the day. Octavian wasn't sure whether Teacher knew he was transgender, though it seemed impossible for him not to.

However, he obviously approved of the cross-discipline approach Octavian had studied. It sometimes came up during Octavian's work on Replika, and Teacher always assumed Octavian could do what needed to be done, whether it involved magic of the masculine discipline or of the feminine. This was a rare and open-minded trait for such a strict curmudgeon.

"Check Replika's internal sensor readings," Teacher blurted out of nowhere.

Octavian jumped in surprise, unsure when he'd zoned out.

"I did that before I left last night," replied Octavian.

"Then do it again."

Octavian rolled his eyes as he deactivated the display of his notes and started a recording of his day's work.

Performing these tests again was quite necessary, and Teacher had made it clear that one of two things could happen if done incorrectly. One was an explosion, which was terrifying. The other was shorting out the whole system, causing them to have to rebuild many parts of Replika's technology from scratch, the most notable being her power core.

All Octavian knew about the core was that it used magic in a way never seen before. Once turned on, it generated its own energy. To deactivate it, the core would need to be removed from its auxiliary systems, a process that was quite tedious and would ruin many of Replika's internal systems.

The information about the manufacturing of the core was a well-kept secret. There had never existed anything like it in the world, and Octavian didn't know exactly where it was made, who it was manufactured by, or how long it took to create.

He didn't intend to find out. He was doing everything he could to ensure that her activation was a success, and he may have had a few fingers and toes crossed for extra luck. Even magicians need luck sometimes.

Octavian's curiosity had once led him to engage Teacher in a discussion about the power core. He had pursued Teacher when he left the lab without a word. He'd even knocked on the door when Teacher locked himself in his office.

Teacher had proceeded to send a text to Octavian telling him to go home for the day. Instead, Octavian went for way more comfort food than he should have eaten and was sick for the rest of the night.

"After you're done with that," Teacher interrupted as Octavian worked, "we should check the alignment of Replika's stabilizers, both for the core and peripheral systems. Since they've been on for a few days, I want to be sure they don't show any signs of strain."

Teacher paused to consider Octavian, though Octavian didn't know what he was being considered for.

"I suppose," Teacher said, drawing out the words in clear reluctance, "you should start considering which journal you want to submit to."

Was this an attempt at caring about another human being?

"I may need help with that," Octavian said, trying not to sound as unsure as he felt. "At first I thought a robotics journal would be best, but then maybe biomedical would be better. Could you—"

"You don't need my help," interrupted Teacher. "Figure it out."

Teacher's expression made it clear that the conversation was over.

Octavian sighed, though he wasn't surprised by the response. So much for caring about another human being.

"We'll finish our final tests this evening, and get her up and running first thing tomorrow morning," Teacher said.

In other words, there would be no sleeping tonight.

"Do you really think we can finish today?"

"We will."

It wasn't strange to work through the night, but something about the way Teacher's gaze shifted when he said it made Octavian uneasy.

"Good thing I brought a change of clothes."

Teacher rarely left the lab building and had transformed some of the unused areas of the floor into a full-time living space. Octavian even had his own sleeping and washing space, which he used far more often than he would like.

"Focus on the details as you work," Teacher continued as if Octavian hadn't said a thing.

"Of course."

"And today, I'll need to approve every procedure checklist as you complete them."

"Really?"

Teacher had never even looked at his checklists before. It was adding to the oddities of the day and not helping Octavian's nerves.

"Octavian," Teacher grumbled in a warning tone.

"I'm sorry. I mean, yes, of course."

And so, Octavian got back to work while Teacher didn't do much of anything at all.

3

DID HE DIE, THO?

The day turned to night, and Teacher showed signs of fatigue, though that didn't stop him from giving Octavian orders. Teacher ordered food from a nearby 24-hour restaurant, but by the time it arrived, Octavian's stomach was in knots.

As they ate, Teacher's eyes drifted around the room, his foot tapped, and his hands shook. Octavian couldn't help but watch as Teacher seemed to process some private terror. Teacher swallowed his last bite of food.

Out of nowhere, he asked, "Do you remember the Multiple Realities Theory I've told you about?"

The casual mention of this topic startled Octavian so much he almost choked on the food he was trying to swallow. He coughed as he remembered the one and only time this topic had been mentioned, in one tight-lipped and awkward conversation after his first semester in the lab.

Over thirty years ago, the International Council of Exalted Magicians had declared travel to alternate realities as a scientific impossibility. In their short yet blasphemous conversation, Teacher had informed Octavian that the ICEM was wrong in the same breath he had sworn Octavian to secrecy about it.

"Drink," Teacher fussed as Octavian tried to get the food down the right tube. "Now, do you remember or don't you?"

Octavian forced out an answer before taking a sip of water. "Yes, sir."

He took a moment to clear his throat before making eye contact with Teacher again. His mentor was silent, waiting for more, although Octavian wasn't sure what he wanted to hear.

"Well," Octavian continued, doing his best to recall this vague memory. "You told me a fellow scientist had almost completed the magical proof for travel to an alternate reality, but they were unable to complete it because the work was destroyed."

"The proof wasn't almost complete. My dear friend completed the work but was never able to present the magical proof," Teacher corrected, as if this was common knowledge.

"I see," was all Octavian could think to say.

"And then my colleague mysteriously died," Teacher said in grim seriousness.

Octavian's raised eyebrow gave away that, while he was nodding, he did not remember that particular detail. He was pretty sure he would remember something like that.

"Who was this colleague? I must've heard of them."

"No, I can assure you that you haven't. But you will."

"Why? Are you going to present their theories to the ICEM?"

"Don't be ridiculous. I only have bits and pieces of the magical proof. To complete it would be a lifetime of work, and— Well, I'm not getting any younger, am I?" Teacher let out a long sigh before adding, "But you . . ."

The long pause nagged at Octavian's curiosity. "What about me?"

"Listen to me, and stop interrupting."

Octavian hadn't interrupted, but he chose not to remind his mentor of that.

Teacher let the echo of his voice fall to silence before beginning a long and detailed description of the project's history. He spoke so fast and in such minute and opaque detail that Octavian couldn't understand and knew he wouldn't remember.

24

Teacher spoke until Octavian's mind was mush.

As he got lost in his train of thought, he kept going back to how wrong this all seemed. It almost sounded like Teacher wanted him to take this on as his thesis project, which would doom him to failure.

"You've stopped listening," Teacher called out.

"I just don't understand what you're telling me."

Teacher grumbled. "I know. Of course you don't." He shook his head. "I've never told anyone else about the Multiple Realities Theory. But I know you're the right one to tell."

This didn't come across as the compliment Teacher intended.

"I think you're overestimating my abilities," Octavian mumbled.

"Well, you're not the most brilliant magical scientist I've ever met," Teacher grumbled. Then he added, "But, someday, I know you will be."

Teacher had never said anything close to this before, barely even given him a positive critique and definitely never a compliment.

Octavian grabbed his plate and turned away to hide the tears welling up in his eyes. When he stood to take his plate to the sink, Teacher stopped him.

"We can clean up later," Teacher said. "I think it's about time we activated Replika."

Something changed for Octavian, a feeling of dissociation from the physical world. They set up a magical shield around Replika in case anything went wrong. Teacher gave his student very specific instructions. Octavian must have followed those directions, but it was as if he was outside his own body, controlling it more as a puppet than its owner.

He seemed aware—in an incorporeal way—of every inch of space in the lab. The light from the rising sun peeking through the one window of the lab. Every tool on the counters. Every tile on the floor. Every book and knickknack and spare part in the cabinets. And as Teacher prepared the remote activation device and declared that it was time, he became aware that something was missing.

Teacher pulled his favorite old, raggedy chair from his bedroom into the lab. Octavian could sense that something was about to happen, something wrong.

Abruptly, he realized what had been missing. The computer, typically in the cabinets under the window, was now in Teacher's hand. Teacher rolled it around in his palm. He rubbed the transparent casing with his sleeve. He traced the tarnished finishings with his fingers with great care.

The inside of the computer was indeed hollow, at least the top half was. Something about the device was glowing, though he couldn't tell what. But it was beautiful.

"Are you ready, Octavian?" Teacher asked.

Octavian gave a weak smile, but before he could respond, he watched Teacher place his finger at the bottom of the computer. A bright, blue light flashed, and Octavian tried to call out to Teacher, to tell him to wait. But all too clearly, he watched Teacher's thumb push the large button along the side of the device.

Abruptly, the floor seemed to fall from under Octavian's feet. He looked down to see his feet still planted on the ground, yet the feeling of his stomach pulling up into his throat disoriented him.

Teacher's old, unstable chair broke with a loud crack. Just as he snapped his eyes back to his mentor, Teacher's body slumped over. The limp form folded over itself and fell to the floor in a pile.

Octavian tried to call out to the lifeless body of his mentor but found he couldn't move. Small strips of flesh ripped off of Teacher's face and arms. His peeling skin revealed muscle until his body was unrecognizable. The limp muscles tore off bones that melted as they were exposed.

Everything spun as Octavian's vision dimmed.

Dizziness and panic overcame him, then fear and sickness took over. He grasped for anything to hold on to but found no stable structure and no solace. As everything around him disintegrated, only darkness remained.

He tried to force himself to think of Stone Plaza, to think of a future where he, a magician of both feminine and masculine magic, sat on the International Council of Exalted Magicians.

Or just a future where he was alive would be nice.

Any future at all seemed so far away in this moment, so far beyond his reach, that he finally succumbed to the darkness.

4

WELL, LOOK WHO'S AWAKE

With the first moment of consciousness came blackness. Replika couldn't see, but she could hear. Crackles and crunches teased her ears. She knew the sounds were strange, though she wasn't sure why. A hiss far too close made her flinch.

Suddenly, she could feel her heavy eyelids pulled tight over her eyes, weighed down by full eyelashes. It took more force than she expected to part them. Those long eyelashes spread across her vision, widening with effort and clearing the way for sight.

A long, horizontal window above her let in red and pink spots of sunlight. She wondered if it was setting or rising. The bright light made her squint, though she couldn't have known the light was actually quite dim.

Colors and shadows and movement and life danced before her. And she thought to herself that it was the most beautiful thing in the universe.

She smiled, or tried to, but her muscles didn't respond how she expected. She didn't have time to wonder why because the window she had enjoyed for mere seconds was now changing.

As if the molecules themselves were reforming, plaster seemed to morph into stone. Wooden workspaces into metal tables. Linoleum flooring into dust covered tile. This new room she found herself in was even dimmer, so unlike the sunlight that had blessed her cheeks moments before.

There was another figure in the room, hands on his temples and teetering away from her toward a small table full of papers and books. He steadied himself there before standing upright and turning back to face her.

He was a curious figure, with the face of a young man but stark white hair. She tried to speak, a feat that was far harder than it should have been. The young man's eyes widened in surprise when her eyelids moved to blink.

"Are you awake?" Octavian asked, stumbling toward her. "Can you hear me?"

She tried to remember how to move her jaw, her lips, and her tongue. Why wasn't it working? Had she lost her voice?

"Do you know who I am?" Octavian continued. "Can you understand me?"

Blood rushed to Replika's face as her embarrassment peaked. Octavian put a hand up on the surface next to her shoulder, and it seemed to Replika that he was using it to keep his own balance.

"I'm sorry. Take your time."

Again, she pushed the sound from her lungs, upward, outward. She moved her lips and tongue, acclimating to the feeling of their shape. Her coordination came to her bit by bit, and she finally exclaimed. "Octavian!"

A large sigh came from Octavian. He almost lost his balance again but steadied himself. She analyzed his expression: relief.

"What's wrong with me?" he asked, voice shaking. "I should start a new recording for this."

His trembling hands reached up to his neck. He pulled a small, round marble from underneath his shirt, letting it dangle from a chain around his neck. He tapped the marble, and it responded with a green glow.

"Stop current visual recording, and open a new visual recording file."

The room was silent, and Octavian's raised eyebrow made it obvious that something was supposed to happen. He repeated the order, but still there was no response. He tapped the marble again, in a specifically intentional way this time. Bright green symbols appeared in a circle in front of him, and Replika tried in vain to push herself up onto her elbows to see better.

Her attention was forced down when, as she put pressure on the surface below her, it made a clanging sound. She was on some kind of metal bed. It was propped up at an angle such that she was almost standing.

She held onto the railings on the sides of the table, trying and failing to pull herself up. When her eyes returned to her companion, Octavian was navigating the marble's interface.

"Of course," he grumbled. "No recordings from the last twenty-four hours. Just my luck." He looked back at her and gave a half-hearted grin. "At least you're here, right?"

Replika had no idea what he was talking about, and it must have shown on her face because Octavian's brow tightened. He dropped the marble back under his shirt, and the glowing interface disappeared.

"You know who you are, don't you?" he asked her.

"Replika," she forced out as she nodded. It took effort, but was easier than her first word.

"Yes, you're Replika. That's right. What else?"

"Well, I . . ." She trailed off. She was sure she knew more, but the details wouldn't come. "That's all."

Octavian's concern was obvious in his expression, but he didn't say anything.

"What happened to me? Was I hurt?" She looked down at the table, then looked back up at Octavian, who seemed struck silent. Finally able to push herself up and onto her feet, she struggled to find her center of balance.

When she wavered, Octavian reached out to her. She expected him to grab her, but he didn't. He just held his hands nearby so she could grab him if she wanted to.

31

She had so many questions as she wobbled in place. "Why was I on a table like this? Did I go through some kind of procedure?"

Octavian took longer than she was comfortable with to respond, but before she could push further, he brushed off her question.

"You're fine now. Let's not worry about that just yet. Let's focus on getting out of here for now."

Replika looked around, noting the thick coat of dust and papers that lined several tables around the room as well as the floor. Wooden flooring, and perhaps an inlay in several colors, peeked out from under the clutter and grunge.

She squinted. The radial pattern of the inlay seemed familiar. However, she failed to remember it and couldn't see it well enough to continue trying, so she turned her attention back to Octavian.

"Where's here? I don't recognize this place."

"Me neither," Octavian agreed.

Most of the circular room was set a step below an outer ring, which was lined with shelves overfilled with books, boxes, and random odds and ends. The few spaces that sat between shelves were packed with haphazardly stacked boxes that had long ago settled into cattywampus piles.

Something caught Octavian's eye, and he walked over to one of the shelves. He reached out to wipe the dust from the spine of several books, though Replika didn't know what he hoped to find. Peeking into the only window in the room, Octavian announced that it didn't lead outside but instead to what seemed like a kitchen.

"This is strange. There's magic here," Octavian muttered. "The lampfires are magic." He pointed at one and noted that there was no wick or candle. "I can sense magic in the walls and nearby, but I don't sense magic generators and regulators."

Though he said this to himself, Replika heard him loud and clear. She couldn't help her amusement at how annoyed it seemed to make him.

Octavian's instinct was well-founded. Every city in their magical world was powered by magic. Harnessing magic to power homes and modern conveniences had been commonplace for almost 200 years. Harnessing plants were so large and ubiquitous that magicians were almost always able to feel the pull of ambient magic toward them. They were so used to it that the feeling just blended into the background, like a hum in a room that goes unnoticed until it suddenly goes silent.

Magic harnessing plants were welcome employers of NUM graduates. A young magician could expect predictable hours, flexible schedules, a hefty salary, and a great benefits package. Most people loved the idea of repetitive tasks, minimal responsibility, and good compensation. So, when the local harnessing plant sent recruiters to universities, which they did every year, students flocked to their information table.

"So are we in some remote location?" Replika asked.

"Maybe," he said. "Or we've been transported to another world."

"Another world. Like, another planet?"

"No, like an alternate reality," he clarified.

5

ALTERNATE REALITIES ARE A THING

Replika couldn't believe what she was hearing. She didn't know how, but somehow, she knew that traveling to other realities was impossible. Or it was supposed to be.

A memory was bubbling up from somewhere, unable to escape and reveal itself to her.

"That's impossible, isn't it?" Replika asked.

"According to the International Council of Exalted Magicians, it's completely impossible. But according to Teacher, they're wrong."

"Teacher?" Replika couldn't hold in her confusion, although she thought this was yet another thing she shouldn't have to ask. "What teacher?"

Octavian started to reply, but stopped himself. She was just about to ask what was on his mind when he said, "So you know who I am, but you don't remember Teacher?"

She could only shake her head because she had no explanation for it. Octavian's pursed lips gave away a deep worry that he was obviously not ready to explain. Meanwhile, she was still finding humor in someone named Teacher.

"He's my mentor," Octavian said, waving his hand in an explanatory circle. "He's a few inches shorter than me. Old. Gold eyes. An Exalted Grand Magician." He interrupted himself to add, "Oh, and a horrible attitude problem. Does any of that ring a bell?"

Something clicked in her mind, like puzzle pieces locking together.

"The one with no name," Replika said, words forming on her breath before there was thought behind them. Then she spoke up, "I do remember him, I think."

"Okay, well, he was sitting in his scary old chair." Octavian moved over to the approximate location where Teacher's chair had been. "Here. And then things started—" He was waving his hands in circles now. "—changing somehow. Does any of that sound familiar?"

"There was a window," Replika recalled. She pointed upward. "It was up that way. There was a tree, and I heard birds outside." Her face twisted as she tried to put the thought together. "But then . . ."

Octavian nodded, and she felt somewhat silly. Either Octavian's ridiculous encouragement or her inability to explain herself stopped her futile effort to describe what happened next.

"Yes, that's right. There was a window up there," Octavian said. Now he was pointing as well. "But it's a wall now. A solid, stone wall." He put his hands out as if he was holding on to Teacher's chair. "And Teacher is gone." The flustered color that had been building left his cheeks. "What if he's dead? What if my calibrations were wrong and this is my fault somehow?"

Replika wasn't sure what to say, but she supposed she ought to say something. Something comforting perhaps, or maybe empathetic. No, perhaps inspiring was the way to go. She suddenly remembered she was standing on her own, and she took a couple of awkward steps forward.

"Something happened to Teacher," Octavian continued. His voice was quiet. "Something horrible. But now there's no trace of him." He put a hand to his face as tears began to form.

As Octavian continued, Replika used as much of her new-found balance as she could to reach him physically, even as he emotionally drifted away.

"Teacher was just telling me about these alternate reality theories and how they'd been proven by some colleague of his, and now—" His voice cracked, forcing him to stop mid-sentence.

Replika put a hand to Octavian's shoulder as she reached his side.

"We're in this together, right?" she asked. "We should figure out the essentials. Food, water, potential threats. We can't just stay here."

Octavian nodded absently. He took a deep breath and stood straighter.

"I'm sure Teacher is fine," Replika said with endearing optimism. "Maybe he's already figured out a way to get us back and just needs time to implement it. So let's just stay safe until then."

Octavian's long pause made Replika wonder if her attempt at cheering him up had missed its mark.

"And if not?" Octavian wondered.

"We'll find our way without him," she assured him.

Octavian took a few more deep breaths. It was obvious to Replika that Octavian had been through something traumatic. Now was not the time to put him under more stress. Yet here they were, trapped in a strange place, and she had no idea how she could help. After all, she had no knowledge of her skills or Octavian's.

As Replika surveyed the circular room, she noticed a large door dominating one side. It had been behind her when she woke up, and there was so much to take in that she had missed it. She had a feeling it was somehow hidden in plain sight, or maybe concealed.

There were, in fact, spells used to conceal objects. Such spells were time consuming to cast, and were considered, in general, more trouble than they were worth. That's because even a magician of modest talent was able to detect magic and thus would be aware that something might be hidden. These spells were most commonly used in non-magical spaces and entertainment "magic" shows.

As far as this door was concerned, it wasn't hidden in plain sight. Replika had just failed to notice it. She did, however, immediately notice it was missing a doorknob and hinges. And, as far as she could tell, it was the only exit.

"So, how do we get out of a room with no windows and a door we can't open?" she asked.

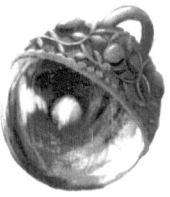

6

Always Look For Traps

Replika ran her fingers along the frame of the oversized door for any small recess that might be hiding something. Meanwhile, Octavian stared at the door as if seeing something she couldn't. She pushed it with a reasonable amount of effort, but it responded with a weak groan.

As Replika moved her hands across it, she noted the texture of the wood seemed rather raw. It didn't have the smell of wood, but she could imagine what it might have smelled like in the past: musky with a hint of sweetness to it. As she continued pushing and sliding her hands across each millimeter, Octavian's eyes had moved on to the woodwork around it.

She looked back and forth between Octavian and the door several times before asking, "What are you looking for?"

"Traps, of course."

Replika tilted her head in confusion.

Octavian explained that traps were the most common type of spell and were made up of two types: triggers and locks. The name was somewhat misleading because locks were a far more common type of spell than triggers. Traps were categorized as low complexity, medium complexity, or high complexity by how many triggers and locks there were.

"In junior magician training, we were taught to detect most traps because they're some of the easiest magic to detect," Octavian said.

There was nothing glamorous about traps, although sometimes magicians added their own flair.

When Octavian first started graduate school, Teacher wouldn't allow him to use the break room refrigerator to store his food. The trap he had used was not trivial, with nine locks and several triggers. Teacher added a visual component, so when Octavian approached, nine glowing locks on a grid appeared in front of the fridge with lines connecting the locks.

"They were bright yellow with a pulsing glow and twinkling sparkle around the locks. Teacher liked to add sparkle to his visual magic," Octavian said.

To finally unlock it took Octavian nine months and far too many uncomfortable conversations with downstairs colleagues about Teacher's shortcomings.

"It was a bit heavy handed, but it was Teacher's way of reminding me that in any unknown situation, you first look for traps," Octavian recited.

"Do you see any?" Replika surveyed the wall he was concentrating on. Between the doorframe and the stonework on either side of the door was a wide application of plaster. But even when she squinted in concentration, she saw nothing but cracking plaster. "I don't see anything."

"There are lots of types of traps," Octavian explained, fixing his gaze on the structure and ignoring her judgemental gaze. "It would take too long to check all of them. So I'm starting by looking for low complexity traps." He let out a small sigh. "But I don't see any here."

Even though he said that, he obviously had found something because his eyes were focused on a single point on the wall. He took rationed steps toward the wall with his arm up as one does when waiting to press the elevator button when the current car is full.

Replika followed his lifted finger to a subtle dimple in the plaster about a foot to the side of the door. Placing his finger against the dimpled plaster, he applied gentle pressure.

There was a loud click, and both he and Replika jumped back. A continuous grinding and a repetitive clicking filled the air as the door dragged itself open into the room. Octavian stepped backward as the huge door swung. When he reached the step down into the circular space below, he slipped, falling backward. Replika threw out her arms and caught him, then pulled him several steps further into the room as the door reached its widest point as it continued its slow swing.

The door dragged along the floor, scraping papers and flinging dust into the air. One click after another resonated through the room until the door slammed into a bookshelf behind it, knocking several books to the ground.

"Was that magic?" Replika asked.

"I don't think so," he replied, regaining his balance. He peeked outside the door. "There's some kind of weird contraption out here that's connected to the door. But however it works, it relied on a magic trigger to open. See? Look here." He returned to the small dimple he had pressed before. "It's a Pressure Point. A magic rod has been placed in the wall that can transfer pressure between two surfaces. The plaster wasn't able to bind to it quite right, so it left this weird spot."

"It must have hit a switch that allowed the door to open," Replika thought aloud. Quite happy with her unfounded detective work, she grinned before turning her attention to the wide opening in front of them. There was a wall a few feet ahead, but an oblique light intrigued her. "I guess now we can explore further."

"You go ahead. I'll see if there's anything of immediate use around here," Octavian replied. "I think a bag I can use was on the desk over there."

Replika ignored him and stayed in the room as he walked over to the desk. As soon as he picked the bag up, Octavian groaned at the thick coating of dust covering it. The metal finishings rattled as he shook it, and he brushed off as much of the dust as he could before opening it.

Octavian pulled out several objects from inside. A small purse jingled, and he seemed content with whatever he found within it. A pair of goggles and a compass looked useful, but the random odds and ends Octavian found did not. Nevertheless, Octavian put it all back into the bag and fastened it shut.

As he started to turn back to the doorway, he was distracted by something on the table. The bag slipped from his grip, off the edge of the table, and onto the floor.

"Is everything okay?" Replika asked, hurrying over to him.

"This can't be—" He said the words in a whisper, but each word was crystal clear to Replika. She looked over his shoulder.

"What's wrong?" she asked.

All she saw was a collection of dust and paper on the desk.

"This is Teacher's handwriting," he said, voice cracking.

"What?"

The papers that were scattered all over the table appeared to be notes. Though they were unorganized, the handwriting on every paper was consistent. Drawings and diagrams had a common sense of style and quality, though Replika didn't recognize any of it.

"I can't believe this," Octavian said, tears coming to his eyes again. "Teacher has been here."

7

TEACHER HAS BEEN HERE

Octavian grabbed one of the pages sitting on the table in front of him. Dust flew into his and Replika's faces. He turned and pushed the paper toward her, using his other hand to wipe away the dust and tears from his eyes.

"Look. This is Teacher's handwriting. Even how he always has to keep his writing within the margins of the page!"

Replika's furrowed brow and puckered lips made him more frustrated than ever at her missing memories. If she remembered Teacher better, she could have confirmed his assertion. With her complex personality matrix, maybe she could even have shared in the anger and sadness and fear that was welling up inside him.

"Are you saying Teacher traveled here, too?" she asked. "Wherever here is."

"I'm saying he lied to me!" Octavian shouted, slamming his hand against the defenseless papers he was holding.

"Well, maybe we're not in some alternate world after all," Replika reasoned. "Maybe we were transported to a secret hideout or something."

Octavian wasn't listening. He gritted his teeth as he flipped through the dust-laden papers. Tears and a quick sneeze tried to slow him down, but he pushed through, recognizing every nuance of the personality within the pages. Key words seemed to jump from rushed sentences: travel, theory, reality, calculation, magical proof, device, malfunction.

"It wasn't some lab accident that transported us here," he grumbled.

He kicked the table before looking over at Replika, who still didn't seem to understand.

"Don't you get it?" he asked. "Teacher sent us here. He knew! This must have been his theory, and he used us to test it." Hands shaking, he put down the papers and leaned forward onto the desk. "My life, everything I've worked for is there, in that reality. I was finally getting somewhere, was finally going to prove to everyone that I was worth something. That I . . ." He trailed off, unable to bring himself to say more.

Replika put a hand to his arm and said his name. He pulled away, grabbing the bag from the floor and throwing it over his shoulder.

"Nevermind. You were right. We need to focus on the essentials. Let's get out of here."

Before Replika could reply, he walked past her to the doorway. He looked back at her to make sure she wasn't going to challenge him.

"I'm right behind you," she said, looking back at the desk full of papers.

Octavian crossed through the threshold and made his way around a wall that obscured an open atrium. Looking up at what should have been the sky, all Octavian could see was a thick layer of fog, though he noted that the visibility on the ground within the walls was perfect. A breeze caressed his face, bringing with it the salty smell of the ocean.

He took a deep breath, trying to clear his mind and move forward physically and emotionally. Sunlight diffused through the fog, casting a soft light into the space within tall walls that lay on all sides of him. The cawing of birds in the distance was drowned out by waves beating mercilessly against some surface beyond the walls.

His courses on ethics, which included lessons on assumptions and unconscious biases, were now at the forefront of his mind. Maybe he was wrong about everything. Maybe Replika knew more than she realized and just needed help accessing that knowledge.

"Replika," Octavian said as she walked past him into the center of the atrium. He waited until she looked back at him. "How could we know for certain whether we've been transported to another location in our reality or we're in another reality?"

"You're asking me?" she asked.

"Yes. Like you said, we could just be in a remote location. I'm sure there are isolated places that are distant from magic power centers."

Not that he knew of any.

"Oh, you mean because we seem to be on an island in the ocean?"

So, she had noticed as well. Despite acting oblivious, she had picked up on all the details he had. And she had reached a similar conclusion, with much less intentional thought. It was a relief to know that her processing was operating properly.

"I don't see anything here that doesn't exist where we're from," Octavian noted. "Magic lamps, wood, metal, water, fog. The architecture isn't foreign, either. Many homes in temperate regions have central atriums. And the atrium has five walls."

"Five walls is significant?"

"It's got a lot of meaning in our culture," Octavian explained, expecting her to remember at any moment. When she did not reply, he continued, "Five-walled rooms represent the balance of nature. It's very familiar."

He said this, but something was off. The typical five-walled room either had one entrance or a door on each wall. But this room was different. The wall they had just entered around was bare, and another bare wall lay to one side. On the other three walls of the atrium were doors, made of similar wood to the lab door, but not oversized. It was different, but not different enough.

45

"Then I guess to figure out where we are, we keep looking until we find something that isn't familiar," Replika said. She shrugged. "And until then, we have multiple hypotheses."

She laughed at her joke—though he didn't understand what was so funny about it—and continued on toward the other side of the open space. With an unintelligible grumble, Octavian walked around the perimeter of the atrium. An initial scan didn't reveal any low-level traps, and the first door he came to was unlocked. He pushed it open with as little force as he could manage, unsure of what he would find on the other side.

Behind the door was a small room with no windows. To one side of the room was a bed, and on the other side was a dresser. Several pages were scattered on the bed and floor in a similar fashion to the papers in the lab. Octavian couldn't help but be curious, but reminded of his predicament, he knew his priorities were elsewhere. He looked back to see Replika leaving the room across from him.

"Is that another bedroom?" he asked.

"No." Her expression was complicated, and she was standing to the side of the doorway as if she wanted him to take a look. "It's some kind of generator room. But it looks like—Well, it looks like it runs on steam."

Octavian raised his eyebrows and repeated what she had just said. She confirmed with a nod. Steam power definitely belonged on the list of things that weren't familiar.

"We'll figure that out once we get food and clean water, I guess," Octavian said. "Let's see what's behind door number three."

As soon as they were both at the door, he turned the knob, but it wouldn't move. He gripped it harder and gave it a tug. When it still didn't budge, he grabbed it one more time and pulled as hard as he could.

No luck. Because of course not.

8

FINALLY SOME MAGIC!

Octavian waited as Replika nudged him out of the way so she could look at the stuck door's knob much too closely. Despite him telling her that he couldn't open the door, she asked, "Is it locked?"

He didn't dignify that with a response.

She tilted her head left and right as she reviewed the door knob again.

"Looks like you need a key to unlock it," she said. "But from the inside? That's curious."

It made sense to Octavian. Every lab at the university controlled access to get in and out. However, they all used magic locks. Since everyone at NUM was trained in the use of magic, a user could simply swipe their hand near the lock to open it—except of course when it was far beyond its obsolescence date. These kinds of magic were called passive, or in the case of the old scanner at the lab building, passive aggressive.

"It isn't so odd," Octavian explained. "Though I see it more often on magic locks."

It didn't cross Octavian's mind that he had seen a physical key in the very bag he was holding. Instead, like many magicians, his first solution to moving physical objects was to use magic. While passive magic was used in magic locks, it would take active magic to unlock this door.

GAIUS J. AUGUSTUS

"This shouldn't be too hard to unlock," Octavian added.

Replika, excited to see what Octavian would do, stepped back as he placed his finger on the keyhole.

Octavian visualized what was called a Gravity Mesh, a three-dimensional visualization taught to undergraduate magicians. A Gravity Mesh was a representation of Nature, allowing users to visualize things such as the planet's pull on objects. He spoke a soft incantation as he bent and twisted the mesh, pushing the locking mechanism out of place.

Once unlocked, he turned the doorknob and pulled on the door. It was stuck from years of disuse, but a sharp tug let loose a cracking sound as the door left its frame.

"That's amazing!" Replika exclaimed as Octavian pulled the door open a few inches.

Her enthusiasm was much bigger than the actual task, which was quite simple. It seemed strange to Octavian because she was supposed to be aware of common uses of magic. He couldn't help but wonder how much she remembered. He pushed the thoughts from his mind, refocusing on the present.

He gave the door a few more yanks before it was open enough for them to fit through.

Putting out an inviting hand, he said, "After you."

Outside the door were thick fog clouds. That sloshing sound was all around them, but little else stood out to him. He looked to his sides at the complex, which was faced with a pale white stucco. The walls stretched out into the fog while still appearing much larger than it had on the inside.

A wooden pier along its base was the only hint of form in their vicinity. The pier also stretched out perpendicular to the walls of the complex, and from that direction came a more uneven beat of water against the piles of the pier and a rhythmic creaking.

He took the bag from his shoulder, putting it instead across his body, and tugged the strap to make sure it was secure. With

48

careful steps, he inched forward into the dense, white abyss before him.

"Careful!" Replika called from behind him.

He looked back at her. She didn't seem to notice the look he was giving her, a look that meant what she said was obvious. Instead, she just kept her worried gaze on him. He sighed, shaking his head, and turned back to his task.

A few feet down the wooden pier, it narrowed to shoulder width. He could feel the water hitting the supports below, pounding one side then the other. The structure seemed sturdy enough, but when the boards creaked below his feet, he found himself trying to decide what he would do if he fell through. He had no idea what to expect. The water sounded close, but he knew he was making guesses as a form of self-soothing.

Placing one foot in front of the other, he crafted a plan to throw his arms out to the side at any sign of failure. Senseless as it was, it made him feel better.

A large silhouette appeared below him in the fog, and he squinted, trying to clarify. Just a few steps more, and he groaned at how obvious what he found was.

"There's a boat!" he called back to Replika. "I'm coming back to get you."

"No, wait, I'll come to you," her voice echoed from the void.

Before he could complain, she was at his side.

"You didn't see the boat before?" she asked with disbelief.

"What? With all this fog? Of course not." A realization came to him, and he pointed out away from the structure. "Can you see land out there somewhere?"

"Yes, of course," she said, pointing in a different direction, "there's land that way, where all the weird looking ships are. Must be inhabited."

Octavian couldn't help smiling. "You have no idea how glad I am that you're here. Do you think this thing is safe?"

Replika merely gave him a useless shrug.

A steep set of stairs led down to the boat. A metal railing held the steps together, and Octavian knelt down before putting his foot onto the first step, placing as little weight on the railing as possible.

Looking down, he guessed the boat had enough room for about a dozen people. An oblong oval, it floated perpendicular to the pier. The ladder was positioned such that he had to climb around some awful looking contraption attached to the back of the boat.

Its flat bottom was made from fine looking wood that was scuffed and worn from years of neglect. His confidence in its stability was waning fast, but, already in too deep, he continued his descent one slow step at a time.

The last step lay a couple feet above the boat. He jumped around the bulky machine, taking in a deep breath as he prepared to sink. The boat drifted up and down, up and down. With no indication of any immediate structural issues or incoming water, Octavian breathed a sigh of relief.

He was somehow still alive. One more miracle to add to today's list.

9

You Gotta Understand To Magic

Finally safe—at least for now—Octavian looked around the longboat. He was feeling proud of himself, as if jumping into the boat was the most courageous act of his life. But he tried not to let it go to his head.

To each side were rudders, which were controlled by an overcomplicated contraption at the head of the boat. He rolled his eyes and turned back to the step ladder to call Replika. However, as he opened his mouth, she jumped down next to him.

A yelp caught in his throat as he bent his knees to keep his balance. "I guess you don't need help," he said.

She smiled. "Thank you anyway."

"Can you figure out how to get that thing running?" He gestured toward what appeared to be a motor at the back, and then added in jest, "I can give you a fire if it's steam-powered."

"It looks similar to the tech inside." She sat next to it and opened a small compartment that sat ajar. "Hey, look. There's a space for a fire. I think this does run on steam power. How did you know?"

Octavian let out a groan. "What kind of people would make something like this?"

"I'll take that fire now," Replika replied mockingly.

He sighed and went over to the opening Replika was pointing to. He was surprised to see not a furnace for a fire, but a small stand with a round groove. Octavian recognized it immediately.

"This is for an elemental marble," he said.

An elemental marble was a small device similar to his Notebook that allowed the limited use of elemental magic in a convenient package. Elemental marbles had gotten smaller since this stand was made, but it was obvious what it was for.

Octavian found it curious. This boat was made to run on steam power, but with magic assistance? It didn't make any sense. When he asked Replika for her thoughts, she seemed amused by how much it annoyed him.

Suddenly realizing water was seeping through his pants from the wet boat, he groaned again before turning his full attention back to the marble stand. He didn't have a fire marble, but as a magician, he didn't need it, at least for their current needs. Warmth built up as he rubbed his hands together and spoke an incantation.

When he opened his hands, an orange orb floated from them. He placed it into the holder, said another short spell, and waited as the fire intensified. The orb changed to yellow.

Upon his nod that the fire was ready, Replika turned the crank at the side of the motor, which—from the sound of it—primed a pump with water. Water in the attached tank started bubbling, and Octavian jumped back when a large click sounded as a gear began turning.

"That means we're ready, I think," Replika said. "Perhaps you should sit down."

"I'll let you handle the rest," Octavian agreed, sitting on one of the benches that lined the boat's sides and gesturing to the front. Replika took her seat at the helm and moved the steering stick back and forth to get the hang of how it moved the rudder. Once satisfied, she put her hand on a large lever and pulled hard.

The boat lurched forward. From the fog, a jetty appeared just ahead of them. Octavian's eyes widened as he clutched the side of the boat. Replika turned hard away from the incoming obstacle. The boat veered toward open water but continued its slide toward an inevitable collision.

Travel between realities was fine, but what they really needed, Octavian thought, was to be able to manipulate time.

It was a foolish and fleeting thought. After all, there was an entire section in his undergraduate freshman year Overview of Magic class detailing the many things that magic could not do.

Manipulating time was on that list. Of course, so was traveling to alternate realities, so maybe that list wasn't as reliable as he thought. The exam on the limits of magical practice was one he'd passed with flying colors. It was a success that, at the time, seemed immense, but now bordered on insignificant.

Still, he was suddenly aware that, though they were rushing toward the dock ahead of them, the seconds stretched.

The world was silent, free of the calls of birds, the rushing waves, and the sputtering boat. The salty smell of the breeze was gone, and droplets of water hung in the air. A familiar mesh appeared around him, much like a Gravity Mesh, but instead of seeing the mesh, he was feeling it. This was a new, different feeling, as if his aura was reaching out and waiting for instructions.

As time stretched even more, the mesh waited for him to manipulate it. His eyes widened as he realized what this mesh was meant to manipulate: time. He was afraid to move, afraid any small gesture would cause time itself to break, but the coming impact was imminent. He had to do something.

Time almost frozen around him, he lifted his hand to orient himself with the mesh, but the water rose up instead. More from instinct than intentional thought, he threw the wave against the boat. He was sure that he had somehow sealed their fate, but the water's force pushed their boat away from impending doom.

And as far as Octavian could tell, he was still alive.

Just as suddenly as the power was before him, it was gone. Time returned to normal, and he continued his fall onto the wet floor. His head whipped down and slammed against the bottom of the boat.

Replika flung herself onto the lever to disconnect the motor. "What just happened?" she asked.

With much effort, Octavian pulled himself up, looking back toward the jetty that was fading into the fog.

They were safe. He grabbed at his head, which pulsed with throbbing pain. Replika knelt beside him, unbothered by the pooled water soaking into her dress.

"It was me," he said, still unable to believe it. "I mean, it was magic. I could see it, but—I have no idea what I just did."

She caressed his head, her brow furrowed. But she wasn't concerned that he had just broken the laws of magic.

"Are you alright?" she asked. "You hit your head pretty hard."

He removed her hands from his head.

"I'm fine. What about you?"

"Yes, I'm fine, too."

She shifted her eyes away from his gaze in embarrassment as she pulled one hand away to brush off her now wet dress. Once satisfied, she looked back at him.

"I'm sorry we almost crashed. If you hadn't . . ." She trailed off before deciding to try a different sentence. "The lever control is binary, either on or off. So it accelerated much faster than I thought it would. Because of that, I believe it should have been docked at an angle pointing toward the open sea."

He allowed her to help him sit up, and he wished his pounding head distracted him from the cold of the water that had soaked into his clothes.

"We could have been killed," Octavian spat. "If this is Teacher's idea of a test, it's cruel."

"Teacher wouldn't try to kill us," Replika paused before adding, "would he?"

Octavian couldn't answer the question. In fact, he had plenty of other things to distract him from thinking about his mentor and chose to focus his attention on the warm, comforting hand Replika had on his neck.

"I guess we should continue on to shore," Replika said.

"Right," he agreed. "Food, water, and all that."

"I definitely could use some of that," she joked, and he gave a half-hearted smile.

Once they were chugging along again, Octavian tried to conjure up the time-warping mesh again.

Magic was not something that worked at some times and not others. It was something that was controlled through a thorough understanding of Nature. Yet the power had come out of nowhere, and he had controlled it instinctively. However, try as he might, he couldn't do it again, and he had no idea how he had done it.

He understood time as it was taught in his physics courses, but nothing he had learned in them came close to explaining this. Racking his brain, he tried to recall any mention of magic for manipulating time. Nothing came to mind.

He couldn't discount the fact that he was distracted by Replika as she entertained herself with a song. She leaned her head back and forth in time as she hummed a tune he didn't recognize. It made it harder to concentrate, especially with his headache.

Octavian was impressed with her, how she seemed to be adapting and learning. He hadn't known Teacher was capable of such an intricate personality matrix, but he was sure it had no equal. Though he was amazed by her social engineering, it bothered him that she didn't know she was artificial. Teacher had never discussed her self-awareness, and so Octavian could only imagine it was a malfunction. But how to correct it?

A different question then popped into his mind: why was the laboratory complex they appeared in on an island? If they had shifted into a new reality, they should have theoretically appeared in the same location. Had Teacher also figured out spatial transport? What else didn't he know about Teacher's magical capabilities?

Octavian began a downward spiral as he wondered if their island arrival point was chosen because the mainland was unsafe. He considered turning back, searching the island complex harder for supplies, even though it was obvious that the complex had been abandoned for many years.

"Replika, maybe this wasn't such a good idea. Maybe we should go back," he said.

Replika turned back to him, head tilted with curiosity.

"What's wrong?" she asked, pointing a finger in the direction they were headed. "Are you worried about the pirates?"

2

TALES OF A VERNIAN YOUTH SERIES

THE *Pirates*
AND THE
MAGIC COMPUTER

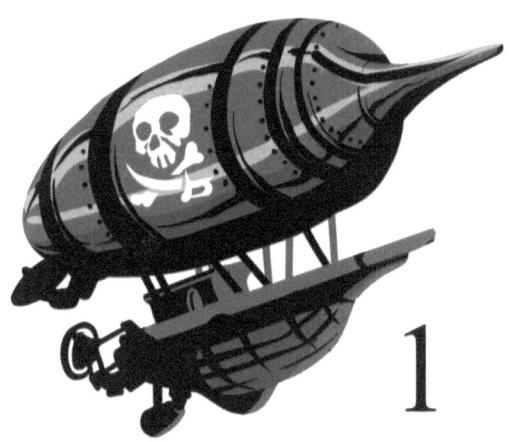

1

THAR BE PIRATES

There was evidence to support that the magician graduate student, Octavian, and the robot who didn't know she was a robot, Replika, were indeed in a reality that was not their own. Their home world was one where magic technology was common and where talented students could attend universities of magic such as the National University of Magic, work on interesting research projects such as building an almost too realistic robot, and, apparently, be transported to an alternate reality by your research advisor.

The world they now found themselves in was different, although they were as of yet unaware of just how different. They'd arrived in a laboratory with magic lighting and a few unique magical items, but as far as Octavian could detect, there was no other magic nearby. Worse yet, the island facility the laboratory sat on and the old longboat they were now traveling to shore on both ran on what Octavian could only describe as an inefficient and ineffective mode of power: steam power.

As the boat chugged along, a cool, refreshing breeze carried the salty smell of the sea. Seagulls called out to each other, possibly gossiping about the newcomers, but more likely calling dibs on that really fat fish swimming near the surface. The fog that had surrounded the island was still thick around them, leaving a dewy moistness on Octavian's cheeks. But that wasn't why Octavian was so uncomfortable.

"Are you worried about the pirates?" Replika had asked.

If there was a hint of concern in her voice, Octavian hadn't heard it. They had been skimming along the water in their steam-powered longboat for a long time now, and though the fog was dense, Octavian knew Replika's robotic hypervision could see through it clearly. Of course, Replika didn't seem to know that her eyes were equipped with multiple modes of visual enhancements, but Octavian was confident she had seen—and not informed him of—evidence of pirates long before she mentioned it.

As if on cue, and before he could find a response worthy of her casual question, the fog began to clear. Octavian barely noticed the rounded coast lined with docks hosting a wide variety of sea vessels, the plumes of steam and smoke that billowed from the factories near the beach, or the cliffs that lined the back of a giant cove where a city stood. He was distracted from the three shelves that had been cut from the cliffs to hold levels of a city. And he missed the strange-looking train cars rolling up and down the cliffside, carrying people from one level to another.

For what seemed like the longest ride of his life, his attention was locked on a skull and crossbones—the Jolly Roger of pirates—decorating a giant zeppelin attached to a large wooden ship that floated above the water. A gangway stretched from the deck of the ship down to the dock, and little dots that must have been real live pirates were moving up and down it. The pirate airship wasn't the only interesting ship docked at the coast, but it kept Octavian's eyes busy. Although he wanted to look away, he couldn't.

All he could think of were the often unprompted stories of frustration Teacher had prattled on about while they worked, specifically those regarding a supposed encounter with pirates. At the time, Octavian wrote off Teacher's fantastical yarns as a means to distract him from his work. His stomach tied itself into knots as he wondered how many of Teacher's even crazier stories might have had some truth to them. Octavian had rarely listened with much interest, and he couldn't remember any details about Teacher's pirate adventure, but he was pretty certain it hadn't been pleasant. He wasn't in a rush to test the accuracy of his memory.

Later, once Octavian felt less in danger, he'd question why a ship would need a zeppelin in addition to traditional sails. He'd wonder how the pirates moved people between the zeppelin and the ship when in flight. And he'd find some amount of forced acceptance that the craft embodied the ridiculousness that this world was accustomed to.

As they closed in on the shore, Replika pushed the lever to disconnect the motor. A reflection of light flickered over the boat's bottom, catching their attention. They both looked toward the source: the pirate ship. Replika returned her focus to guiding the slowing longboat into position.

However, Octavian was focused on the gleaming spot where, when he squinted, he was sure someone with a spyglass was looking their way. He looked back toward the island complex, now just an ominous fog in the distance. Cursing to himself, he wondered if he should have concealed their arrival. By the time he looked back to the pirate ship, the observer was gone, but the chill up Octavian's spine was not.

"Why wouldn't you mention something like pirates earlier?" he grumbled.

Replika either didn't hear him or pretended not to. She turned the boat toward the sea with expert precision and eased it into a jetty with other boats of similar size. They bumped the wooden supports, and both leaned out to grab them before the boat could bounce away.

She nodded to Octavian confidently. As he regretted every second of holding on to the muck-covered wood, she reached down along the side of the ship and pulled out a strange clamp he hadn't even realized was there. She secured the vessel, and they stepped up onto the jetty to head toward land. Replika was unnecessarily cheerful and began pointing out things in the distance, but Octavian was still distracted, and not just by the sludge he was trying to transfer from his hands to his pants.

In empty corners, shady men waited for something as they stared off into fantasies. Others seemed deep in conversation with scantily clad women who laughed at whatever the men said. The warehouses along the boardwalk looked abandoned, with rusted metal plating and broken windows, though the thick smell of soot and the smoke billowing from their stacks proved otherwise. And in the distance ahead of them was a crowd of people and some structures.

Then there they were: pirates. Each wearing the Jolly Roger somewhere on their person, they lined the boardwalk and leered at the newcomers like school bullies.

In this world, pirates were obligated to wear their crew's unique version of the Jolly Roger when off-ship. They were murderers and thieves, of course, but they had their pride. And in this particular port, there was another incentive to identify oneself as a pirate.

Several generations before, the great pirate captain Kiiw and a few later traitorous allies noticed the rapid growth of this city's population. It didn't go unnoticed when a family flaunting their expensive tastes moved into a home there.

Led by Kiiw, the pirates ransacked the city, kidnapped citizens, and threatened to burn down the houses. It was then that the contemporary Mayor Weil proposed a deal. Intrigued, Captain Kiiw agreed to listen. Though Kiiw would often be called soft for giving any leeway to the settlers, no one in the pirate community would deny that the deal he made was downright awesome.

They sat down to chat about this "treaty" over afternoon tea, a time which the citizens held terrifyingly strictly—that's a spooky story for another time. They savored the biscuits, pastries, and sandwiches. They melted at the flavorful masterpiece of homemade tea. And Captain Kiiw fell in love with the city.

Mayor Weil made his offer with impeccable timing. For immunity from further pirate raids, the city would offer their own form of safety. Pirates could come ashore and enjoy food and tea at their leisure, courtesy of the town. The pirates would receive priority for several town services. And while the pirates would only be allowed on the beach level of the town, they were granted a degree of freedom for the pirates to just exist and generally feel like they were on a vacation. Never having had a vacation before, Captain Kiiw accepted the treaty without the input from other pirate captains and with no further negotiation.

That didn't go over very well with the rest of the Pirate community and led to a dramatic and grisly end for Captain Kiiw. Nevertheless, as a matter of pride, pirate captains thereafter enforced the treaty both on their ships and on the shore. And they agreed that the whole setup was pretty cool—a change in mentality that came too late for the pirate who brokered the deal in the first place.

Without the benefit of this little history lesson, all Octavian could do was try to convince himself that the dozens of eyes locked on them were friendly—or maybe just coincidental. Perhaps his mind was making it all up, and no one was looking at them at all, he hoped.

The thing about perhaps is that they are the product of conjecture. Sometimes these perhaps are useful to distract oneself from inaccurate illusions of the mind. This was not one of those times.

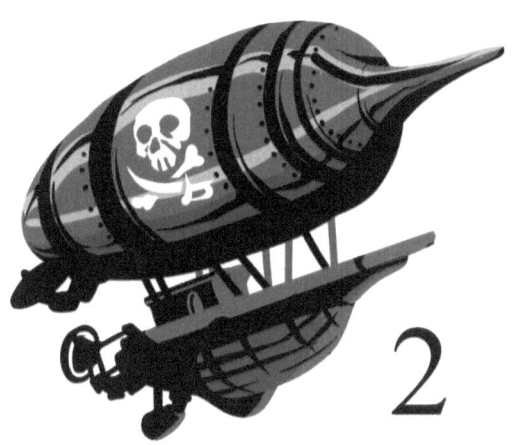

2

CHRONOFORD, STEAM CAPITAL OF THE WORLD

Were the pirates just ahead staring at Octavian and Replika? Or was Octavian just having a really rough day and seeing danger where there was none? Whatever the truth was, Octavian's fluttering stomach wouldn't settle down.

Some figures lined the boardwalk's railing while others spoke in small groups, blocking most of the walkway. None were shy about the weapons they carried at their hips, chests, and thighs. One let out a loud, teasing trill, causing Octavian to jump and bite the inside of his cheek. He moaned at the pain as laughter erupted around them.

"Are you okay?" Replika asked him. "Does your head still hurt?"

He had almost forgotten his head and the bottom of the boat had collided when the longboat had bolted into action. His head ached, but the pain was dull and not his primary concern at the moment. After allaying her concerns, he shifted the conversation to a large engraved sign just ahead made of wood with metal accents. There was a silhouette etched into it of three vertical pipes with steam rising out of them. The words read:

"Welcome to Chronoford
Steam Capital of the World"

There wasn't a place called Steam that this city was the capital of, nor was the city world-renowned for the quality or quantity of its steam. The contemporary mayor invented the self-proclaimed title because of a mix-up with the engraving. The pipes and steam were half the size they were supposed to be. The engraver had mixed up two orders and luckily stopped before he inscribed, "*Dedicated to my mother, a woman only a son could love.*"

When the Mayor alerted the city council to the error, they refused to fund another cut of the rare wood the sign was made from. They had additional concerns about the cost associated with redoing the engraving at the bottom of the sign, a required 255-character notice to pirates regarding the terms of their treaty with the city.

Octavian didn't read this fine print, but he did feel as if the universe—or was it now the multiverse—was smacking him in the face with the city's name. Chronoford, as in Chronos, the personification of time, or so thought an ancient civilization known in his world as the Greeks.

It seemed almost too coincidental that less than an hour earlier, he had commanded a new form of magic related to controlling time. And he had no idea how he'd done it, how to replicate it, or how it was even possible.

He thought now would be a great moment to stop time so they could escape all the pirate-y eyes leering in their direction. The strong collective gaze hinted at a job that needed doing, and he wasn't keen to learn what that job was.

"Let's lose them in the marketplace," Octavian said in a hushed tone as he grabbed Replika's arm.

"Lose who?"

"The pirates."

"But we have nothing for them to steal," Replika noted as he pulled her along. "What are you so worried about?"

"Just come on," he groaned.

The Chronoford Market at the Docks was large and unorganized. Carts and small wooden booths were haphazardly placed around a large courtyard. Loud clonks, clanks, and shings rang out with every step anyone took, a deafening and quite annoying repercussion of the wooden boardwalk the whole market sat on. Children zigzagged between legs and screamed when their parents got hold of them. Yet in all the chaos, Octavian finally relaxed—not completely, but enough.

He took in the variety of goods, though if he had looked around better, he would have seen the locals' looks of surprise at the couple who had just arrived. When his grip on her arm weakened, Replika slipped her hand into his and pulled him along instead. She squealed in delight as they made their way over to one of the booths.

As his adrenaline rush took a quick break, Octavian realized there was a chill in the air. Teacher had kept the lab a similarly chilly temperature but had also directed Octavian not to wear anything over his work vest. Octavian had often attempted to push the boundaries of his allowed wardrobe: a hoodie, a thin sweater underneath his vest, a sweater with no shirt under it, two shirts layered on top of each other, et cetera, ad nauseam.

The first time Octavian had shown up to lab out of dress code, Teacher sent him home to change. When he returned to lab, Teacher demanded he work through the night "to make up for the lost time." Not one to give up, Octavian brought extra clothes to change into the next day, only to be told to change. Teacher had seemed almost disappointed when Octavian didn't have to trudge all the way home.

Octavian didn't let these missteps stop him from attempting to keep himself warm in the lab. One day, he had worn a neoprene wetsuit under his clothes. Teacher had definitely noticed. Octavian could tell from his crossed arms and long look. But that day, his advisor hadn't said a word, which felt like a win to the young graduate student.

Unfortunately, it was an uncomfortable win, so Octavian had to weigh his options: extreme discomfort from the wetsuit or extreme discomfort from the cold. Octavian chose the comfort of his armpits and nether regions over the comfort of his hands, mainly because putting on and taking off the wetsuit wasn't worth the effort.

Now that he was aware of the chill in the air of the open market, it seemed to stick to him. Octavian wished he had a sweater or a shawl or a blanket. He rolled down the sleeves of his dirty button-down shirt. To his dismay, they were still damp from their eventful boat ride. Looking from cart to cart for something that might help, he realized the technology was far behind what he was used to.

There weren't screens displaying today's specials, customers weren't tapping their marble computers to confirm a transaction, and vendors weren't using a holographic interface to track their sales. Instead, people were reading prices from hand-painted signs, handing over metal currency, and receiving hand-written receipts. The currency was familiar, and he recalled the pouch of coins he had found at the island complex. He patted the bag at his side and nodded to himself as a metallic clinking answered back.

He took in the airships lining the cove docks, another indication that they were indeed in another world. The pirate ship didn't stand out as much when it floated next to two dirigible cruise ships and a vast number of smaller, more conventional wooden vessels. It was still menacing and disconcerting, of course, and Octavian was no less concerned for their safety.

Replika had continued forward while he gawked at his surroundings. As he rushed to catch up, Octavian realized the level of technology wasn't the only thing different about this world. He felt validated for questioning Teacher's fashion choices as he confirmed how out of place Replika's knee-length cupcake dress was. Passersby wore long dresses and top hats, corsets and canes, even one person with all four. Some people wore simple brown and beige working clothes, similar to those Octavian had on, while others flaunted feathers and a very specific set of vibrant colors.

It almost seemed as if he'd been transported back in time, though he was pretty sure that in his home world, watches didn't let off steam no matter how far back in time you went.

The thought jarred him enough that he had to take another, longer, more awkward look. Passing him was a man who was minding his own business and checking the time on his wristwatch because he was late for an appointment. But the simple act of lifting his wrist caught Octavian's attention and left the magician with questions.

So many questions.

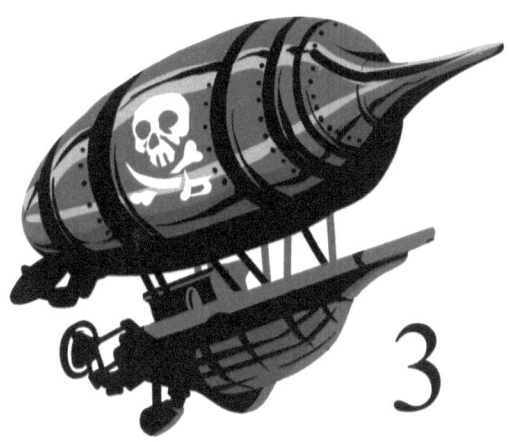

3

Two Point Free

The act of lifting one's arm in order to check one's watch is a common gesture and certainly not one that would—under normal circumstances—cause Octavian to stare longer than is socially acceptable. But the wisp of steam rising from the watch was quite unusual, at least in the reality Octavian was from.

He followed the man's arm movements, confirming that he wasn't imagining it. The watch looked normal enough, although clunky. But when the man's cuff pulled back further, it revealed a chamber on the underside of his wrist, presumably for water. He couldn't believe what he was seeing and didn't want to think of what this meant.

However, his mind was already speeding ahead with questions. Why would anyone design a steam-powered watch? Was there fire inside it somewhere? What fuel source could it be using? Was there enough water to power it for long? Octavian had so many questions but a much stronger sense of annoyance.

He was on his way to accepting this strangeness when he noticed a vendor nearby wearing a pack on his back. And surprisingly—though less so than it would have been a minute earlier—steam was coming out of it. It just got stranger as Octavian realized that the man was walking in place on a stair-stepper type device. As the man pedaled in place, two mechanical arms sorted herbs into teabags. After a minute, the man stopped to make a few adjustments, and when he started it up again, the mechanical arms created a different tea blend.

It was exhausting to watch him. Octavian didn't want to think too hard about how the whole device worked, and, as if flipping a "nope" switch in his mind, he returned his attention to Replika, who had gotten quite far ahead of him yet again.

"It all looks so good!" she exclaimed as soon as he caught up to her. "See? Aren't you glad we came ashore? Taking care of basic needs is always a good place to start."

She didn't wait for him to answer as she picked up a few pieces of fruit and pointed Octavian toward a display of bread.

"I don't know how much we can buy," he whispered to her.

"Then ask," she replied in a loud, matter-of-fact whisper.

He sighed and got the attention of a woman on the other side of the table as she finished up a previous transaction.

"Somefin' I can 'elp ya wiv, dearie?" she asked. She gestured to his empty hands.

The fact that she spoke English surprised him. He didn't know why he was surprised since the sign for the city had been in English, but surprised he was. The woman recognized that he was distracted and repeated her question. He apologized before responding.

"We're not from this area, and I was hoping you could give me some idea as to the value of your currency." He pulled the bag from his waist and retrieved the coin purse. He opened it and scooped out one coin as if the woman couldn't see the weight of the purse. "A friend gave me this to get started," he continued with a white lie.

The woman's eyes were wide, and he got the feeling he should have been less conspicuous with the currency.

"My word, this'll las' ya qui'e a while," the woman replied. "Each one a these would pay for a hear'y meal for the bof a ya, an' then some."

"What? Really?" he asked.

"I ain't no swindl'r, sir. Sure as rain, ya've got a fine friend wha' gives ya this kind a small fortune."

When he turned back to Replika, she was humming and filling up a cloth bag with food. They enjoyed a sampling of their purchases as they went from booth to booth, selecting from the assortment of fruits, berries, cheeses, and baked goods. As she was placing a purchase into Octavian's bag—since her new bag was now full—a loud bang echoed through the market. The noisy crowd went quiet, and Octavian looked around, trying to gauge how normal a sound like that was.

It wasn't normal.

Replika looked toward the commotion, eyes full of curiosity. But something else had caught Octavian's eye. Five pirates were heading straight toward them. Even though he tried to convince himself that the group was just headed in the duo's general direction, their eyes were locked on the newcomers.

There was no more perhaps about it. He had to do something.

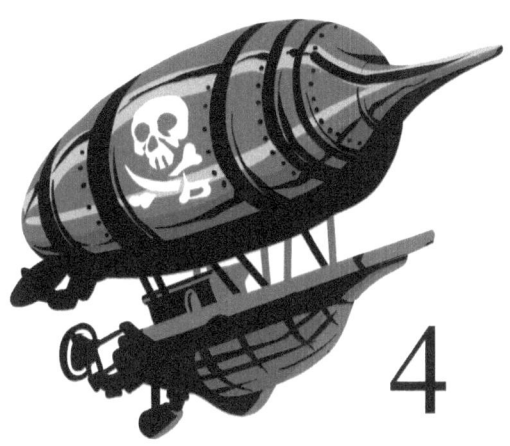

4

THE GENTLEMAN

Fearing the pirates would be on them in moments, Octavian opened his mouth. Replika grabbed his arm just as he was reaching for hers.

"Something's going on over there," she said.

"Let's check it out," Octavian agreed.

As she pointed to the people gathering at the end of the market, he pulled her toward and into the building crowd of voyeurs.

He thought it might be a show of some kind. To his surprise, steam was billowing out from beneath the ground with force. Long pipes rose from the ground in the distance, and one by one, metal flaps covering the pipes opened, erupting with huge plumes of dangerously hot vapor.

This was no normal underground.

The door near the front of the crowd had a label, but Octavian couldn't make it out from where he stood. Spoiler, it was literally a funicular maintenance door, but it held a discovery that would open a figurative door to many more questions. Octavian's attention was transfixed on it, as if he knew a mystery sat dormant beneath his very feet.

The crowd was uninterested in mysteries and resorted to comments ranging from fear of not being able to return home to badmouthing the transport's quality. The maintenance door swung open, banging against the outer wall, and a worker in heavy layers of clothing rushed out. The crowd's tune changed to one of worry and feigned sorrow for the crew's safety. The worker's clothing layers varied in thickness, appearing to be made to resist heat. He wore thick, cumbersome gloves, making it clear to Octavian that he wasn't doing detailed work below ground.

Another loud bang shocked the onlookers, who gasped. Two more workers came running out of the opening, followed by a plume of black smoke that obscured the doorway.

As the smoke began to clear, Octavian pointed beyond the maintenance doorway. "What's that?"

"Looks like a tram of some sort," Replika said. "I noticed them as we were approaching the city. Two sets of tracks. One tram goes up while the other goes down."

Octavian couldn't remember why, but he knew "tram" wasn't the right word for this.

The word was funicular, and this particular funicular was the main mode of transportation between the three levels that had been carved from the seaside cliffs.

"Necessity is the mother of invention, I guess," he said, adding, "as long as it isn't steam powered. Those are more like the excrement of invention."

Replika laughed before moving on to another question, pointing at the first cliff that the funicular was supposed to climb. "It looks fun, don't you think?"

"Yeah, actually," Octavian couldn't help but agree. "It does."

The three technicians who had come from the underground tunnel were now talking to an older gentleman. With a stiff collar and tight brocade vest, he stood in sharp contrast to the dusty men and woman who were telling him he'd be losing money and making a lot of people angry today. The man took a deep breath, looking at the crowd for comfort. Octavian didn't notice, but his white hair caught the gentleman's attention. His pause only lasted for a moment before he cleared his throat and approached the throng.

"My apologies, fair citizens," he said. His voice was crisp and light, with an aristocratic air that made every member of the crowd silent in suspense. "It seems it will take longer than expected to repair the funicular."

"That's the word!" Octavian exclaimed in a loud whisper directed at Replika. He was absolutely correct about the word but absolutely wrong in his timing to point it out.

"Be assured. My best people are hard at work to get you all safely to your homes," the fancy man continued. "Now, if you please, break up the crowd." He clapped his hands as he walked from one end of the group to the other.

Octavian didn't move as the people dispersed. When he turned toward the market, glaring pirate eyes stared right back. His breath caught, and he looked back at the gentleman, who was walking away.

"Excuse me, sir," Octavian called.

The gentleman turned to look at them. As if he hadn't seen them before, his attention seemed spellbound. To be clear, he was not bound by an actual spell, but instead by a recognition. Not the shallow recognition that comes with a passing encounter, but a deeper, richer, and more meaningful one.

However, Octavian's attention was on who might be behind him, not on who was in front of him.

"May I offer my assistance?" Octavian asked.

"Assistance?" the man replied. "What's your trade, boy?"

"I'm an engineer." Octavian hoped engineers existed in this place. "Allow me to have a look."

"Are you kidding?" one of the technicians chimed in.

"He's jus' a kid," another laughed, hitting the first in his arm. "Wha's he gon' do?"

The gentleman scoffed at them before turning his attention back to Octavian.

"Have a look," he said, seemingly amused by the prospect. "These fools can't seem to figure it out."

The laughing from the technicians stopped.

"Guess that means we can go relax some," one said as she crossed her arms over her chest.

"Good luck, kid," another jeered.

Replika leaned toward Octavian and whispered, "Do we need protective suits?"

What had he gotten them into?

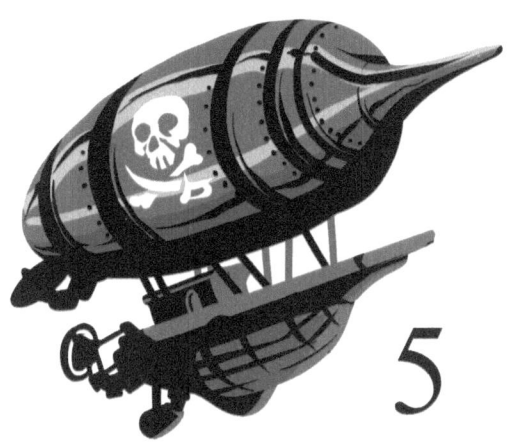

5

THE WHOLE WORLD IS SKETCHY

Octavian questioned his life choices as the funicular main-tenance workers walked off, laughing and discussing what they'd brought for lunch. The gentleman waved Octavian and Replika to follow him. As they made their way closer to the door to the underground facility, Octavian noted that the smoke had settled.

"And how might I refer to you and your . . . companion?" the man asked.

When Octavian answered the question, the man introduced himself as Mr. Pennybottom. It was a peculiar name and one that might have made Octavian laugh in a less dire situation. Not that he was one to laugh at others' names, at least not out loud.

"Down the stairs, you'll see the inner workings of the funic-ular. I'll be back to check on your assessment in an hour or so. I have another pressing matter to attend to." He finally looked at Replika. "You both be safe down there, and try not to break it further."

"Yes, sir," Octavian said.

"You didn't ask about the protective suits," Replika com-mented as they stepped over the threshold into a tunnel with stairs leading down into darkness.

Once he shut the door, Octavian said, "I have magic. And you're . . ." She was heat and fire-resistant, but he couldn't say that. "You're safe. I'll cast a protection spell on the way down."

He looked back at the door one more time, worrying that they'd be followed down. Much to his surprise, there was a large valve that moved a lock into place.

"You're locking the door?" Replika asked as he turned it.

"Those pirates were—"

"The pirates again?" she interrupted. "Why do you think they're so interested in us?"

Octavian groaned. "Do you think I imagined it? I swear they were watching us. I think it's because we stand out wearing these unusual clothes." He meant her unusual clothes, but he knew his stark white hair wasn't helping them blend in.

"How do you even know the people you're talking about are pirates?"

"You're kidding, right? They were wearing the Jolly Roger!"

"I don't even know what that is," Replika said in a matter-of-fact tone.

"The skull and crossbones. They were wearing it like a gang sign. That's the sign of pirates!"

With a disbelieving smile, Replika responded, "I'll just have to trust you."

On a landing several steps down sat a lantern, its warm glow bathing the walls of the tunnel. She picked it up and started down the stairs with bouncing footsteps and a quiet hum. Octavian trudged a few steps behind, grumbling with frustration.

"If you ask me, you should be more worried about that gentleman," Replika said.

"Pennybottom? Why?"

"As soon as he saw us, his whole mood changed. Then, he stood around, as if he was waiting for us to approach him. And it's weird that he's letting you try to fix what is likely a very sophisticated system. Even weirder now we know we can lock ourselves down here. And—"

"Okay!" Octavian interrupted. "Okay. I hear you. He's sketchy. The pirates are sketchy. That boat we took to shore is sketchy. This whole world is sketchy!"

"Are you satisfied that we're in another reality?"

"Let me put it this way. I can't imagine any place in our reality insane enough to use steam power instead of good old-fashioned magic."

Replika laughed, and Octavian found it quite infectious. Despite himself, he found himself half-smiling.

At the bottom of the tunnel was a long semi-circular hallway, which sat perpendicular to the stairs. It was long, extending quite far in both directions. To the right, pipes, tanks, gears, and valves filled the space. Metal walkways with short railings ran along the walls, which added to the cluttered aesthetic. Conversely, the way to the left was empty.

Replika brimmed with excitement as soon as the contraption to the right entered her field of vision, but Octavian was drawn to the empty end of the hall.

"Can you believe this?" Replika exclaimed as her counterpart started down the other end. "The walls are hot. I don't see any fuel source down here. I'll bet there's some kind of natural heating being used. What if there's an active but dormant volcano nearby? Wouldn't that be something! It heats water—I think they're heating water right from the ocean. Sure smells like sea water."

As she continued her trip to the right, Octavian did the same in the opposite direction. His footsteps echoed, emphasizing just how empty the space was. He could still hear Replika fawning over the machinery behind him, but he wasn't listening.

Octavian lifted his hand and lit the dark tunnel with a magic light. A door sat off in the distance with red writing on it. Octavian couldn't read it yet, but he was closing in.

"Definitely sea water," Replika called. "They have capture areas for the distillation waste."

Her momentary silence gave Octavian pause.

"Everything seems to be fine over here. It looks like the workers released some pressure. Maybe the gauge is inaccurate? Thank goodness they were wearing protective equipment. Octavian, you find anything?"

The door was just ahead of him now, with a yellow square outlined on the floor in front of it. The door read "*MANAGEMENT ONLY*". Octavian knew it was locked before he reached it, and not with a normal lock.

"Octavian?!" Replika called out again.

Octavian finally responded. "I'm down here."

"Why? It was empty over there."

"There's a door."

"A door? Like to a custodian closet?"

"That's oddly specific," Octavian mumbled. Then he called back, "No."

Replika's footsteps echoed around the hall as she rushed toward him. He watched as her afropuffs and dress bounced with each step, marveling at how graceful yet ridiculous she looked.

"Do you think there's something important in there?"

"Yeah." He waited for her to get closer and pointed back to the winding pipes, gauges, and valves that she had left behind. "I think all that is a distraction, and this whole thing is running on magic."

6

Magic Warnings are Useless

Replika quickened her pace to a run when she heard magic might be nearby. Anything that could connect them to their home world would surely be useful, she assumed. Plus, running was fun. Octavian seemed excited, waving his arm to tell her to hurry.

"You said there's magic here?" Replika asked when she reached his side. "I thought you said there was no magic away from the island we were on."

"That's not what I meant," Octavian corrected. "The power generators back home are so ubiquitous, you can feel a background level of magic everywhere. When the magic noise of power generators was gone, I knew right away they were missing. It's like a hum in a room that suddenly goes silent." He pointed to the door. "But what we have here is clearly magic."

It was a door. There wasn't anything particularly peculiar about it. It was metal and a thick layer of dust and rust had built up at its base. So, not just a door, but an old, rarely used, poorly maintained door.

Confused, Replika raised her eyebrow at him.

"This door is locked with a magic trap," he said. Before she could ask if that was strange, he added, "It's strange. They put a magical warning around it so a magician would be wary as they approached. I sensed it as soon as I hit the bottom of the stairs."

GAIUS J. AUGUSTUS

Warnings in their magical world were most often used as teaching tools, and other uses were considered amateurish. During a time when they were more common, the largest technology company in the world, NF Tech, had outfitted their computers with a comprehensive warning system. Unfortunately, almost every function triggered one warning or another to the user. The company soon became known as "NF"icient (inefficient) Tech throughout the world. Despite well-meaning updates to reduce the quantity and frequency of warnings, the company never recovered financially and several years later sold to a competitor.

The CEO wrote a book about the failing years of the company, which sold more copies and made more money than the failed computers had. Warnings lost favor after the incident and were often replaced with other forms of magic, most often trap spells.

To Replika, who hadn't heard about the fiasco, warnings didn't sound all that bad. She'd just have to trust Octavian that the warning was nothing to be concerned about.

He took a deep breath. "This will probably take me a while."

"What do you think is inside?" Replika queried.

"I don't know. Whatever it is, it's masked by the trap."

"Couldn't it be dangerous? There was a warning there, after all."

"There are much more effective ways to keep people clear of danger. I can't imagine why a warning spell would be someplace like this. I don't understand why magic is here at all, and we won't know until we get through that door."

"Mysteries upon mysteries," Replika said. She wanted to know more, but she sensed Octavian was eager to get started. "I'll leave you to it," she said with a smile.

Heading back toward the pipes at the other end of the hall, she realized how many details she had taken in without noticing. When they first entered, she had expected these tunnels to be completed with some kind of concrete. Instead, a fine tile lined the tunnel's curved ceiling. Below her, pentagonal bricks lined the floor. When she neared the stairs, the brick changed to a wider square. It was an awkward transition, with many of the pentagonal bricks cut to form a line where the square bricks started.

The heated water system began mere feet on the opposite side of the stairs. A salty smell filled the place, and the air was hot and sticky compared to the cool, breezy day on the surface. Thick metal pipes ran from the walls and floor into several large tanks, each with two release valves nearby. For the largest tank, one valve was open. When she closed it, the reading on the gauge above it didn't change, not even when she flicked it with her finger like a true professional.

Although they had heard an explosion, there was no evidence there had been one. She leaned down to peek under the pipes and tip-toed to look over the tanks. Nothing. It was as if the blast had never happened.

Much of the water was filtered in smaller tanks. Sand and salt lay in trays below the filtration tanks, a clear sign to Replika that clogs had been a problem in the past. Crouching down next to the tray, she realized she had a small bag strapped onto her thigh. She lifted her skirt and opened it. Inside were several vials of different sizes and colors, all empty. She placed samples from the collection trays into them.

She checked over the system one more time, yet there was nothing to explain why it wasn't running. Not that she knew what she was looking for. But the only thing that seemed out of place was that open valve she had found and perhaps a faulty gauge.

It didn't make sense to her. A broken gauge couldn't explain the malfunctioning funicular. All she could think to do was to tinker with it. However, without the proper protective equipment, tinkering seemed foolish, even with whatever protection spell Octavian had enchanted her with.

She didn't know what she was looking for. So instead, she looked back toward Octavian.

He was still standing in front of the door at the other end of the hall. His assertion that the whole water heating system was a distraction seemed unreasonable. Why would anyone create such an elaborate ruse? Every piece of evidence in this little mystery supported that this system worked until a short while ago. A gut feeling told her it was no coincidence that the funicular system stopped working as soon as they arrived, but she had no evidence to support such an intuition.

A bright, purple light suddenly gleamed from Octavian's end of the hall, and his voice came just after. "I've got the first trap down."

7

PSYCHE PARTICLES

Replika rushed back through the maze of pipes, the lantern swaying with each step. Though Octavian was at the far end of the tunnel, every detail of his face was as clear as if she was standing right next to him.

Deep in concentration, his eyes seemed to glow. She had noticed this intense look before, each time Octavian used magic. It made her heart race to think of how beautifully the gold swirled in with the brown of his eyes.

She somehow knew that as magicians grew stronger, their eyes turned sparkling gold. She was sure it was a sight to behold in any magician, but Octavian's changing eyes matched an inner beauty she sensed deep within him. He was quite lovely.

A bright purple cage stood between the door and Octavian. Crossbars formed nine boxes at eye level. And by the time she reached his side, Octavian was grinning.

"What happened?" Replika asked.

"There was a trigger point where the grid is now," he said as he gestured toward the glowing cage in front of him. "It was masked, but luckily, I aced every class on traps in my undergrad." Proud of himself, he pointed toward the door as he continued. "There are nine locks behind this trap, one on each corner of the grid. Once I get past this, I should be able to get those unlocked pretty quick."

"What does this mean?" Replika asked, mirroring his earlier gesture at the puzzle.

"This is a lock, and—you may think this is strange—I've seen a lock just like this before," Octavian said. "Teacher used it on the breakroom fridge during my first year."

Replika couldn't believe it. Octavian's suspicions of Teacher seemed more founded by the minute. Her memories of Teacher were vague. Her gut told her Teacher would never put them in danger without reason, yet they had found no evidence explaining why he may have sent them there.

She shook the thought from her mind. Now wasn't the time to get lost in the theoretical.

"The weird thing is," Octavian continued as he turned back to work, "I've never seen any other lock like it."

"Then you're thinking Teacher set this trap?" she asked.

He nodded, putting his hands on his hips and reviewing the cage in front of him. She watched him stand and stare, but nothing was happening.

"If you've done this before, why isn't it open yet?" Replika asked.

"I'm working on it," he grumbled, though his tilted head made him seem more frustrated than upset. "It's just a very precise process. The idea is to create a homogeneous array of magic over the grid, but the lines of the grid have to be devoid of particles."

"Particles?" She paused for a second. "You mean psyche particles?"

"You remember!" he exclaimed, looking at her with a broad smile. "Or, at least, you're starting to. That's right. The fundamental particle that allows magicians to do magic. Psyche particles."

He returned his gaze to the glowing purple cage. Squinting his eyes, he paced from one side of the cage to the other. The glow in front of them faded abruptly, and Octavian laughed at his success. Replika couldn't help but feel excited, too.

"You said there are nine more locks?" she asked.

"They're easy. Don't worry. I'll have this open in a few minutes."

Replika watched as he placed his hand on the top-left corner of the door. She looked down at her own hands, wondering if she could control magic, if she should be able to see these psyche particles, or perhaps feel them.

Psyche particles can't be seen, and if they could, it would be difficult to see anything else. The particles exist in a multidimensional field. Early humans had learned to sense this field, and later learned to feel its movements. Doing so allowed them to make predictions about many aspects of nature and sometimes was touted as the best way to decide what to wear for a date.

Much, much later, a magician commonly referred to as "The First Magician" decided it wasn't enough to feel it, they needed to control it. The legend goes that The First Magician climbed to the top of the tallest mountain in their homeland with nothing but a journal and an extra pair of trousers. Once at the top, they studied the psyche particle field. They observed how it acted and reacted to changes in the environment: weather, movement, sound, touch. And as they learned about its interactions with the physical world, they discovered ways to manipulate its connection.

No one knows what happened to The First Magician, though many believe they jumped to their death in an attempt to fly. Sometime after, others happened across a journal wrapped in trousers, and one thing led to another. Before long, the study of magic became of powerful influence. The journal was now held in the tower of the International Council of Exalted Magicians, but the trousers were lost to time.

Once Octavian removed all the locks, he held a hand out to the door, inviting Replika to open it. She turned the knob and pulled gently. Much like every door in this world, the door was stuck. More determined, she handed Octavian the lantern.

She placed both hands on the doorknob and yanked it toward her. The door swung open, and with it, the doorknob broke into Replika's hand. The other side fell to the floor and rolled away.

"Sorry," Replika said with a sheepish grin as she took back the lantern.

On the other side of the door was a small room with a large tank in the middle. A pipe ran into it and another ran upward out of it, leaving only enough space for them to walk single file around the edge. They walked in opposite directions, as it seemed quite awkward to do anything else.

Octavian's face lit up when a small compartment on the backside of the tank caught his attention. "I knew it!"

Replika leaned down to get a better look, though there was barely enough room to bend her legs.

"A pilot light?" she asked.

"Just like the one on the boat."

"What's so special about it?" Replika asked.

"That little groove. It's meant to hold a fire marble."

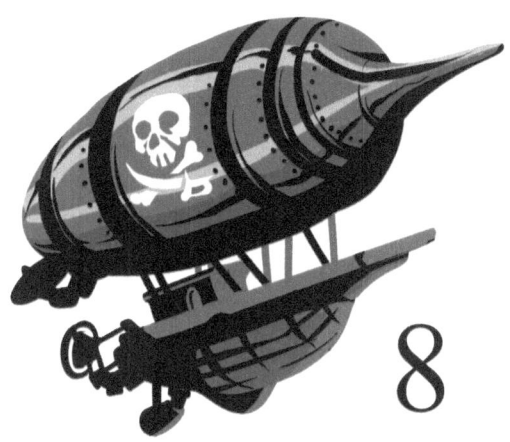

8

TINY ROOM BIG TANK

As Octavian said the words "fire marble," his eyes lit up. Replika wanted to share in his excitement, but she couldn't recall what a fire marble was. He waited as she put the pieces together in her mind.

"A fire marble. Right. Which is . . ." She paused for a moment as if checking her memory to be sure, ". . . magic?"

"Yes. Exactly!" Octavian exclaimed. "There's no magic anywhere here, but somehow there's a magic-powered heating mechanism for a steam-powered transportation system hidden underneath a steam-powered city. That cannot be a coincidence."

"Octavian, I checked the mechanics on the other side of the tunnel. It's been in use and is well-maintained. I didn't find any evidence of an explosion, either. Everything on the surface was just for show. I'm starting to think someone intentionally shut down the system."

Before she could share the rest of her hypothesis, Octavian said it out loud.

"Shut down so we could find it?"

She nodded.

"As for who would do this," Octavian continued. "I think that's the perfect question for our gentleman friend, don't you?"

Octavian didn't wait for her to answer. His attention seemed focused on the mechanics of the tank, all the joy transformed into intense concentration.

"What are you doing now?" Replika asked.

"I think we'll have more leverage if we fix this gizmo."

Replika was smiling now, too. She couldn't help it. It was as if Octavian's momentary giddiness was contagious. As Octavian did . . . whatever he was doing, her attention shifted to the walls of the room. Next to the door, she noted a small hatch with writing above it. It was hard to read, and she couldn't tell if it was worn down by time or whether it was covered with dust. She placed her hand on it and wiped a couple of times, but it didn't do any good.

Abruptly, something strange happened to her vision. She took an instinctive step back, running into the tank. It was as if she could see through whatever dirt was there and pick up what lay underneath.

Surprised, she looked toward Octavian, only to find that the whole room looked different. She was no longer seeing color but instead was seeing something beyond color. She had no words for what was happening, but somehow, she had some sense of what it meant. She looked back at the wall, at the writing that had been so unclear just moments ago.

"*System Override*"

Octavian peeked around the hulking metal mass taking up most of the room to see what she was doing. He stood up as he followed Replika's gaze to the wall.

"Is something there?" he asked, leaning closer.

"Octavian, this system looks pretty old. Do you think that this was built at the same time as the mechanical system on the other side of the stairs?"

"No idea," he replied. "But if Teacher was here at some point, he could have installed this."

Replika didn't like the answer, and she lifted the lantern to make sure he could see her pursed lips.

"Well, we won't find any more answers here," he said. "Once we've got this working, we can ask Mr. Pennybottom some questions."

Replika used her finger to clear off the dust and grime from the door's cracks. Digging her nails behind it, the door opened with a crack, revealing a lever inside. A glance at Octavian ensured he was watching, so she pulled the lever up. When nothing happened, she pushed it down. To her surprise, it went past its starting point with a loud click.

Another small panel on the wall below her flew open. She squatted down as best she could. It was a small locker, and what was inside was less surprising than it would have been an hour earlier.

"What's that?" Octavian asked as she pulled out the contents.

She held it up to him. It was a small, round device that looked somewhat larger than the marble Octavian hung around his neck, except it was red and a few centimeters larger. She peered inside and it seemed to come alive as fire danced this way and that, round in circles, trying to free itself.

"It's a fire marble," Octavian answered his own question. "Well, that saves us some time."

"Can I install it?" she asked.

At his agreement, they returned to the other side of the tank. She held the lantern up to examine the marble stand her counterpart was pointing at. It was a small indentation, the perfect size for the marble, down to the nanometer. She reached out and placed the marble into the indentation.

"Now secure it with that hinge cover," Octavian said.

She found the cover he was talking about and swung it around until it was firmly against the marble. A small latch locked it in place, and when she looked back to Octavian, he nodded. She had done it correctly.

"It's not on," he noted. "Something should have happened."

"Let's try the lever again," Replika said.

Replika returned to the lever and within moments of switching it upward, a bubbling sound bounced around the small room. Steam started flowing up the exhaust pipe, and the machinery hidden above them creaked and moaned. There was a hiss as steam pushed its way up the exhaust, and a pressure gauge on the tank wobbled in the safe zone.

"Well," she said, wiping her hands together for a job well done. "One mystery solved."

"Only a million left," Octavian added.

9

STEPPING IN FECES IS THE LAST STRAW

When they emerged from the tunnel a short time later, a crowd had already coagulated near the station. The writhing mass of riders seemed quite ready to head to the flats above the beach. The bobbing waves of heads made Replika's skin crawl, and she turned her attention to the steady wisps of steam that were rising from pipes nearby, routed from the tunnels below to the safety of the open air.

Murmurs started as the steam pipes released a melodic note, then another. Much to Replika's delight, the pipes played a tune, though it was either pathetic or the bad kind of charming—she wasn't entirely sure which. Even though the song was mediocre, she found its creativity endearing.

Octavian's look of disgust made her smile. Actually, she was quite comfortable with him, despite being unaware of who she was or how she came to be in his company. She was in awe of Octavian's magical ability, like a beacon of light in a dense fog. She had a strong feeling that, whoever she was, he was an important part of her life.

Octavian's gaze shifted away from the pipes to Mr. Pennybottom, who was walking toward them from the market. As soon as he reached them, and without hesitation, he pat Octavian on the back.

"Good job, my boy. Fine work," he laughed.

"Sir, I have a question," Octavian said, interrupting the man's celebration.

"Are you worried about payment?"

"No, don't worry about that. I'm wondering who built that machine down there. The one behind the door."

The man's face became solemn.

"Ah, I see," he said. He didn't look or sound surprised. His eyes drifted to a distant memory.

An entirely different memory, though not entirely unrelated, involved stories his parents told him about his ancestors. The first Pennybottoms who came to this town were wealthy entrepreneurs hoping to be part of something innovative. Though their wish came true—for what was more spectacular than Chronoford, the city carved from a cliff, the apparent steam capital of the world—the city's transportation was less than ideal, and it was often described as horrible, dangerous, and unsanitary.

The carved switchbacks were originally meant to carry supplies and equipment for creating the flats, but after the work on the city was complete, the walled pathways remained the sole way to get between levels. This was a problem because rocks fell from above, the road wasn't smooth, and the pathway wasn't wide enough for mass use. If that wasn't bad enough, once citizens were regularly using the switchbacks, the waste they dumped on the ground not only spread disease but also smelled awful.

When one patriarch of the Pennybottom family stepped in feces for the n minus 1st time, he exclaimed something along the lines of, "If I have to step in shit one more time . . ."

And soon after, he stepped in feces for the n-th time.

He had learned of a failed attempt to create a lift system between flats. Unafraid of spending exorbitant amounts of money on things that were not for the greater good, the Pennybottom family commissioned lifts to each city level, accessible exclusively to the family and their guests. The Pennybottoms used their superior mobility between flats to secure an influential place of power in the town.

Replika watched as Mr. Pennybottom pulled himself from his different but not entirely unrelated memory. He took a deep breath and pulled Octavian off to the side. Replika tried to follow, but the man held a hand up to stop her. She crossed her arms over her chest and pursed her lips. After a minute that dragged on forever, Octavian thanked the man and rejoined Replika.

"Well? What did he say that was so important I couldn't be a part of it?" Replika asked. She huffed, pursed her lips even harder, and crossed her arms even further.

"I'll tell you when we get onboard," he said, gesturing toward the funicular station. "But it's good news."

He was smiling, but something about the situation worried Replika. She looked back at the gentleman, who was smiling his own strange smile at them. The look in his eyes betrayed that he was hiding something, and Replika really wanted to know what it was.

Octavian led her to the so-called station, which was more of a gated platform, despite what the sign at the entry said. They walked right past the crowd, Octavian flashing a piece of paper at the attendant, and onto the funicular car.

"Don't we need tickets?" Replika asked Octavian as they sat in two seats by a window.

"Mr. Pennybottom gave us this." He held up the piece of paper he had held up outside. "It's a VIP pass for me and any guests I want to bring along. He owns the funicular system."

Though it looked like a fallen train car from the outside, inside was homey with tiered seating at an angle matching the steepness of the incline. The decor was opulent, with striped wallpaper, chair railing, and even curtains around the windows. There was a light floral scent, odd since the only flowers Replika had seen since they arrived were those being sold at the market.

"That's very generous of your new friend, but where are we going?" she asked.

"The 'Third Flat,'" Octavian said.

10

Funiculars Save Lives

Despite Octavian providing his own air quotes to the words "Third Flat," Replika didn't know what that meant. When she asked, Octavian leaned forward and pointed to the three tiers that sat below the original cliff's full height.

"The three levels of cliffs above the beach are called flats, and we're headed to the top one." Octavian lowered his voice down to a whisper. "He said the man who designed the magic system in the tunnel—probably Teacher—frequented an antique shop on the Third Flat. I figured we'd head there and see if we can find out anything else about what Teacher did while he was here."

"Seems convenient," Replika commented. "Did you confirm it was Teacher?"

"Well, no." He sighed. "But you're right, of course. I should have asked, just to make sure. Although I don't know what name Teacher would have used, and I don't know what color his hair and eyes were when he was young."

Octavian glanced around, and Replika wondered if anyone would even care if he brought up magic. Everyone appeared to be minding their own business, so Replika just moved on.

"That's true, but if he knows anything about Teacher, it could be helpful."

"I'm sure we can find Mr. Pennybottom again if we need to ask more questions. He seems friendly."

"What?" Replika asked, genuinely surprised. "You still don't find him suspicious?"

Octavian paused to think, putting a hand on his chin and raising his gaze to an invisible thought bubble. Replika wasn't sure whether he was humoring her or giving this real thought.

"Secretive, I'd agree with," he finally responded. "But not suspicious."

Replika found his demeanor quite charming, so she left it at that. She turned to look out the window as the car accelerated. They rolled up the tracks, and the squeaking of the wheels matched a rhythmic clunking. As they ascended, she noted a heavy smog that covered the town, making it difficult to see the horizon to the west.

She shifted her focus to their island, which she could still clearly see despite the smog of the city and the fog surrounding the island complex. It was far off, yet she could see it so well that it made her wonder—

The First Flat came into view, distracting her from her previous thought.

The city itself was sizeable. Near the tracks, each flat was filled from the back cliff wall to the front cliff face with buildings, courtyards, and pathways, but there was still room to grow toward the far end of each cliff. As they paused at the Second Flat, she noted that each level had a large station to accommodate the traffic of people traveling between levels.

When Chronoford was first accepting citizens on the flats, most housing was clustered at the northern side of the cove, where the switchbacks were. To reduce costs—or, more correctly, to increase profit—the mastermind behind the city, Horatio Castille, forwent other plans for transportation between flats.

His crew suggested a simple solution as a proof of principle: a lift system between the beach and the First Flat. They argued the switchbacks could become deadly with too much use, and

Mr. Castille argued that a lift would require excessive mainte-nance to remain in working condition, effectively bankrupting him. They struck up a bet, and six months—and quite a few deaths—later, the crew won, earning themselves a hefty raise. However, despite the bet and regular deadly reminders of the danger of the switchbacks, no other public transport system was completed until the funicular. After its inauguration, almost all citizens migrated their homes and businesses close to the rails.

Like the citizens, the transport system had caught Replika's fancy. The starts and stops were much smoother than she imag-ined they would be, and she couldn't help but note the sharp con-trast between it and the longboat's jolting mechanism. Each flat brought with it excitement and curiosity, so much so that Replika was disappointed when they reached the final stop.

They followed the passengers out into a large pavilion. Though its simple post-and-lintel construction was sound, it seemed obvious to Replika that it needed repairs. The rail went through two similar pavilions on the other flats, but they were much grander. Whereas the paint on the walls was peeling in the Third Flat Station, the coat of paint looked recent on the First and Second Flat stations. The roof of this pavilion was missing win-dows she'd seen at the other stations, which let in a lot of natural light. And, though Replika couldn't verify this for the other sta-tions, this one had a certain smell that didn't sit right with her.

As soon as they left the pavilion, they were in the hustle and bustle of a string of shops. From bakeries to clothing boutiques, Replika marveled at the variety of items available. A strong breeze brought with it the smell of fresh, sugary delicacies from a confectionery store, which had a line of people waiting to buy. A few more meters and that smell was replaced by smoking meat so perfectly cooked, it was falling off the bone as customers ate it. Her gaze then fell on a shop of beautifully arranged flowers that lifted her spirits from the disrepair of the Third Flat's infra-structure.

She was effectively, practically, and successfully immersed.

11

CHEERY AND CLUTTERED, A WINNING COMBINATION

Replika took in everything she could as they walked down the wide, cobbled street of the Third Flat of Chronoford, Steam Capital of the World. The countless footsteps that had tread across it had worn down the stone. At regular intervals in the roadway sat small seating areas with long-dead flower beds and benches that, while clean, had seen better days.

One such bench had been blessed by the great Detective Quinn Frumingham, who was world renowned for zir most famous case, inappropriately named the "Chronoford Killer" case. The case began when a series of city construction workers became ill and died. The newspapers of the time, if you could call the informal writings of gossips a newspaper, convinced its readership that these deaths were caused by poisoning. Through thorough analysis of throat throughput, Frumingham deduced that the culprit was merely the result of a mix of dietary habits that led to dehydration.

Never missing a chance to sensationalize, the newspaper prepared a special edition that was, through a series of coincidental and sometimes comical circumstances, redistributed around the world. Frumingham became a household name and sat zir bottom on this very bench on the day it was dedicated in zir honor.

In zir later years, ze lamented about not being well known for solving true murder, larceny, arson, and missing person cases, but instead had become famous for having some "gosh darn common sense." Ze complained to students at the New South Coast University College of Forensic Science, saying "one doesn't become a detective for the fame, but if one does accumulate popularity, one hopes it would be for one's best work."

Zir final words as ze bled out from a knife wound inflicted by the later-named Frumingham Foiler were "Maybe solving this one will finally set my record straight." On zir corpse, investigators found evidence that led to zir murderer—who ze had been tracking for over a year for other murders—and a notebook full of statistics about zir lifetime of spectacular detective work.

A biography published ten years after zir death, *The Real Detective Frumingham*, revealed zir brave and insightful exploits to the world with the respect and dignity Frumingham wished for and deserved. Unfortunately, the reviews were lackluster compared to another biography published a few months later, *Killers in Our Diet: A Deep Dive Into Detective Frumingham's Most Iconic Case*.

Frumingham's bench in Chronoford was in no better shape than any of the others. Despite their disrepair, many of these benches were full, whether it be from shopping bags and boxes or from large families fighting over where to go next. If Replika and Octavian had been visiting Chronoford for pleasure, they would have enjoyed relaxing on one of these benches and people watching. However, they had a destination to get to, though Replika had almost forgotten that.

She was distracted by the narrow width of the street, the contents of the shops, and every other observation she had made since exiting the funicular car, but Octavian's voice pulled her back into the present.

"There it is," Octavian said.

After a moment to remember what he was talking about, she asked, "Where?"

He was pointing down the road, where the shops were dwindling and replaced with empty buildings and professional services. Among them was a little rundown place attached at the back to a large warehouse. The front door sat in an alcove surrounded by windows, which displayed a variety of antiques.

The display windows were cluttered with a myriad of intriguing but random items, some looking worn with age, while others looked as good as new. Mannequins modeled clothing, and items for the home sat on tables and display shelves.

"I wonder why a magician would frequent a place like this," Replika said.

Octavian shrugged and opened the door to the shop. They were immediately confronted with three things. First, the hollow, dull ring of a bell that was hanging by a thread just above the door. Second, the musky smell of items of varying age and quality. And last, a maze of potentially purchasable items that seemed to offer a challenge to get anywhere in the store.

As Replika took in the cluttered mounds of treasure, a voice called out from somewhere.

"Hello! Welcome!" The voice had great energy but little in the way of evidence as to its source.

Behind piles of odds and ends was a long glass counter, and behind the counter was a tall curtain covering a two-story archway. The voice had come from beyond this curtain. Just as Replika was wondering if she imagined the voice, a person emerged.

"I'm Jonny," they said with waving arms and a cheerful grin. "Please. Please. Come on over. Don't be shy. What can I interest you in today?"

They wiped their hands on their apron, adding dust to the stains that already sat near the pockets. By the time Octavian and Replika found their way around the obstacles and over to the counter, the shopkeeper had blabbered out several questions about what they were looking for, leaving no time for them to respond.

Replika took a deep breath, ready to interject when the opportunity came available.

"Hello," she blurted when Jonny took a breath.

As if surprised, Jonny paused.

"We're hoping you can help us find someone. We heard he frequented here," Replika continued.

"A frequent customer?" Jonny laughed. "That is rare. Tell me more about this someone."

Replika struggled to find words to describe Teacher, so she urged Octavian to take over with a long look.

"He helped build the system that runs the funicular," Octavian said. "Mr. Pennybottom said you'd remember him."

"Oh!" Jonny exclaimed, their laughter seeming more nervous now than before, though they were still grinning. "Mr. Pennybottom, you say? Why, yes. Yes, I understand now what you're looking for! Wait right here. Wait here!" They put up their hands and backed away.

"But we're not—" Octavian couldn't finish his sentence before Jonny disappeared behind the curtain.

"I guess you hit a nerve," Replika said with a shrug. She turned around and waved her arm over the crowded shop. "Sure is a lot of interesting stuff in here."

"Yeah?" Octavian asked, a doubtful look on his face.

"Yeah. Kitchen items. Some toys and instruments. And, of course . . ." She paused and wiggled her hand toward something. ". . . whatever that is."

That something she was wiggling at was an old prototype which used steam power to assist in the pulling of carts. It was invented by none other than James L. Pennybottom, our Mr. Pennybottom's father.

He had noticed that far too often, traffic in the switchbacks was stalled because of excessive loads on carts. Horses needed time to rest as citizens tried to cram as much as they could on their travels between flats. It was quite an annoying delay for travelers, both because of the malodorous smell of the switchbacks and because, without fail, they would end up in uncomfortable conversations with the strangers either in front of or behind them.

The invention, aptly called the Cart Assist, used steam power to ease the burden on the horses, however it had several drawbacks that led to its discontinuation. First, it didn't replace the horses needed to pull carts, it only eased their burden. Then there was the fact that cost estimates were quite expensive. But the most important reason was that the weight added by the water needed for the device to function negated its effects, rendering the device useless. Details, details.

The invention earned James L. Pennybottom the name "The Bottom Penny," since no one wanted to spend a penny on his invention. Luckily, his other work, along with his family's continued wealth and influence, restored his reputation as a brilliant and innovative inventor. This particular trade and notoriety was passed on to his son.

Octavian's imagination ran wild with speculation, none of which came close to the ridiculous splendor of the Cart Assist. He chuckled, and Replika let out a small, accomplished laugh.

"Here it is!" Jonny called out, their voice muffled through the curtain and piles of treasure.

There was a loud scraping sound and then a jumble of bangs and booms and possibly a bam or two. As Jonny slipped through the curtain, Replika realized the clutter problem wasn't isolated to the shop's storefront. They held up their find. Upon seeing worried faces, Jonny waved a hand at their customers.

"Everything's fine," they said with the same grin they'd had on their face since Replika and Octavian had entered the shop.

They placed a small leather bag on the counter, and Replika recognized it straightaway. It was the same as the bag she had on her thigh.

Just as she was wondering what was inside, Octavian asked, "What's this?"

"Take a look," Jonny urged.

Octavian slid the bag across the counter to sit in front of him. It was small, just too big to hold in one hand's grip. He loosened the strap holding it shut, then pulled on the tied knot that secured the closure. His eyes widened as he revealed what was inside.

12

GOTTA HAVE IT

Octavian was too surprised to notice when Replika leaned forward, trying to get a look at the contents of the leather pouch. He pulled the round object from its bag and turned it this way and that to get a better look at it. When he noticed Replika, he held it out to her, hoping she would recognize it without him needing to say anything.

A computer.

A bona fide magic computer.

He couldn't believe it.

The bottom half of the sphere was clad with metal, but the top half was hollow, covered by a piece of thick, clear material. It was smooth like glass, but Octavian knew it wasn't. Three strips of metal, each fabricated to resemble ornate vines, stretched from the metal base around to the pole, dividing the top half into three parts. Where the three met, a large crystal sat, chiseled with seven facets.

Octavian peered into the transparent portion of the device. There was a flat plane with several axes drawn, though there was no indication of what the axes were measuring.

It was all too familiar to Octavian. Although he'd never gotten a close look, this looked almost identical to the computer that sat in the glass cabinet in Teacher's lab. The same computer

Teacher was holding—and had pushed a button on—right before they were thrown into this reality.

There were dozens of companies that manufactured computer marbles, but only three had been around when computers were this large: NF Tech, MaGeek, and Phyre. These early marbles were designed with a sentiment resembling "trying too hard." They included intricate detailing, innovative—yet rapidly obsolete—accessories, customized user interfaces, and non-standard sizing. With a mere two millimeter diameter difference between the brands, it was easy to, for example, accidentally pick up the wrong toilet virtual assistant for your particular computer, leading to the general consensus that toilets should be manually controlled and virtual assistants have no place in the bathroom.

After years of innovation followed by years of standardization, there were only a few differences between modern marbles that most people were interested in. The first was color, with the most popular being beige, although several new tech startups refused to carry such a color. The second difference of interest to most people was sheen: gloss, eggshell, luster, or matte. And last, computer marble users were divided on whether marbles should be transparent, translucent, or opaque. Arguments on this divisive topic had resulted in fractured families, riots, protests, and the occasional flier or graffiti in public restrooms.

Octavian's computer marble, creatively called "Notebook", was translucent, iridescent, and eggshell, but that's neither here nor there.

The computer sitting in front of him didn't conform to any standard size or design from the three major brands likely to have manufactured it. Not only was it somewhat larger, but the opulent detailing had tooling marks and irregularities. The glass-like material that encased the marble's interior had many imperfections, making the axes on the interior of the device a bit warped from certain directions. These details hinted that the computer had been handcrafted.

13

THE SNITCH

Despite having a magic computer marble within his grasp that was almost identical to the one Teacher had kept locked away in a cabinet in the lab, Octavian couldn't think of any way to keep it. He had tried bribing the shopkeeper, which he couldn't do properly without knowing the actual value of the coins he had. Jonny didn't seem interested in bartering anyway. Perhaps he could offer his services, as he had to Mr. Pennybottom. It seemed like as good a plan as any, though he worried about what it would take to convince the shopkeeper.

Suddenly, Replika grabbed his arm and began pulling him.

"Don't worry," she said as she dragged him through the maze of items toward the door. "We'll figure something out."

"Wait. We can't leave yet," he argued. He wasn't fighting her tugs. Though he wanted to, he knew there wasn't anything left for them to do.

"Let's just do some more shopping before heading back home," Replika urged, speaking louder than she needed to and pulling him harder than he could resist. "We'll come back tomorrow."

Something was off, and it wasn't that she called the island complex "home," although doing so was disconcerting.

As she dragged Octavian out the door, he looked back to see Jonny shaking their head while chuckling in some perverse amusement at his dismay. He dropped his head back, leaving his fate in Replika's firm grasp.

The sun peeked through the cloudy sky, then was gone again. A gentle breeze was interrupted by a gust of wind, bringing with it the salty smell of the sea. He wanted to enjoy it, but instead, he kept ruminating on what he could say to get a hold of that computer. No solutions came to mind. One thing was for sure, he had more questions now than when they entered the shop.

It's probably obvious to say their sudden departure from the store was suspicious. What was equally suspicious was the figure who had been nearby since the funicular car on the beach. After the figure observed what happened in the shop, they rushed to one of the Pennybottom homes, where they had used a bribe to gain access to the lift there.

Once they made it to the Second Flat, they exited from around the back. Mrs. Gupta, an elderly woman who recognized the figure, called out to them. She fussed when they kept running, and they couldn't bring themself to ignore her. After all, she'd gone out of her way the week before to bake them their favorite flavor of pie.

"This is the trouble with you young folx," she said. "You're always in such a hurry. Well, in my day . . ."

It went on this way until the figure finally talked themself out of the situation. Now behind their self-declared deadline, they pushed through busy streets and crowded corridors until they arrived at another Pennybottom property.

"Oi! Mate!" a voice came from behind.

The figure rolled their eyes. It was John "the mouth" Mecklenburg. Despite the figure's objections, John told them all about the bar fight they saw the other night, where a tourist from one of the vacation boats had tried to pass himself off as a local. Except he didn't know a lick of English and his travel translation book wasn't in his native tongue. After throwing out some friendly and unintentional insults, he learned that a pub probably wasn't the best place to try to fit in as a local, especially in Chronoford, where pirates were welcome.

John "the mouth" Mecklenburg laughed and laughed through the entire story, and when he was done, the figure gave a polite chuckle before continuing on.

After being forced to eat a sample at several food shops, ripping their coat on a branch whose bite was as bad as its bark, and getting mud in their boot after stepping in a puddle that was deeper than it looked, finally they reached the next lift.

It was no easier getting through the First Flat or the beach, and when the figure reached their destination, they were questioning why they put themself in this situation to begin with. Their parents had wanted them to become a doctor, but did the figure listen? Of course not. And now here they were, explaining a suspicious scenario to a suspicious soul with a spyglass, who would use the information to do who knows what. And then they were given a hefty coinage, and suddenly it was all worth it.

Back on the Third Flat, Octavian was realizing he hadn't slept in over a day. And then he realized something else. Although Replika had mentioned shopping, she didn't stop at the sweets shop she had drooled over earlier or the clothing store with the childish dresses she was programmed to love. She pulled him right past them, heading straight for the funicular station.

He wasn't excited to shop, although he reminded himself he still wanted a sweater. A bright color would be nice, with a soft inner lining and extra-long sleeves. It brought back memories of being bundled up, playing in the snow, and subsequently tripping on ice. He then remembered how much he hated the cold.

In fact, how could he even think about the cold when they just lost their only remaining clue about how to get home, his real home? He wondered if Replika was feeling the same way.

Worried, he tried several times to ask Replika what was going on, but she interrupted him to point out a contraption that a street worker was using to light the streetlamps or a piece of luggage chugging along behind a person, letting off gentle streams of steam for some despicable reason.

By the time they were off the funicular car at the beach level and exiting the market, Octavian had suffered enough of her avoidance.

"What are you doing?" he asked. "We can't go back to the island yet. We need to get answers."

She continued pulling him along the boardwalk toward their boat as if he hadn't said anything. He repeated her name several times before she responded.

"We came out here for supplies," Replika replied in a forced, bouncy tone. "We got them. We can return tomorrow to ask more questions."

"There's no reason to rush like this." He sighed. "Replika, please. At least let go. You're going to bruise my arm."

She stopped and complied. She turned back toward him. If there was ever a reason to suspect someone, the look on her face now was that reason.

Her look was the kind of look that the famous reality show star Babra Rondelle gave his daughter as he refused to allow her to pursue her medical gender transition because her doctors were sure that, due to a pre-existing condition, she wouldn't live through it. Or the look that his daughter gave to her father as she went into that very surgery.

It was a look which was quite different from the one that both father and daughter put on when the world found out that the whole thing had been faked and she had never been in danger during any of her five gender confirmation surgeries. And none of these looks spared the reality show from being replaced by the equally fictional show called The Exalted Council, which was canceled halfway through its first season after a lawsuit from several Exalted Grand Magicians.

"Now tell me what's going on," Octavian demanded.

"Well, you see—" she started, now seeming quite coy.

Before she could continue, two arms grabbed Octavian around his shoulders. He tried to look behind him as two more arms flew into view to wrap around Replika's torso.

He'd been distracted. Too distracted. Way too distracted. But no amount of reminding himself how distracted he had been would loosen the grip on him.

14

THE SHOT HEARD 'ROUND THE DOCKS

Octavian thrashed back and forth, trying to break free of the hold around his arms and torso, but another set of hands grasped onto him and turned him around.

Beside him, Replika threw an elbow into the stomach of her attacker. As Octavian struggled to break free of the firm grasp he was in, she dropped, spun, and struck the man straight in the jaw. The man fell backward and let out a curse. It wasn't the kind of curse that Octavian would have expected, such as a word or two of anger or an insult directed toward Replika. Instead, it was a series of jumbled up words that seemed solely connected by their tone of negativity. Replika didn't seem to notice as she turned her attention to Octavian's predicament.

A hand reached for her wrist as she took her first step toward him, but the hand and the attached human fell away when she slammed her palm into his nose. His nose bleeding, he took a couple steps backward, only to trip into the arms of the first man Replika felled.

It wasn't the first connection the two men had shared, but it wasn't the connection either was looking for at this moment.

Replika then stomped over to Octavian's assailants, who were backing him away from her, one fiddling with her knife while the other struggled to keep in control despite Octavian's wiggling.

His arm broke free, and he scratched at the face behind him. Hot breath met his neck as the man holding him screamed. Wrenching away, Octavian freed himself before falling forward onto the ground. As he rolled over, Replika seized the man's arm with one hand and punched him in the stomach with the other. She grabbed the woman who had retrieved her knife and threw her to the ground. Replika stomped on her hand, causing her to let go of the weapon with a strong yelp.

Octavian focused on getting out of there in one piece, but a small part of him wondered what the hell Teacher was thinking when designing this "medical innovation." If there had been time for him to question the decision to add combat to Replika's repertoire, he may have wondered why her offensive moves were overpowered and why her defensive moves were so evasive. While there wasn't time at present to ask these or any follow-up questions, a seed was planted in his mind that would continue to grow with time.

Replika pulled Octavian off the ground and along the boardwalk until he had his balance back. They could hear the pounding of footsteps on the wooden boards behind them as their attackers got their bearings and carried on with their pursuit.

After jumping into the longboat herself, Replika held out her hand to help Octavian in. He clutched it to get on board before looking back. That was a mistake. Attached to the sleeve of each of their attackers was the Jolly Roger. These were pirates. Because of course they were.

Was he hoping Replika was right when she said the pirates weren't interested in them? Of course.

But was he surprised that they were the ones perpetrating this attack? Absolutely not.

Octavian was so unsurprised that, despite being terrified, he wanted to laugh at the whole ridiculous situation.

He tried an internal laugh.

Ha ha ha, he thought.

But it just wasn't satisfying.

Just beyond the pirates, leaning against a nearby post, stood a large monster of a man with a full beard and a tricorn hat, golden chains dripping from his neck and wrists, while a spyglass hung at his right hip. Octavian couldn't be sure, but something in the man's smug smile and relaxed posture made him sure this was their leader. All he was missing was an eyepatch and a peg leg. He took slow, calculated steps, unafraid of losing his prey.

Replika called for him. The fire had gone out, and he rushed over to relight it. His heart was racing. He glanced back. The pirates were walking down the jetty toward them, staying a step behind the large bearded man.

"Any time now," Replika urged.

"I'm trying," he replied with urgency.

"Then stop looking back. Just concentrate. I'll take care of them."

He looked up into her determined smile. The butterflies in his stomach subsided, and his pounding heart slowed. He allowed the ocean breeze to overcome him. Wisps of wind brushed through his hair. As the waves sloshed against the boat, its buoyancy bobbing him up and down, up and down, up and down. The water hissed as it crawled onto the shore, only to be pulled back out to sea by sticky hydrogen bonds. The calm and bustle of Nature was all around him, yet he was in control.

He closed his eyes. The molecules moved in their stochastic rhythm, and he knew how to manipulate them. He pulled them closer, moved them faster. The psyche particles were at his command, igniting the air and then holding and controlling it. It was just him and the flame.

Once ready, he placed it into the area for the pilot light. Bubbling water pushed a spinning disk, ready to release its power into movement. The world came back into focus and with it, the sounds of pirates. They were cheering on their captain, the bearded man, as he attempted to pull Replika out of the boat by her arm while laughing out some kind of arrogant self-adulation.

She punched him in the face, pushing him a step back. Using the leverage to brace her foot on the edge of the jetty, she kicked him in the knee, causing him to recoil.

His grip loosened but didn't release, and he pulled her along with him. She grabbed at the nearest bollard, not allowing him to drag her out of reach of escape.

A large clacking sound rang out as the captain pulled his pistol from its holster. He said something Octavian couldn't hear and which he wouldn't have understood had he heard it. In one large effort, Replika threw all her weight against his thumb, which loosened his grip just enough to free herself. She fell into the boat and slammed down on the lever in the same motion.

A shot rang out.

The longboat lurched forward, masking the crying gasp that came from Replika's robotic lungs. The clamp that had secured the boat to the jetty destroyed the support post it had been attached to, and the structure collapsed. Octavian fell backward onto the bottom, knocking his head once more on its sturdy wooden planks.

The motor churned out steam.

The waves pounded against the boat's front.

Seagulls cried out in the distance for some unrelated but well-timed reason.

But somehow, for Octavian, it was silent.

15

BLOOD IS RED

Fear gripped Octavian as he laid on the bottom of the boat. A part of him didn't want to see the result of the gunshot, but he knew he couldn't just do nothing—as tempting as it seemed. As soon as Octavian regained his composure, he clamored to gain some footing, pushing himself up onto damp knees and sloshing towards the bullet-pierced robot.

"Replika! Are you okay?"

She had been shot, so it was quite the loaded question and bordered on insensitive.

Luckily, Replika wasn't listening.

She was on her back, clutching one shoulder with the opposite hand. He pulled her body up into his lap, cradling her head in his arm. She didn't writhe in pain or grimace at his touch. Perhaps she wasn't in as much pain as he thought she would be. Still, she was not moving or responding to him.

"Replika, answer me. Say something," he begged. He leaned down. "Look at me."

Big purple eyes jerked over to meet his gold and brown ones. Her mechanical irises closed and opened to adjust to the changing light as his shadow wavered.

He was shaking, even more than the boat's bouncing could explain away. He worried she could feel it, that she could sense the terror in his heart. But he decided the backlighting of the sun and the jumpiness of the boat were enough to cloak his tells.

"You're going to be fine," he said with as much confidence as he could muster. "I promise. So, just say something."

She struggled for a moment. Her mouth moved, trying to form words, as she had when she had first been activated. And finally, she spoke. "What's wrong with me?"

"You were shot," Octavian said.

He felt dumb for stating the obvious, but what else could he say?

Her lips curled up a moment, a half smile, but it was gone before it fully developed. His mind spun, trying to remember what kinds of tools he'd seen in the island complex. He could barely breathe as he tried to figure out how he would dock the boat, transport her up onto the dock, and carry her into the complex. He struggled to remain calm as panic threatened to take over.

"It doesn't hurt like it should," she continued. "And . . ."

She held her hand away from her shoulder to show him the silver lubricant that was seeping from the wound. Besides the hole in her shoulder, she also had a gash on her lower arm, which was also leaking.

"I'm pretty sure blood is red," she added.

Octavian swallowed the lump in his throat. Why did it have to happen like this? He berated himself for not telling her she was artificial when he had the chance. He should have told her immediately. Could her body handle this kind of damage plus emotional shock?

Teacher and Octavian had planned out testing strategies for Replika post-activation. Tests of both her emotional systems and physical limitations were part of those plans, but a battle royale with a band of pirates wasn't what he had expected. Octavian couldn't think as he hovered somewhere between "panic," "almost panic," and "pretty much panic." He was combing his memory, trying to recall anything in her documentation that would tell him something about her prognosis.

After a few deep breaths, he calmed enough to assess the amount of fluid she'd lost. It wasn't an excessive amount, and he reminded himself of her regenerative functionality. Finally, his panic faded into the realm of "ready to panic at a moment's notice."

"If you can move," he said, "we can get back to the lab. I can repair you once we're there, but I need your help."

"Repair," she repeated. "Am I a mechanical doll of some sort?"

Teacher didn't program her to know his name, but he programmed her to know the phrase "mechanical doll?" Really? How preposterous. It was another odd design choice, similar to how he programmed this medical innovation to fight for no reason in particular. When Teacher had told Octavian that Replika was designed with a full personality, he thought he understood what that meant. He had even done some work on the system, but he hadn't scratched the surface.

If he had believed Teacher was still alive, he would have made a mental note to have a serious chat with him about all this. But he didn't, and so he wouldn't. Instead, he focused his attention on the matter at hand.

"Let's talk when we get back to the island. I'll explain everything."

"You promise?" Replika asked.

"Of course. I promise."

Finally, a true smile came to her face, which gave his heart an endearing tug. She allowed Octavian to help her into the seat next to the controls. Nodding her head toward the approaching fog, she used her uninjured arm to steer them toward the island that it concealed.

By the time they docked, Octavian could tell Replika was less anxious. Although she was still in pain, her posture showed very few signs of tension. She was able to dock the boat with little effort and climb the steep stairwell without help. Not that he didn't offer, but she rightfully pointed out how awkward such a task would be.

Inside, he left Replika in the small, windowless bedroom he'd found when they were exploring the space. Rummaging through the laboratory, Octavian filled his bag with tools. He rejoined Replika, and, sitting next to her on the bed, he took her arm in his hand. With a gentle smile, he pointed to her shoulder.

"May I?" he asked.

She nodded, and he reached behind her to unfasten the ties at the back of her dress. Once opened, he helped her remove her arm from the sleeve.

His first task was to assess the damage. What had originally seemed like a hole blown through her shoulder now appeared to have been a much shallower wound. The casing of her shoulder had taken most of the blow, so her inner workings were intact. The gash on her arm was longer and there was damage to her muscular fibers. This would weaken her, but she should still have her full range of motion.

This was good news, both for her recovery and for his shaky hands.

"As I guess you've realized," he said as he took up his tools and began working, "you're a robot. You may remember I'm a graduate student who works in Teacher's lab at the National University of Magic. Your activation was the goal of my first grad school project. But, of course, you were designed by Teacher."

"Why?" she asked. "Why was I made?"

"Teacher designed you to advance the medical field."

It was a white lie.

Teacher had explained to Octavian some of Replika's more impactful advances, which were all focused on improving medicine. However, he had never divulged his original purpose in designing and building her. Octavian could only guess from the insights he had gleaned while working on her systems over the past few years.

Her senses were enhanced, and she was stronger than a human. Her mechanical precision was fine enough for microscopic surgery. And several of her systems were advancements that Octavian believed would have revolutionized the industries of prostheses, artificial organs, and diagnostics if they hadn't been cast from their world into this ridiculous steam-powered reality.

Of course, Replika's most exceptional and groundbreaking feature, her unique power core, generated its own energy with magic so complex that he wasn't sure even those in the International Council of Exalted Magicians could understand it. Every inch of her seemed to hold a technological marvel, and there was so much about her he didn't know.

"You're the most advanced robot in our world," he told her.

"But in the end, I'm just a machine." She said it in such a dismal tone that he couldn't find it in himself to keep working.

But what could he say?

16

THE SKY SHIELD

Octavian's stomach bunched into knots at Replika's dismissal of herself as "just a machine." He looked up from her wounds to meet her gaze, but she was looking away from him. He put a hand to her chin and turned her face toward him.

She had tears in her eyes, and Octavian's furrowed brow drew in tighter.

"You aren't 'just' anything. Having robotic parts or being powered by magic doesn't change that. Every living thing is a machine. You and I aren't different. I even have a prosthesis of my own."

Replika brought her hand up to her cheek to hold his in place. She seemed content with his answer, but he couldn't be sure. Was she honestly okay?

He bit his lip before continuing. "Now that you know. I hope you can help me."

"How can I do that?" she asked.

"Well, the good news is that the wounds look worse than they are. I've created a temporary seal that should help for the meanwhile. The bad news is that without access to schematics and documentation, doing a real fix is going to take a while, if I can do it at all. But if you can access your plans, we can figure this out together. Do you think you can try?"

She thought about it. He couldn't help but be concerned for her. Not only had she just gone through a physical assault, but her world had just been turned upside down. He cursed Teacher for putting her through this. Her usual energy and smile were gone, and Octavian felt sure she was exhausted. He certainly wasn't thinking as clearly as he would like.

"I can do it," she replied with a gentle smile of pride.

Or maybe she was fine, and he was just being a big baby.

In fact, neither of these was true, as they realized when a loud boom sent chills up Octavian's spine. Before either could take another breath, another loud boom echoed from above. They both jumped again, and Octavian rushed to the atrium. Out of nowhere, a giant cannonball came hurtling down through the fog toward his very non-big baby face.

Physical cannonballs were quite rare outside of museums in Octavian's world, but historically, all civilizations have found some way to send objects up so they can see how fast they come down.

One notable example was the Ponsoi, a cult that once laid claim to 500 acres of land bordering the countries of Chalsinia and Palo. The Ponsoi had negative views of all magic, and they sought a homeland where these activities were forbidden.

After their surprising claim to the land, the two bordering countries held an informal conference on the subject, which mainly consisted of laughing at the Ponsoi's expense. Even more surprised by this turn of events were the 150 or so Chalsinian and Palovi people who lived on the stretch of land. In honor of the Ponsoi "liberation," the locals organized a satirical celebration where they set off fireworks, employed entertainers to imperson-ate the Ponsoi, and had varying degrees of success at getting drunk.

When the leader of the Ponsoi blessed the event with his presence, he was enraged to see "magic" in use as fire appeared in the sky from nowhere and clowns pulled flowers from their small sleeves. The Ponsoi released a statement telling the world they would show no mercy to those who planned and attended the social gathering. The Chalsinian and Palovi leaders, sides still hurting from laughing so hard, ordered the immediate removal of the Ponsoi cult.

The Ponsoi readied their projectile weapons and shot them into the sky in retaliation, aimed at their enemies. And, like all civilizations, they watched them come down, but that was about all there was to see. The projectiles were thwarted with ease. Within hours, the Ponsoi subheading of the related chapter of history was closed, and the world was forced to go back to the lackluster existence that was everyday life.

Octavian's negative outlook on a lackluster existence had shifted in the last twenty-four hours. Before then, he might have wished for some excitement, but now he believed that a lackluster existence was probably quite nice. Although studying the masculine disciplines of Offense or Protection and Healing would have been beneficial at this moment, it didn't occur to him to wish he had majored in either. Instead, he took the last few moments of his life to curse the pirates with scurvy. The thought was problematic, as this was a major public health concern in the pirate community, but as far as last thoughts go, it wasn't so bad.

He flinched as if it would help him fend off the cannonball, turning his head as another boom rang out. When he opened his eyes a few seconds later, he wasn't dead. Instead, the cannonball had stopped just above the atrium. It rolled downward and away, as if the complex was surrounded by a dome.

He put his hand to his face and laughed in relief.

"A sky shield," he muttered.

"What happened?" Replika said as she reached his side. "What's a sky shield?"

"What are you doing? You should rest."

"How am I supposed to rest when we're under attack?" She looked back up as another loud boom rang out. "Octavian!"

As the next cannonball came raining down, she prepared to pull him away from its path, but he braced against her. A second later, it stopped in midair and rolled away, seeming to have forgotten where it was headed. She gasped.

"That's a sky shield," Octavian explained. "I didn't realize there was one here. It must stop well above the complex or I'd have seen it."

"We're protected from overhead attacks, then?" Replika asked.

"Yes."

"Only overhead attacks?"

His jaw dropped as her meaning dawned on him. They were open to attacks by land.

17

FACE TO FACE WITH THE PIRATE CAPTAIN

With the impending threat of pirate invasion, Octavian didn't have time to question why he had thought the island would be safe. In his haste to avoid this line of inquiry, he may have assumed he was just trying to return to something familiar. The truth was more along the lines of instinct, which connected him to this place, much like gravity pulls two objects closer to each other.

He rushed back to the bedroom, threw the tools into his bag, then pulled Replika toward the laboratory.

"Can you help me close the door?" he asked.

After quite a lot of pulling and even more forceful pulling plus some additional pushing, the clicking lock of the latching door echoed through the room. Octavian breathed a sigh of relief that was cut off by more dropping cannonballs. Despite the noise, he felt safe, for now.

He turned to her and held out his arm. "Here, let me help you get your dress on."

She turned her head away as she realized that a side of her camisole was exposed. She nodded, and he pulled her arm into her sleeve.

"What do we do now?" Replika asked, trying to change the subject as Octavian tied her dress up.

"You're asking me?" Octavian replied with exasperation. "I can't believe they followed us here. What could they even want?"

He asked the question as if no one had asked it before, despite Replika having questioned this very thing several times while they were ashore. Unknown to Octavian, Replika had a plausible answer to this very question.

She obviously decided not to share this because her next statement was, "Well, we can't stay in here forever."

The booming of cannons stopped.

He took a few deep breaths to calm himself. They proved to be in vain as the sound of an army of footsteps on the wooden docks outside made its way through the solid lab door. The front door to the complex burst open with a bang. The captain was shouting, and Octavian was finding it difficult to concentrate. They were closed in, trapped in a cage of his own making, with only a door—albeit a very large and sturdy door—to protect them.

Despite his best efforts, or at least the best he could do under extreme duress and limited time, Octavian couldn't think of any options to escape. He cursed himself for not taking the magic offense workshops that Teacher suggested. Little good it would have done, he thought, given that when they were attacked back at the docks, he hadn't even recalled the defensive training he had learned in his required Physical Magic class.

Without a better understanding of the layout of the complex or island, he had no reason to believe there was another way out. He was left with footsteps growing louder, a heart pumping faster, and his breaths getting shorter.

He was panicking, which wasn't very useful in this particular moment as it not only didn't solve the problem, but it made him feel worse. It was a painful reminder that he also hadn't taken the Meditation for Crisis Situations training—another oddly relevant suggestion from Teacher.

"It's only him," Replika said.

He looked back at her. "What? Who?"

"It's their leader. He's walking this way. But he's alone. The others don't want to follow him inside. Something about a curse?"

Suddenly, a memory came to him. Teacher had once mentioned that pirates were afraid of magic. And then, just like that, an idea!

"Let's open the door," Octavian said.

Replika paused, looking at him deeply and carefully to make absolutely, positively, and completely sure he was not joking. Then she nodded her reluctant agreement. She went over to the wall next to the large door and pressed the Pressure Point. Octavian took several steps backward, down into the recessed area of the lab. Replika joined him as the door clicked open.

Octavian expected the confident captain to come rushing in, but instead, the bearded giant stood outside the doorway with a wary squint. Octavian drew his chin down, his spine up, and his shoulders back, trying to appear more confident than he felt. The clicks of the door continued until it slammed into the shelf behind it.

With a loud jingle, the Captain took one large step forward. He pulled his arm up from his side and pointed his ready pistol at Octavian. With his other hand, he pulled out a dagger from its scabbard on his hip.

"Don't you want to know why we weren't destroyed by your cannonballs?" Octavian asked.

"I know yer magic, lad," the man said with a suspicious squint. "This island's always been infestered with magic, far as I know."

"You're alone against magic, then," Octavian said. His palms were sweaty, but he kept himself steady. He started rubbing his fingers together, building up heat with the friction. "I'm guessing your lackeys were too scared to risk coming in here. But you couldn't pass up a chance to prove how brave you are."

"I'm 'ere fer that, ye snivelin', wretched piece o' pigskin," was the response as the good captain pointed his dagger toward Replika. "T'ain't no wench. That thar's a mechanercal doll. And yer gonna hand it o'er."

"Not gonna happen," Octavian said with a quick shake of his head.

"T'wasn't a request."

18

A Pirate's Diplomercy

With large, slow steps, the pirate captain stomped toward them, pistol in one hand and dagger in the other. Octavian took a deep breath, pulling and shaking the molecules around his hands. Hot, orange flames ignited above them with an exciting bounce, and Octavian gave himself an internal pat on the back at his success. The large man stopped in his tracks. Octavian's intense glare masked his exhaustion as he held the flames steady.

After almost an entire minute of silence, the captain sheathed his dagger and put his pistol back into its holster. He let out a loud sigh of defeat and then a careful laugh. Out of energy, Octavian allowed the flames to die.

"I see yer willin' ta fight fer yer plunder." The pirate put out a hand and waited, as if he wanted to shake hands. "I'm Cap'n Egnaro. Known as much fer me diplomercy as fer me ruthlessness."

"Diplomacy?" Replika asked, raising a single eyebrow.

"Aye. Fer example, how 'bout I don't kill the both o' ye thievin' spit weasels, an' the cyberg do a job fer me?" Egnaro continued, placing his rejected hand onto his hip.

"We all know you can't kill us," Octavian said, lip curling up in disgust. "And what the hell is a spit weasel? And wait, who are you calling thieving? You're a damn pirate!"

"Ye denyin' what stole ye li'l dolly thar?"

"What?" Octavian asked. "Say that with some sense."

"Even if I couldn't kill ye, I ken turn ye in fer thievin'. Ye see, I've got me relations with the authority in port here."

"Are you saying you're going to frame us for stealing?" Octavian said.

"Actually," Replika spoke up from behind him, drawing out the first syllable.

He glanced at her before returning his attention back to Egnaro.

"Ye got yerself a lyin', thievin' mechanercal doll, laddie," Egnaro said with a laugh.

"I didn't lie," Replika insisted, turning to Octavian. "I was going to tell you."

Replika pulled up her skirt and untied the pouch from around her thigh. Octavian took it from her and gave Egnaro a stern glare of warning before releasing the fastener on the bag. His eyes widened as he pulled out the sphere that was inside.

"Replika!" Octavian cried out. "You stole the computer?!" He turned back to the pirate captain. "And you had your people following us?"

"What ken I say?" Egnaro said. "I make it me business ta foller suspicious knaves."

"So you can blackmail people," Replika said through pouting lips.

Octavian couldn't help the smile on his face. "I've never been happier to be in the room with a criminal." Now confident for real, he turned his full attention back to Egnaro. "I'll tell you what, Captain. I will make a deal with you after all."

Octavian took a look around the messy room. Upon seeing a metal chair knocked helplessly onto its side, he sat it back up—which immediately gave it a sense of dignity—and moved it closer to one of the metal tables nearby. He held his hand out for Egnaro to sit down. With an amused smirk, the pirate took the seat, and Octavian jumped to sit on the table next to him.

"Wat're ye thinkin', lad?"

"We'll do you a favor if you do one for us. The next time you need it, you can use my magic and my partner's strength."

Replika opened her mouth to say something. Octavian made eye contact to hear her out, but she stayed silent.

"And what favor might ye be wantin' in return?" the captain asked.

"The shop owner will know who took this trinket. And I assume we'll need to go back to town at some point. Put in a good word for us with your friends of authority. And we keep the device."

Egnaro crossed his arms over his chest.

"That's mighty odd, lad. Why shouldn't I just take the toy fer me own uses? Must be valuable fer ye ta offer yerselves."

"Because only a magician can use it. It's useless without me," Octavian lied with pure confidence. At least, he thought he was lying at the time.

It would be quite the exclusive device if all magic computers were limited to magicians. Magicians were quite rare in Octavian's world, mainly because people thought the subject was too hard. Before computer marbles existed, computers tapped into the power of the local power generators, meaning they needed a physical connection to the power source. These desktop computers, not yet shaped like marbles, were very popular, as they brought convenience and connectivity to the world.

Magicians were the first to harness wireless technology because they had the knowledge to affect the world through the manipulation of psyche particles. A huge advancement came from the usual source, the great minds of graduate students. All magic was possible through the understanding of Nature, and the bulk of a magician's early training came in the form of magical proofs, logical statements that showed a magical ability was possible.

Most young magicians and often advanced magicians with less than optimal training relied on proofs in their everyday use of magic. However, following up on several education-focused studies on magician training, many universities had changed their curriculum's focus from memorization of magical proofs to hands on, kinesthetic training, using the proofs as auxiliary.

The idea was to cultivate an environment of innovation, and that was certainly the case for graduate student Lisa Turnhall.

While out drinking with her friends one evening, Lisa Turnhall of Engineering & Technology—that's E&T to those in the know—was quite inebriated, as happens when graduate students go out drinking. Her friends, also students in the feminine discipline, were arguing with her about whether one can practice magic just as effectively while under the influence.

They could have taken this discussion inside, where they could have sobered up with a mediocre burger, underseasoned french fries, or overpriced cheese and crackers. They could have taken their questions to their research advisors, who would have made up answers in order to not lose face before suggesting they write a literature review. They could have just let the whole thing go, but they were already an hour into the debate, so that seemed out of the question.

Instead, the drunk young woman and her friends made their way up to the rooftop bar to get another drink.

There, the E&T student claimed you could program an object or device to run magical proofs on demand, effectively democratizing magic. Lisa Turnhall took a napkin and a pen, then went to work through her thoughts with as much care as one under the influence can muster.

19

MAGICIAN REQUIRED

While Lisa Turnhall, the Engineering and Technology graduate student, was busy writing a magical proof on a paper napkin at a rooftop bar, her friends waited—as much as you can wait while you go to the dance floor and enjoy yourself. The deep beats and addictive Backwards Slide line dance were too much fun to miss, and if they didn't keep moving, one of them would end up falling asleep against a random stranger again.

But when she was done, Lisa Turnhall had filled thirteen napkins with writing and filled herself with more alcohol. Her friends sensed something different about the napkins, as if they had some quality that they couldn't pin down. They started to believe that their drunk friend was more brilliant than usual, and they wondered if she was brilliant because she was drunk or if they thought she was brilliant because they were drunk.

In reality, they were all pretty drunk, but her brilliance and their acknowledgement of that brilliance were absolutely on point.

Although they were later convicted of assisted suicide, her friends witnessed the first recorded example of a functional magic object unconnected to either magic infrastructure or a magic user. As the E&T student jumped to her death, she paused for a moment in midair, which was part of the magical proof she had written on the stack of napkins she was holding.

Lisa Turnhall's hypothesis was correct, and it is believed she would have revolutionized the E&T subdiscipline had she lived. Instead, her research advisor, Grand Magician Auklord Smith, swooped in to claim the accomplishment and set up a multimillion dollar computer company. Twenty years later, when the friends were released from prison, they sued Grand Magician Auklord Smith and won. They spent the rest of their lives sober and rich, two things that don't always go hand in hand.

Octavian knew his history and had even received the Lisa Turnhall Memorial Scholarship during his undergrad, which allowed him to stay in school when his family situation went sour.

In Octavian's world, this huge advancement in technology allowed non-magic users access to many benefits previously only available to Magicians. So when Octavian told Egnaro the stolen computer required a magician, he thought he was lying. It would only be moments before he realized the device had yet another unique characteristic which set it apart from a manufactured marble: it required a magician.

Egnaro looked to Replika for confirmation of Octavian's claim, and she put her hands to her hips and nodded much too emphatically. He turned back to Octavian, squinting his eyes. Octavian held out the computer. The pirate captain considered his options before relaxing back in the chair, which creaked but thankfully didn't break.

"Aye," he said. "I'll help ye. But only if ye ken show me proof o' that li'l ball bein' magic."

Octavian smiled. He knew it. The pirate was afraid of magic, so much so that he dared not touch the device.

He held the computer up and placed his finger on a concave indentation at the bottom. When nothing happened, he paused.

This was the moment of realization. Every magic computer marble was touch-activated and powered by certain magical proofs that allowed non-magicians to use the technology. However, this computer wasn't using magic that way. In order to power it, he had to actively channel magic through it.

Of course, he didn't know this at first. The computer didn't give him any instructions, but as soon as he realized his touch hadn't activated it, he somehow knew what he needed to do.

Hiding his surprise, he channeled magic through the device. A light glowed from underneath the glass exterior. A second later, a blue light shot up from inside and through the crystal at the top. All around them, a field of glowing points flashed into existence. Some had symbols around them, others had an X crossing them out. Assuming this was a tactile interface, Octavian tried to touch them, but the symbols were unresponsive. His eyebrows were drawn down tight as he gave up on using the visual interface with his hand.

He turned back to the pirate captain, whose jaw was hanging down in amazement.

"Is that proof enough?" Replika asked.

"By the light o' the moon, that thar's the dark arts," the captain replied in a loud whisper.

Octavian was deep in thought. He turned his attention to the buttons on the side of the device. There were nine of them, and the center one was larger than the others. He recalled Teacher holding his computer marble in his hands, a computer marble too similar to this one for comfort.

Teacher had pressed a button, and then Teacher had been torn to pieces.

He wasn't keen to repeat Teacher's mistake—assuming it was a mistake. Perhaps Teacher had done it on purpose, but why? Without knowing more, he was quite reluctant to press any of the golden buttons.

He couldn't help but feel like he was grasping for nonexistent answers. But one thing was for sure. This device was magic, and it required magic. Okay, maybe that was two things. But he was sure of them. He needed to figure out how to use it so he could access its information. And he hoped that information would lead them to a way home.

"Ye want me ta risk me reputation fer a map? Must be quite the treasure," Egnaro chuckled.

"It's not a normal map. It's a . . . star map or something," Replika argued.

"Now yer tellin' me ye can fly ta the heavens?"

"Try the buttons," Replika urged in a heated whisper, though not low enough that the Captain Egnaro couldn't hear her.

Octavian rolled the device in his hand. His thumb finally made it to the large central button. One of the dots in the room started to glow brighter, but Octavian was too nervous to notice.

Egnaro was entranced by the shifting image around him. The focus moved to another dot, then another, Egnaro following them with a discriminating eye. Abruptly, he stood, pulling his gun from its holster and shoving it against Octavian's throat. He didn't seem to like what he saw, or perhaps he sensed the danger that awaited.

"Ye want ta die, lad? Talk. Wat's this device fer? Wat's happ'nin'?" Egnaro yelled.

"Don't worry," Octavian said. "It's not dangerous. You told me to prove it used magic, right?"

Egnaro paused, reluctantly lowered his pistol, and placed it back in its holster. The movement above them stopped, leaving a glowing dot with an X over it highlighted. Octavian didn't know what was going to happen, but he had to try something. With a deep breath and a healthy dose of fear, he pressed the large button on the device.

The world began to spin. Egnaro dematerialized right before them, molecules rearranging into a new configuration. They were changing worlds again. As the nausea took over, Octavian could only see darkness. Where could they be now?

The newly forming air was thick, and he soon realized something was wrong. The space around him was crushing him. He held in the air left in his lungs, but the pressure pushed back. He waved his arms, trying to find anything to grab onto, and found himself kicking as well. There was nothing around him. No walls, no floor.

A light trickled in from above, and as he forced his eyes up, the space above him rippled. It was dark, but familiar. He was underwater. How far up was it? Could he make it? He could barely make sense of his thoughts as he struggled to find any kind of form to give him context.

He tried to push his arms down against the water, but he didn't have the energy to ascend to the surface. As he drifted into a black, empty unconsciousness, the computer slipped from his loosening grip, sinking into the depths below.

3

TALES OF A VERNIAN YOUTH SERIES

THE *Silence* AND THE RARITY OF HUMAN LIFE

1

MEMORIES AND MEMETTES

R eplika, the mechanical doll, stared out at the ocean from an alcove of a giant, black pillar of rock jutting out from the water's depths. The waves beat against it with a steady rhythm, and she allowed herself to be distracted by its music. She didn't want to remember her magician companion, Octavian, sinking lifelessly, and she needed a distraction from the pain in her wounded shoulder. There wasn't much else to occupy her time.

The surface of the water bobbed up and down, as if it hadn't just rudely tried to drown Octavian. No amount of staring was going to get her an apology, but she threw all the shade she could at its lapping waves.

Finally, she took a break to look at Octavian, wet clothes still clinging to his form. It had been well over an hour since she pulled him from the water and resuscitated him, but the humid air was thick around her. She knew he would be unhappy at his damp situation, and a small smile spread across her lips as she imagined his annoyance or disgust or—well, anything. Seeing him awake would be enough.

A sharp pain reminded her she'd been shot by a pirate, of all things. If she hadn't experienced it herself, she would have found such a thing hard to believe. But when she tried to stretch her arm out in front of her, the pain was all the proof she needed, perhaps even more so than the hole in her dress. Octavian had stuffed some kind of padding into the holes in her skin, but he hadn't had a chance to do any repair work before the pirates attacked.

She didn't think to curse her creator, an Exalted Grand Magician known as Teacher, who definitely deserved the blame—at least in part—for her predicament. Not one stray negative thought of him crossed her mind. This may have been because she was a nice person, or she could have been programmed to think only positively of Teacher. But more likely, she was busy trying to remember how exactly she had gotten them both to safety.

Replika's first moments in the ocean of this new world had left her with burning questions. Once she had realized she was under water—she had immediately looked around for Octavian. She floated upward while he sank. She swam down to him and, finding him unconscious, pulled him up with her.

That was about all she remembered clearly. Everything else was a blur. A strange, far off blur, as if she'd been on autopilot. She'd been mindful of his biometrics, even the amount of water in his lungs. Yet it happened so quickly that it seemed like a dream.

She'd made her way into a conveniently placed alcove in this pillar of rock. Tool marks revealed that the recess wasn't natural, but there was no indication of who or what did such a thing. The slick and glassy rock reminded her of obsidian—though she wasn't sure why she knew about obsidian in the first place—but the tall, columnar shape was uncharacteristic of the volcanic material. And Replika had seen many more pillars jutting from beneath the ocean waves as she pulled Octavian into the alcove.

After a solid five minutes of intense thought, Replika had decided to call the rock Black Mirrorite, despite it not being shiny enough to act as a mirror. Still, something about the words reminded her of the material, and there was no one else available to discuss it with, so she figured she could call it whatever she wanted.

Octavian took a deep breath, and Replika leaned toward him to check. She hovered above him, listening to his steady inhalations and matching it with her own. She had done the same after she had ensured Octavian's safety, moments before she had regained control of her consciousness. Saving Octavian had seemed like instinct, like something she was compelled to do. Is this what it meant to be a robot? Did she not have free will?

In their homeworld, free will had been quite the hot topic in robotics. Engineers would argue with each other about whether robots had free will. Engineers like to argue, especially once they have already discussed the latest breakthroughs, the weather, and whether jeans should be allowed at professional conferences.

In one camp, self-proclaimed gods insisted that by programming a robot, they had, in effect, dictated all future actions made by that robot. Their opposition claimed a robot's creator could not predict every scenario, and thus free will must be responsible for the response of a robot in a situation.

This debate was the central premise of the court case Krystankzovic v Free. Hermann Free, despite his name, didn't believe robots had free will. His fame originated from a video clip that had circulated around the globe and images from it accompanied by humorous text (called a memette) had even become widely shared.

The prosecutors in this particular case represented the victim of a crime committed by a robot of Free's design. They faulted Free, using the argument that the robot didn't have free will.

The case dragged on for months, and Free became the subject of some of the most enduring memettes of the time. In the end, Free conceded that it was possible for a faulty robot to act in a way consistent with the idea of free will. Despite the statement, they sentenced him to ten years in prison for the crimes of the robot.

While the Free memettes had been buried within Replika's memory banks, the answer to whether she had free will had not. Unbeknownst to her, she was unique in ways only Teacher knew, and he was in no condition to share anything with anyone. She did, in fact, have as much free will as any human, just as she had trauma responses when someone she cared for was in mortal danger.

But for Replika, it seemed like her memory was flawed. She worked hard to remember something—anything!—from before she woke up in the laboratory with the window, her only memory from their home world. There had to be more to her past. Try as she might, the memories remained out of reach, as if she'd merely forgotten everything before.

She remembered an elderly man with eyes that shimmered in gold, even where the pupils should be. This was her creator, but she didn't remember his name, even though it was on the tip of her tongue. Octavian called this man Teacher, and he seemed convinced Teacher had exiled them from their own reality into these alternate worlds.

Replika had no concrete memories of Teacher. She could merely picture him in her mind. However, she did have the memory of emotions tied to him: warmth and safety. So even though she didn't **know** for certain, she **felt** certain they had shared touching moments. Among the strange recollections about Teacher was a clear memory of his hands: rough and confident, yet gentle and cautious.

The more she pushed herself to put words to these feelings, the more sure she became that Teacher wouldn't have sent them into the unknown without good reason. The cognitive dissonance burdened her. She didn't know why she thought highly of him when the evidence made Teacher's role in their current situation pretty obvious.

Her memories of Octavian were even stranger. She could see clear but incomplete visions of him in her mind. One particular moment stood out to her. His hair was longer and unkempt, completely different from the short, tidy cut he currently had. They were in a green space of some kind, perhaps a park, but she couldn't quite tell. And Octavian was laughing. Even though she couldn't see it, she sensed the warmth of his hands as they intertwined with hers. The longer she thought about it, the more the physical pieces of the memory came to her. Her cheeks were cold as a chilly breeze blew over them. There was a soft, fluffy fabric wrapped around her neck, and she was pulled off balance. What followed was hot breath on her face and warm but chapped lips on hers.

How long had she been active? Was she supposed to have feelings like this? Why was she unable to remember more? She had so many questions, though she was far more comfortable facing these queries over the concerns she had about their health and safety.

Her primary concern—when she chose to address it instead of escaping into impossible memories—was that she didn't know if she was able to swim to shore. She couldn't see the shore from the alcove they were in, but she could tell the tide was rising and knew it was further than she dared to attempt, especially while holding onto Octavian. Though the breeze carried a chill with it, the weather was actually quite warm. It would be safe to stay in the alcove of the Black Mirrorite pillar for a while longer, though she was unsure what the weather would be once the sun set.

She refocused on what she could be sure of. They needed a plan to get to shore.

2

BENEATH THE WAVES

B eneath the waves, the black pillar where Replika and Octavian aired out stretched down to the ocean floor. There,
organisms of many shapes and sizes swam, scuttled, and
sank. An octopus waved its body this way and that in a mating
dance unique to this world, while the octopus at the other end of
the dance wished the dance didn't exist at all. A young, whale-
like mammal swam with their mouth opened wide to engorge
themself with food, while their mother fussed at them to slow
down. And crabs busy nipping at each other were snatched up by
three bipedal mammals—human-like but around half the size.

They swam together, all with gray-blue skin and webbed
toes. Together was a strong word for this situation, as they
weren't coordinated and didn't seem to pay much attention to
each other. They swam in a predetermined route, occasionally
looking around to make sure the others were within eyesight.
When necessary, one would return to the surface for a new breath
of air before swimming down to continue their work.

While their primary goal was to collect food for their village,
one of them had a knack for being distracted by novelty. She had
once found a rock shaped like a certain body part and had spent
days taking it all around the village so everyone could see. The
village leader, after noticing she was slacking on her duties, had

the rock smashed. Within days, she had a new discovery: a deformed seashell that looked like it was smiling.

On this particular day, she found something quite different. Unlike many of her previous discoveries, which were met with—at best—mild amusement, this would be different. She must have realized that from the moment she saw it. Or she was just drawn to its shiny exterior.

The spherical object was like a rock but quite unlike any rock she'd ever seen. She swam down and looked it over carefully without touching it. That squid incident a while back had taught her you should always be careful of what you touch. After unstrapping the rod secured at her hip, she poked at the rock.

Nothing happened.

She poked it again.

Nothing happened again.

It wasn't covered in muck like her usual finds. So, she figured, it had to be highly mobile or new to the ocean, both of which were extremely intriguing.

She poked it again, harder this time, causing it to break free from the flora it was stuck in and roll down a hill. She swam downward after it, though was distracted by an especially chunky crab that she'd save for herself later. Then she was back at it, looking dutifully this way and that for the strange rock.

A school of fish whizzed past her, fins slapping her skin as they fought to keep up with the group. She waved her arms in frustration but doing so just made it harder for the fish to evade her.

Once they passed, she hurried down to the bottom of the hill. The rock had to be here. She checked between creatures, behind a boulder, and within long, swaying kelp, but it was nowhere to be found.

That is, until she noticed something familiar, a large barnacle-covered mound. It wasn't familiar because she had gone there before but because she was strictly forbidden from going there at all. She slowly pushed herself backward, but just as she did so, the light glinted off an object laying right at the foot of the mound.

The mound split horizontally, revealing that the object was laying not at the figurative foot, but at the literal mouth of it. It thrashed its body against the ocean floor, freeing itself from underneath the sand.

The gray-blue person propelled herself around a large boulder. She waited a moment before peeking around the corner. The creature was swimming now, methodically retracing its path. The shiny rock, if it was still there, was probably under a bunch of sand and debris. She peered hard, sticking her neck out as far as she could and squinting her eyes.

But she didn't see it.

Disappointed, she gave up on the rock and returned to her work. As she turned back around, she was met with the enormous eye of the creature just unburied from the sea floor. Its mouth opened wide as it raced toward her. She pushed off of the boulder she had been hiding behind and kicked her legs hard, flicking her webbed feet for an extra dash of speed. She grabbed at rocks on the floor to pull herself faster, pushed with her arms, but she could feel the mouth of death getting closer.

Something closed around her leg, but she pulled it out as she made a sharp turn. Darting left, then right, she stayed just ahead of her pursuer. Her breath was getting short with the effort, but she couldn't risk swimming upward into open waters.

She turned again and headed back toward a wall of rock near the hill she had descended. Using every muscle to its fullest, she pushed herself hard.

The wall came closer, closer, closer.

She reached her arms out in front of her and abruptly pushed herself down into the sand and seaweed at the floor. Above her, the carnivorous fish gave pause. It threw its body back and forth to turn around. It swam in long, slow circles above her. And then, finally giving up, it turned and swam away to its next favorite hunting spot.

Relieved, she exited her hiding spot and took a long, careful look around.

It was safe.

She resolved herself to swim up to the surface before rejoining the others, but just as she turned, a gleam of light caught her eye. It was the spherical rock, sitting at the base of a large barnacle-covered mound.

3

Don't Drop Important Things

The unconscious Octavian groaned and attempted to roll from his side. Replika put her foot behind him to keep him from getting too close to the edge. It wasn't the first time he had tried to plunge himself back into the water. This time, though, was different because it appeared he was now awake.

"Replika?" he asked with a pained raspiness.

"Octavian!" She moved across the small alcove to sit closer to him.

His eyes fluttered open. "I thought I was going to die."

"I wouldn't let that happen."

He had no response, or perhaps couldn't get it out. There were tears in his eyes, and he put his hands to his face to hide them from Replika. He cleared his throat and apologized.

"Octavian, it's okay. We're together, and we're safe for the time being."

He looked like he had more to say, but the pain so evident on his face stopped him. She encouraged him to sit up and helped him lean against the rock. He ran his hand through his hair before looking at his hands.

"Where's the computer?" he asked.

Replika hadn't thought about the spherical device at all. "You have your bag on you. Is it in there?"

"I was holding it when we changed worlds." He let out a loud groan. "Did I drop our only way home into the ocean?!"

"Maybe I can swim down and find it," Replika offered, but Octavian immediately shook his head.

"You're already hurt. Being immersed in sea water probably already damaged your wound. I need to do at least some basic repairs, but even after that, you aren't graded to go deep diving. Especially—" He interrupted himself with a coughing fit. "You get it."

"Then what's the plan?" she asked.

"You tell me," he replied.

He was pale, and there was no way he could swim to shore by himself. Yet, she worried that if they were caught unprepared, the setting sun might bring a frigid cold with it. They needed shelter that wouldn't become a danger when the tide changed or the sunlight faded.

"I'll swim us to shore," she said. "It's mostly cliffside, but there's a beach if we go north a bit."

"How long are we safe here?" he asked. "I'd really like to make repairs before you try to do anything."

She had hoped he would say that. When she agreed, he gestured for her to turn around. He untied her dress and helped her pull her arm from its sleeve, not letting on if he was bothered by how damp the dress was or how difficult it was to peel from her skin. She sat silently as he retrieved the tools he needed from the bag secured to his waist. His hand touched her arm, much warmer than she thought it would be, and a shiver ran through her.

"Does it hurt that badly?" he asked with obvious concern.

"No, it's fine. I mean, it hurts, but I was just—" Unsure of what she wanted to say, she tried a different sentence. "You're warm. It feels nice."

Octavian's voice was low as he struggled to speak over the water pounding against the rock, but he spoke with a gentle kindness that calmed her. "You've been through a lot. I'm sorry your first day of life had to be like this."

"First day?" Replika asked. "Wait, I was activated yesterday?"

Octavian replied, "You saw the window of the lab turn into a wall, remember? That was right after you were activated."

"So we've . . ." She trailed off, and a glance at Octavian's furrowed brow told her she was worrying him. "We've never been to a park together?"

"I would have loved to spend our first day together at a park," Octavian said, "instead of all this. But no. Why?"

"I thought it was a memory, but it was just a feeling, I guess."

The difference between memories and feelings isn't as straightforward as it might appear. For example, it may seem like feeling sad is quite a different experience from remembering sitting in a park with your favorite person. However, if you feel sad because you remembered this was the last time you ever saw your favorite person, the question becomes more difficult to answer.

Exalted Grand Magician Arthur Chale set out to operationalize this distinction, chronicling his work in a ninety-nine-volume series named *Magic's Role in the Human Condition*. While much of the series read more like an encyclopedia full of mansplaining, there was enough useful and provocative information for the later Exalted Grand Magician Dara Rezaei, Director of the Office of Behavioral Sciences at the National Institute of Magic, to put out a request for proposals for research on the topic.

Of the resulting funded studies, Exalted Grand Magician Dara Rezaei found one of particular interest, which ze fought to continue the funding for long after ze left zir position. The premise of the research was to create artwork infused with psyche particles in a particular inactive state, and then to excite those particles through an interface with a person's mind. Zir hypotheses were that feelings would invoke abstract color changes in the art, that neutral memories would invoke imagery, and that strongly emotional memories would create vibrant art beyond all but one person's imagination.

The National Institute of Magic funded the study for over twenty years with contradictory and sometimes offensive results. Of the thirty principal investigators who were involved in the project, twenty-two required long-term therapy, ten made permanent career changes, and one started a very successful art gallery for dick pics, which seemed like a smart move given how often that seemed to come up during research sessions.

Additionally, three crimes were inadvertently solved during the research. Though the resulting art was not admissible in court, the pieces were seized by the authorities and destroyed due to their graphic nature and gaudy color palettes.

Despite the challenges, the project made some headway in understanding the link between memories and emotions—at least everyone thought so until one ambitious graduate student actually read every volume of Exalted Grand Magician Arthur Chale's series, after which she reported that everything they had "learned" was already recorded within those pages. An abridged version of the series was produced, and there were many exasperated sighs to go around.

As Octavian continued his work on Replika's arm, she found herself letting out a sigh of her own. She couldn't be sure if it was tied to her feelings, a memory, or just simple boredom.

Other than asking for her to check her systems in certain ways, her white-haired companion kept his speech short. She had the feeling he felt worse than he let on. So, she silently waited as he worked at his own pace, using the time to enjoy the beautiful view, which she was starting to forgive though she'd never forget.

When he announced he was finished, he followed it up with instructions. "That'll have to be good enough for now. The wounds are already healing, so your immune system seems to be functioning adequately. It'll be a day or two before you'll fully replenish the lubrication fluid and regenerate all of your connections, so moving might hurt a bit until then. Once we get to shore, you should minimize the use of your arm. Maybe we should make a sling for it. And we'll—"

He interrupted himself to cough, and Replika turned to put a hand on his shoulder.

"Let's worry about one thing at a time," she said. "Can you hold on to me?"

"I can swim," he replied, then added quietly, "I'm a pretty strong swimmer, actually."

She was surprised enough by his response that she said, "Then why—" She stopped before she finished her question.

Octavian's face gave away his shame, and he had obviously been waiting for her to ask why he hadn't been able to swim to safety.

"Maybe there's a way to get to shore without swimming?" she asked instead.

"Replika, I shouldn't have needed you to save me," he said. "There are a dozen spells I could've used down there. Spells I thought I could do in my sleep." He ripped his gaze away before continuing. "I don't know how I'm going to survive this."

She took one of his hands in hers. He leaned his head down into his arm, obviously losing control of his composure but unwilling to show Replika. As he cried, she squeezed his hand in support. After a few minutes, his breathing settled, and he peeked up from his arm shield. She smiled gently at him.

He wiped his face, cleared his throat one more time, and stood.

"Let's walk," he said firmly. "I'll create an ice bridge."

Replika made sure to express how impressive this was, and Octavian seemed satisfied with his choice. And although he didn't say it, she was confident in his joy at avoiding the water and its moist dampness.

4

HE HAS REGRETS

With the decision made to get to shore by walking on water—frozen water, that is—Octavian lifted a hand and spoke words Replika didn't even try to understand. The ocean water around them hardened, and when Octavian put a hand out, she stepped carefully onto it. The ice crackled under her feet, but didn't crack.

"We should hurry, though. It'll start melting as soon as I stop concentrating," he informed her.

She took his hand and, with both care and speed, followed the growing ice trail.

Replika knew walking on water wasn't something Octavian invented out of necessity. Ancient Magic theorists claimed early humans used magic to cross the Singh Strait, and they often faced scrutiny from mainstream researchers who believed a natural land bridge facilitated their migration. While there was little evidence to suggest one group was correct, the fact that Ancient Magic theorists made a habit of attributing every ancient marvel to a sometimes completely personified and capitalized "Magic" made many people hesitant to support their hypotheses. Still, the *Ancient Magic* documentary series aired for twenty seasons, which supports that, at a minimum, their ideas were entertaining.

Hand in hand, Octavian and Replika took one step at a time until their icy path met a sandy shore backed by a sheer rock face.

The sand was littered with rocks and debris. At the top of the cliff was a thick layer of trees, leading Replika to hypothesize that the mess on the beach came from above. The cliff was composed of the same black mirrorite as the pillar they had taken refuge on.

They walked along the beach, the tide rising steadily as the sun dipped down toward the horizon. It was already noticeably cooler than when they had arrived, and the powerful gusts of wind increased the bite of the cold.

Knowing they would need a fire at some point, Replika picked up pieces of plant debris to use as tinder. It was as the sun touched the sea that she finally noticed a break in the rock. Though still a ways off, every step improved her certainty that it was a cave of some sort. She found herself bounding toward it, leaving Octavian behind her, yelling at her to slow down as if she was a naughty child ditching her parents.

By the time he caught up to her, she believed this was their best option for a night's rest. The cave's opening had a turn in it that would keep the wind from blowing directly on them. The wall of the cave had soaked up the warmth from the sun, and its ambient heat made a noticeable difference in the cave's temperature. There was only one problem, one that Octavian noticed as soon as he arrived.

"Someone's been here?" he asked, pointing to the circle of stones that lay at the center of the cave.

"There are toolmarks, see? I think it was carved out by someone, but I don't think we have much choice. Who knows where the next break in the rock will be? And the light is fading."

"True," he muttered.

She assumed Octavian had magic workarounds for most of their problems, but they both needed to rest. This seemed like as good a place as any.

"Besides, it's a good thing," she continued. "The ceiling looks like it's handled its fair share of heat from fires, and the shape directs the smoke up toward the entrance of the cave. With the regular wind here, I assume the airflow stays steady so the smoke doesn't build up too much."

Satisfied, or perhaps too tired to argue, Octavian loosened the bag from his waist and dropped it.

"There's still some food from the market that we might be able to salvage in here," he said. "Do you mind trying to make something out of nothing?"

"Are you going somewhere?" she asked as he hovered near the entrance.

She wanted to cozy up around a fire, and she couldn't imagine Octavian was enjoying his soggy shoes. He considered her question for a minute, as if he didn't know the answer.

Finally, he responded, "I'm going to set some traps."

Octavian kicked a mound of sand as he walked down toward the water's edge. He let out a frustrated groan, looking back toward the cave and hoping Replika couldn't hear him. Taking a deep breath of salty air, he tried to push away the memory of the water constricting him, of holding the device loosely in his hand, of his body feeling out of control. Creating an ice bridge to shore hadn't kept his mind as busy as he had hoped, and he went over the scenario in his mind, remembering the myriad of ways he could have saved himself.

He wasn't a novice magician. He had years of training and many hours of experience under his belt. Because magicians were pivotal to keeping his homeworld working, all training magicians volunteered for a mandatory year of public service, where they could choose a track to pursue. Octavian had chosen the emergency management track. In addition to learning spells such as those to change the density and viscosity of liquids, he had been on one of the emergency teams during the South O'er earthquake, one of the largest in recent history.

Yet today, he had almost died. No normal death, either. He'd almost drowned, a scenario he'd been trained to handle. Except, of course, for the changing realities part.

It was the horrific end to a terrible day. A day that started as a major milestone in his future career as a magician had turned into a series of cortisol-inducing episodes that likely shortened his life by several years.

He was almost to the water, and he forced himself to step forward. A small wave washed up over his water-logged boots. He was looking forward to letting them dry out once the fire was started. Everything needed to dry out, now that he thought about it.

The sound of the ocean and the smell of the salty air filled him with a bittersweet nostalgia, and he closed his eyes to enjoy the chill that it brought. Almost out of nowhere, he realized the depths of his exhaustion. He felt heavy and weak. His muscles ached, and his head throbbed. He would definitely sleep well tonight.

A hissing sound got his attention, and he opened his eyes to find himself somewhere different, somewhere indoors. And not just any indoors. The smell of machinery, lubricants, and old, cluttered stuff was so familiar, he could cry. He was back in the lab, Teacher's lab.

5

BACK IN THE LAB

O ctavian's astonishment left him speechless as he realized where he was. He'd know this lab anywhere. After all, he had spent far too much of the last few years here. But despite the strong emotional response resonating through him, his body didn't respond to his panic-driven instinct to look around. Without his command, his gaze moved downward. He was ankle deep in water, and an uncontrolled look around did not reveal a source.

Frustrated at his body's independence from his brain, Octavian lamented as he leaned down. He looked around tables, chairs, benches, and some random items that probably shouldn't have been there, as if looking around would make the water stop. When his body straightened, he saw an early version of Replika lying on the table nearby. Thoughts that weren't his entered his mind. The water was sure to ruin some of his materials.

Were these the worries of this useless body?

He sloshed through the water one step at a time. Even though he had no control, he could feel the water's hydrogen bonds sticking his socks to his feet. It was so frigid it made his feet sting. The cold was enough to make him want to puke.

Or was that his body's anxiety?

He jumped as the door to the lab swung open. A panicked whip of his head brought his gaze in line with the bright gold eyes of an Exalted Grand Magician. The water formed a shelf at the doorway, which Teacher was safely beyond.

"What's going on here?" Teacher barked.

"I don't know!" Octavian's voice replied. Was that a squeak in his voice? How embarrassing. "There's a leak somewhere, but I don't know where."

"I'm well aware of the leak." Teacher put his hand out, as if to present the water to Octavian. "What I'm asking is why haven't you taken care of it?"

Octavian felt his mouth quiver, but it offered no response. He was seldom one to let Teacher have the last word. More often, he would ask questions, trying to squeeze out a hint toward the answer.

"Useless," Teacher grumbled. "Watch carefully."

Teacher put his hand out in front of him, arm straight and palm facing down. As he lowered his arm, the water seemed to retreat. He bent his elbow, which forced his arm to move inward. The water lifted from the ground but was more viscous. Moving his hand with precision, Teacher guided the water toward the sink across the room. He loosened his magical grip, allowing the water to drain into the metal sink, which made loud glugs as water ran through the drain.

Octavian noted a string of viscous water flowing from the sink to a nearby wall. His body was clearly missing it, and he cursed at its ineptitude. He looked back at Teacher only to find Teacher pointing at the same wall Octavian had noted. When his uncontrolled gaze met the wall, he found its molecular configuration altered so he could see through it. This was Teacher's doing. Water was flowing down the inner wall, most likely from a leak above. And then, the flow of water stopped.

Octavian looked back at Teacher, who was stepping into the dry room with his arms crossed over his chest.

"Describe what I did," he demanded.

This bumbling version of Octavian stumbled through an explanation, getting many parts right but some obvious things wrong. Teacher corrected him when he was mistaken but otherwise waited until he finished.

"And then . . . well," his own voice stumbled, "somehow, the leak stopped?" His pitch went up at the end of the sentence, one of Teacher's peeves.

"Somehow," Teacher grumbled. "You rely too heavily on your physical senses. Every quantum of space and time has a signature to it. You don't need to see it, hear it, smell it, touch it, or taste it. You just need to tune in to the physics of what's happening. Didn't your professors teach you this?"

His body gave no response.

Teacher grumbled something that Octavian couldn't understand. The Exalted Grand Magician was motionless for quite a while before Octavian realized something had changed.

When he tried to look down at his hands, it worked. He was back in control. At least, he thought he was. Then, suddenly, Teacher was mere inches away from him.

"It's not safe," Teacher said.

Octavian staggered back a step.

"What do you mean?" he asked.

"You cannot continue to hop universes without direction."

"I don't have a choice," Octavian replied. He grabbed at his throat in surprise as his voice escaped. He really was back in control! He savored the feeling of being in his own body, free to speak and look where he wished. "You trapped us here. You locked the computer's functionality."

Teacher's gaze demanded his attention, and Octavian stopped talking.

"There are many worlds," Teacher said. "There are infinite realities and variations. Human life is a rarity, and most realities, I'm afraid, are uninhabitable. It will not be enough to plug the leak. You must be proactive to ensure your survival—and hers."

"I couldn't even save myself," Octavian replied. "And I lost the computer."

"The Reality Tuner is a tool," Teacher continued. "You cannot rely on it to guide you. Instead, you must become its guide."

What the hell did that mean? The computer—the "Reality Tuner"—was gone, and how could he guide anything if he couldn't even rely on his own magic. As soon as he realized he was underwater, he should have triggered magic. He'd practiced the scenario so many times that it should have been second nature to him.

Teacher reached out and grabbed Octavian's face with his hands. Octavian tried to pull away, but he couldn't. Teacher's grip wasn't tight. Octavian merely felt stuck.

"You have the tools. You have the mind. Get them working together before you get yourselves killed," Teacher demanded.

Teacher's eyes were wide with panic, but within them, Octavian saw something, a clue. It was a clue to the answer.

The clue he needed.

6

BRINGING THE OUTSIDE IN

The phrase "bringing the outside in" bounced around in Replika's mind as she paced around the spacious hut she now found herself in. Somewhere in her memory banks, she knew there was an explanation for the phrase "bringing the outside in." She was even more sure that the phrase didn't apply to this hut—despite the grass bed where their captors had deposited Octavian, the woven vine walls, and the thatched roof. Even so, the packed dirt under her shoes was so raw that the phrase jumped right to the front of her mind.

She couldn't have known that in Teacher's spare time, he enjoyed watching home and garden shows. Every Saturday, he locked himself in his office-turned-bedroom to watch the charismatic Tania Dunn take a boring grass or dirt lot and magically—figuratively speaking—transform it into a beautiful and functional space.

Her approach was caring and thoughtful, but her demeanor was brash. Regularly on the show, her clients would question whether her final result would serve their purposes or would simply add another eccentric design to Dunn's portfolio. However, they were never disappointed in the end, and follow-up episodes recorded several years later featured families who recounted how Dunn had changed their lives along with their yards, complete with sappy music.

Over the years, Dunn had taken many types of clients and projects, but of particular interest to Teacher were episodes about mixed use spaces, such as a garden dining room or a vacant hut acting as a makeshift jail.

Replika and Octavian's hut wasn't much of a jail. Of all the places they could have ended up, this definitely was not the type Replika had expected when she was surrounded in the cave by small, bipedal people with just enough humanoid features to be disturbing.

She had considered fighting the small invaders, but she was pretty sure she had invaded their cave. To make matters worse, as she had exited the cave in response to a jab in the side with a sharpened blade, Octavian was being half-dragged from the beach.

A dozen of these people had surrounded her, and with nowhere to run, she had decided to bide her time until she understood what the heck was going on. Of immediate concern was how these individuals had snuck up on her. She hadn't noticed even the slightest deviation in the noise profile of her environment.

She went back over the memory again. There had been wind with powerful gusts every forty-five to sixty seconds. It blew through the cave and channeled upward through holes drilled into the outer wall. The sea's crashing waves were audible, overlapping with varying intensity. Her dress had made a rustling sound as it moved across her skin, petticoat, and, at one point, the cave wall.

Octavian's footsteps had drifted into the distance, drowned out by the wind and waves. Oh yeah, and she had been humming a song, which she couldn't place but which seemed to fill her head when she was idly doing things.

No, there had been no warning at all. One moment she was alone, and the next, spears, sharpened sticks, and stern stares were all pointed her way.

They had led her down the beach to an odd set of stairs carved from the cliff, and she grimaced at seeing how roughly they accordioned Octavian's long body up to the top. Her hurried footsteps had crackled and popped on the forest floor. But never once did she hear a sound from her attackers.

She had considered the possibility that they were ghosts, but she couldn't reconcile a ghost's inability to affect the ground it walked on with an ability to hold Octavian's head just barely high enough to avoid an impact with a large rock, thank goodness!

With no proper explanation, she had turned her focus to trying to gauge the threat. The small people had brought them to this village, which had sixty-three huts arranged in circular rings around a central raised platform. Now inside one of those huts with several guards outside the door, she used her fingers to spread the shoots and vines that made up the wall and peeked outside. The platform was empty, and she tried to imagine the silent shows the silent people might put on. She laughed internally at the thought of mimes acting out famous scenes of Shakespeare, Lorraine Hansberry, or Exalted Grand Magician Symphoni Marshall.

Though the stage-like platform was empty at the moment, the village was not. Dozens of people, all at around half her height, were making their way around, none making the slightest sound. Though it was dark, her enhanced vision and sophisticated processors calculated a range of skin tones, from reds and blues to greens and grays. Correlated with their skin colors were unique morphological differences as well. For example, one reddish figure walking by had textured skin that reminded her of tree bark, while their dark green companion had smooth skin and large, dark eyes.

These people went about their business as if nothing was out of the ordinary. Maybe they met and captured new people every day. Maybe this was all part of some incredible cultural experience that all newcomers to the area had to endure. Was it leading up to ritual sacrifice? She didn't see a sinkhole, volcano, or violent whirlpool of doom anywhere, though her view of the stage didn't allow her to rule out bloodstains that could be there. Perhaps they were going to be kept as pets or servants. Or maybe the villagers just needed time to warm up to the universe jumpers. And since these people obviously didn't value verbal conversation, maybe this was their way of showing hospitality. After all, they had left a generous supply of finger foods—fruit and grasses, with some berries and nuts thrown in—by the entrance soon after they arrived.

She smiled and laughed at her own optimism, wishing Octavian was awake to raise a doubtful eyebrow. Octavian seemed to have a unique and creative way of looking at the world. Even though he came across as pessimistic, she could sense that he had the same curiosity and interest as she did.

She knelt next to the grass bed where he lay. Her own breathing slowed to match his, and she waited. The silent people had deposited him, snatched away their belongings, and left, returning only to leave the food. She confirmed he was still breathing, as she had done every few minutes since they arrived. She grabbed the blanket on the dirt next to the bed and covered him with it, also as she had done every few minutes since they arrived. Though she had never witnessed him throwing it off of himself, it kept ending up back on the ground.

Finally giving up on willing him awake with her stare, she looked back at the door to the hut. Calling it a door was a bit of a stretch, since it was actually just a break in the shoots and vines covered by a thick cloth tied tightly against the exterior of the wall.

She let out a frustrated groan before falling back into her hum, that "bringing the outside in" thought timed to the beat. Just as she got into the rhythm, Octavian shot up, scurrying backward until he hit the wall behind him.

7

Very Quiet People

Replika jumped as Octavian awoke in a panic. She half-expected the whole hut to shake when he hit the wall of shoots and interlaced vines, but the structure was more stable than she anticipated. Octavian's grip on reality returned, and he calmed as he saw Replika's worried expression.

"Sorry," he said, putting his hand to his chest to help him catch his breath.

"Just so you're aware," she explained before any misunderstandings arose, "we've been captured, and we're being held in a hut in a village of very interesting and very quiet people."

"Um, okay," he responded.

That was all she really wanted to say at the moment because she was quite concerned about Octavian.

"How do you feel?" she asked.

"Wait." Octavian put a hand up, clearly not satisfied. "We were captured? By quiet people?"

"Very quiet people," she corrected.

Replika sat next to him on the bed and gestured for him to follow her lead. She parted the flexible wall and urged him to look. Outside, the villagers made their way from hut to hut, yet not a single sound came from their steps. Octavian leaned closer, and Replika looked through the opening with him.

"What in magic's name," he said.

"They don't speak," she replied to a question he hadn't asked, "and their footsteps don't make a sound."

"That's magic," Octavian said. He was holding the wall material and trying to point. Neither was necessary nor useful as he continued. "They're affecting gravity passively."

"Does that mean they're making themselves float?" Replika's eyes were wide and possibly sparkling more than usual.

"Not exactly," he said noncommittally. "Non-magic users call it a levitation spell, but that's not it either. It doesn't really matter. What matters is that these people may use innate magic. That's extremely rare in our world."

He was awfully excited over something that Replika thought sounded boring. She was still trying to wrap her head around it when he looked back at her.

"What were they like? Did you talk with them?"

"What are they like?" she repeated for effect. "They're the kind of people who sneak up on you, knock you out, and drag you and your companion back to their village without any explanation."

She wasn't angry, but she did feel like what she was saying, though obvious, needed to be said. Perhaps Octavian wasn't thinking straight because of yet another blow to the head—his third in the last day. Maybe he was being open-minded, not making an assumption about their situation. Either way, she reconsidered her words.

"Well," she said, "they didn't kill us, so that's something. And no, they made no attempt to communicate except threatening me with weapons."

"I wonder how we could talk to them," he murmured.

"What do you want to talk to them about so badly?" she couldn't help but ask.

"Well, to let us go, for starters," Octavian answered.

Admittedly, she hadn't asked for them to be released. She had decided not to speak unless spoken to, and thus no speaking had been spoken. She wasn't entirely sure if he was serious about asking their captors to set them free, but that didn't keep her from feeling a little silly for not trying to speak with them.

He leaned against the wall. After a deep breath, he let his head fall back against it. He scrunched his face, apparently not finding the wall as comfortable as he would have liked.

Long ago, the villagers had attempted to make their walls more comfortable by coating the vines with different materials and creating different weaving patterns. Unfortunately, nothing seemed to work.

One citizen, a black person with skin as shiny as black mirrorite, came up with a solution: forget the walls. After finding a bramble in his bed of foliage, he swore to never settle for less than a marginally comfortable furniture experience.

He and his family cleared a section of forest to plant soft grass and trees with fluffy leaves. With these materials, he began making furniture, first for his family, then for his neighbors. His furniture became such a sensation among the silent villagers that he took up a permanent role making things more comfortable.

Even after years of service to his people, the shiny person struggled to solve the most basic of obstacles to comfort, the knobby walls of their huts. On his deathbed, he looked around at his family, wishing he could provide them with the answers. They diligently worked the orchard every day, and many suffered from aches and pains.

Suddenly, it came to him. He reached out to one young child to help him out of his soft, flower-filled bed. With everyone's eyes trained on him, he walked over to the wall, turned his back to it, and began rubbing. The knots of vines dug into him, massaging his tight muscles.

It had been his final and most wonderful gift to his people, and since that day, all villagers used the hut walls to tease out aches and pains. Their tensions could now be easily relieved so they could focus on what really mattered, which was probably something like kidnapping intruders and being really quiet.

One of their intruders, Octavian, looked like he could use something to help ease his tension, but the look on his face after leaning against the wall made Replika relatively confident that a vine massage was not the best approach.

"Guess we need to figure a way out," she said.

"Have you noticed anything else that could help us?"

Replika joined him on the wall. She had a lot of questions about these people. How complex was their non-verbal language? How many variations were there to their adaptations? Were there other villages or other races that they traded or communicated with? The long list of questions hadn't been answered, and the answers she had gathered weren't useful for their escape.

Unless . . .

"Oh!" she exclaimed.

Finally, something useful.

8

LEVITATION SPELLS

Through all the questions running through Replika's mind about the colorful, silent people who were holding them captive, she finally thought of something useful.

At least, potentially useful.

"Oh?" Octavian asked.

"They're sensitive to sound."

"You mean, they hear well?"

"Exceedingly well," she confirmed. "When we got into the forest, one of them split off from the group while the rest of us waited. When they came back, I figured it was nothing. But when we started walking again, they gestured at some kind of animal in the distance. I think they heard the animal from where we had stopped, at least a mile away, and plotted a path for us around it."

"Was it some kind of predator?" Octavian asked.

"I think so. It looked like it to me," she replied.

"I guess sneaking out won't work?"

"Oh!" she exclaimed again with her hands together and her shoulders raised.

"Go on," he said when she didn't continue.

"You can make us float like them!"

"Uh . . ." He paused. "No."

"What?"

"No, I can't."

181

"Why not?" She puckered her lips into a pout.

"It's way too long to explain."

She let her shoulders drop and then flopped onto her back on the bed of plant matter.

The explanation was long, especially to someone who had traveled to two new universes, been chased by pirates, bargained with the captain of said pirates, almost drowned, been captured by eerily quiet people, and—let's not forget—lost the one device that could get them home.

In their home world, two schools of thought existed on implementing an "anti-gravity," "levitation," or similarly named spell. The first focused on applying an equal and opposite force counter to gravity while the second focused on manipulating a—theoretical at the time it was first proposed—Gravity Mesh around an object. When the Gravity Mesh was theorized in a paper released by the Consortium of Theoretical Physics and Applied Argumentation, the scientists noted that the force of gravity being exerted on an object couldn't be altered because the planet's mass couldn't—and probably shouldn't—be changed by a single magician. However, a magician could alter the meshes around objects and many properties of their environments.

The magical proof required comprehensive knowledge of every atom affected by the spell. With this, a magician could theoretically manipulate the effect of gravity on an object or group of objects. Modern objects that used these "levitation" spells affected the environment around the object, effectively changing its buoyancy.

The first public attempt at a levitation spell in Octavian's homeworld was by Villano the Magician, a popular entertainer at the time. He fashioned a heavy box that he filled on stage with weights. He had an audience member come to the stage to verify just how heavy the box was.

"Very."

Villano the Magician explained he would make the box levitate by condensing the weights down to a small center of mass.

Doing so would allow him to modify the gravity mesh and levitate the box, or so he thought.

The death of the brave volunteer and their last word was immortalized in a song by Sandra Nguyen, which was performed during a fiftieth anniversary memorial in the same theater. Unrelated to levitation, this event also ended in the death of an audience member. However, this person was not immortalized in the memorial plaque placed outside the theater a week after the concert.

Back home, Octavian had owned a levitating bag, which had also been his favorite bag. It had used a similar logic to the heavy box, but in a much more manageable and much less deadly way.

Replika didn't want to take no for an answer. In the short time between saying the idea and the idea being rejected, she'd gotten her hopes up about walking on air. The forced frown on her face was no match for Octavian's exhaustion.

"I could do it if we just needed to lift a small object nearby. But moving a whole person is way beyond my skill level." He gave her an apologetic smile. "But it was a good idea."

"Maybe there's another way to get out of here without making a sound," she said.

"Do you have something in mind?"

"Do you?"

Neither did.

9

ALMOST ESCAPE

While they waited for an epiphany on how to escape from their silent captors, they ate—and even enjoyed—the food left for them. They both kept an ear out for any sound coming from outside. There was the occasional chirp of a bird, the rustle of the leaves as the wind passed through them, but nothing else, so they eventually went back to snooping through the thin walls of the hut.

The sun had set, but the silent people didn't look as though they were heading to bed anytime soon. Torches remained lit throughout the village, and even the flames made more noise than the villagers. Many looked to be preparing to leave the village, while others were returning from elsewhere. Guess it's a shift change, Replika joked to herself.

A group emerged from the forest led by a girl holding a shiny, round rock, and Replika could just make out the people's gestures of excitement and urgency. A few others came to see what was going on. After a moment, they reached out to others with the same urgency. The mass of people slowly crawled toward the central platform, and it grew until they were a large group at the center of the village.

Replika hit Octavian, who had taken a break since he couldn't see well in the dark. He peered out to see what she was looking at.

"What's going on?" he whispered.

"Don't know," she said. "But it looks like an opportunity to me."

It took Octavian a minute to catch on to her point, but once he did, he shot up onto his feet. He threw the remaining food onto the small blanket that he, while sleeping, had refused to be covered by. After securing it around his waist, he waved back at Replika and made his way to the entrance.

He stood next to the tightly secured fabric, and Replika peered through the walls to check on the guards. It was dark out, and the only movement resulted from the wind.

"There's no one out there," she whispered.

"The guards are gone?" he asked.

She nodded. The trees rustled in a gentle breeze, and it gave her an idea.

"Can you make the wind blow harder?"

He nodded, waiting for her to elaborate.

"It could be loud enough for us to sneak out of here," she said. "What do you think?"

His face lit up. "I think it's brilliant."

Words she couldn't understand slipped effortlessly from Octavian's lips. He placed his finger against the fabric door, and as he slid it downward, the fabric ripped, leaving a hole for them to exit through.

Just as Replika pulled the fabric apart to give Octavian space to exit, the rustle of leaves got louder. The branches of nearby trees waved this way and that, bending to the wind's will. They stepped out of the hut, and a powerful gust swept over them. As leaves flew into their faces, they lifted their arms to shield against the debris. She looked back at Octavian, who was grimacing. He didn't seem to have control over how much the wind speed varied, but they had what they needed, a camouflage of noise.

Replika led the way, taking careful steps away from their prison. She glanced toward the village center and noticed that the crowd had grown much larger. She wondered if the whole village was out there, and if so, why.

Instead of heading directly out of the village, she circled around several of the huts. With a quick glance, she made sure Octavian was still with her, which he was.

Another powerful gust of air blew her dress up, and she pushed her hands along her sides to keep it down. She looked back at Octavian, who was focused on his work. He was following her without hesitation, and she wished she could tell him what she was thinking.

Then, a new sound echoed through the air. It wasn't loud, and she instinctively knew it was out of Octavian's range of hearing. It was a buzzing sound which, with a few turns of her head, she localized to the village center.

Looking around for her next move, she turned to see two figures leaving a nearby hut. She put her hand out to stop Octavian. The two were yellow and gray, and they were making gestures that reminded her of sign language, which she suddenly realized she knew. She looked back and forth between Octavian and the colorful pair several times. They were engrossed in silent conversation, but she and Octavian were in their periphery. The wind masking their steps died down and was replaced by a gentle gusting that oscillated like breath. Replika smiled and made sure her breathing matched its frequency.

What would she do if they turned toward her? Could they call for help? They didn't have any weapons on them, so perhaps she should just knock them out. However, not knowing anything about their physiology, she was concerned she might seriously injure them.

Just as she was about to take a step closer, the two small people noticed what was happening in the village center. They rushed away, completely unaware their lives may have been in danger.

"Safe," she mouthed to Octavian, also signing.

"You can sign?" Octavian answered in sign.

"**You** can sign?" A cheesy grin slipped across her face. "Good call on the wind change, by the way."

"What now?" he asked.

She looked past him at the thick forest, which could provide some shelter. But the ocean was on the opposite side of the village. She considered whether it would be better to attempt crossing the village now, while the citizens were distracted.

She pointed behind him. "Forest." Then in the direction of their capture. "Ocean."

"Ocean, to find the computer?" he asked.

She nodded. With a nod of agreement from Octavian, she turned toward their target. The wind masking their steps, she led him around the village one hut at a time. Much to her happy surprise, there were no more encounters or near misses, which would also have surprised her, but in a much less happy way. She took the chance to move toward the inner ring of huts, where she could see the gathering. There were over a hundred people at the village center, and that buzzing sound grew more intense the closer they got.

A purple-skinned figure, taller and more stout than the others she had seen, stepped up onto the platform. This was a village meeting, and she figured something big was going on. This didn't seem like the kind of village to have impromptu parties. Other than sudden bouts to play out Hamlet in mime. Replika held back a laugh at her own inside joke.

Nevertheless, it seemed too much of a coincidence that this village gathering was happening soon after their arrival.

Octavian tapped her. She looked back to see what he wanted, but he barely started his sentence before his jaw dropped. He hit her as if she wasn't already paying attention to him and pointed back to the gathering. She turned, unsure of what could have gotten his attention. But as soon as the stage came into her line of vision, she saw it.

The purple-colored figure was holding up the computer.

10

LOUD AND PROUD AT 110 DECIBELS

Octavian struggled to hold in his surprise and excitement at seeing the computer he had rudely deposited at the bottom of the ocean. Yet there it sat, in the purple hand of a figure who he assumed was the village leader. In their other hand, which was just as purple but larger than the first, were their bags. His priorities shifted, and a shared look with Replika ensured they were on the same page.

They were going to retrieve their belongings.

In his surprise, his concentration broke, and the wind stopped. An unconscious shift in weight caused a few leaves to crackle under his foot. Even if these villagers hadn't had super hearing, they still would have heard the loud crunch that echoed through the silence.

Suddenly, hundreds of eyes were on them.

"We should run," Replika said out loud, taking a few steps backward.

"Yeah, let's do that," he replied.

They both turned, and without looking back, dashed toward the village edge. Octavian pulled his computer marble, Notebook, from under his shirt, thankful it hadn't been taken when they were captured. With a quick command, it created a moderate glow to light their way. It was enough for him to see and to jump over the thick branch he almost tripped over.

"I don't think this is going to work," Replika said as she held back to stay beside him.

"What?" Octavian called with a heaving breath.

When was the last time he had run? It wasn't as easy as he remembered.

"We're at a disadvantage," she continued. "They know these woods. They've got incredible hearing. And who knows how good their other senses are?"

"And?" Octavian said, trying to make it obvious that he was open to another plan but already too out of breath to say it.

Replika looked back, but he couldn't risk doing the same, lest he trip or choke on his own spit.

"And, in case you were wondering, they're also very fast," she confirmed. "It's actually pretty incredible."

"Replika! Focus! Please!"

"Focus. Right."

She pretended to focus on dodging a pile of rocks in their path, but he could tell she was at nowhere near the disadvantage he was. The treeline came closer and closer. He didn't think they were going to make it. His breath was already short. His legs burned. He swore to himself if he got out of this alive, he'd get back in shape.

Since he had been knocked out on the walk from the beach to the village, he had no idea what to expect of the surrounding area. On top of that, his white hair made him stand out among the foliage, he wasn't a very good climber, and he was already pretty tired of being dirty. He shuddered as he remembered the mucky dock, the slimy bottom of the longboat, the feeling of wet shoes from his near-death experience, and the prickly texture on his skin when he awoke in the hut. He longed for a hot shower, some strong aromatherapy, and a nice loud playlist of fast-paced music.

He stopped in his tracks, pun intended.

"What are you doing?" Replika asked when she noticed. "Shouldn't we keep running?"

He smiled and gestured back toward the incoming mob.

"Follow my lead." He tapped his computer marble. "Notebook, play *Loud And Proud* at 110 decibels."

As the song queued up, he started running back the way they came, Replika right beside him. The villagers were closing in fast. Abruptly, pounding bass erupted around them. The villagers just in front of them dropped into crouching positions, hands over their ears.

Octavian's ears framed a big smile, and when Replika reached his side, he saw she was equally amused.

"Let's do this," he signed.

Every villager they passed was overloaded by the sensory input. He lifted his arms and spoke magic words, drawing clouds in the sky toward each other. A loud clap of thunder rang out as they collided. One after another, the noise immobilized the villagers.

Replika left his side and ran ahead, where a group of villagers were still standing. She let out a loud scream—which surprised Octavian just as much as the villagers, but he refused to stop. When a brave few silent people stood their ground, Replika dug her feet into the ground and kicked dirt into their eyes. They were still reeling with pain when Octavian passed by them.

His favorite song was playing louder than he'd ever heard it, and he regretted never going to a concert. The band, Last Ones Standing, were well known for their mix of gentle lyrics and aggressive musical arrangement.

Their lead percussionist, Hanson Lockhardt, had been an engineer who graduated from the National University of Magic. While working for a tech startup, he became engrossed in a pet project trying to map the frequencies of oscillating psyche particles to musical notes. Doing so required a special facility, one that didn't exist and that he didn't have the money to build.

Like any good entrepreneur, he reached out to colleagues from the university, donors of the university's foundation, and anyone else with money to burn. While in prison for fraud in association with his method of raising funds, he raised enough money to build the facility he needed. It was conveniently finished just in time for his release.

A few years later, Last Ones Standing released their first album, featuring a magic instrument that reacted to the psyche particle field in the room and was modulated through the unique talents of Hanson Lockhardt. Their first single, *Can't Hold Ones Back*, was at the top of the charts for months and was the top grossing single ever, until they broke their own record five years later.

Octavian's favorite song, which was currently offending the ears of every villager it met, was the first dynamic single of all time. The track reacted to the mood of the listener. When Octavian was sad, the song played in a melancholic pace and key. And when he was racing to triumphantly retrieve his best chance at a way home, it was loud, confident, and as aggressive as Replika, who was enjoying kicking up dirt a bit too much.

The song was an innovative masterpiece that inspired Octavian in his quest to integrate masculine and feminine magic because it was about being true to yourself publicly and unabashedly. And in this moment, every note was pumping pure power into his veins.

As they closed in on the stage, the crowd of remaining villagers stood ready to fight. Replika paused and waited for Octavian to catch up. It was obvious the music was still affecting the silent people, but its effects seemed somehow diminished. Reluctance was clear on Replika's expression.

Something had changed, but what?

As he reached her side, the fires around the central stage lit Replika as she signed, "It's the buzz."

11

Buzzkill

Octavian barely heard her when she whispered it, but he understood as she signed the words.

"When they're all together," she continued, her voice cutting through the silence, "they let off a buzzing sound. It's protecting them somehow." She grimaced. "It's awful."

He couldn't hear the sound she was referring to, and he thought it was probably better that way. He could only imagine how creepy all the eyes on them would be with a terrible buzz ringing in his ears.

"Any ideas to get through?" he asked.

The crowd collectively began to move, like a swarm of insects gravitating toward a beam of sunlight. The leader, still standing on the stage, was making direct eye contact with Octavian, as if directing the villagers with their gaze.

He and Replika took steps backward as they each strategized a way out. The villagers they had left behind gathered around them. They were surrounded, and to make matters worse, Octavian's favorite song was changing key.

He tapped Notebook to stop the music.

"Ideas?" he asked.

"One."

"Sounds better than none. What is it?"

"How confident are you that if we get the computer, we can get out of here?"

A group of villagers with spears and knives cut through the crowd, figuratively. But their hostile gestures made it clear that they were quite ready to literally cut through the intruders.

"Fifty-fifty," Octavian replied.

"Good enough for me."

Replika crouched down. Confused, Octavian lowered himself as well. Replika's gaze was focused on the purple-skinned leader on the stage. Octavian slid away from her as he anticipated her next move.

Abruptly, she launched herself into the air. A scream escaped her, sounding more fearful than her antagonistic ones earlier. Every pair of eyes was transfixed on her steep ascent into the sky and her subsequent descent toward her purple target.

The stage crunched under her as she landed at the leader's side. She yanked the bags from their larger hand. They tried to pull the computer away, but she grabbed their arm and squeezed it hard. They dropped the computer. She scooped it up and launched herself back into the air again with a heavy grunt.

When she landed next to Octavian, she grabbed at her ears, dropping the computer.

"Ugh, that buzzing," she grumbled as it rolled away.

Octavian ran forward to stop the computer with his foot. But before he could pick it up, sharp points dug into his clothes from several angles. He lifted his eyes to see far too many staring back. Not really looking forward to being stabbed—although he did consider it—he stayed completely still.

Calm, intentional words slipped through his lips. They carefully crafted a spell one syllable at a time. With extreme accuracy and crystal clear intention, he set down the framework necessary. As he let out the final word, the computer flew from the ground into his hand. With no hesitation, he powered it up and pushed the large center button on its side.

The world shifted, leaving the already nauseous Octavian dizzy and sick, afraid of what would come next, and yet ready to leave this world behind.

The new world appearing before Replika was dark. Extremely dark. Even darker than the village they'd just been standing in, where at least there had been torches.

She shifted her vision, trying to find some kind of internal setting to help her see. Moments later, something changed within her, and suddenly her surroundings were somewhat visible. She felt it happen but didn't know how she'd done it. Despite the change, it was still hard to make out what was around her. She squinted, peered, and cocked her head to the side.

There was a table, maybe two. A cot off to the side, against a wall. A toppled chair. Odds and ends scattered across the ground and surfaces that she couldn't make out.

Everything was still except a lone figure, who she assumed was Octavian. It was a guess she confirmed when he ran into one of the tables, letting out an "oof" followed by a characteristic grumble.

"Replika?"

Three dim lights came aglow around them. Her eyesight adjusted again, and things became clearer. The furniture was reminiscent of metal laboratory workbenches, and paper strewn over them had overflowed onto the floor. This reminded her of the laboratory island complex in the first world they'd visited.

She looked up to get her bearings. What she initially thought was a closed off room was actually a shallow cave. The walls of solid rock arched upward about thirty feet. And around a gentle curve was an opening to the world, which was just as dark as inside the cave. Octavian stood at the very back wall, stumbling toward the cot. He wouldn't be able to see the mouth of the cave from there.

She took a few steps toward the opening, struck speechless by the view before her. All she could bring herself to do was put her hands up to her mouth as she tried to take it all in.

12

STORM FIRES

A s far as Replika could see, the land was flat, making the sky look huge. And filling the sky were stars, so many stars. It was breathtaking. She was sure it was the most beautiful thing ever.

But that wasn't accurate.

One of the few things arguably more beautiful than a sea of stars is a storm fire. Only two known examples of storm fires existed in their home world. The entertainment company InFire FX was commissioned by a small but upscale resort to develop an innovative show of some kind. The patron company loved pyrotechnics, so it was clear that the effects should be physical.

InFire FX's design made use of magic to stabilize a field of combustible material in the sky. Controlled ignition of fires throughout the show would create a beautiful and unique experience. The tests they ran were all successful, and by the time the first show was scheduled at the resort, the media lauded it as the most anticipated event of the year.

Rich and famous people from all over the world flocked to the resort. This included ten members of the International Council of Exalted Magicians, who, while definitely rich and famous, were allowed free entry to "the show that would change the world."

On the day of the show, clouds coated the entire sky. Unknown to InFire FX, the field they had created was not as stable as they thought. Over the course of the day, the combustible material from the field both seeped into the clouds' puffy embrace and fell, giving a lightly coated hug to the resort.

When the show started, everything seemed fine at first. Then, suddenly, a bolt of lightning shot from one cloud to the next, igniting a fire with deadly results. Though the Exalted Magicians were able to protect themselves and many guests, no one survived the storm fire without permanent injuries. Onlookers from off-site and those watching live remotely described the conflagration as "amazingly beautiful, but not worth the money."

The resort and InFire FX both went out of business soon after the incident. Unfortunately, seven years later, another resort attempted to use the technology again, with similar results. After this tragedy, which left no survivors, experts determined how the lightning had triggered such a terrible cascade. Though several countries attempted to develop something similar for military use, they were unable to reproduce the effect. Thus, the world was spared another deadly instance of the beautiful storm fire.

Of course, stars are also beautiful and are also fires, but they are, more importantly, at a much safer distance. So, while Replika couldn't think of anything more beautiful herself, she wasn't really missing out on anything.

"You need to see this," she finally said to Octavian.

"I can't see anything," he replied. "The room is spinning."

Hearing his dismay, she rushed over and steadied him.

"I feel like I'm going to pass out," he said, "or throw up. It's hard to tell."

She helped him sit on the cot nearby, placing his bag beside him. He was gripping the computer tightly. Based on their experience in the last world, she couldn't imagine how scary this transition must have been for him. And although she squeezed his hand to help him relax, his clutch on the computer didn't falter.

"Why don't you try to get some sleep," Replika offered. "It's nighttime, and we appear to be safe for now. You can sleep off the nausea and recharge."

Octavian didn't put up a fight. He laid down and took a deep breath.

"Wake me if anything interesting happens, please," he said, sounding half-asleep already.

"I will."

She squeezed his hand again before returning to the cave entrance, where she tried to grasp the immenseness of the universe from the tiny glimpse she was viewing.

Octavian awoke to a gentle rumbling beneath him. He sat up, squinting at the bright sunlight coming in from the cave opening. He placed his feet on the ground, and before he could figure out what the rumbling was, it faded away.

He decided he must have imagined it.

The bright light wasn't helping his dull headache, so he shielded his eyes. When he tried to stand, his legs wobbled, so he let himself fall back onto the bed. Calling out for Replika yielded no response, so he let out a sigh.

It was unclear to him how long they'd been gone from home. Was it only yesterday that his biggest problem was having his academic plan approved? Now, he feared for his life whether he used the computer—the Reality Tuner—or not. Abruptly, he realized his hands were empty. The Reality Tuner was gone.

13

THREE HARD PROBLEMS

Panicked at the thought of having lost the Reality Tuner all over again, Octavian frantically looked around. Heart racing and fear rising, he soon found the computer wedged between the cot and the cave wall. He snatched it up, as if pulling it away from a thief. Those sneaky cave walls.

Holding the computer gave him some solace, almost as much as if he had taken a deep breath or two. This was his only way home, so a bit of panic was natural, or so he reasoned.

His fingers started to hurt, and he realized he was clutching the Reality Tuner, causing the detailed filigree to dig into his flesh. He tried to relax his grip, but as his mind wandered, he unconsciously clung to it.

He was overwhelmed with everything that had happened, and he found it difficult to stay in the present. One moment, he was thinking about the terror of a device that allowed them to travel between realities. The next moment, he was wondering why none of the people in the previous worlds were transported with them.

He was too distracted to notice the small, wedge-shaped devices lodged into man-made cracks in the cave walls. He didn't bother to look at the stagnant magic needing to be restored. And though he was currently pondering how to stay alive, he ignored the technology he needed in order to do so, though he didn't yet know his life was still in danger.

Octavian had three things on his mind.

First, the computer needed a better name than the Reality Tuner. He took a moment to brainstorm, but nothing came to him. He groaned. That was supposed to be the easy one.

Next, he needed to learn how to make it work. Considering an operational definition of work, he decided it wasn't enough for the device to just transport them to random universes that may or may not be suitable for human life. Instead, the definition of work had to include the ability for them to control where they went.

He lifted the Reality Tuner to his face and looked carefully at the workmanship. It was astoundingly similar to the computer Teacher had kept in the lab: a solid half and a transparent half, elegant vine-like metalwork reaching around to the top, a flat plane inside with a grid and symbols he didn't recognize, and a crystal at the top. Never having counted the buttons on the computer in Teacher's cabinets, he gently ran his finger across the nine buttons on the side of the Reality Tuner. They weren't labeled, so he couldn't guess what they were for. The large center button seemed to trigger the reality jump—at least so far—but he wasn't sure how the device decided where to go.

Octavian scoffed as he remembered Teacher grumbling when he suggested labeling things in the lab. This was the perfect example of why labels were so important.

He centered himself as his pulse quickened. Nothing was going to happen until he powered it up. Though the thought of doing so terrified him, he certainly wasn't learning anything new by staring at it. He placed his finger on the bottom and directed a flow of psyche particles—the key to magic—into it.

The crystal at the top glowed white, and a display similar to a star chart filled the room. None of the markings near the points on the chart looked familiar. He looked closely around the entire map, but nothing suggested how to control the tuner. It could be deceptively easy to transport them to a universe with a toxic atmosphere, no atmosphere, or maybe no planet at all.

And that was the third thing on his mind. He needed to figure out how to protect them when they universe hopped. Reality jumped? What about just tripping?

Deciding what to call the process was a problem for another time.

Bringing himself back on task, he reasoned that if he could control where they traveled to, he could avoid universes where the planet was inhospitable, as most realities probably were. As Dream Teacher had said, human life is rare, and worlds compatible with human life, while theoretically less rare, weren't likely to be much more plentiful.

He stopped the flow of psyche particles powering the device, and the glow dimmed to nothing. He slid his thumb across its glass-like casing. It was almost as if the universe—well, the multiverse—was whispering to him, hinting at what he should do.

Listening, he let the question float freely in his mind without forcing an answer. The field of psyche particles ebbed and flowed around him, connecting him to the universe and the universe to him. He closed his eyes and waited as the natural current of energy moved and transformed the information he needed.

The answer flowed toward him until it was just out of reach. He waited patiently for it, not reaching or grasping, as it drifted closer.

And then the answer was there, plain as day.

Fire marbles.

14

THE DISCOVERY OF PSYCHE PARTICLES

Long before the invention of magic computers, magicians recognized the need to store energy and matter for later use. They understood that the natural properties of the universe were linked, but the magical proof needed to map these complex relationships into a stable and manageable device eluded them. The limiting factor was the psyche particle, the discovery of which paved the way for items like fire marbles. Though this knowledge was foundational to magic technology, the discovery itself was shrouded in mystery.

Octavian had learned about this in a weekend crash course on astral projection. Astral projection wasn't a skill taught to contemporary magicians. Many magicians claimed it was impossible, while almost all magicians insisted it was impractical for reasons not relevant at this point. Although Octavian wasn't ever successful at astral projection, he did learn about the legend of Imo, a magician and spiritual teacher who followers believed was the first to discover psyche particles.

There were no historical documents proving that Imo ever really existed. Yet her followers existed in such numbers that they had formed a small nation of individuals who studied her practices. Their religious text was a set of journals supposedly authored by Imo some 2500 years earlier.

In these journals, Imo documented her astral projection journeys. She meditated eighteen hours a day, six days at a time, with one rest day between. Most of her meditation time was spent on astral projection, during which she studied the nature of the universe.

She was obsessed with questions such as how do the clouds know which way to go? Why do people show unilateral handedness? And why, when hanging the clothes out to dry, does one sock always go missing? The answers, of course, are the clouds are at the mercy of the wind, because brains aren't great at being used to their fullest ability, and because paired socks, more often than not, hate each other.

On one night, she projected herself to the mountain peak where the Holy Trousers were discovered. There, she decided on a whim to look up. It wasn't an odd thing to do, but she suddenly realized she had never thought to do it while astral projecting. She expected to see stars—which was a perfectly reasonable expectation—but instead she saw a glimmer. It wasn't the kind of glimmer that someone glancing at the sky without purpose might have noticed. It was a kind of glimmer only noticeable by someone as thoughtful as Imo and with as much free time as Imo had.

At first, she assumed it was more stars and that somehow, when she was outside of her body, she could see further. But as she squinted to see it more clearly, she found that it was more than just a glimmer.

It was a dynamic field of glimmers.

During what was to become known as the Long Sleep, she lost all concept of time. The longer she looked, the more ubiquitous the particle field appeared to be. And the further she studied, the more connections she found: between the particles and the clouds, between the particles and the socks, and between the particles and the human mind.

These particles came to be known as psyche particles, and as human understanding of the particles increased, so did the ability to manipulate them. Such is the way of magic, where understanding is key to mastery.

For later magicians interested in containing energetic information, the connections psyche particles allowed were key. One prodigious magician named Xiang Bu theorized that one could condense the matter and associated energy of just about anything into a small container. It could be encased in a material that stored information regarding the environmental variables, which could later be used to recompile the matter and energy into their original form. In other words, one could make a container and cram it full of stuff. Then, when needed, the stuff could take on its original form based on instructions in the container.

Xiang Bu and his successors experimented with this idea over generations until finally, EnviroJars were born.

Octavian called them EnviroJars as a sort of inside joke, in part because it sounded cool and in part because neither Percoarcted Reduction Of Matter Entangled In Nanostructured Data Repositories nor its abbreviation PROMEINDR rolled off the tongue.

Fire marbles were a form of EnviroJar, but theoretically, EnviroJars could hold just about anything. Octavian had studied the magical proof during his Theory of Magical Items course in undergrad. Given the right materials and enough time, he knew he could figure out how to create an EnviroJar that could save their lives if the need ever arose.

Octavian finally loosened his death grip on the Reality Tuner and pulled his bag up onto the bed. He dug his hand into it and reached around. When he felt a small chain, he pulled it out. He rolled his eyes at the tangled mess of cord, chain, and string. Or maybe he was rolling his eyes because it was still slightly damp. Either way, with exasperation, he freed the chain from its knots, pushed it through the small loop on the side of the Reality Tuner, and secured it to his belt loop.

That would do for now.

He stood up and stretched his arms above his head, leaning backward to deepen the stretch. Finally taking a proper look around, he noted papers strewn across work surfaces, chairs, and the floor. Before he even checked, he knew whose handwriting he'd find on them. He flipped through those on a nearby table, skimming for information on the world they were now in or perhaps information about the tuner.

A crumpled up paper near the far corner of the table caught his eye. He was drawn to it, and his hand trembled as he reached for it—perhaps from his rumbling stomach, perhaps from fear. But he ignored the feeling, picked up the paper, opened it, and read the far too familiar handwriting.

15

THE NAMING OF WORLDS

Octavian couldn't believe what he read on this random crumpled up piece of paper.

"I am trapped and alone, looping through these universes. If some other being somehow finds this here, they must also know that they are trapped as well. There seems to be no way out, especially no way without"

It stopped mid-sentence, interrupted by a gruesome tear through the paper. Reading it sent a chill through Octavian. Maybe he'd been wrong all along. Perhaps Teacher hadn't intentionally sent them here, and this was just some big accident. His heart raced at the thought of being trapped in these alternate realities, just as Teacher had been.

Octavian had wanted to change the world—his own world— and to conduct transformative research that would improve people's lives. Replika was supposed to be his ticket to success. She was a first step toward using magic for many unmet medical needs, from reconstructive brain surgery to body modification. Magic had brought his reality so much innovation, and he had planned to add more inclusive medical technology to what already existed.

None of that was possible now.

He stopped an impending downward spiral, reminding himself to stay present. After all, if Teacher had been trapped here—and the other universes he and Replika had seen so far—then he had also escaped somehow. Early messages of being trapped meant nothing. Teacher had made it back to his world somehow. That fact alone meant escape was achievable.

He was still haunted by Teacher's final moments. It differed from when Captain Egnaro or the small, silent people had disappeared. Instead of atoms rearranging themselves, Teacher had been ripped apart one layer at a time. Bile rose into his throat, and he fought the urge to throw up.

Octavian couldn't keep denying the truth. He wanted to believe this was unintentional, but Replika's programming and his connection to the Reality Tuner were damning evidence. Teacher's expression just before expelling them from their world had been complex, but he knew something was going to happen.

There was no doubt in his mind that Teacher planned this. Maybe not everything—that seemed impossible—but Teacher had purposefully sent them into a web of alternate realities, a trap he himself had once been ensnared in.

What Octavian couldn't figure out was why. If this was all a test, what did Octavian need to do to pass it?

He chided himself. If he kept thinking that way, he would suffer for it. After all, if he assumed this was a test, that meant Teacher would come help them at some point. Octavian couldn't keep hoping for Teacher to show up. Instead, he had to assume they were on their own.

A sound startled him, and he spun on his heels. Replika walked around the corner into the cave, shaking her dress roughly to remove the dirt from it. He breathed a sigh of relief.

"I didn't mean to scare you," she said when she saw his surprise. "Are you feeling better?"

"Yeah. Thanks."

She smiled, and her furrowed brow relaxed. "We seem to be in a desert." She made her way over to him. "I looked around, but I didn't see any sources of water or food. This rock structure is the only thing for miles in any direction."

"I guess that means we won't be staying here long. We'll need to use the computer—the Reality Tuner, as Teacher apparently called it."

"You sound worried," she stated, though the shine in her eyes seemed to give away some excitement at having a name for their universe hopping-jumping-tripping device.

"We don't know where we'll end up," he answered. "It could be better, or it could be worse." He suddenly remembered his idea to build EnviroJars. "I may have a solution, but I need materials that probably don't exist in an empty world."

"I said it was a desert, not empty," Replika said, a grin widening across her cheeks.

She pulled something from her back. It was a makeshift envelope bag folded from the cloth that had wrapped their original food purchase. Plopping it triumphantly onto the table, she unfolded it and held her hands out in pride.

Octavian gawked at her finds. Among some tools that she must have found lying around the cave-turned lab were samples of a few dozen rocks and minerals.

"I'm calling this universe the Material World," she proclaimed. "There is so much geological diversity out there. I'm sure you can find something useful."

This was outside of his area of expertise, but he had taken a lapidary course as an elective in his undergrad. Maybe Replika had data on materials such as those she had gathered.

"Do you know what these are?" he asked.

"Nope," she said, still smiling widely with her pride fully intact.

So much for that.

He picked up a crystalline sample and held it up to the light coming in from outside. It had impurities, but it could be useful for an EnviroJar.

"Will that work for your solution?" she asked.

"I don't know. Maybe. Are you able to analyze its composition or structure?"

Her demeanor was suddenly coy. "I can try."

He felt a pang of guilt for pushing her. He grabbed a few familiar-looking samples and separated them from the others. "Hey, don't worry about it. Maybe it'll come naturally when you need it."

"Sure," she muttered. "Maybe."

Octavian didn't want to push too hard, so he did his best to look interested until she continued.

"Actually, that's happened before. When we were fixing the funicular in the Steampunk World, out of nowhere, I suddenly saw things I couldn't usually see. And then, when we appeared in the Silent People's World, I somehow pulled you out of the water and resuscitated you. It seemed automatic, somehow."

The Steampunk World and Silent People's World, huh? Replika seemed much better at naming things than he. Thanks, Teacher.

"Well, then. If you're up to it, take a look at these samples, and tell me what's different about them."

She looked at them closely, picking them each up and turning them this way and that.

"I've got nothing," she said.

Octavian gave her a tight-lipped smile. "Thanks for trying."

He picked up a layered, translucent material from the collection. It looked similar to a mineral from his world, except that attempting to scratch it with his nail left it unharmed. This could work.

"There was a lot of that," Replika spoke up, sounding cheerful again. "Would you like me to gather more?"

"I think it's an exceptional find," he encouraged. "Would you mind?"

"Not at all!"

He couldn't help but grin at her enthusiasm. "I'll get started prepping things here. We don't need an excessive amount. Maybe ten samples of this size would be ideal."

The ground shook, and Octavian looked around to see if he was imagining it. Metal clinked against metal as the table, chairs, and bed eased back and forth.

Something was coming.

16

THE WORLD'S A'SHAKIN'

The ground beneath Replika's feet wobbled. She had sensed similar shaking since she'd started exploring that morning, but it had gone as quickly as it arrived. The tremor was stronger this time, but her analysis of their surroundings gave no clues to its source.

"The sooner I get you those samples, the sooner we can move on, I guess," she said in response to the tremor.

"Yeah. Let's hope it doesn't get worse," Octavian replied. "Do you want me to go with you?"

"No, it's not far, and it won't take me long. You just focus on whatever preparations you need to do."

She grabbed her makeshift bag and rushed off before he could reply.

Once out of the cave, she looked back. Octavian had followed to the mouth of the cave and now was scooping sand into a bowl. She couldn't imagine what he was going to do with a bowl of sand. For a moment, she wondered if she should have asked more about his plans.

She laughed to herself as he struggled to pick the bowl back up before turning her attention back to her task. She got her bearings. The horizon stretched out around her in all directions, interrupted by a far-off range of mountains to one side and the outer casing of the cave on another.

Something was odd about this world, almost as if it was artificial. The cave had a small mouth, and it concealed an interior larger than it appeared from the outside. The ground was dry and cracked but heterogeneous, and fine sand atop rock and packed earth covered the area around the cave. It seemed to her as if someone—one guess which someone she was thinking of—had intentionally crafted this formation to use as a workspace. But that was impossible.

Her current destination was almost a thirty-minute walk away. There, concave pits interrupted the rocky ground, each with a different sort of mineral deposit. In some areas, the rocks had been weathered away to reveal large, sharp crystals. In others, material jutted out of the ground. One such protrusion held the mineral she needed to collect. Shoots of rectangular minerals jutted out of the ground in a field of several square meters.

She arrived at the deposit and congratulated herself for remembering her way back. Unaware of the big mineral farming industry in their home world—or the Magic World, as she was calling it—she was intrigued at the almost perfect distinction between the different mineral deposits. However, the concave pits that sat at regular intervals across the area were clear signs that these formations were unnatural.

Similar to agricultural farms, there existed mineral and gem farms across the globe in their world. One of the most notable was the Micah Mica Mecha, where different varieties of crystalline and silicate materials were grown through the magic-assisted processing of natural materials. Though the Micah Mica Mecha was the principal supplier of the material used in the outer coating of marbles, their tourist industry was no slouch at bringing in profits.

Seventy-five acres of land were dedicated to an amusement park themed after the different products manufactured by the Micah Mica Mecha. Millions of guests each year enjoyed the roller coasters, dark rides, entertainment venues, and splash pad. Mineral Mountain, the most popular of the roller coasters, was world renowned for its exciting twists and turns. However, unknown to most guests, excluding the Micah Mica Mecha Fanatics Fan Club and also Teacher, the vibration from the popular coaster was harnessed by magic power generators around the frame, making Mineral Mountain completely self-powered.

It was an interesting and relevant factoid about an otherwise over-commercialized and environmentally unsustainable tourist attraction. But they had won a lot of awards for their colorful rock candy delights, so who cares about that other stuff?

As Replika got to work obtaining her samples, she continued what she had been trying to process since they arrived. She had some basic knowledge of her own systems and was picking up more as she dug deeper. Yet she had vague memories of personal experiences and feelings that she couldn't place, especially knowing that she'd been activated just moments before she and Octavian were thrown into their first alternate reality.

She had figured out how to access her diagnostics while Octavian was repairing her arm, yet every diagnostic she ran came back clean. There was no reason for these memories to be vague. They had to have been pre-programmed into her, didn't they? If they weren't her memories, she wondered if they were the real memories of someone else. What purpose did they serve? Perhaps they provided her with a more realistic perspective of the world. If so, why did they seem to sit just out of reach?

Maybe it was a bug needing to be addressed. Or perhaps they were purposefully displaced by Teacher.

She tensed at the thought, but it wasn't anger that held her. She had an innate love and trust toward Teacher. Despite the evidence pointing straight to the Exalted Grand Magician as having purposefully trapped them here, she was sure he had a good reason for it. Unfortunately, she didn't have a single clue to explain that reason. Still, it didn't sit right with her to think poorly of him.

A novel texture amidst the shiny, gray mica caught her eye. Slamming down the hammer-like tool she'd found in the cave, she noted that this material was harder than its surroundings. She crouched down, tucking her skirt under her bottom as best she could, and wiped the obstructing debris away. This was the first instance she had seen of minerals mixing in these deposits. She hammered away at the surrounding mineral.

The new sample was crystalline, and the more she revealed it, the more colors it held. Waves of green, blue, purple, and black swirled across it. Touching it sent chills through her, but neither holding it up above her nor holding it close to her face revealed why. She broke off a large piece and placed it in her bag. Somehow, she knew it would come in handy.

Once she had gotten enough of the samples she'd come for, she pulled the makeshift pack onto her shoulder and started back toward the cave. A sound boomed behind her, and she turned to identify it. It was thunder, evidenced by the immense cloud in the distance. A wall of detritus stretched from the ground into the cloud. The barren landscape looked in desperate need of rain, and Replika smiled as she determined it was moving in their direction.

The memory of refreshing rain on her skin made her take a deep breath, and she closed her eyes to keep a firm hold on it. The storm answered her relaxation by throwing lightning down. A clap of thunder accompanied the shaking ground. The storm was moving slowly, but this fact only momentarily comforted her.

Another bolt of lightning crashed into the ground, but this time was different. The storm cloud turned red where the lightning had run through it. A scar spread, and within seconds, the entire storm and debris field was on fire. She gasped at the terrifying beauty that rivaled the dark night she had marveled at when they arrived. The fire burned red, then blue, then white.

She looked back at the cave, estimating with sufficient and unnecessary accuracy the distance and time it would take for the storm to reach it. Looking back at the storm and getting a feel of its speed, she got her answer.

The storm would be upon them within the hour.

17

ANCHORS ARE COOL

The ground rumbling was getting worse, Octavian noted. He wondered if a big earthquake was coming. He had never felt an earthquake before, although he had been protected from the quaking motion of an earthquake by magic stabilizers. Still, he knew earthquakes were preceded by smaller foreshocks.

He abandoned his project and looked around the cave to assess its ability to support a shield. As was standard practice before doing any magic work, he first checked the structure for traps. There were none, but the search yielded a surprise. Someone had embedded magic anchors into the walls of the cave.

Lots of magic anchors.

Magic anchors were classed into two types: material, like those in the cave walls, and immaterial. Octavian had been preparing to create immaterial magical anchors, which even a magician-in-training could set up on a small scale. However, when physical objects were used as anchors, they were conceptually similar to EnviroJars in that they encapsulated a predefined set of variables. Unlike the static nature of an EnviroJar, which was only practical on a small scale, anchors allowed for stability in even extremely dynamic environments.

For example, when a tsunami threatened the city of New Tokyo in Nihon, Exalted Grand Magicians set up anchors around a community center where citizens had gathered. Each Exalted Grand charged up to five anchors, giving the building and its surrounding area a bubble of protection from the crushing flow of water that hit the coast.

Yursi Stovanki, a tourist from Chalsinia who was not within the protective shield but saw it as ze narrowly escaped death, described the bubble in this way:

"It was as if the building and the people were themselves water. As if I was the odd one for being flesh and bone. I thought it seemed like a nice way to be, especially since I also thought I was about to die."

Yursi's incredible account of zir experience was made famous in zir book *The Wave That Almost Killed Me*, which hit bestseller lists around the world. The book notably did not make the bestseller lists in Nihon, where most believed the book made them look bad. Despite record sales, a movie deal, and a Broadway musical based on zir book, Yursi became best known for another strange adventure involving a dozen ping-pong balls, fifty magical anchors, thirty magicians, a football field, and a football field worth of comic books.

Octavian was surprised and appalled to find over fifty anchors in the cave, though he should have been thankful not to have ping-pong balls or a football field worth of comics. He couldn't imagine how Teacher could have installed so many on his own or why he would have in the first place. A larger rumble shook the ground below him, and a wave of understanding washed over him.

The number and distribution of anchors needed for any given task varied based on the necessary shield size, the stress they were intended to respond to, and other such factors. Most magicians at Octavian's level of expertise could only place one anchor at a time.

Each additional anchor after the first was significantly more difficult to place nearby, especially if placed by the same magician, because the unique resonance of a magician's essence was leveraged when setting up a new anchor. After the first anchor, each additional anchor had to recognize the other anchors and interweave with their stability mesh. Compatibility with another magician's anchor was easier because the base essence of each magician was unique. Even so, most magicians chose to work alone when setting up a field of anchors because of a sense of superiority, imposter syndrome or, on the rare occasion, both.

For a magician such as Octavian with a few years of graduate-level training, it would be impossible to charge over three anchors total in such a small area.

He had only seen a large field of anchors once before, on a tour of a Global Defense Force facility. The Global Defense Force were the Magic World's leading shield experts, and that trip had a special place in Octavian's memory. Not only had he been forced to act as an "audience participant," but he'd also been unable to charge the small anchor he was directed to. His stage fright had never been worse, a skill he improved in the years after.

Before his life-changing participation in the stage show, the tour guide had taken the group to a viewing deck that looked out over a large open area. Dotted across the landscape were anchors—the tour guide claimed there were one-hundred-twenty-one—placed equidistant from each other. Stretching high into the sky was a tube, where water from underneath the shield was pumped up before tumbling down over the transparent shields in the most overengineered fountain in the world.

Octavian was reminded of the fountain because this field of anchors also appeared to be overengineered. The density of the anchors in the cave implied a more dire threat than an earthquake. But everything seemed calm and peaceful here. The deep rumble of thunder was an ominous disagreement.

The magician noted that these anchors had lost most of their magic reserve. As with everything else he had seen since the start of this little adventure, he concluded that the anchors were originally placed many years earlier. For so many anchors to exist in this small area, Teacher must have charged them over time, though even that seemed like an insurmountable task. Octavian couldn't ignore the evidence, though.

Three anchors would take Octavian all day, and with their limited food and no water, he wasn't confident he could even do that. Something nagged at him not to ignore the anchors, but that nag refused to disclose why.

He returned to the samples Replika had collected. There, he narrowed in on the sample he had noticed earlier, a black mineral giving off a magic resonance. It was theoretically possible to leverage that energy to magnify his own abilities. He had heard of minerals in his world that were known for their benefits of focusing magical energy. Maybe it would be sufficient to charge enough anchors to cover himself and Replika.

Biting the inside of his cheek, he tried to run through a magical proof in his head. He brought up a three-dimensional sketching interface on Notebook and began working out the details. This was going to take a while.

Tired and hungry, his mind wandered back to the EnviroJars. Could he charge the anchors, complete the EnviroJars, and power the Reality Tuner? All the while needing a decent meal and probably another year of sleep? He groaned as he considered his options. One option was to focus on the anchors so they could rest and eat, but he had no guarantee he would be able to do so before whatever calamity hit. Perhaps they should take their chances and just hop to another world while they could.

The rumble of thunder continued.

Replika's voice struck Octavian's ears like lightning hitting the ground.

"We have to leave," she said.

"What's wrong?"

"There's a big storm coming this way."

"You're worried about a storm?"

She moved her arms in big circles as she emphasized her point. "A **BIG** storm."

18

TRUST IS HARD

Octavian didn't doubt that the storm Replika referred to was big, maybe even **VERY** big. He was just uncertain why it mattered when they seemed pretty safe inside their cave. It was doubtful there would be flooding because of how flat the land was, and even if the wind blew rain into the cave, its shape made it impossible for that rain to make it to the back.

The only logical answer was that Replika was leaving out an important detail.

"And?"

"And," she said with great emphasis on every word, "it's on fire."

"As in literal fire?" Octavian asked.

"As in literal fire," Replika insisted.

"And it's headed toward us?"

Replika put her hands on her hips and nodded as big as she could. Octavian looked at all the papers he hadn't gotten to sift through. He had noticed an entire section devoted to the magical potential in this reality's geological diversity and had made a mental note to read it later.

"How long do we have?" he asked.

"A little over half an hour, by my estimation."

He absolutely trusted her estimation. The thunder was getting louder, and the ground began trembling again. Unsure of their next steps, he went to the mouth of the cave to see for himself. Even if the desert beyond hadn't been eerily flat, he would have seen the monstrous wall of flames fading from shades of red and orange to blue and white. It was a storm fire, something he never thought he'd live to see. As beautiful as it was, he wasn't thrilled about it heading their way.

"We should use the computer," Replika insisted. When she saw his discomfort, she asked, "Right?"

"I'm not keen on traveling again until we have some kind of plan in place. We've gotten lucky so far, but who knows where we'll end up next?"

"But you said you had an idea."

"I do," Octavian said with a nod. "It's like a fire marble, but instead of holding fire, it would hold a temporary bubble of environment. If we end up someplace awful, we could trigger the bubble, which would give us enough time to jump to another universe."

"And you can make that?"

"I think so, but a prototype will take an hour, at least."

"We don't have that long," she reminded him.

He groaned his agreement. As he tried to think of a better way to make this decision, Replika looked around, her mouth open as if she had something to say. But instead of saying anything, she closed it again and put her hand to her chin. She walked over to the table and picked up a piece of paper.

"Is this normal paper?" she finally asked. "Not enchanted or anything?"

"As far as I know, yes, it's normal."

"Then why is it still here?"

He wasn't following her. With a furrowed brow, he cocked his head to the side and lifted a hand to encourage her to enlighten him.

"I don't think that crazy storm thing . . ." She paused as she tried to find a better word.

"Storm fire," Octavian assisted.

"Right. I don't think that storm fire is an isolated incident. Some of the mineral deposits nearby have been under extreme heat and pressure."

He wanted to ask how she knew that if she didn't have any mineralogic analytical instrumentation, but he figured now wasn't the time.

"So you're saying storm fires are normal here?"

"It could explain the lack of vegetation," she added. "Yet the items here in this cave are unharmed."

"What's your point?"

"There's an entire landscape out there that's pretty much barren, and yet this little lab, all Teacher's stuff, everything here is in decent shape. Doesn't it make sense that Teacher built some kind of protection into this place? Maybe we're safe here."

Octavian looked up at the anchors. He pointed. "I see what you mean. There are shielding anchors in the walls, a lot of them. But they're running low on power. Even if they've protected this place in the past, I doubt they can now." He went over to one and put his hand up to check the power level. "That's strange. I swear I checked this earlier, and it was at two percent, but now it says it's at five percent."

"Did you do something to it?"

"No," he said with a shake of his head.

A loud clap of thunder boomed, and the ground shook even harder. The power fluctuated, moving upward to eight percent.

"No way," he laughed. "It's going up."

The power climbed to ten percent before the ground stopped shaking.

"I don't understand. How?" Replika asked.

"I'm not sure, but what if this is how Teacher designed it?" He ran his hand through his hair. "What if he didn't place and charge all these anchors? What if he placed the anchors and the vibrations from the storm charges them?"

"That would work?"

"Maybe," was the best he could offer. "If there hasn't been a storm fire in a while, or if the storm fires deplete the charge, that could explain why the power is so low."

"So you agree," she said matter-of-factly.

He blinked as he tried to figure out what she was talking about. "Agree with what?"

"That we should trust Teacher."

Octavian wasn't sure how to respond to that, so he moved on. "I might be able to use some of the material you found to speed up the charging process."

"And what if you make a mistake? Isn't it complicated and dangerous to rush something like this?"

She was right, of course.

"So we just . . . ." His voice trailed off, not wanting to enumerate their lackluster options.

"Do nothing," Replika said, "or leave."

Octavian didn't like either, but the loud boom and the following blaze that shook the ground from the storm all the way to the cave pressured him to concede.

"Okay," he said. "We trust Teacher."

They peered out of the mouth of the cave, where the world had transformed into a different kind of empty. This emptiness was like a fog, with flashes of light pounding into the ground and sending shockwaves through every particle of matter around. The whole cave shook, and tiny pieces of rubble shook loose from the cave walls and ceiling. This did nothing to alleviate Octavian's anxiety. Replika grasped Octavian's arm. He wrapped his arm around her as another boom quaked, and she pulled him closer.

They held each other tightly as slightly less tiny rocks broke free above them and fell to their feet.

This trust thing was hard.

19

SURVIVING THE STORM

T he minutes passing by seemed like both hours and seconds. Time stretched as if to torture Octavian. Time condensed as if to add pressure to their stress. The storm fire was moving towards them, pounding the ground with an onslaught of debris and heat. The anchors embedded in the cave's walls were slowly charging. Since Octavian had never seen so many in one place and because he had never experienced a storm fire before, he had no idea what was required to protect them from it. He hated that his best option was to trust a system he knew very little about set up by a person who had trapped him in this alternate reality, but here he was.

The air was getting hotter, and Octavian didn't think that was a good sign.

But still he waited.

The storm would be upon them in minutes, and the anchors, charged by the mechanical energy released by the storm, neared fifty percent capacity. He placed his hand on the Reality Tuner and questioned how quickly he could get them out of there if he needed to. He was pretty sure that by the time he realized they were in imminent danger, it would be too late to do anything.

Yet still, he waited.

Just as he thought he could take a deep, calming breath, another lightning bolt burst from above and hit the ground just in front of the cave, sending a shockwave through the whole area. In its place, the lightning left a fire that ignited the ground and the air above it. The fire shot up and out from its origin, throwing itself toward the cave opening. Octavian grasped Replika and closed his eyes, never more unsure of his future.

The ground shook as the storm swallowed the cave with the magician and the robot inside. Outside, flames spread and heated until they were white hot. Steam and sand pounded down onto the structure. Though with each moment, the cave structure threatened to collapse under the storm's might, it was merely a new chapter in a war that had been waging for many years. The protective shield, at seventy percent power, was charged enough to face its greatest enemy.

When Octavian looked at Replika, he saw that her eyes were closed.

As if realizing that he was looking, she opened them. She smiled widely and threw her arms around Octavian in less of a death grip and more of a hug.

"We're alive!" she exclaimed.

He returned her embrace, yet was genuinely out of words.

"What now?" she asked.

"I guess I make an EnviroJar."

"Oh, my goodness. Is that what you're calling them? How clever!" She spoke as if their lives had never been in danger. Her joy was overwhelming, and he couldn't help but smile.

"But then what? Do you feel confident using the Reality Tuner?"

"No, I'm not confident at all, but . . ." He pulled the Reality Tuner from his belt and held it up. ". . . I noticed something earlier." He turned the Tuner so she could see the buttons on the side. "Most of the buttons work how you would expect. You push them in, and then, when you let go, they return to their original position. But the two outermost buttons are different."

He pointed to the row of buttons on the side. The large button at the center had four buttons to each side. He was pointing to the ones on the ends.

"These buttons stay in when you push them. Then if you push them again, they go back to their original position."

Finally, he tapped the center button, clearly confident with the device as long as it wasn't being powered by his magic.

"And the center button, which is the one I've been pressing, doesn't just depress in place. You can push in just one side or another, and so I think it may work as a kind of joystick. I mean, if I could get it to work at all."

"You've tried them all?"

"When we were in the—" He paused to try to remember what she had called it. "When we were in the Steampunk World, with Captain Egnaro, I pressed a couple of them, thinking that they would navigate around that star map."

He waved a hand in front of him as if reminding her that the device had created a three-dimensional visual interface of points. It had looked like the star maps one might see at the NUM planetarium, where an immersive show of holograms gave tours—popular among regional schoolchildren—navigating the solar system, the galaxy, and different astronomical areas of interest.

"But they were unresponsive?" Replika asked.

Octavian nodded.

"I guess we'll just be pressing that center button again," he said.

"At least we'll have an EnviroJar as a failsafe," Replika said.

He nodded and glanced at the anchors. They were eighty-five percent charged. He shook his head at the brilliance of it.

"Do you mind monitoring the charge, just in case?" Octavian asked. "I don't want to risk getting distracted and becoming a pile of ash."

Octavian showed her how to check the charge indicator, which appeared when it sensed an organic object nearby. Replika took up a position next to one of them, and Octavian gathered supplies to start crafting. The charge of the anchors steadied at ninety-two percent, and the two traded hypotheses about this and that while Octavian worked.

Placing his finger over one of the samples Replika had brought back, he pressed down. A line formed on its surface, then the piece snapped in two. Repeating this step a few more times, he created six pieces approximately the same size.

He leaned forward in his chair and placed one hand to each side of the first sample. Ten long minutes later, the sample began to look wobbly. It reddened, and Octavian used a flat tool to place it in a small bowl. He rolled the sample around, and after a while, it took on a round shape.

For a long time, he alternated between heating the sample and rolling it. Once he was satisfied with its shape, he placed it on the end of a metal rod. He spoke the words of a spell, taking his time to ensure each syllable made his calculations clear. When he was sure the spell was complete, he let the marble cool. He added additional layers to the marble, going through the same cycle of heating, rolling, and casting his spell. Once he was satisfied with it, he used a cooling spell to rapidly chill it.

He held it up to Replika. She had been watching intently, or at least pretending to, which surprised him almost as much as the sparkle of excitement in her eyes.

"How do they work?" she asked as she marveled at its beauty.

"When you need to use one, you just break it. They should break in the palm of your hand if you squeeze them." He squeezed it, and it broke more easily than he had hoped.

As soon as it cracked, a gust of wind rushed through the cave. Papers whipped into the air, dancing around the cave. Replika laughed in delight.

"Wow, that's amazing!"

"Something like that," Octavian said, his mind already trying to figure out how to make it more difficult to break.

"We'll each hold one when we travel," he explained. "If you detect a hostile environment, you activate yours, since you fare better when we shift realities."

"How long will it last?"

"A few minutes. Enough time for me to try the Reality Tuner again."

"Sounds like a plan!"

Octavian wondered if she was a bit too excited.

The second marble he created didn't break when he squeezed it, and Octavian ended up stepping on it to get it to crack. His third attempt struck a balance, just difficult enough to break that it would be safe in their bags, but not so difficult that it would be impossible for him to crack in his hand.

Now that he had the density correct, he could cast the spell to place the proper environment into the EnviroJar. The spells were more intricate, taking much longer to form as he specified the composition of the air, the pressure within the bubble, the size of the bubble, and so on. But he didn't rush.

When he was finally done, he held the EnviroJar out and squeezed it hard. The air around them cooled to a comfortable temperature. He took a few deep breaths and asked Replika to take a few readings of the air. He was satisfied with the result.

After much sweat, several terrifying thunderous booms, and plenty of magic, he held up two lopsided orbs, EnviroJars, each about two inches in diameter. Replika took her marble carefully, and Octavian didn't correct her. She was stronger than him, and he guessed it would be much easier for her to break it.

Under better circumstances, he could tailor an EnviroJar to her, but for now, he was ready to leave. The storm fire showed no signs of weakening, and although the anchors were relatively stable, they'd dropped down to almost eighty percent again. They packed up their things, and Octavian argued with himself about whether to add Teacher's notes to his bag. At some point, Replika had gathered the papers into stacks, protected by tools she'd found around the cave. He knew he couldn't take everything, and he worried that they would be ruined quickly during their travels. With a frustrated sigh, he left them. Replika found her own bag under the cot—how it got there was anyone's guess—and filled it with the materials she had gathered.

Once they were ready, Octavian powered on the Reality Tuner as he had each time before. The map appeared above them, transmitted through the crystal at the top of the Tuner. As they had discussed, he tried the smaller buttons, but nothing changed. He depressed the sides of the center button, but again, nothing.

"Nothing happened." Replika was certainly talented at stating the obvious.

"So, the center button, then?"

Replika nodded. They both looked down to confirm the other had an EnviroJar in one hand. They were ready. With a deep breath, he pressed it.

The world began to change, and Replika put a hand to Octavian's shoulder to help stabilize him.

But if there's one truth to moving between realities, it's that stability and stochasticity maintain a fragile balance in the multiverse.

The ground underneath them in the new world was made of metal that moaned as Replika shifted her weight back and forth. Glass circles were dispersed around the floor, allowing viewing access to an elaborate system of conduits, walkways, and structures below. Metal tables lined every wall and a row of tables ran down the middle of the room as well. Everything looked old and worn, but there was no rust to be seen. On one table sat a box-shaped device. On top of it sat an even larger box with one black side.

"What is it?" Replika crossed over to it. She leaned down and followed a cord that was coming out of the back of it, down the wall, and into a socket of some kind. "I think it's some kind of electronic device."

Octavian leaned in and placed his hands on the box.

"No magic," he confirmed. After another moment, he withdrew his hands, totally offended. "There's live electricity running through this."

"The lights look like they run on electricity as well," Replika said, pointing at the bulbs beaming harsh light down onto them from the ceiling.

"That's so dangerous!" Octavian exclaimed. "But I suppose if this world hasn't harnessed magic, it's a logical step in technological advancement."

Just as Replika was reaching to investigate the box further, there was a loud bang. A door to the far side of the room swung open, and two robotic creatures burst into the room, pointing menacingly in their direction with pointy objects as they each spouted their own demand.

"Cease all current activities."

"You're coming with us."

THE *Robots*
AND THE
CHRYSANTHEMUM

1

A Stable Configuration

Many things can only exist in a stable configuration. For example, the most stable configuration of an atom is when its outermost shell of electrons is full. Realities, no matter how alternate they are, only exist when that reality is in a stable configuration. So, while the possibilities are infinite, each possibility exists within a field of probability. The location of an electron around an atom also exists as a probability, but the actual location, much like the location of a particular alternate reality, is difficult to determine.

A robot—such as the one jabbing its pointy arm extension in Replika's general direction—is not an atom or an alternate reality, and the most stable configuration of a robot comes down to engineering. This robot looked sturdy enough, with its oversized frame sitting low to the ground. However, its range of motion was limited, and its visual sensors faced perpendicular to the direction of its wide, clunky movement, which made even the most threatening of gestures seem awkward. As if to accentuate its flaws, the poor thing knocked into tables as it tried to make a turn. It continued its attempt at appearing threatening, and Replika questioned whether the most stable configuration was really the same as the most effective design solution.

The magician and the mechanical doll—Octavian and Replika, respectively—had appeared in this new alternate reality from what Replika was calling the Material World. The reliance on electricity in this universe had been obvious. They had appeared in some kind of lab, just as they had in most of the previous realities. However, this was the first lab they had visited where papers weren't strewn about. Every surface was bare except for electronic equipment.

One of those pieces of equipment, though ancient and worn, had alerted someone to their presence.

Thus, the awkward robot and its partner, a cylindrical, rolling robot with four arms held out in front of it, had burst into the room, knocked into just about everything possible, and commanded the attention of the intruders.

Despite the oddity of two robots demanding that Replika and Octavian cease all current activities, Replika grinned. She looked to Octavian—who also seemed unimpressed with the two robots' display of force—before shrugging and putting her hands up.

"We have ceased," Replika said.

"Decontamination procedures are required," the awkward robot said, holding out a pointy object that was clearly not meant to be pointed at people. It couldn't turn its visual sensor array toward them, but it could still point the pointy bit in their general direction.

"Um, okay," Octavian replied.

"You will follow us," the robot commanded.

"This way," the other added.

It took almost two minutes for the robots to wiggle their way out the door, giving Replika time to ask questions.

"Should we really go with them?" she asked Octavian in sign language.

"I don't think we should fight them, if that's what you're thinking," Octavian replied.

She wondered how he knew that's what she was considering. It was as if he remembered how delighted she'd seemed fighting a band of pirates or kicking dirt into the faces of small, silent people.

"They're not built for fighting," she signed back.

"We don't know where we are, how many opponents we would have, or how we would escape."

They followed the robots into a hallway, where red warning lights strobed. Replika stared at them until she became dizzy, then turned her attention to the rest of her surroundings. The walls, floor, and ceiling were all clad in metal that clanged and sometimes even boomed as they walked forward. If it had been narrower, she would have guessed it was ductwork, but the hallway was five feet wide and seven feet tall.

They turned a corner and came to a doorway. It opened to another, wider hall with a metal floor and glass walls and ceiling. Beyond the glass lay a maze of glass and metal passageways, skybridges, and structures. Above everything was a huge, transparent dome stretching over a mile in each direction. The sky outside the dome was red and full of clouds as the sun dipped down behind the buildings.

She now agreed with Octavian's assessment of their situation. This dome was massive and complex, and despite the poor design of the two robots they were following, the design of the outer wall of the dome hinted at a sophisticated level of technology. They needed more information before taking any drastic actions.

Abruptly, the awkward robot turned its sensors toward her—ish. As unimpressive as the robot was, she could sense its sternness. She didn't want to offend, so she held back her protest.

It turned its attention to its partner, and they made some beeping and whirring sounds at each other. As they approached a perpendicular hallway, the cylindrical robot pushed Octavian to the right while the awkward robot pushed that pointy object into Replika's side, urging her leftward.

"Hey!" Octavian protested.

Replika spun to see one of the robot's appendages holding Octavian by the arm. However, just as she pushed against the pointy object at her side, she made eye contact with her travel companion.

The magician shook his head.

"It'll be fine," he signed to her. "And if it's not, we'll find each other."

She bit her lip as the sharp object urged her again to the left. With unenthusiastic reluctance, she nodded.

Octavian made a gesture toward her that wasn't sign language, but she didn't have time to ask what it meant. The cylindrical robot used its many arms to drag him through a metal door, and she kept her eyes locked on Octavian's until the door closed behind them.

She put her hand on the sharp object.

"Please stop. I'm complying," she said in her firmest voice.

"Move forward," the robot said.

"Move forward, please," she corrected.

"Move forward," it repeated.

She placed her other hand on the sharp object and pushed her hands against each other, twisting the metal back on itself to remove the sharp edge.

The robot's visual sensors examined her handiwork, then returned its focus to her.

"Please," it said.

She smiled, stood up tall and proud, and sauntered in the general leftward direction. With some forceful directions from her guide, she arrived into a narrow hallway of doors. The hallway had only one entrance, and she had just arrived through it. A sense of panic arose within her. She turned to leave, but the robot shoved her against the first door. The door gave way behind her, opening into a small room that she stumbled backwards into.

The sideways robot pushed her further inside and said, "You will speak to someone soon."

It took her bag, then closed the door, locking her within. She remembered the route they had taken when they left the lab, but what use was that? Knowing nothing about this place, she had no idea how to find Octavian. She lay her head on the nearby wall and let out a defeated moan.

Why would they separate them? How much trouble were they in? What were the robots going to do to them? And who should she be preparing to talk to? The questions tried desperately to overshadow her fear for Octavian. She could imagine a thousand different ways they could hurt him, and she was powerless to help. How would she even know he was in trouble? She wiped a tear away as it escaped her eye.

It dawned on her that she was alone, and the feeling weighed on her. More questions bombarded her mind.

What would she do if something happened to Octavian? Would she be stuck here? Did she even want to travel without him? Nothing else seemed to matter to her in that moment other than finding him and making sure they could stay together.

The door swung open. It slammed into the wall, and Replika let out a yelp in surprise. A figure whirred into the room, the same size and shape as the doorway. The bright light from the hallway beyond backlit it. Visual sensors glowed red from the face of the figure. It zoomed toward her and stopped sharply. She gasped, averting her eyes and covering her ears.

She was alone and terrified, and that was perhaps the least of her worries.

2

SOME ANSWERS

Octavian sat alone, knees to chest, in the corner of a small, metal-lined room. The only openings were small one-inch holes near the top of the door the robot had shoved him through. He hadn't wanted to be separated from Replika, but at the time, it had seemed like their best option. After all, they appeared to be in a self-contained structure without a strategy or any knowledge of their captors. They didn't even have the element of surprise.

The lock on the door was electromagnetic, and disrupting the electrical current running through it would be enough to unlock it. Even so, Octavian wasn't feeling prepared to venture out and explore.

He thought it best to bide his time, especially since his captors had removed his outer clothing. He'd been able to keep them from removing his underthings, but they had taken his bag and the Reality Tuner.

He still had his Notebook marble somehow, perhaps thanks to the cloaking spell he'd attempted to put on it but most likely because getting it off him was more trouble than it was worth. While he remained uncertain of many aspects of his current predicament, he was certain he'd been in this small metal room for far too long without a shirt, vest, pants, socks, or shoes. Because although the metal cell was spotless, it wasn't comfortable.

His body dysphoria wasn't doing him any favors, either, so the best he could do was curl up and wait as the rude robots—and whoever might control them—decided his fate.

Unknown to Octavian, no one controlled the robots. There were no humans within the dome at all, a fact that may have disturbed him if he'd known it in this particular instant. However, he would later be comforted to learn that despite the initial encounter's flaws, the robots had attempted to be congenial and gentle with him. They didn't often interact with fragile, fleshy things, and some robots just had worse manners than others. The denizens of the dome—artificial life forms, except for a few exceptions—were unwavering in their diligence to keep their home sterile, and having intruders—especially organic intruders—was a grave concern.

Word of their arrival had already spread to all inhabitants through a central communications network, and they had held a meeting to discuss how to handle the situation.

Their first order of business was to assess the possibility of biological contamination. This wasn't the first time organic life had entered the dome, though it had been a long time since any humans had set foot inside. Humans had built this structure, and since then, breaches had sometimes let in invaders of the organic kind.

The first major breach had come ten years prior, when a small robot specializing in the assessment of microfractures came across a crack in the outer wall as well as thousands of insects that had come in through it. The insects had attacked the poor thing and were carrying it off somewhere before it thought to alert others.

It had taken thirteen days to assign a unique identifier and nickname to each insect, assess all the insects for contaminants, evacuate them after they were cleared, and reseal the breach. Afterwards, the small robot took up an office job in data entry and was never quite the same.

Octavian wouldn't be the same after this experience, either. For now, he grumbled about the lack of comfortable positions in the metal surroundings.

After many hours of complete silence on the other side of the door, the sounds of movement beyond the door caught his attention. He tucked his feet in close and crossed his arms over his chest as a series of muffled beeps made their way through the wall. A loud click preceded the opening of the door.

A red-eyed beast came rolling into the room, motors whirring and fans roaring. Octavian winced and squinted at the hallway's bright light blazing in after it.

What followed was a sight for sore eyes: Replika. She rushed to his side and, unaware of his discomfort, threw her arms around his head.

"They took your clothes, too," she said, waving her hand at her own lack of floofy dress, though she still had on a petticoat and body slip.

As if realizing what Octavian's body language was screaming, she turned to the gigantic beast—which was actually a door-sized robot—behind her.

"I'll take one of those blankets now, please," she said.

It beeped and made a loud grinding sound before a compartment opened. Octavian stared in disbelief as Replika retrieved the blanket and thanked the robot. "For now," she said as she handed it to Octavian. "They're working on the clothing part."

"What's going on?" Octavian asked, wary of her casual manner with the robot beast. "Are we free to go?"

"Not exactly," Replika said with a twisted grimace. "It's a long story. Come with me. Let's sit somewhere comfortable. Maybe have something to eat?"

He nodded and followed her, that strange, loud, red-eyed thing rolling behind them. Their destination was a long room with a table in the middle. A series of bowls sat on it, each with a different color of mush within.

"I know it doesn't look like much, but it's edible. I promise," Replika assured him.

He scooped some of the mush from one bowl onto his finger and tried it. He nodded at her, satisfied, and sat down.

"Now tell me more," he said.

Replika sat across from him and smiled.

"I've learned a lot already. For example, there aren't any humans here. Just robots."

"Yeah?" he asked.

"Yes," she said.

She didn't say anymore, so he said, "Replika, tell me about our situation."

"Sorry. Right. Well, this won't surprise you, but that room we appeared in? It's a lab used by none other than Teacher."

"I'm ceasing to be surprised by that one as of right now. How'd he spend time here without them knowing?"

"They did know," she corrected. "They set up the lab space for him, and they worked together on some technology."

"What kind of technology?"

She paused for dramatic effect. Octavian was unimpressed.

"My power core," Replika stated.

Now Octavian was impressed.

"What do you mean, your power core? Teacher said he worked on it with a specialist out of Deutschland."

"That's a lie. He created it here, with these people. They call themselves the Progeny. Anyway, when he completed the core, instead of giving it to them like he promised, he stole it."

Octavian couldn't believe what he was hearing. Teacher, a con? A thief? This man, who was a world-renowned magician, who was well-respected, and who had a name for being brash but honest, stole technology from a world that no one even knew existed?

The revelation of alternate realities and Teacher's personal encounters in some of these realities were equally mind-boggling. But it seemed like there was always something new to discover about Teacher's enigmatic past.

"So, Teacher was coming and going at will between our world and these other worlds?" he asked, pulling the blanket around himself as he tried to hold on to it while eating.

"I don't think so," she replied. "He stayed in this world a while, according to the Progeny."

"So why steal from them?"

"I don't know. But at least we understand why the Progeny don't trust us," Replika said.

"Because Teacher deceived them," Octavian asked.

"Yes. But on the plus side, they said they think of me as family because I carry their technology."

Finally, some good news!

"That works out well for us." His excitement was apparent in his voice, and Replika grimaced.

He sensed a "but," and he really hated buts.

3

Y'ALL SHOULD PROBABLY TALK ABOUT THIS

Replika propped her elbows onto the table and leaned her head into her hands, a clear indication to Octavian that she was about to ruin her good news with a bad "but." He continued to eat, waiting for her to continue.

He stole a glance at the large robot standing at the door nearby. It seemed deactivated, or at least unresponsive, and he couldn't help but wonder just how tight the surveillance on them was. Did they really think of Replika as one of their own?

"Except," she finally said, "they want me to stay here with them when you go."

He paused and looked up from his food at her.

"What?"

"They say I belong here. You know, because I'm a robot. Because I'm artificial. And because I have parts they designed."

Octavian couldn't believe what he was hearing. His heart pounded with agony and fear. What was he supposed to say to this?

All he could think of was how precious she had become to him, how lonely he would be without her, and how meaningless getting home was beginning to feel.

Later, he would wonder why the two of them were the only ones transported to each world despite being in the presence of others, such as the pirate captain Egnaro and the small, silent people. He would then move on to hypothesize that he and Replika were somehow tied to the device, which might make it difficult to leave her behind, even if either of them wished for that. Before going further, he would be distracted either by something very beautiful or something very terrifying, but for now, his mind was trapped in his current worry of loss.

"What do you want to do?" he asked, swallowing the lump in his throat.

"I want to stay with you," was her reply, as simple and innocent as the moment she was activated a whole two days ago.

She put a hand to his, and he smiled.

"Then I'll stay here," he said.

"No." Replika shook her head as she said it. "I want to know why we were brought here. I want to know what Teacher had planned for me. And I want to help you get home."

"How are we going to do that if they insist you stay?"

"I'll think of something. Don't worry."

"Maybe I'll think of something first," he joked.

He took her hand in his and squeezed it.

A loud thud rang out as the nearby robot slammed its mechanical arm onto the table. They both jumped, and Octavian grabbed at the blanket as it tried to slide off his shoulder.

"You must stay," the robot commanded Replika. "And the organic must go."

"You promised to treat him with respect," Replika argued.

"You told us you would properly consider staying in our world."

She sighed. "We will come to a solution that we all can be happy with. You have my word. But for now, we need rest. Can we talk about this tomorrow?"

"You do not require sleep."

"I do so require sleep," she insisted.

It was quiet as the robot seemed to process the statement, and Octavian looked to Replika for some guidance. Receiving none, he waited as it processed the information.

"Agreed," it said abruptly. "You will rest for nine hours, and afterwards, you will meet with the Leadership Committee."

Replika smiled and thanked it. Octavian turned his attention to the food in front of him. He was no longer hungry, but he wondered when the next time they would eat would be. He sighed heavily, as was his best way of dealing with frustration, and stood to join Replika at the door.

A small metal box on wheels was just outside. At a crawling pace, it led them to a room with one large glass wall. Octavian was surprised to see how far from ground level they were. When they had been in the glass skybridge headed toward the detention rooms, or whatever those cells were, they had been just above the ground level. He remembered some gentle slopes here and there, but had they really traveled several stories up?

There were two makeshift beds that had thick blankets and something resembling clothing folded on them. Octavian thanked the robot, which seemed to just ignore him and leave.

Octavian went over to the window. The same red sky they had seen earlier hung above them, but he could finally see the ground, the outside ground, which was alive with a diversity of flora. As he watched, flora shifted as beasts brushed against them. In the distance, he noticed another dome, and as he became aware of it, more seemed to appear. The large facility they were in was just one of many, and he couldn't help but wonder why they were there.

"Wow," he said. "I thought perhaps this dome was because the outside was uninhabitable, but it looks beautiful out there."

"I didn't get a lot of context about their situation," Replika replied, "but they're very hesitant to interact with the outside world."

"Strange. Do you think they're afraid of it?"

"I'm not sure," she said plainly before changing the subject. "Octavian, are we going to talk about this?"

"About what?"

"Our current situation."

He walked over to one of the beds and held up the "clothes." It was just a length of fabric with several holes cut in it, and he put his head through one of them and his arms through the other two. Then he used a long stretch of fabric that he found underneath and tied it around his waist.

"Which part do you want to talk about?" he asked as he sat on the bed.

"Well, first of all, are you really okay?" She sat down across from him on a second bed before continuing. "Being stripped down and locked in a small room alone couldn't have been the best experience for you."

"I'm fine," he assured her.

She pursed her lips. "You know you don't have to be fine, right? You've been through an awful lot the past couple of days, and there's nothing wrong with letting everything settle in."

"How can I let anything settle in?" he asked. "I don't have time to process any of this. Too much is happening."

Her expression was gentle as she reached out and put her hands to his legs. "We're safe here. It might not seem like it right now, but after talking with several of the Progeny, I think you can relax for the time being."

"This may come as a surprise, but I haven't relaxed in years."

"That is quite surprising," she replied with a laugh.

The last time Octavian had truly relaxed was almost three years before, when he had driven across the country from his apartment near his undergraduate campus to an unfamiliar city where he would attend graduate school under the tutelage of one of the most powerful magicians in the world, known only as Exalted Grand Magician Teacher. The trip had taken him five days, and he had taken time to check out some of the interesting magical monuments that were near his route.

The furthest was a monument that was fifty miles north of a more desolate stretch of highway, in the middle of a large field that sat in the middle of a forest of enormous trees. At the center of the field was a deep impression and an oblong boulder 100 feet across. No ordinary boulder, this rock had a series of cracks that had been chiseled into its surface. Though its history was unknown to the people of the Magic World, the plaque claimed the cracks were actually a spell placed there by the native people of the area, who still owned the land and operated the monument's site and gift shop.

Known as the Field Stone, the meaning of the spell had been lost to time. Locals theorized that the boulder was the reason trees didn't grow in the large field. Others thought the boulder's spell was responsible for the good weather and harvests that blessed the area each year. Neither hypothesis was true, and yet Octavian's experience at the site was tied to the truth behind the boulder's presence.

4

THE FIELD STONE

When Octavian drove across the country for graduate school, he had stopped at a magical monument. Essentially, it was a big rock, but a spell had been inscribed on its surface. However, the meaning of the spell had been lost to the Magic World.

The rock's true history began with an indigenous magician and his wife, who had seen the boulder at the top of a hill overlooking their land every day. The hill sat to the east of their home, which the magician's great-great-grandparents had built way back when. Each morning, the sun would rise over the hill, yet the shadow of the boulder blocked its rays from hitting the home for an additional hour.

They had many conversations over the years about their frustration with the boulder, of how it blocked their view of Nature's precious morning light. Plants that preferred light at that time of day refused to grow, animals struggled to keep their schedules, and days seemed shorter. The boulder was composed of a marble-like stone that the locals called heatstone because it absorbed and held heat well. Unfortunately, it also let off heat, which led to a quite annoying temperature gradient across the field.

While trying to redefine their planting strategy for the next year, the couple grew frustrated with the unique conditions that they had to consider, which limited their options for crops, flowers, and casual wear. They traveled to visit the elders of their tribe. The elders were aware of the problem because the magician's ancestors had shared the same frustrations over the years.

There was a legend that a Nature spirit had left the boulder to watch over the magician's family, so as frustrated as previous generations had been, they had never been willing to take action. However, the magician was the first in his family trained in magic, and the elders saw this as an opportunity.

They instructed the magician to travel to the top of the hill and meditate there alone for five days to seek the guidance of the spirit that had placed it there, so the magician and his wife returned home with conviction.

As they packed provisions for his quest, the wife began to worry. What if they angered the spirit by questioning its gift? What if it removed its protection from their land? And what if the spirit took everything away, but still left that dang boulder?

Despite her fears, the magician resolved himself to fulfill the task that the elders had set before him. So, with a kiss goodbye, he set off for the hill.

On the first day, he asked the spirit to speak to him, but received no response.

He asked again on the second day, and birds gathered on the hill. He watched them respectfully, but nothing happened except for the stinky evidence left behind by the birds.

The third day brought even more birds, and though he tried to focus on his meditation, the birds pecked at his toes, dug into his bag, and were just plain annoying.

On the fourth day, he begged the spirit to speak to him, but all he received was an icy wind. It was an odd feeling with the heat of the rock on one side of him causing him to sweat and the frigid wind on his other side causing him to shiver. Yet he stayed where he was and continued to meditate on how that boulder had plagued his family year after year.

On the fifth day, distraught and exhausted, he cried out to the spirit to hear him. That annoying flock of birds landed nearby, and he thought to shoo them. However, just as he reached out his arms, an enormous shadow descended over him.

The largest bird he had ever seen landed on top of the boulder, its talons digging into the hot stone. The magician froze in fear, humbled by the bird's presence. They shared a long look, then a longer look, and then an even longer look. Then, with one large swoop of its wings, the bird pushed itself off of the boulder.

The boulder wavered. Wind from the beating of the giant bird's wings threw the man backward.

The boulder tipped. The bird released a deafening squawk that shook the ground.

The boulder toppled once, then twice, and then began to roll uncontrolled down the hill. The magician rushed to his feet, and, seeing the boulder headed for his home with increasing speed, he summoned his creativity and cunning.

With a burst of magical energy and impromptu words of a spell, he threw out his arms. The boulder lifted from the ground, but its forward momentum hurdled it forward. Panic welled up as he thought of his wife, who was in the home that the boulder was still flying toward. He was overcome with grief as every second stretched longer and longer.

For reasons that may never be known, everything was suddenly still: the wind, the birds, the boulder, time. The magician didn't hesitate. He weaved a spell into the boulder, carving deep markings into its surface. As time slipped back into its normal pace, he threw a force down on the boulder, shoving it into the center of the field where it still sits today.

The Field Stone was not a popular magic monument, although it certainly would have been if people knew the truth about its origins, but when Octavian examined the boulder with those intentional markings covering its surface, he sensed something from it. He could sense the engravings in the rock, even those he couldn't see from the other side of the stanchions. Ev-

erything else faded away, and a sense of calm, comfort, and stillness washed over him that he'd never experienced before. The
markings were etched into his memory, and even though he soon
put it to the back of his mind to focus on his research, it was impossible to forget the power he had inadvertently touched during
his visit.

The week-long drive from the east to west coast for graduate
school had given Octavian time to decompress before he started
the next hurdle of his life. He'd received no such transition time
when he and Replika were thrown into an alternate reality, and it
seemed strange when she suggested he could relax.

It was perhaps her suggestion that inspired him to take a
deep breath and let himself fall onto the stiff bed in this world of
robots. He grunted when there was no bounce, though it was better than a cot in a cave or a heap of grass and leaves, so he
thought it best not to complain.

He recalled how much complaining he had done while under
the tutelage of the Exalted Grand Magician known as Teacher.
Although Octavian was still certain Teacher was responsible for
their current predicament, he wondered if he could have been a
better mentee. Perhaps he should have listened more, or at least
not have argued quite as much. How much more could he have
learned? How much more prepared would he have been for this
situation?

Wait . . . how prepared was he?

"I know what we have to do," he said, his mouth pulling
tight into a smile of realization.

"To escape?"

He let out a laugh and clapped his hands together before
rolling to look at her. "No. To gain their trust."

5

DRAGGING CHAIRS AND CONTROLLING LAUGHTER

R eplika wondered if she had misheard Octavian, but she knew that she hadn't. Octavian's claim that he had come up with a way to earn the trust of the robots of this world, the Progeny, left her curious about what it could be. Especially given his dramatic pause after saying it.

Or maybe he was joking. He wasn't quite the joking type, but he had surprised her several times before.

"Besides being upstanding citizens?" she asked with a wry smile.

The joke didn't seem to phase him. His eyes were intense with determination, and Replika's curiosity took over. She didn't need to ask him what he was talking about because he started speaking before she could get around to it.

"You said Teacher helped the Progeny build your power core, right?" Octavian asked.

"Yes. They made it seem like he worked on some other projects with them, too, but I'm not sure what."

"Okay, and why did they need his help? What did he know that they don't?" He sat up. "And more importantly for us . . . " He paused, holding his index fingers up in front of him. "What do I know that they don't?"

Replika wasn't following his logic, and she wasn't sure if she was distracted by his sudden return of energy or by the fact that they were pretty in the dark about the Progeny's technical capabilities.

"I don't understand the question."

"Magic, Replika."

Her eyes widened. Why hadn't she realized it? She hadn't seen anything indicating the Progeny had magic proficiency. But she still wasn't quite sure how that helped them.

"I don't think they can do magic," Octavian confirmed. "I don't sense it here at all, and everything here seems to run on electricity, which is limited. So, if they don't trust me because Teacher stole something from them, then maybe I can gain their trust by helping them build something that needs the magic they can't access."

Replika couldn't believe what she was hearing. Octavian was offering to help the robots who had taken him prisoner and who were insisting she stay behind when he left. She could see in his eyes that he wasn't trying to deceive them. He trusted her when she told him they were safe, and he truly wanted to make a difference. His genuineness made her heart ache, and she smiled warmly.

"Well?" he asked.

"I think it's genius," she said, trying to hold back joyful tears.

"Hey, what's wrong?" He reached over to take her hands, and she grasped them.

"Octavian, when they separated us, I was afraid. And when they told me I had to stay here, I thought I might never see you again. I can tell they mean well, but I was so scared they'd keep us separated." She pulled a hand away to wipe away an escaping tear. "I want us to stay together. I want that more than anything."

She was surprised when he jumped over to her bed and pulled her into a hug. Throwing her arms around him, she clutched him. She reveled in the smell of him, in the feeling of his firm form, in the softness of his hair against her face.

"Me, too," he whispered.

Thoughts clouded her mind, as if a long-lost memory was gaining new life. The memory of a hand reaching out toward her, of a tightness in her chest. The vague remembrance of being embraced, kissed, and held close to a smooth, warm body. These thoughts lingered, but they didn't make sense. Where did this come from? What was she supposed to remember?

No amount of questioning brought answers.

Replika and Octavian awoke to a robot—who was clearly unaware of the concept of waking up—insisting they stand and follow her immediately. She led them through a maze of hallways to a medium-sized room where a line of robots waited for them.

Replika hadn't met any of them the day before and was surprised to see a diversity of designs and materials. She had assumed there was some kind of standardization in the robots' designs, but each was unique and easily identifiable.

The few robots she had met the day before were obviously not diplomats. They had made demands and expected those demands to be met. The five robots she now found herself standing across from—and who appeared to be in positions of authority—were different. Somehow, they let off an air of concern, gentleness, and wisdom.

The room itself was empty, just a metal box with a door at one side. Unlike the room they had stayed in the night before, there were no windows to distract them. Replika wasn't sure whether to think of it as an interrogation room or a meeting room.

When the robots offered to procure chairs for Octavian and Replika, both visitors graciously refused. However, the robots insisted.

A knee-high, short-armed robot whirred from its position at the end of the line. It was small for the job, but left the room to retrieve the chairs. After several minutes of awkward silence, a loud scratching sound rang out from the hallway beyond the door.

Replika looked at Octavian, hoping they could share a look of shared humor at the strangeness of the situation. However, Octavian held his gaze steady, moving his attention from one of the five remaining robots to the next, holding his professional composure despite the squeal of the dragging chair becoming louder and louder beyond the door.

The sound stopped, and the door opened. With only a second more of the grating sound, Replika jumped into action, rushing over and taking the chair.

"Thank you," she said, "I'll take it from here."

The robot nodded, looking somehow relieved, and turned to leave the room. She put the chair next to Octavian, who gave her a quick glance before urging her to take the seat with a quick hand gesture.

As the silence from the robots across from them continued, Replika's mind returned to the night before.

It had seemed strange to rest. She hadn't been tired at all. In fact, she had been quite restless. To calm her, Octavian had offered to sleep beside her. The bed was small, so they laid side by side, him behind her. He gently placed his hand on her waist, and she had interwoven her fingers with his.

She had pulled his arm further around her, and he scooted closer until he was pressed against her. She could feel his heartbeat, and every breath hypnotized her with its rhythmic pace. And then, well . . . then she must have fallen asleep because things became strange.

As the silence dragged on, she tried to recall the mishmash of feelings, the flickers of visions, and the onslaught of fragrances, but it was too chaotic to make sense of. She was unsure if these were more vague memories, or if this was what dreams were like.

The renewed song of a dragging chair pulled her back into the present, and she struggled not to laugh. She put her hands to her mouth to keep it from escaping. Another glance at Octavian confirmed he was somehow holding his poker face.

Maybe he didn't think this situation was comedic. Maybe he thought it was completely justifiable that they had sent the small, awkward robot with short arms to retrieve two chairs, one at a time, and drag them each several minutes down the hallway to the meeting room where they had convened. She fought to stop another laugh as a squeal echoed into the room from down the hall.

No. There was no way Octavian was immune to the humor of this moment. She was sure this was a learned skill and clear evidence of a masterful magician.

Her assumption that magicians were trained to hold their composure in ridiculous scenarios was not entirely unfounded or divergent from reality. About fifty years prior, in their home world, a notorious criminal had appeared whose modus operandi included the application of a substance to his victims that increased their emotional response to stimuli. Victims of the Hysteria Killer were often found with strained lungs and diaphragms, with faces covered with tears and snot, and with elevated cortisol levels.

The Hysteria Killer was so elusive that the police requested the assistance of a private investigative firm of magician detectives with extensive forensic analytical chemistry experience. However, they lacked experience in investigating homicides.

In an attempt to gain more information about the Hysteria Killer, the firm decided to do several tests on the substance without the oversight of the police force. This was against the agreement they had made with the precinct, which required them to remain under police supervision for the duration of their investigation. Instead, they snuck out a sample of the substance, which had been found on one of the victims, and set up the test in a secluded office where they wouldn't get caught.

Unknown to the firm or the authorities, the Hysteria Killer was aware of the test and exposed all the present magicians to an aerosolized compound that reacted violently with the substance they were testing. The recording of the unfortunate test haunted the citizens of the city until one year later, when the Hysteria Killer was captured thanks to a serendipitous bout of diarrhea and a magician detective who had no sense of humor.

The case was often taught at the undergraduate level in an elective course on controlling emotions and retaining one's composure. Though the story was used to stir up excitement for the course, most professors who taught it were so good at retaining their composure that they bordered on emotionless. This made the course very useful but very boring. Had Replika known such a course existed, she would have decided Octavian had taken and aced the class.

When the second chair made it to the door, Octavian retrieved it from the small robot, giving it an encouraging smile and nod. Replika could have sworn she detected a smidgen of humor in that smile as he turned around and their eyes met, but his composure quickly returned as he put the chair next to hers and sat down.

"Lovely," one of the robots in front of them said. "Let's begin."

6

THE HISTORY OF THE PROGENY

The five robots standing across from Octavian and Replika introduced themselves and allowed them to do the same. Then, with no prompting, a bipedal humanoid robot named Yestary spoke.

"It was many revolutions ago," it said, putting an arm out as if to display its story, though no display appeared. "Long before the teacher arrived."

Well, this backstory was going further into the past than Replika had anticipated.

"We lived alongside the Organics, humans who were our creators and our friends." It had a malleable face that allowed it to show a variety of expressions, and its center of gravity was low, coming across as a bit of a gut.

Replika was enamored by its round form as well as its obvious aptitude for storytelling. But, on the basis of trying to appear sincere, she fought back a grin.

Yestary continued, "The Organics sought to reverse the damage their industrial might and corporate negligence had caused on the ecosystems of the planet, but their efforts came too late. The human Organics perished as the world fell into chaos, but we were still here. We created a community of Progeny and dedicated ourselves to restoring some semblance of balance to the organic world."

It paused, and another robot, Eraea, took over. "The planet now teems with organic life."

Eraea was beautifully proportioned, with four long arms and a long conical base. Her face had large almond eyes that projected bright green eyes, a finely crafted thin nose, and lips that would have put super models to shame, had any still been alive. However, unlike Yestary, the material used for her exoskeleton was susceptible to fading and rust. It was clear from chemical staining at her joints and the variety of metal patches of differing color across her body that her maintenance was an uphill battle.

"We found ourselves at a crossroads," she continued.

A strange buzzing sound accompanied her voice, but it didn't detract from the rich tone that each word expressed. Her song-like speech was a poor match for her patchwork body.

"It was amid our research into more sustainable and scalable power options that the teacher arrived. He had a strange technology that we had never seen before and could not harness ourselves."

"Magic," Octavian said. "The manipulation of psyche particles."

"Yes," she replied.

"You know of it?" another robot, Noe, asked. Its humanoid body shone with a bright copper color, although from its awkward movements, Replika could tell that it had a very limited range of motion.

"I do," Octavian replied. "Replika told me that the man you spoke of, Teacher, didn't leave under the best circumstances. Can you tell me about him?"

"He appeared from nowhere," said a fourth robot, Pirdeo, a blue sphere hovering over a rolling cylindrical base with an expression projected onto the sphere's surface from within. "From a place beyond this world, but equivalent. He said that he had become lost between worlds. When we asked if he was trying to find his way home, his response was, 'something like that.' It was quite strange, but we thought nothing of it at the time.

"He stayed a long while, saying that we could help each other. We treated him as a guest with the utmost respect. He was the first human organic many of us had ever seen. Together, we designed a technology that generated a dynamic energy field."

The last of the robots, Chope, who had not yet had the chance to speak, looked like it brimmed with words that could spill out from its articulated mouth at any moment. It held its cupped hands together as it wiggled around in small circles.

"It was beautiful!" Chope interrupted. "It was more than technology. It was art."

The face projected on Pirdeo's spherical "head" moved around to face Chope, whose round head retracted down into a compartment between its shoulders with embarrassment at its interruption. Replika found herself enamored with Chope's shyness and excitement and fought to keep from letting out a loving sound in Chope's direction. She was mostly successful.

The face returned its attention to Replika and Octavian, and she snapped her gaze up from the adorable fifth robot to appear as if she was the epitome of attentiveness. At this, Replika failed spectacularly.

"Our facilities run on solar arrays and chemical exchange arrays," Pirdeo said, "and over the years, the organic life beyond our walls have overrun those arrays. With the teacher's help, we hoped to harness a new sustainable method of power."

"What about the other facilities?" Replika asked. "We saw other domes like this one outside."

"There are similar problems across our network," Eraea said, "though each has its own unique obstacles."

"We placed many resources into our plan with the teacher," said Noe. "We overextended ourselves because we realized how immense the rewards would be."

"And then he left," Octavian said.

Each of the robots nodded, did something that resembled nodding, or did something else that wasn't nodding but that Replika decided was agreement nonetheless.

Octavian stood with such force that his chair screeched backwards several inches.

"Please accept my assistance to address your power concerns," he said. "Allow me to stay here with Replika and make up for the wrong that Teacher did."

"You have the same device," said the sleek, bipedal robot, referring to the Reality Tuner. "You could slight us in the same manner as your predecessor."

It was an odd statement, seeing as they had confiscated the Reality Tuner and hadn't yet returned it. Replika thought Octavian might correct the error, but to her surprise, he took a different approach.

"Yes, I could," Octavian admitted, "but I won't."

"And why not?" one of the robots asked, though Replika wasn't sure which.

Her gaze transfixed on her travel companion. His eyes—which had begun their transition from brown to gold long before she was activated—were literally and magnificently sparkling while he let off a figurative, gleaming aura of confidence. She half expected a burst of magical light to erupt from within him, but nothing so flashy was typical of Octavian's style of magic.

Instead, he just stood there, shoulders back and chin lifted. The robots seemed both suspicious of Octavian's intent and curious why he claimed he wouldn't steal from them as Teacher had.

"Because that would be wrong," Octavian replied.

"We have nothing to offer you," Chope said, head still sunk down into its body.

"None of us has anything to lose," Replika spoke up, "but we all have so much to gain from working together. I think it's a wonderful idea."

"We will discuss," Yestary said. "Please retire to your room. We will provide sustenance and hydration, and we have set up a waste disposal unit in the room adjacent to yours."

"Thank you for your consideration," Octavian said politely, bowing his head.

Replika bowed her head, too, then followed when Octavian headed to the door. It opened, and the same robot they had followed the evening before met them just outside. Replika peeked behind her at the robots to whom they had just spoken. The shy fifth robot, Chope, was peering out from within its body, and she smiled and waved. Its head rose, revealing a pleasant expression that Replika thought was positively adorable, and she bounced after her small escort with hopeful expectation.

Once in their room, Octavian let out a loud sigh. He flopped onto the bed face first, and it was so firm that he didn't even bounce.

"Ow," he said.

"You did amazing," Replika assured him.

"I'm not so sure. Should I have offered some kind of collateral? I said something stupid, didn't I?"

"Were you nervous?"

"Of course." He lifted his head to look at her before planting his face into the bed. "Weren't you?"

"No." She sat next to him and placed a hand on his head. "I knew you could do it."

He let out a groan, then another sigh, before rolling onto his side.

"Thanks," he said. "I just hope I can deliver. I didn't ask how much power they need or what they intend to use the power for. Maybe I should have." He shrugged as best he could in his current position. "Anyway, I just hope they don't make that poor robot drag those chairs back to wherever they came from."

"Right?" Replika exclaimed.

An incredible shaking reverberated through the structure, interrupting her thought. They both jumped to their feet and rushed to the window. Down below, red and orange flames reflected on windows, walls, and a sea of debris.

"A fire?" Replika asked.

"No," Octavian said. "That felt like an explosion."

7

PASSING THROUGH WALLS

Octavian rushed into the hall, Replika at his heels. He gestured for her to take the lead. As the robots had led them through the halls, she had unconsciously created a map. Octavian must have known she could more easily navigate to the fire, and she kept her pace slow enough for him to keep up with her as she ran.

She came to doors with locks and kicked them open. Sure, she could have let Octavian use his magic, but this was an emergency. And it felt incredible!

The halls twisted and turned, often with glass walls that revealed that the fire was spreading. At the pass of a window, she saw a handful of robots spraying a substance toward the fire. When her next chance to peek arrived, the size of the fire was— well, it was pretty much the same.

Robots rushed by them in every direction, filled with purpose and far too busy to worry about the two strangers. She was thankful they wouldn't need to force their way through any opposition.

Finally, she paused in a glass skybridge that sat ten feet above the ground level. After a moment of internal arguments over whether to keep going and hope for the best, she turned to Octavian. "This is as close as I can get us without guessing."

Octavian pushed himself up against the glass. His face, reflected in the window, was full of concentration. He took two careful steps backward and widened his stance before taking several long, deep breaths.

"Jump through the glass," he said.

"What?" she asked.

He didn't repeat himself, and Replika didn't want him to. It sounded crazy enough the first time. Instead, he chanted, moving his hands in calculated patterns. He was sweating, his brow furrowed. The sparkling gold in his eyes seemed alive, swirling with motion that wasn't typically there.

Gathering her resolve, she took a deep breath in, as if she was about to jump into a pool of water. She pushed herself toward the glass wall of the skybridge, throwing her hands in front of her face to shield it from broken glass, but she didn't break through. Instead, she merely passed through, as if nothing was there. She plummeted toward the ground below, twisting to prepare to land.

Her feet hit the ground, and she allowed the momentum to work through her as she rolled. She popped back to her feet and looked up at where she had jumped from. Where the glass should have been, there was a hole, as if nothing was there at all. She backed up a few steps to see if it was a trick of the light, but no. The glass was gone. Not broken, just not there.

A body plunged through the hole. As if by reflex, she bent her knees and jumped upward, towards the falling man. She caught Octavian and returned to the ground holding him. He was smiling as he climbed out of her arms.

She looked up at the skybridge to see that the glass was now intact. It almost seemed smug, as if it had purposefully allowed them through just to deny them the pleasure of breaking it. This wasn't the case at all. Not only was the glass not sentient, but if it had been, the entire experience would likely have been traumatizing.

"Come on," Octavian said, panting as he rushed toward the growing flames.

She met his stride. "Did we just go through solid glass?"

"Yes," he replied in sign language.

"Are you okay?"

"Yes."

She wasn't convinced, but she didn't push any further.

Within a few minutes, they were in front of the blaze. The heat was intense, and she expected Octavian to jump in and whip up some hardcore magic to quell the flames. Instead, he waved at her to follow him as he jogged toward a robot who was directing several others.

"Replika," Octavian said, out of breath.

As the other robots dispersed, presumably to follow this robot's instructions, the supervising robot turned to face the incoming magician and mechanical doll. As soon as xe realized that they weren't more backup but were instead the visitors from another world, xe threw xir appendages up in surprise.

"What are you doing here?" xe said. "This entire sector is evacuating."

"We're here to help," Octavian signed.

Replika spoke the words for him as he fought to catch his breath.

"Help?" xe repeated.

Octavian and Replika both nodded.

"But you are organic. You are susceptible to damage from exposure to smoke inhalation and—"

"He is insisting that he can help," Replika interrupted as Octavian urged her to correct xir. "And he's asking you to trust him."

The robot paused, obviously skeptical but not wishing to push the matter further.

"Do you know the source of the fire?" Replika asked as Octavian signed the words.

"Well," the robot faltered. Xe regained xir composure and said, "We've been having small electrical fires in this sector over the past few months. Nothing like this. We did an inventory analysis and identified some ignitable substances being stored here, but we hadn't yet moved them."

"Is everyone out?" Replika translated, then added, "I think he means, has everyone been evacuated?"

"We can't be certain," the robot replied. "We haven't set up a check-in yet. That's being handled by another team."

"Do your people require oxygen to function?" Replika asked, gazing at Octavian in confusion at his odd question.

Luckily, the robot understood what Octavian was asking.

"Many of us use aerobic processes in our functions, but none will be unsalvageable without it. But this fire has grown so fast that it'll take time to—"

Octavian rushed off toward the fire. Replika thought to follow, but Octavian had his hand out, palm perpendicular to the ground, moving it in repeating downward strokes. It wasn't sign language for "stop", but it was close enough that she decided to wait.

"What's he doing?" the robot asked.

"I don't know," she admitted.

"He's going to get himself killed."

She shook her head but remained silent, unable to disagree but unwilling to write Octavian off so easily. He had just gotten them through a solid wall of glass. Who knew what he was capable of?

As long as she could see him, she could be sure he was safe and could get to him if something happened. Butterflies danced in her stomach. A lump caught in her throat. Her chest was tight. Octavian continued his race toward the inferno, and she brought her hands to her mouth.

In a large, secret room attached to one of the research labs of the burning building, a humanoid robot was hard at work. She had received the transmission to evacuate the area and had proceeded to ignore it. No, she wasn't suicidal. She had an important task to complete. At a computer console, she frantically typed the last set of commands to execute. She rushed to a large dolly on the other side of the room that held a metal crate. She pressed on a pedal to unlock the dolly wheels and rolled it over to the platform sitting next to the console.

With another press of her foot against the pedal, the dolly dropped an inch, and the sides of the crate retracted into the dolly, leaving only the frame of the crate and the egg-shaped contents within. It sat in a nest of cushioning material. She lifted it carefully and with great effort. Her arms ached as she inched over to the platform and lowered the object onto it.

Abruptly, it sprang into a vertical position, hovering a few inches above the platform and spinning a few degrees. The humanoid robot placed a hand on top of it to steady it and smiled.

With a few more strokes on the keyboard, she pulled the dolly away from the platform, left the secret room, and sealed the door shut behind her.

8

Into The Fire

O ctavian was still out of breath, yet he raced onward.
The blazing fire had spread further since he first saw it. At that first moment, he'd been consumed by the memory of being underwater in the Silent People's World, where he had almost drowned. The helplessness and fear tried to overwhelm him, but this time, he pushed those feelings away. He needed to act before the fire grew even larger. With intense intention, he turned his thoughts to his emergency management training and, more specifically, fire emergency management.

He was sure the Progeny could handle the situation, but he had a skill that was especially useful and seemingly unique in this world.

The Magic World—Octavian and Replika's home reality—had a wide variety of tools for managing fires, including wet and dry chemicals and water disbursement. However, the National Central Authority for Fire Management dictated that an active center of emergency magic management with at least three certified fire specialist magicians must be present within ten miles of every fire department in the Ledina nation.

When the fire department arrived at a scene, the situation was assessed, several environmental measurements were collected, and the data was entered into the Fire Estimation and Arson Registration System (FEARS)—an unfortunately named international tool to estimate whether one or more magicians should be deployed to the scene. If a magician was deemed necessary, the closest center of emergency magic management was notified and a certified fire specialist magician was dispatched to the scene.

The regulation around fire specialist magicians was a controversial topic for decades. Critics claimed that the time it took to categorize an event would cost lives, that magicians weren't cost effective, and that it would put the fire department out of work. There was even a sect of magicians who opposed using magic for fire management, although their reasoning was far stranger.

Their leader was a man named Theodore Therrington, and he was the epitome of a loud voice that stood out in a crowd. Nevermind that he thought it necessary to use voice amplification magic whenever he spoke, one of the eccentricities that characterized his colorful history.

Theodore Therrington was a businessman who specialized in fire response. In short, he profited from doing what the center for emergency response was supposed to do for free. He argued that privatizing magician services such as those he provided ensured magicians weren't taken advantage of by government agencies, who pay much less.

As part of his campaign, he traveled the nation and held rallies to gather support for his platform. And it was at one of those rallies that the inevitable happened.

Inevitable not because spontaneous fires break out at fire safety events, but inevitable because despite all Theodore Therrington's knowledge of fire management business, he refused to cover the cost of fire specialist magicians at his rallies.

The source of the fire forever remained a mystery, but its ending was grim. Well, except for the fireproof confetti, streamers, and deflated balloons that survived to decorate the wreckage. It was quite fitting that this rally led to an expedited approval of the National Magic Fire Management Act and a boom in sales for fireproof party supplies.

Octavian was as close to the fire as he cared to be, and there was no fireproof decor to be found. The heat of the flames made his skin feel like it was burning, but the proximity allowed him to reach into the plasma with his senses. He could feel the pressure and temperature changes that were allowing it to spread. He took deep breaths, attempting to focus his attention on the one thing he wanted to manipulate, the oxygen feeding the flames.

The area was large, too large for one magician, but he tried to convince himself that even a small reduction in the fire's footprint would give the Progeny time to put it out.

He tried to focus but was distracted by the memory of the window he had jumped through minutes ago, then further by his undergraduate training, when he had tried to apply his understanding of elementary particles with no success. Back then, both his body and ego had been bruised several times as he tried to pass through solid objects.

What was different this time? Was it just that he had more perspective from the years of training since his Quantum Magic class? Or was it his resolve to make a difference in this world?

He shook his head as he dismissed the thought. Magic didn't work by emotion, especially not desperation. A magician was only as strong as their knowledge of Nature. Somehow, he had improved his understanding enough to apply that knowledge.

That wouldn't help him here. Even with the most talented fire specialist magicians, an event of this size needed at least two people, who would work from opposite ends. There was no way he could hope to match that, despite his deep understanding of the nature of fire.

The building groaned as its structure bent. Then, from inside, voices cried out. He shot into the building, where the ceiling was bowing downward. Beyond searing flames was a small group of Progeny huddled together in fear. Their finishes looked warped, and they were struggling to push forward.

He threw his arms out toward them. He yelled a loud spell, ignoring the burning in his throat. The group looked at him and, as the flames receded, rushed toward him.

"Get out," he said. "Are there others?"

"This is everyone who gathered in the hall," one robot said as she held her face plate together. "We tried to check the labs again, but the heat—"

"I understand. Go."

As the robots went out the door he had entered through, he looked up at the surrounding structure. He could hear something, a melody that seemed to pierce through the cracking, groaning, and whooshing of the fire. There was no direction, and no time to figure out where the sound was coming from.

He had to do something, and he had to do it now.

9

Taming a Flaming

No matter how powerful the magician, it's impossible to know the location and speed of every atom in a dynamic environment, such as the raging fire encompassing the large multi-floor structure where Octavian now stood. He knew he needed to act, but such a feat required the processing of too many forces at work, too many stochastic variables to consider, and too many numbers to crunch.

In the Progeny World, there was a legend of a computer that could accurately predict 94.487252% of future events for the following twenty-four hours. Newly activated robots were often told stories of the Great Computer, its prophetic talents, and how one time, it saved the world from an incoming asteroid just by informing the Organics to all blow really hard in one direction all at once.

So pervasive was the legend that every year, the robots held a special innovation challenge in the Great Computer's name. The competition led to incredible but not always useful advancements. One such winner had developed an algorithm that could create fifty years worth of computer-generated film noir video content in just under a minute, though the completely necessary deletion of that content took much longer.

Yet none of the robots or their innovations could calculate the location of every atom relevant to Octavian's current task.

Such was the complexity of fire management magic. However, Octavian hadn't rushed into the billowing flames without a plan.

The plan was not to put out the entire fire single-handedly. That was beyond the power of one magician. Instead, he hoped to do what he had learned during his fire emergency management training: give emergency teams more time to get people to safety, stop the flames, and secure the structure to prevent further damage.

Octavian took a moment to survey the surrounding space. The open area stretched up four stories, and walkways spanning the distance from one side to the other were twisting in the intense heat. Railings were warping. Walls were crumbling. The glass windows and doors that lined entrances to laboratories and offices weren't looking so great.

Octavian focused on the fire. He could feel the waves of heat. Tendrils of glowing gas consumed and oxidized everything in their path. Their billowing breaths emitted heat and debris. It was stochastic yet organized, and when he concentrated on a small enough area, he could predict its movements enough to starve it.

With deep, steady breaths, his consciousness reached out to the oxygen in the air, the ever-increasing temperature, and the building materials that were fueling its continued growth. Sweeping his arms in practiced motions and crafting a precise spell, he altered the temperature and pressure. He isolated the fuel, disallowing the fire access to it, first within a small area, then steadily forming a bubble around himself.

The bubble itself was invisible, but the distinct lack of flames inside would have made it obvious to onlookers, if there had been any, that something awesome was happening. As he continued the motions, one side of the invisible bubble grew larger, keeping the fire from expanding and subduing it as it pushed forward.

His mind was clear and laser-focused, and things were going quite well. Of course, it was only a matter of moments before an interruption threw him off.

"Octavian!" a voice rang out from behind him.

He spun on his heels to see Replika rushing in his direction. The bubble burst. Heat swelled as the fire renewed itself. Flames flew down from above. Just as windows in the hallway burst from the sudden change, Replika threw him to the ground, covering him with her body.

His breath was forced out of him. He couldn't find the words he needed to say. Replika didn't say anything either. She just held him firmly down as glass rained down around them. A groan echoed from above, louder than the fizzing and crackling and general noisiness of the fire. The groan was joined by moaning and crunching sounds.

This was not good news.

Replika jumped to her feet. She leaned down, grabbing Octavian under his arms and pulling him up with such force that he tripped over himself. He grasped at her. Just as he got his balance, a loud boom erupted. The walkways overhead collapsed on each side of them.

Wasting no time, she grabbed his arm and started to pull him toward the exit. Octavian didn't stop to wonder if she planned to bound over the obstructing pile of rubble or burst through it.

"Wait!" he yelled, pulling back against her. He endured the pain that came with defying her. "Trust me!"

She paused, and he shared a long look with her. Her eyes were wide with worry and brimmed with tears. Her lips were drawn tightly together. As the moments stretched and stretched and stretched, Octavian noticed the silence around him. Fires don't know the meaning of a whisper, so it hadn't suddenly decided to be polite. Beyond Replika's form, the fire sat static, unmoving.

It was then that he realized it. Time had stopped.

This had happened before. Had it only been days ago? It seemed like forever. Now that he was aware of stillness, he could sense the same Time Mesh he had manipulated on the longboat in the Steampunk World. That time, he had moved the water, affecting an opposite force on the boat that kept it from crashing.

Octavian clung to the power. He was unable to control when it came or went. His mind raced as he tried to formulate an ad hoc magic proof that would save them and perhaps anyone else in the building.

He raised his hand, a slow, dragging motion that felt like he was immersed in a thick syrup. Swiping his arm to the side, he applied a force to the collapsing ceiling debris threatening to collide with them. It shifted, ready to scatter away from them when time was restored. As he desperately tried to determine the next step in his plan, he realized the Time Mesh wasn't the only new element of Nature he suddenly had access to.

This new thing was hard to describe. It wasn't a sensation, yet he could feel it as if it were part of him. He was used to reaching out with his mind and manipulating the psyche particle field. This was how magicians interacted with and manipulated the natural world. But the range of such a skill was limited.

Magical theorists and theoretical magicians alike believed that three things determined this range: a magician's level of ability, the dynamics of the local psyche particle field, and some universal limit that no magician could exceed. That third bit had been elusive, and the only substantive evidence for it was that no magician had ever sensed the psyche particle field to infinity. While many had tried to write mathematical and magical proofs to determine this theoretical limit, the most common consensus for the limit's value was an unenthusiastic shrug.

In this moment of stopped time, as Octavian's attention was pulled from the Time Mesh, he found himself able to sense more properties of his surroundings and further than ever before. He could see the properties of the burning building, the dome around them, and even into the organic world beyond. These sensations weren't vague or distant. It all seemed tangible and malleable.

Though he couldn't explain where it had come from, with this level of power, he could stop the fire.

Yet with his attention divided, his grasp of the Time Mesh was slipping. This may have been because he was trying to use other magic at the same time, or perhaps this was just the natural way in which the Time Mesh worked. Either way, this problem couldn't be solved with the elusive time magic, and he'd only get one chance to do it right.

With conviction, he loosened his slipping grip on the Time Mesh and instead focused on the increased range of his senses. With a simple lift of his chin, he suffocated the fire. He placed his hands in front of him, fingers spread, and eased them away from each other. He spoke a spell that made the environment inhospitable to fire kind.

The edges of the flames flickered as time gradually returned to normal. He could feel the pressure and temperature dropping. Turning his head to look around took a greater effort than moving his arms, but he didn't even try to understand that oddity. Instead, he watched as the fire dissipated around him.

Beyond his visual range, each spark and flicker went out until only the core of the fire remained, the hottest part.

He closed his eyes and moved his head and hands in careful, precise motions. The color of the fire, clear in his mind, dulled and dimmed. And finally, it went out, leaving its physical and emotional devastation to the survivors.

10

GOLD RUSH OF THE EYE VARIETY

Octavian had quelled the fire threatening the dome-shaped home of the Progeny. Unsure what else to do, Replika helped Octavian out of what remained of the buildings, where he collapsed into a magician-y mess on the synthetic ground.

She was worried, but somehow, she knew he was merely exhausted. Around them, the robots were in a frenzy, trying to make sense of what started the fire and what stopped it. It wasn't long before the outsiders were noticed, and before she knew it, a robot claiming to be an expert of organic human physiology was at their side.

As they tended to Octavian, Replika's eyes scanned the collapsing structure. While most denizens steered clear as they waited for the emergency response team to report on their efforts, one robot stood at the base of a now flameless building. It had been scanning the crowd, but now just stood, looking up at the misshapen walls.

The humanoid robot was a familiar shape, and she recognized it as one of the robots they had spoken to earlier. Yestary was its name, she assured herself, and she was correct.

"Would you like some assistance returning him to your room?" the would-be medic robot asked her. "I have requested a gurney."

"Oh, thank you," Replika replied. "He'll be fine, right?"

"His biometrics are within an acceptable range, so I do not suspect he inhaled too much smoke. However, I would like to come check on him when he awakens."

"As . . . would . . . I," said another as it rolled up to them. It was the robot Octavian called "the red-eyed beast", who they had met while being detained.

"Hello, Sestym," Replika replied.

"Why . . . was . . . visitor . . . in . . . fire?" it asked. "I . . . will . . . investigate."

"He is in no condition for one of your interrogations," the medic said.

"And I'll have you know, Octavian is the one who stopped the fire," Replika said firmly, crossing her arms.

"Impossible," Sestym said.

"With magic," Replika added, as if that made it all make sense.

"I . . . will . . . investigate," Sestym repeated.

"Fine. I look forward to seeing you at our quarters later on, then."

"Nice . . . seeing . . . you."

"You as well," Replika said, despite the entire conversation being pretty awkward.

"Have a good day," the medic added.

When Octavian awoke, Replika noticed something different about him. The sparkles of gold in his eyes had changed. It was difficult to pinpoint, but his eyes were definitely sparklier, more golden, and—she hesitated at the thought—more commanding. Her heart raced, and she found descriptive words difficult to grasp.

Even if Replika didn't have the words, she knew it was atypical for a magician's connection with the magical field of psyche particles to spontaneously increase in intensity. A magician's magic stemmed from their knowledge of Nature and the processes derived from it.

It wasn't uncommon for a magician to spend fifteen or twenty years in training, then look at an old picture and think, "Holy magica, is that what my eyes used to look like? Also, why did I think that haircut was cool?"

The eyes of Grand Magicians such as Octavian's former academic advisor, Grand Magician Kastra, were mostly gold except for their pupils, while those of an Exalted Grand Magician such as Teacher, Octavian's research advisor, had a haze of gold even over the pupils of their eyes.

Grand Magician Kastra had never stopped to consider that his haircut wasn't cool, nor his gaudy fashion sense. He was so egocentric that when his second wife complained he took up too much closet space with his wardrobe, he took that to mean he needed not only an additional walk-in closet but also more expensively designed variety in his clothing choices. While that's not the only reason she divorced him six months later, it was on her list of grievances.

Teacher, on the other hand, had more important things to worry about than his hairstyle choices in old pictures or his goldening eyes, important things which were not entirely foreign to the struggles facing Octavian and Replika.

Replika wasn't sure if etiquette necessitated she inform Octavian of his ophthalmic change, and before she could make a decision, Octavian spoke.

"Do I smell food?" he asked. "Or something masquerading as food, at least?"

The food had arrived a few minutes before Octavian awoke. Smiling, she served him a bowl of the provided sustenance before eating her own. Replika thought it tasted much better than the Progeny's first attempt, though Octavian didn't seem convinced. Even so, he ate a bowl of it and seemed re-energized.

Between bites, he had a lot of questions about what happened, and she answered each in turn. It wasn't until after she answered all his questions that she was comfortable asking one of her own.

"Why did you run into the fire?" she asked.

"I'm sorry if I worried you," he replied, putting a hand on hers. "I thought the only way to put the fire out was to start at one end and suppress it section by section. And I knew if I could start on one end, then the response team's job would be easier."

"Section by section? That's not what happened."

"Believe me. If I knew I'd be able to put the whole fire out at once, I wouldn't have gone inside the building at all." He shook his head in disbelief. "I'm still not sure how it was possible. It shouldn't have been possible."

"Then how did you do it?" she asked.

"It was . . . " he paused, waving his hands in small circles as he tried to find the words. "It was that Time Mesh thing again."

"You mean like when you stopped us from crashing our boat in the Steampunk World?"

"Sort of like that, yeah," he said with a nod before scooping more food into his mouth. "But more than that. It was like I could sense further and deeper."

She cocked her head to the side and furrowed her brow.

"Replika, it was amazing and overwhelming and unbelievable and . . . " He paused, again lost for words.

He held up his bowl of food and then placed it in front of him.

"This bowl has food in it," he said. He held up the spoon-like object he was using to eat. "I can eat the food because I can reach from the bowl . . . " He scooped up a spoonful and put it to his lips. " . . . to my mouth."

When Octavian handed her the bowl, she took it from him.

"I can't reach the bowl anymore," he said, holding up the spoony thing again, "even though I still have the tools I need to eat."

He let go of the spoon, and with a flick of his finger, it floated over to the bowl, scooped up a bit of food, and delivered it to his mouth. Grabbing the spoon again, quite proud of his metaphor, he smiled.

"The limitations of my reach were expanded," he said. "I wasn't using magic I didn't understand. I was using the magic I know in a context and scope that's beyond what an individual should be able to do."

"That's amazing," Replika said, dazzled by both the demonstration and the implications. "Can you do it again?"

He shrugged and went back to eating his food.

Replika twisted her lips to the side. That was not a proper answer. Even so, her heart felt full at seeing this side of Octavian, one filled with wonder and excitement.

There was a soft knock on the door. Replika stood to answer it, but two loud banging knocks followed. She jumped. Shaking her head, she stomped over to the door and threw it open.

Sestym stood beyond, almost exactly the right size to fit through the doorway, with its red sensor light beaming toward her.

"I . . . will . . . investigate."

11

AN AMICABLE AGREEMENT

Sestym, the large, boxy robot with one big, red, eye-like sensor, asked Octavian many questions, and Octavian answered each in earnest. As the questions continued, the would-be medic robot interrupted them, checked on the magician, didn't have any further insights to give, and left again. Replika could only watch in amazement at Octavian's patience as, slowly, the tension eased from the room.

"Thank . . . you . . . for . . . your . . . time," Sestym said in its usual rhythmic cadence.

"Of course," Octavian replied, standing up to lead it to the door.

Beeping at a steady rhythm, it backed up until it was outside the room.

"Until . . . next . . . time."

"Take care," Octavian replied.

"You are so good with people," Replika mused as Octavian closed the door.

"Yeah?" he asked, laying on the bed with an exhausted sigh.

"Absolutely."

"Well, it's still tiring." He covered his mouth as he fought back a yawn in vain. "I doubt those robots we met earlier will see us again today. They probably have their hands full with the aftermath of the fire."

"Probably so," Replika agreed. "Is there something you want to do?"

"Yeah, actually."

"And what might that be?"

"Just relax with you," he said with a smile. "I feel like we've been in mortal danger since you were activated. Wouldn't it be nice to just—I don't know—get to know each other?"

Her face felt hot, and she put her hands up to cover her cheeks.

"Yes. I'd like that, too."

Octavian and Replika talked through the day, the evening, and into the night. They spoke of Octavian's time with Teacher and of Replika's known and potential abilities. Replika admitted her interest in pirates, and Octavian admitted to being curious about the silent villagers.

Sharing their experiences over the last few days seemed, to both of them, like reminiscing on a lifetime. It seemed fitting. Both were so comfortable that it was almost as if they had known each other for a lifetime. While Replika settled into the feeling with great comfort, Octavian was apprehensive. After all, it was his mentor who had built her, had trapped him in these alternate realities with her, and had laid the groundwork for almost every action they had taken since this little adventure began.

Perhaps it really was a test, but not for him. Was it possible that Replika was the key to getting home, and he was just her engineer? If so, why make her so lifelike, so personable, so beautifully curious?

Perhaps Teacher had expected to bring them home, but something went wrong. Octavian was still plagued by the memory of Teacher's body being torn apart. Something had gone wrong in that first reality shift, although Octavian suspected that may have been intentional. He had nothing but a gut feeling as evidence, which amounted to almost exactly no evidence at all.

For now, all he could do was enjoy this time of safety and make the most of every day, both to learn about their situation and to learn about each other.

The next day, they were again called before the group of five robots, the Leadership Committee, and Replika was relieved to see that the chairs were still there for them. She wasn't sure she could contain her laughter if they repeated the ordeal of dragging them from their storage area again. There was something else missing, though: the humanoid robot named Yestary, who Replika had seen outside the fire after Octavian extinguished it.

The present robots introduced themselves again as if for the first time, and Octavian and Replika did the same.

"There's someone missing today," Octavian observed.

Replika was surprised he mentioned it. He hadn't seen Yestary the day before, and there was no indication that its absence would cause any delay in their negotiation . . . or whatever it was they were doing.

"Yes, this is true," the blue ball, Pirdeo, replied.

"Is everything okay?" Octavian pried.

The robots exchanged looks.

"Yestary was personally affected by the fire," Chope, the small robot with the retracting head, finally responded. "It suffered a significant personal loss."

"I was afraid you'd say that," Octavian mumbled, head lowered and fists tightened. He took a deep breath and returned his gaze to the committee. "How many casualties were there?"

"Three," replied the patchwork robot with the beautiful voice, Eraea. "We understand that we have you to thank for extinguishing the fire."

Replika was relieved to hear they recognized his heroic action. She took back every mean, suspicious, or otherwise negative thing she had thought about Sestym. Octavian didn't look nearly as relieved.

"I'm sorry I couldn't do more," he said.

"Upon arrival and initial assessment of the situation, the head of our emergency response team estimated a minimum loss of thirty-two Progeny," Eraea said. "He then reported that the fire was spreading much faster than anticipated and updated that estimate to fifty-one. We have categorized your contribution as significant."

"However," the copper robot, Noe, said. He paused, and the robots looked at each other again, perhaps engaging in a conversation that neither of the visitors could hear.

"Forgive us," Eraea said. "It's not that we don't appreciate what you've done. But we hold Organic life to be of the utmost importance."

Octavian's brow furrowed as she continued.

"The loss of your life in the fire would have devastated our community. We cannot condone you risking your life in such a way."

"I didn't risk my life," Octavian interrupted. "Maybe from your perspective, organic life is fragile. But I did not intend to die when I entered that building."

"But you collapsed," Chope said, head lowered into its body slightly.

"I exhausted myself," Octavian said, then added, "**AFTER** safely exiting the building."

The robots exchanged gazes again in silent conversation. After a minute, they returned their attention to the reality jumping, universe hopping, tripping duo.

"Our apologies for the miscategorization," Eraea said. "We understand that the best way to learn about you and your limits is through experience, and we believe you are sincere in your wish to help us."

"We propose," Pirdeo continued, "that you assist us in the project left by your predecessor. We will provide you with proper clothing, food, water, and supplies. When the project is complete and we have gotten to know you better, we will revisit our discussions of future plans for both of you."

"What about me?" Replika asked.

"You are our family," Chope replied with an obvious sense of cheer that Replika still found adorable. "You may do as you wish."

"Dangerous words," Octavian muttered in jest.

Replika laughed as she gave him a push. Did this mean he was feeling more comfortable here?

The copper robot, Noe, left the group and walked up to Octavian.

"Allow me to escort you to the core of the Independence Project," he said.

"Independence?" Replika asked.

None of the robots responded, and Noe took quick, small steps toward the door. Replika shared a look with her traveling partner.

"Independence from what?" she asked Octavian, as if he knew any more than she did.

Octavian shrugged.

"Only one way to find out," he said, looking intently at their escort before hurrying to catch up.

12

THE CORE

Unfortunately, after Replika and Octavian were led underground to a large work area, after they were introduced to the team members who worked on the Independence Project, and even after one of the team members offered them a tour, they still didn't have an answer for what the Progeny's Independence Project was attempting to gain independence from. It seemed to Replika that this was quite a large omission. After all, when one named something, the name usually implied a meaning of some sort.

In the Magic World, at the turn of the last century, the International Council of Exalted Magicians had announced an initiative called PETS. There was wild speculation about what PETS could stand for. Environmental activists claimed it stood for a Planetary Environmental Transformation System that would help combat growing issues related to environmental sustainability. Meanwhile, the political sector insisted the acronym stood for a collection of initiatives for Public Engagement and Trust.

Public debate sparked a huge media response. Every news venue published editorials, interviews with panels of experts, and trivia contests related to this mysterious initiative. For every person who spoke up on the suspected bravery of the ICEM for speaking out on this topic, another spoke up about their suspected closed-mindedness for cracking down on that topic. All the while, no one had any idea what PETS was or what the announcement had meant, and attempts to elicit a response from the ICEM were met with canned, vague word salads and several well-meaning shrugs.

When the initiative went live a few months later, pretty much everyone was surprised to learn that PETS was part of a leaked internal memo. It communicated to Exalted Grand Magicians that they would be allowed to bring their pets to the local headquarters one day every week as an internal community building exercise. Even most of the Exalted Magicians were surprised, since very few read the memo before sending it to the virtual recycle bin. An excitable intern had capitalized the word for emphasis.

During these weekly events, it became clear that, when cute animals are involved, names often don't hold a lot of meaning.

The Independence Project may have been a misleading name or related to animals, but both were not true. As far as Replika and Octavian were concerned, it was one giant mystery.

As they concluded the tour, their rolling guide with way too many appendages paused in front of their final stop. They stood on a metal grate balcony overlooking an enormous maze of machinery. Computers and engines were mixed in with things Replika couldn't identify, and at the center was a large, cylindrical tube with clear piping going down its length. She assumed it lit up, but whatever it was, it didn't appear to be active.

"We Progeny have spent many years trying to perfect a method of power generation," the robot, named Neasso, said. "Despite how disparate this all looks, at the heart, we have a generator connected to a diverse array of energy sources. This is the core of the Independence Project."

"Is it functional?" Octavian asked.

Replika eyed him. It was obviously not functional, but she could tell Octavian was reaching for something more. Everything they had seen until now seemed fully operational, though many systems were in need of some upgrades. This core—whatever that meant—had to be what they wanted him to work on. But why?

"No, it's not yet functional," Neasso replied.

"Why not?" Octavian pushed when the succinct robot didn't continue.

"Because the Organic who came before stole the power core."

Octavian did a double take. "Are you saying you were building Replika's power core to run this entire dome?"

"And more," Neasso assured them. "The system requires a substantial input of power to initialize. The core would have provided that, and then continued use would have been auxiliary."

Replika could only guess why that was so astonishing, but Octavian's face gave away how excited he was. Maybe it was just her, but she could swear the gold in his eyes was sparkling more than usual.

"I'd like to get an overview of what you have so far," Octavian said. "And I'm sure I'll have questions."

He turned to look at Replika.

"You don't need to hang around here if you don't want to," he said.

Replika almost spoke up to say it sounded fun to learn about whatever it was Octavian was so interested in. But, after a moment of thought, she realized that would be a lie.

"Okay," she said. "I'll see you later, then."

"At dinner?"

"Sounds good."

Another team member offered to escort her to the main level, but she declined. She knew the way, and she didn't want to take up any more of their time.

When she exited the underground area, she was surprised to find it was early afternoon. Neasso was definitely meant for detail work and not for speed. She noted a pair of doors that she guessed led outside . . . at least, to the most "outdoor" area of the dome that existed.

Looking around to get her bearings, she rounded a corner and found the charred remains of a building. It was one of the structures burned in the fire. Emergency teams were still combing through the wreckage, reinforcing the structure, and disassembling the broken pieces.

Among the twisted metal, crumbling walls, and charred debris, she noticed a structure still stood that was entirely intact. It was a small brick building big enough to house a few labs. In this structure, a hidden elevator led to a secret room that no one alive and functioning, except perhaps one, was aware of.

"Replika?" a voice called.

She turned to see the humanoid robot who had been missing from their meeting with the Leadership Committee.

"Yestary, hello," she responded.

"What are you doing here?" it asked.

"Octavian and I were getting a tour of your underground facility, and Octavian wanted to dig deeper into the details. I was just taking a look around and ended up here."

She paused as it considered her words.

"I heard you lost someone in the fire. I'm sorry to hear that," Replika said. "I know Octavian is, too."

"No need," Yestary said before she could say more. "What you both did was brave, and you saved many lives. I know that Reya would have been proud to call you our friends."

"And who was Reya?"

"She was my partner, in research and in life."

"I didn't know you were a researcher."

"All of us on the Leadership Committee hold what we call Positions of Inquiry," Yestary explained, gesturing for Replika to walk by its side as it led the way. "We each have an area of expertise and a hunger to explore."

"Explore. As in, outside the dome?"

Yestary's body began to wiggle and a strange rhythmic sound escaped it. Replika was eighty-seven percent confident it was a laugh.

"No, of course not," it said. "Explore information. Possibilities. Understanding."

"I see. And what is your area of interest?"

Yestary paused, and Replika stopped beside it. Yestary's face was expressive. Not as finely crafted and lifelike as Replika's, but she could see the pain in its furrowed brow, the pensiveness in its tightened lips, and an odd hint of mischief in its light gray eyes.

"My research," it said, "is on Organics."

13

THE PROGENY POWER PROBLEM

Octavian was equal parts enthralled and appalled at the specifications he was reviewing. The Leadership Committee had said they used only solar and chemical exchange arrays to generate power, however, they had built several other sources of power, according to these documents. Each source was supposed to feed into a central power center, where the power was stored. The distribution of the power was calculated using a complex algorithm that took into account time of day, live tracking of population density, and dozens of other variables.

For example, some high-traffic areas had been outfitted with devices that converted the robots' kinetic energy into electricity. However, since the robots were each made of different materials, they each had different physical properties, and the engineers had designed some magnificent ways of leveraging those properties to increase the output. Based on the known locations of each Progeny robot, they could scale the power generation systems to focus on the types of robots that were in that area.

While this was widely acclaimed by the Progeny, there was a small sect of robots led by one named Godin who erroneously believed the systems would have adverse effects on the Progeny, such as slowing down their movement or even harming their internal systems. Octavian was much too new to the system to have an opinion on this matter, and he wasn't sure whether to be more suspicious of a robot conspiracy theorist or of Neasso, the engineer who spent far more time than necessary explaining why Godin's gang was wrong.

Octavian was surprised such an effective and efficient electricity-based system could exist, and he had said as much to Neasso. And he asked, quite bluntly, why they hadn't activated the system yet.

The answer came with hours of explanation and both figurative and literal hand waving, but to put it succinctly, the issue was that the stolen power core had been the lynchpin of their plans. The core was intended to jump-start the system and was designed with a fundamental magic power generation technology.

Octavian couldn't believe the power core that Teacher had claimed to be secretly designed in Deutschland was, instead, built by Teacher and a bunch of robots from an alternate reality. Of course, whether he could believe it or not, it was the truth. So all Octavian could do was grumble at Teacher's deceit.

Teacher had designed many amazing technologies over the years. How many of Teacher's other inventions were stolen?

"So you see," Neasso explained, finishing the long-winded explanation, "we've been unable to turn the system on because we designed it to use the core."

"Yes," Octavian replied.

"We've tried to find a replacement power source, but have been unsuccessful thus far. The power requirement is just too high."

This was the other thing Octavian was all grumbly about. These people might be robots, but they were as good at topic pivoting as any old-fashioned politician or Exalted Grand Magician. He had asked the next question ten times—or maybe it was a million . . . he really wasn't sure anymore.

"And why is the initial power requirement so high?"

"The system's power distribution panel is divided into . . . "

Oh . . .

My . . .

Magic . . .

Neasso was going to explain the entire thing all over again
. . . again.

"Wait," Octavian interrupted, fighting an eye roll so hard his
vision blurred. "I understand the system architecture well
enough. I'm pretty sure I understand the basic requirements and
the big picture. What I don't understand is why the power needs
to all be channeled into one system. It seems like you could manage it in a modular way, which would be more sustainable and
serviceable anyway."

He sifted through the papers Neasso had given him. Despite
being a digital race of beings, the Progeny were devoted to keeping analog records of many things. When asked, one of the robots
had told Octavian "it just **feels** better."

"Look here," Octavian said as he found the relevant page.
"According to this, if you isolate the power generation of this
system, you could sequentially activate each sector based on its
necessary input potential."

"It won't work," Neasso insisted without so much as a
glance at the papers. "It's all or nothing for the project."

"The Independence Project?" Octavian clarified.

Neasso nodded.

Octavian didn't even bother to ask. Before he could grumble, his stomach did it for him.

"What is that?" Neasso asked in surprise. "Are you ill?"

"No," Octavian said with a smile. "I'm getting hungry. I
need food. Sustenance. Fuel."

"Ah, fuel," Neasso said, waving zir arms as ze liked to do.

Octavian hadn't figured out why ze sometimes did this. He
got the feeling that Neasso thought that it made zir explanations
more acceptable. It didn't. It was just distracting.

"Would you like me to call someone to take you to your accommodations?" Neasso asked.

"What time is it?"

"62598," the robot replied.

Octavian blinked, as if clearing his vision would make sense of the numeric answer. "Uh, how close is that to dinner time?"

"I'm unsure what constitutes a dinner time," Neasso said.

Octavian scratched his head absently. "Maybe I should head back. I don't know when Replika was hoping to eat, and I must admit, it's strange not knowing how much time has passed."

"Don't worry. We'll still be here tomorrow," Neasso joked in enough of a monotone that Octavian didn't register it as a joke.

Octavian viewed these people as individuals, but he couldn't shake the culture shock. Each robot was unique. Some had fully expressive faces and bodies, while others were rudimentary. Some had a wide variety of emotional responses, while others seemed to be task-focused and stoic.

He didn't want to assume any of them were less sentient than the next, but he was struggling to figure out how to best respect their diversity. For now, he merely took each opportunity as it came to him and hoped for the best. Had he recognized the joke for what it was, he would have pretended to laugh.

As he was led to their quarters by a shy robot who looked back every few seconds to make sure he was still there, Octavian wondered how well Replika was adjusting. She seemed comfortable being on her own and interacting with the Progeny, so maybe it was silly of him to worry about her. Yet here he was.

They passed through the door to the hallway where their room was, and laughter bounced echoed through the space. He put his hand out to touch his escort.

"Excuse me," Octavian said.

The robot turned to look at him but still said nothing.

"I've got it from here. Thank you very much."

The robot made a quiet series of beeping sounds before hurrying off the way they had come.

Octavian crept closer to the doorway. It was cracked open, and Octavian peered in.

Replika was seated on the edge of the bed, bouncing heartily as she chuckled. Across from her was another figure, seated on a chair that hadn't been there when they left the room. Octavian couldn't make the other figure out.

His stomach felt like it had lifted into his throat as Replika laughed again. Doubt clouded his mind, and he fought back triggered memories of abandonment. He took a few deep breaths, stood up as straight as he could, and pushed the door open.

14

The End Of The Organics

Replika spun as the door opened. Her eyes lit up when she saw Octavian, and his fears melted away. He could now see that the other figure in the room was Yestary, a member of the Leadership Committee of the Progeny, who also appeared to be glad to see him.

"Octavian! Come sit," Replika said. "Welcome back. Did you have fun?"

"It's amazing," Octavian said with a gentle smile, "but strange."

"Strange how?"

"We can talk about it later." He turned to the visiting robot. "You're Yestary, right?"

"That would be me," the robot said with a jiggle that Octavian assumed was a laugh. "And please don't apologize for my loss."

Octavian closed his mouth, which had been poised to do just that.

"I'm thankful for what you did," Yestary said. "I can't express how grateful I am that you stopped the fire. The loss could have been far greater."

"Yestary and its partner, Reya, study organics," Replika explained. "Reya even did biological research, and she had live cell

313

cultures in storage in those facilities. Yestary told me earlier that most of their samples survived intact."

"And those samples wouldn't have survived had the fire continued to spread."

Octavian nodded, not sure exactly how to respond.

"Where did you get live tissue samples?" he asked without thinking. "Did Teacher provide you with them?"

"We did work with Teacher, but no. The samples are all preserved from the time of the Organics."

Octavian and Replika asked two questions simultaneously.

"What did you work on with Teacher?" Octavian asked.

"How long ago did the Organics live?" was Replika's question.

Yestary chose to answer the latter.

"The last of the humans, who we call the Organics, died several hundred years ago. It's a sad story, really. They chose technology and convenience over sustainability and living in harmony with Nature. The world became inhospitable, and settlements fizzled out until all the humans were gone."

"How do you know no one is left?" Octavian asked.

"Well, we suspect it, from the data available to us. The Organics set up a network of satellites, relay stations, and sensor arrays all around the world which relay information to us. We serviced all of that technology until about fifty years ago.

"There were also some societal changes in the last hundred or so years of their existence that lowered their fertility rates."

"What?" Octavian blurred.

"Mm." Yestary confirmed with a nod. "As I said, it's very sad. We don't have a lot of information about how or why it happened, and that question has been of particular interest to Reya and me."

"And Teacher helped you with whatever you're working on that was related to that?" Octavian asked.

He looked to Replika, who seemed just as riveted by the story, and then back to Yestary, who didn't look like it was prepared to say anything more about it. Why were these robots so secretive? Had Teacher done more sketchy stuff than just stealing the power core?

Octavian's mind took this very moment to remind him that Replika had stolen the Reality Tuner. Well, that choice made a lot more sense now.

Before anyone could say anything more, noise came from the hallway. The far door to their hall slammed shut. Squeaky wheels drew closer. And a questionable aroma drifted into the room.

Yestary stood. "It seems your dinner has arrived. I'll leave you to it."

"I have more questions," Replika said, also moving to her feet.

"I would be worried if you didn't." Its humanoid face was kind as it added, "Come find me whenever you'd like. I'll gladly answer what questions I can."

"How do I find you?" she asked.

He pointed to a console that was tucked behind the door.

"You can use that interface to contact me for now. Since you both will be with us for a while, I'm sure we can equip you with an MID. That is, a mobile interface device. I'll speak with the others on the Leadership Committee about it tomorrow."

It waved and left just as a wheeling cart arrived at the door. Octavian was able to stave off the humor of the small robot that was directing the cart without being able to see over it. They thanked it for the meal, and it rolled on to its next wheeling destination, just as blind but well-calibrated to its environment.

Octavian shut the door behind it and waited. Replika raised an eyebrow, and he knew that she knew that he wanted to say something.

"Something's going on," he said once the hallway door slammed shut.

"Something?"

"Yes. Something."

315

"Like, a serious something?"

Octavian opened his mouth to reply, but Replika interrupted.

"Or maybe an exciting something."

"R—"

"Oh, what about an amazing something?"

"Replika," Octavian said. "Do you want to know what happened or not?"

She grinned and nodded.

He let out a sigh before gathering his thoughts. "After you left earlier today, I got the runaround from Neasso about the power concerns for the Independence Project. And you must've noticed how Yestary avoided my question about the project he worked on with Teacher."

"I'm sure they'll come to trust us soon," she assured him. "But I do find it odd. Maybe if I could learn more about their history, I'll get a better idea of why they're so secretive."

"Worth a try."

He sat in front of his meal and gave it a thorough review. He thought it was bread with some kind of soup inside it, and he worked up a cautious optimism. It looked much better than the mush they had gotten since they arrived, though the smell was still dubious. And the mush they had received thus far wasn't horrible. The consistency was just very odd: a bit gummy, with a knack for sticking in the back of his throat.

With a preparatory sip of water, he picked up the spoon-like object, which he desperately needed a better name for. Perhaps he should just stick with "spoon."

"At first, I thought they were being secretive because I'm an Organic or whatever," he said, dipping his spoon into the soup. "But I'm not sure. I get the feeling something happened that makes them very cautious of outsiders in general."

"Something?" Replika said with a wry smile.

"Don't even start." Octavian couldn't help but grin.

"By 'something happened,' I assume you mean besides Teacher stealing from them, right?"

Octavian half-shrugged half-nodded to show that she'd made a good point, but yes, that was what he meant.

"I agree," Replika said. "They haven't said it directly, but they've closed themselves off from the outside world. Yet they don't strike me as xenophobic."

"Me, neither."

Replika braved eating a bite of the spoony substance, so he followed suit. The consistency was thick and smooth, but there were chunky bits. He bit into them, and a wave of flavor exploded from them. Satisfied, he shoveled more into his mouth.

"Wow," Replika said. "This is delicious!"

Octavian just nodded, mouth full.

"Let's just keep our ears and eyes open for now," Replika said.

With another nod of agreement, Octavian drank a refreshing gulp of water. The water was unexpectedly unnecessary, since the food's texture was rather pleasant, and he savored the feeling of drinking not for thirst, but for enjoyment. With that out of the way, he dug into his very welcome, delicious meal.

15

CHRYSANTHEMUM

Replika twisted her lips to the side in frustration as she touched the unresponsive screen again. In obvious defiance, it remained black. She pushed her finger harder against the screen, causing it to light up before going black again. Extra defiant, Replika decided.

Octavian had left just after finishing a breakfast that was surprisingly fresh and flavorful. Their hosts had also provided them with a change of clothes and protective foot coverings for Octavian to wear while in the engineering levels. The clothes were more refined than the original outfits they'd been given, which were simply stretches of cloth and ties to hold them together. This fabric was softer and more comfortable, and the Progeny had sewn it into clothes-like shapes. Although baggy, Octavian had seemed satisfied with the pants. Replika thought they'd work well enough until the Progeny finished whatever quarantine they were doing with the clothes they arrived in.

After getting ready, Octavian had left Replika alone with this infernal device. Not that he knew there'd be any issues getting it to do its one job, but she had a feeling he could fix it. She assumed it was supposed to be a simple touchscreen interface, and the glimpses she had gotten so far looked straightforward enough. However, she'd spent the last several minutes trying the same thing over and over while expecting the results to be different and definitely feeling a little insane.

She crouched down to look at a panel under the screen. Wedging her fingernails between the panel and the wall, she wiggled it until it popped open. Inside, cables wrapped around each other in bundles, but Replika was quick to identify a cause for the issue.

Several of the cables had been chewed through. This was equally curious and distracting. As far as Replika knew, there were no organic life forms within the dome. However, the bite marks along with the droppings at the bottom of the panel proved otherwise.

She leaned closer, pretending she could gauge how old the evidence was with closer inspection. Despite being hundreds of years old, the Progeny kept the dome and its inhabitants well-maintained. Even the doors swung with silent ease, which was more than Replika could say for the doors in a certain other reality she had visited. So why hadn't anyone noticed this outage?

Uninterested in teaching herself anything about electricity, her mind wandered to the myriad of creatures that could have created this damage. Did it have sharp teeth? Was it carnivorous? Was it dangerous, with bright red eyes, cat-like reflexes, and a vampiric taste for blood?

She needed to reel that imagination in a bit and get back to the task at hand: the screen.

Remembering another panel in the hallway, she hurried to it. She hummed as she popped it open. Inside was what she expected, an emergency repair kit, but she was pleasantly surprised to find another screen interface like that in their quarters.

And even better, it worked.

A tap activated the interface, and she navigated to a map of the dome, titled "Chrysanthemum" and subtitled with a sequence of numbers that she assumed indicated its serial number.

She was mostly wrong. The Chrysanthemum was one of eighteen structures built across the landscape by the Organics, each named after a flower and collectively called "The Bouquet." The number on the screen indicated the date the dome passed its initial inspection, the year it was intended to receive its next regular maintenance, and the number in sequence that it was built.

Of the eighteen structures, this one was the last to open. Unlike the short delays seen in the Rose and Tulip domes due to failed inspections, the delay for Chrysanthemum took four years because local citizens refused to concede to naming it Geranium. The anti-Geranium protests that broke out caused tens, perhaps hundreds of dollars in damage and cleanup costs. Despite their obvious respect for others' property, their protests proved persuasive.

This was mostly due to one Organic named Georgie Gourdy. Ze was a self-proclaimed anthophile and the president of the local flower enthusiast's club. After a heart-pounding debate over the superiority of orchids and a vote that was far too close for comfort, the club, who had no real authority, had announced that the dome was to be named Chrysanthemum.

Led by Georgie Gourdy, they brought their decision to the Federated League Of World Empowerment and Respect, who were the organization responsible for making these kinds of decisions. The FLOWER representatives who met with Georgie Gourdy and zir Carnation Cabinet were unprepared for the 157 member group to pack themselves into the office, much less to do so while squabbling and gossiping. Perhaps this was why they couldn't hold back their laughter at the proposal.

Not only were Chrysanthemums far less popular than Geraniums, they argued, but the name was twice as long. That meant all name plates would need to be twice as big and they'd need to pay for twice as many letters to be painted, etched, or however else they planned to display the name.

Well, Georgie Gourdy wouldn't take no—or laughter—for an answer. They stayed in the FLOWER offices until the authorities were called to haul them out. Within hours of zir release from the precinct, Georgie Gourdy organized an almost constant barrage of protests, petitions, and patronizing people at the build site, the FLOWER offices, and sometimes even the homes of officials.

"Compared to all that annoyance," a FLOWER representative retrospectively recalled, "changing the name didn't seem so bad."

Replika thought the name was lovely, even if it did take up every pixel of the horizontal space allotted for the text. A flashing dot on the map indicated her position in a building labeled "*Dormitory A*" that sat near the southeast edge of Chrysanthemum. A red triangle pulsed over it.

She swiped at the screen to zoom in on the building and tapped the triangle icon. Dozens of dots appeared: some green, one yellow, and a smattering of red.

She was willing to bet that wasn't a coincidence. With the impulse control of a toddler, she broke into an excited sprint to go check it out. She rushed up two levels, turned left, took the second right, spun in a few circles to get her bearings again, and continued straight down to the other end of the hall.

Her heart raced with exhilaration as she closed the distance between her and the objective.

"—cannot keep doing that."

She stopped.

It was a voice. A small voice with an electronic hum underlying each syllable. Triangulating the position of its source with her superior senses, she rolled onto the balls of her bare feet and crept toward it. She took each step with careful intent, testing the metal floor for creaks before placing her full weight onto it.

Slowing her breathing, she inched around a corner. Light spilled out of an open door, interrupted by a moving shadow. She crept closer, one step at a time, each breath slower than the last.

"Is it good?" the voice returned.

She jumped. After an uncontrolled gasp, she held her breath in, but the room's inhabitant didn't seem to notice.

Her curiosity pushed her forward to the doorway, and she peered around it. There, at the far end of the room, a cylindrical robot with long tube-like arms and legs huddled over something.

Zir hand was flat on the floor, and in it sat a small mammal of some kind. Not a feline with sharp vampire teeth as Replika had imagined, but a rodent with a fluffy tail and ear tufts. She had some understanding of the creatures of the Magic World, but not enough to pass judgment. So she just stared in awe as the large rodent ate from the robot's hand.

As she peered around the room for scale, she realized the robot was likely almost seven feet tall. Zir head was shaped like a bullet, but she could tell it was on a neck of some kind because it rolled around as ze made small, loving sounds directed at the rodent.

Replika leaned forward further for no good reason, bracing herself against the door frame. With a loud crack, the metal frame broke from the wall. She tumbled toward the ground and, turning her attention to the incoming metal floor, shifted her weight to catch herself. In the moment that her attention diverted, the robot lunged in her direction, eyes drawn thin and glowing red.

She turned her gaze up to look into zir face, into zir enormous and ominous form hovering over her, and let out a simple but poignant, "Oops."

16

MEPTOR AND THE MUSCRITE

Even as the giant robot's glowing red visual sensors and ominous form loomed over her, Replika didn't regret investigating the potential source of bite marks that broke the touchscreen display in their room. She did somewhat regret alerting this robot to her presence, but she was far too busy being intimidated to notice.

"The dormitory is off-limits," the robot boomed in a loud but high-pitched voice.

"Um," Replika replied poetically.

The robot paused.

"Wait. You are the robot that came with the Organic." Ze didn't wait for her to respond. "I am very sorry. I thought you were—"

"I'm guessing you aren't supposed to be here, either," Replika said.

"This was the dormitory for the Organics. It does not have the necessary functionality or accommodations for the Progeny. But I maintain it, so I am allowed here."

"And your friend?" Replika asked, gesturing toward the rodent, who was far too busy nibbling on a piece of fruit to care about this conversation.

"Ah." The sound came out as a strange robotic stutter.

"I do not know where she came from," the robot said, "but one day she was here, and so I fed her. Now, she appears every day."

Replika couldn't hold it in any longer. Her laughter erupted, even causing the rodent to skitter away a few feet. The robot took a step backward, unsure what to make of the reaction. Replika tried to stop, but she couldn't.

Something about this giant, menacing robot caring for a small, helpless rodent just tickled her.

The rodent was called a muscrite by the Organics. Though this muscrite was rather large when compared to similar rodents in the Magic World, the average size of a muscrite had been reduced by about half since the Organics were alive. This particular muscrite was of average size, average weight, and average intelligence. In fact, this rodent was nothing special at all except that she was in a certain place at a certain time and was thus able to experience an environment and amount of pampering that very few muscrites ever would.

Several months earlier, there had been another containment breach at ground level. Between a buildup of moisture, plant roots, and a variety of animal life plus some seismic activity, a crack had cut its way through to the interior of the dome. Within hours, an army of ants and a battalion of beetles were spreading their territory and scaring the living daylights out of the Progeny.

A massive initiative was organized to return the beings to their former exterior habitat—after proper decontamination and cataloging, of course—and to check the entire dome for possible structural weaknesses. Five distinct areas were identified as at risk and repaired. However, unknown to the Progeny, several larger animals, including this muscrite, had also made their way inside.

This particular muscrite had been burrowing and eating bugs she found along the way when she suddenly found herself encased in a solid tunnel full of dirt. Not built for backing up, she continued onward. She was rewarded with several extra-juicy beetles that she wouldn't have eaten except that they were rare at that time of year.

She had emerged just inside the southeastern wall of the dome and was both terrified by the enormity of the structures around her and curious as to their contents. With a few brave sniffs, she ran as fast as her chunky little legs would take her into the nearest building, her fluffy tail waving like a little flag behind her.

She tried tasting many new things, including some very chewy cords that, while not the yummiest thing she ever tried, looked too good to pass up. A week after her arrival, this robot had found her. They became fast friends, and the muscrite had been fed and spoiled ever since.

After at least two minutes of continuous laughter, Replika finally pulled herself together. Apologizing several times, she took deep breaths.

"I'm Replika," she announced.

"My name is Meptor," the robot replied.

Meptor was an odd personality, but once ze opened up, ze was a well of knowledge. Replika learned that, while most of the buildings within the dome had an incredible amount of sensors to track things like temperature, pressure, and humidity, the dormitory was much less sophisticated. The Progeny were sentimental about the building. They kept it well-maintained but had not installed the upgrades they had in the rest of the Chrysanthemum.

Ze especially liked the sensors that reported population density because then ze could avoid crowds. Meptor was quite the introvert, preferring the company of the little muscrite to zir fellow Progeny.

When Meptor found out that the interface in the visitors' quarters was broken, ze insisted on fixing it posthaste. Waving goodbye to the muscrite—who was busy cleaning herself and didn't much care now that her meal was over—ze led Replika on a serpentine path through corridors, across a bridge to another building, and down a level. After getting supplies from a utility closet, they made their way across another bridge, back into the dormitory, and down another level.

This place really was a maze. Good thing Replika's system created maps without her consciously thinking about it.

The panel was on the floor where Replika had left it.

"I always tell her not to chew cords, but she still seems to do it every so often," Meptor mused.

Ze looked at Replika and cocked zir head to the side.

"Do not worry," ze said. "I will have it fixed soon."

"Thank you," Replika replied. "It surprised me to see something broken. Everything seems to be in good working order here."

Ze released the screen from its housing. A loop on the rear side allowed zir to hang it on a hook tucked behind the screen.

"Well, most of us are designated for maintenance, but I am the only one who works in this dormitory. It is a bit more complicated than other areas, and the sensors that alert me to damage are not very reliable."

Meptor pulled the cables from behind the screen and tossed them aside. Then, crouching down to the panel below, ze pulled the stretch of wire that had been severed from the wall. It was odd to see the large robot's form trying to fit into such a small space, and Replika couldn't believe this was what ze had been built for.

"That sounds like it could be frustrating."

"For others, yes. But I enjoy the work," ze said as ze pulled materials from zir bag. Ze paused to look at Replika. "What about you? Do you like it here?"

"You mean, do I intend to stay here?"

"My understanding was that you must stay as part of your agreement with us."

Ze returned to zir work replacing the cables.

"I know," Replika replied, "and I do enjoy this world and the people I've met." She paused, unsure whether to go on.

"But you prefer the company of the Organic?" ze asked. Ze wobbled zir head this way and that, a motion that Replika now recognized as a happy one.

Replika knew she wanted to stay with Octavian, but there was more to it than that. Being restricted to the dome felt suffocating, especially compared to the multiverse of realities to explore. She got the feeling Octavian was terrified by the wealth of experiences the opportunity provided, but she found it exhilarating.

She opened her mouth to respond, but Meptor spoke instead.

"I can understand preferring an organic to your fellow Progeny. You are in good company."

"You love the muscrite, don't you?" Replika asked.

"Yes," ze admitted freely. "She is very special to me. Organic life from outside is forbidden, so I am afraid the others will find out about her and send her away."

A sound startled them both, and they whipped their heads to the doorway to see a figure standing there. A robot figure, with a concerned grimace on its face.

17

RETURNING THE REALITY TUNER

Replika hadn't heard the door at the end of the hall open. She hadn't heard anyone approaching. And she hadn't heard the cracked door slip open. It wasn't until Yestary made a sound resembling clearing its throat that she realized someone was overhearing the private and problematic conversation she was having with her new friend, Meptor.

Replika wasn't sure what to say, but she knew the conversation was not one Meptor had intended to be eavesdropped on by another of the Progeny. Ze seemed equally speechless, and they both just stared as the awkward pause became longer and longer.

Then, in a valiant and successful attempt to break the silence, Yestary pulled its hand from a bag at its side and held out a familiar round object to Replika.

"This device allows you to travel between realities. Is that correct?"

Her eyes were already wide with surprise, but they might have widened just a bit more.

"The Reality Tuner!" she exclaimed.

"I spoke with the Leadership Committee. They're checking over your other belongings, but I've asked them to expedite their return."

She rushed over to Yestary and threw her arms around its neck.

"Thank you," she said.

As she pulled away, Yestary's gaze met Meptor's.

"Meptor," Yestary said with a nod.

"Good day, Yestary," Meptor replied cautiously.

"I . . . " Yestary paused for a moment, considered the words it was about to say, and started again. "I assume I may speak without my words being repeated to others."

Yestary's tone sat somewhere between a question and a statement. Replika and Meptor both nodded, assuming their agreement kept their own conversation confidential as well.

"When Teacher arrived, he had a very similar device," it said, "and he said some odd things while he was here. Things that, at the time, I considered premonitions or predictions.

"He told us—Reya and me—that one day, another Organic would come who could tap into the psyche particle field, and that they might need help to understand how to use the device. He asked me to promise to share my knowledge with him.

"I don't know how much help I can give, as I'm unable to use the device, but I believe he was speaking of Octavian."

Replika took the device. "You know how to control it?"

"Teacher showed us the basic functions, yes, although there were many questions still in his mind about 'universe hopping,' as he called it."

She looked back at Meptor, who had resumed zir repair work while pretending not to listen.

"Thank you. We'd appreciate any information you can give us," she replied when she returned her attention to Yestary. She had the distinct feeling there was more to it than that, but wasn't sure how to ask. "Would you like to have a seat?"

"No, I have other matters to attend to, but perhaps after you've settled in, you and Octavian will visit me for dinner."

"Dinner? The Progeny have dinner?" Replika asked.

Yestary jiggled with humor. "We have gatherings, but not meals in the way the Organics used to. Even so, I'd be delighted to prepare a meal for you."

"That sounds nice," Replika said.

Yestary pulled the bag at its side open and rummaged around. After a few moments, it made an excited sound and pulled out two handheld devices.

"Here," it said. "One for each of you. They're the MIDs I mentioned before. Mobile interface devices. You can send text, audio, or video messages or start a live call. And there are other functions as well."

They were round, puck-shaped devices about a quarter of an inch thick. Replika noticed a button on one side and pushed it. The screen on its front lit up in response.

"*51228*" the screen read.

"What's this?" Replika asked.

"The time. There are 86400 seconds in a day."

"Oh!" Replika said with a laugh. "I see!"

"Is this not how you measure time where you're from?" Yestary asked.

"No. We divide days into twenty-four hours, each with sixty minutes, which each have sixty seconds."

"How arbitrary," Yestary said, obviously intrigued. "I look forward to learning more about your world and customs. I must go now. Say hello to Octavian for me."

"I will."

Yestary peered around her at the robot doing zir best to look busy. "Nice to see you again, Meptor."

A vaguely friendly grunt came from Meptor in response, and Yestary went on its way. Replika waited until the hall door shut before speaking.

"Do you not get along with Yestary?"

"It is not that," Meptor said. "When the other Progeny talk to me, I just do not know what to say."

Ze stood up and snapped the panel into place. After removing the screen from its hook, ze reinstalled it into its shell.

"You've done fine talking to me," Replika said as Meptor turned to her, wiping zir hands on a cloth.

"You are easy to talk to. Like an Organic."

"I could help you, if you'd like. To talk to others. Maybe we could find new friends together."

"That sounds . . . " Meptor paused.

Replika leaned in with anticipation of what word ze would choose. Exciting? Fun?

"Terrifying."

Replika laughed.

"But nice," Meptor continued.

"And in return," Replika said, "you can tell me more about the history of your world and the Progeny."

The robot's head wobbled in happiness. They had a deal.

Octavian hadn't expected time to go by so fast. He spent much of his days trying to work out a magical proof to meet the Progeny's power requirements. Then there was the time he spent trying to piece together why that power requirement was so high.

After presenting several options to the engineering staff, he had finally determined they were one hundred percent, completely, immutably, and—in Octavian's opinion—suspiciously uninterested in making what they already had work. The Progeny's focus remained on finding a method to reach their massive system start up threshold, and they refused to share why.

Once he accepted that limitation, things had become even more frustrating. Replika's perpetual energy core was very much a mystery to him, and he didn't feel comfortable examining its properties while active. The Progeny had also denied his requests for Teacher's notes, so Octavian was on his own.

If that wasn't bad enough, the Progeny preferred for notes to be written in analog. As in, by hand. On . . . paper. And don't ask where the paper came from because the Progeny refused to answer that question as well. Octavian's hands hurt from the manual effort. He found himself duplicating his work in his Note-book, which was much faster and easier but didn't relieve his frustration. Still, it was worth the extra time to have a copy for himself.

Despite the setbacks, he would soon gather some informa-tion. Whether he could classify that information as useful was a matter of perspective. When left alone, Octavian used his magic to unlock the three file cabinets in Neasso's office and look through documents he found within. He'd never been explicitly barred from inspecting the files, but the fact that they were locked probably should have been evidence enough.

While Octavian's regular perusals revealed things such as an increasing rate of outer hull breaches and an external ecological reliance on the dome, none of this information told him anything about why Teacher knew how to create a perpetual power core.

In other words, the information was useless to him, at least for now.

Replika, on the other hand, was gaining a lot of information. She met with other Progeny regularly, both on her own and with her robot friend, Meptor, who was always far too nervous around Octavian to say much. Through these interactions, Replika was learning much about the Progeny's culture.

Morning and evening meals were the highlights of every day. The duo exchanged stories, caught up, and enjoyed food of ever-increasing quality. The Progeny brought them new clothes regularly, which also improved in design and construction with each iteration. Although their belongings were returned, both travelers continued wearing the Progeny's clothes out of respect and appreciation.

One day, over a month after their arrival, Octavian took note of a door near the entrance of the engineering level. It was a nor-mal door except that it was the only locked door he had come across since his release from detainment. And yes, he had tried to open it once, though he'd so far quelled the urge to use magic to unlock it. Still, he often wondered what lay beyond.

It may have been his throbbing fingers or perhaps frustration about his lack of progress, but today, that locked door seemed to mock him. Days had stretched into weeks, and if he didn't do something, they could end up staying here for years.

He hurried to their quarters, his anxiety rising. How had he become so complacent? He still needed to find his way home, still needed to become an expert in his field, still needed to prove to the Magic World that he was worth something.

He didn't have time to dwell on this much longer because Replika wasn't in their room when he arrived. In her place, a note lay on the table. His brow furrowed as he read it.

18

IT'S GETTING MUSHY IN HERE

Octavian again read the note Replika had left on the table of their quarters. It held detailed directions, although the note didn't say where to. He pulled out his MID and opened a chat with her.

"Is this some kind of puzzle?" he messaged.

But he received no response. He tried to locate her MID with its built-in functionality, but hers wasn't active.

Steeling himself, he reviewed the directions a few times and headed out to follow them. The sun seemed to descend faster than usual as he followed each turn.

Upon reaching a dead end, he retraced his steps until he found his mistake. He chided himself. How did he not know where he was after being here so long? He couldn't even do that right!

As he begrudgingly ascended each ramp, he cursed his own arrogance at thinking he could solve the Progeny's troubles. He couldn't even comprehend Teacher's expertise, much less hope to match it. What he had set out to do was impossible for a magician at his level, and he was a fool to think otherwise.

Each step left him questioning his vector, and those after had him considering if he had ever been on the right path in the first place. This was a literal question in his mind, but also a philosophical one. Not that he was coherent enough to see the parallels.

After forty-five minutes of this, he reached the last step of the instructions.

"Go straight up the ramp and through the doors. See you soon!"

Though he'd had plenty of time to prepare for the many possibilities of possible destinations, none came close to what he found.

A rooftop balcony lay beyond with a dim string of lights draped across the railing. The scent of steamed mushrooms stuffed with a cheese-like substance and fresh vegetables wafted up from a basket on the ground. A large blanket sat underneath the basket with two plush pillows on either side.

Standing at the railing, body facing away but head turned in profile, stood Replika. She was backlit by pink and purple clouds and the setting sun. She was exquisite, and it brought a smile to his face.

All of his doubts and worries melted away as they shared a long, intense look. Even though she'd been waiting, she seemed surprised to see him, probably because it took him so long to get there. But her gaze softened as a synthetic breeze rustled the blanket and her skirt. He realized that, for the first time since they arrived, she was wearing a skirt that poofed out in a teacup shape.

He was about ninety-five percent confident she had requested that particular wardrobe item. Even though it was ridiculous, it suited her better than the slacks and long skirts the Progeny had been providing since their arrival.

Her hair was loose, but the tight curls were clipped behind her ears. Her bright, round eyes reflected the sky, making them an even brighter shade of amethyst than normal. Through a wide smile, her full lips parted to speak.

"You made it."

"You gave good instructions," he replied, despite how long the journey had taken him. "What's all this?"

She waved for him to come over and then gestured at the sky. "I thought this would be a perfect place to view the sunset."

"It is," he agreed. "How'd you find this place?"

"I went looking," she said with a light laugh. "I looked for flat roofs on the western side of the dome. But I admit, I was surprised to find something like this."

He reached her side to gaze at the unobstructed sunset, and she leaned her head onto his shoulder.

"It's wonderful," he said.

"How was work? Any progress?"

"No. I just don't know enough about using psyche particles for power generation. Without Teacher's notes, it's slow going to parse out the math and magic myself." He took her hand in his. "What about you? Any answers about what the Independence Project could be about?"

She lifted her head to look up at him. "Just more nice folx who won't share their people's most important secrets."

Octavian let out a small chuckle. "How dare they," he joked before reveling in her laugh.

"Well, that's why we're up here. You've been working hard for weeks now, and I thought it might be nice to do something special."

"This is incredible," he said. "And . . . "

And it was pretty damn romantic. He couldn't bring himself to say it out loud for fear he would end up stammering in embarrassment. Instead, he avoided eye contact and her questioning gaze.

"And I appreciate it," he finished.

"Are you hungry?" she asked.

"Yeah, sure," he replied.

They sat across from each other in the dimming light, and Replika served them. On the blanket, Replika had placed many of the mineral samples she'd collected in the Material World. The sunlight gleamed against the samples, casting pink and red light onto the surrounding surfaces. It was a very nice touch.

One of the samples caught his eye, and he leaned over to pick it up.

"I'm not sure I ever showed you that one," Replika said. "I found it while gathering materials that last time. There wasn't much of it, but I thought it was pretty."

It had a crystalline structure, and as Octavian held it up to the light, he sensed a shift in the psyche particle field around it. The waves of color that drifted through the stone seemed like, at any moment, they could begin to ebb and flow.

But there was something else happening, something he couldn't quite put his finger on.

He closed his eyes and examined the surrounding psyche particle field: how it moved, its flow pattern, where it pooled. It seemed like it could pull him in, but not in a terrifying way like the Grafton Vortex, a natural phenomenon in the Magic World that could shred most organic tissue to dust.

This was a disruption in the psyche particle field, a well of sorts that attracted particles, held them loosely, and then released them at a steady pace. He had sensed this before, but where?

He opened his eyes and snapped his gaze to Replika. Without warning, he rushed to her side. He hovered a hand in front of her torso, where her power core was embedded deep within. Completely immersed, he missed her calling out his name.

The way the magic flowed to and from her core was similar to the sample. Far too similar to be coincidental. Beyond the basic properties matching that of the stone, Octavian could feel forces at work. Not just any forces, but intricate spells with a familiar flair. Teacher's work.

When he opened his eyes again, he found her large pools of amethyst gazing back at him. It caught him off guard, but he couldn't tear his gaze away.

"What's wrong?" she asked.

"Nothing," he said. "Sorry."

"Is the sample important? I had a feeling it was," she admitted.

Was she leaning closer to him, or was he leaning closer to her? He wasn't sure. His head was spinning. One moment, he was unraveling a potential solution to the Progeny's power dilemma, and the next, he was distracted by how perfectly Cupid's bow described Replika's top lip.

"Um," he stuttered.

"Octavian," she said, each syllable causing his heart rate to increase.

"This mineral has the same properties as your power core," he got out. "It's sort of like a battery that charges and depletes itself, except its power source is the psyche particle field, which exists everywhere."

Her hand lifted from her side and touched his cheek. Tingles ran down his spine as her light touch moved down his jaw and around to the nape of his neck.

His breath had quickened, and he struggled to get it under control. His mind was racing. He'd thought of her in this way before, but they'd been in mortal danger since he activated her.

Every muscle in his body was ready to pull her close to him and enjoy the taste of her lips. But all of his neurons were telling him they hadn't had enough time to figure out their feelings for Replika because they were too busy trying to keep him sane in their turbulent and dynamic situation. Poor neurons.

Just as he was failing to make a decision for the tenth second in a row, a chime rang out from both of their attire, where the Progeny had recently discovered the joys of pockets. They both paused and pulled out their MIDs.

"Would you care to join me for dinner tomorrow evening? Perhaps at 65000?"

19

Finally Making Progress

Yestary's well-timed dinner invitation sent Octavian and Replika into a laugh. He lost his balance and fell backward onto his rear.

"Do you want to respond, or should I?" Replika asked as she wiped a tear from her eyes.

"Maybe we should wait a month before answering," he replied.

Their laughter returned in full force.

"And you thought he forgot!" Replika said.

"I just thought—" He couldn't finish the sentence as he started laughing again.

When they regained their composure, they decided to message Yestary in unison, accepting the invite. Replika picked up one of the stuffed mushrooms she'd served herself.

"Here's to tasty food," she said.

Octavian was overwhelmed with flavor when he took the first bite. "Did you make this?"

"It took me three days to convince the head chefs that I wasn't insulting their cooking," Replika mused. "Chef Ayd kept saying things like 'just because you've been helping in the grow labs doesn't mean you know how to cook.'"

"Well, this is amazing," he replied, ignoring her award-worthy impersonation. "I didn't know Teacher knew how to cook, much less that he'd given you any cooking protocols."

"So you think this is his favorite recipe or something?"

"No, nothing like that," Octavian said. "I was kidding, but if I'm honest, I'm not convinced he's the one who programmed you."

"What do you mean?"

"Well, the Progeny helped with your power core, right? So who's to say he didn't get help with your personality matrix?" He shoved another bite into his mouth.

"I guess that could be true. You don't think he was capable of it?"

He shrugged and finished chewing. "I don't know if you're aware of the level of robotics in our Magic World, but there was nothing even close to your level of sentience out there."

He watched Replika think for a moment, and it was almost as if she was trying to recall the previous year's winner of the International Advancement for Robotics' annual competition in the Magic World.

The winning entry had been the XMedia 50T, a human form robot whose greatest talent was balancing really, really well. It had no personality at all, though it was touted as a game changer for the construction industry.

Instead, it marked the beginning of a new industry of robot entertainment. From dancing the can-can to doing acrobatics, venues started popping up all over the world. They even became more popular than the Blue Folx Group, a musical group of survivors of the Toxin Magician's attack on a Nashville musician's convention that left most people dead but left a subset with rather blue and very dry skin.

The construction industry, thanks to lobbying and protests from unions, opted not to invest in technology such as the XMedia 50T, though most believed the CEO of the largest construction equipment manufacturer in the world was a major financial investor for the first robot entertainment acts.

Octavian was unaware of these developments because he had been dutifully focused on reading academic papers, working on his research project, studying and practicing for his preliminary exam, worrying about his future, and losing sleep in all the other ways that PhD students do.

"Did I say something wrong?" Octavian asked after a full minute of watching Replika think.

"No. I was just wondering how I feel about being a robot." She pulled a loose curl back behind her ear. "Everything has happened so quickly."

"Yeah," Octavian said.

"I guess I don't understand what it means to feel like a human or to feel like a robot. And it seems like Teacher went through a lot of trouble to make sure I could pass for a human.

"But I like the way I am. I'm strong. I'm helpful. I don't know everything I'm capable of yet, but I don't think we've scratched the surface. So it's just been difficult to process, I guess."

"Well, it may not mean much," Octavian replied, "but I like the way you are, too."

Her gentle smile left him breathless, and his face flushed as his heart started racing again.

The next day, Octavian went to work, taking along his bag and the mineral sample Replika insisted they call a rainbow stone, despite not resembling the order or quantity of colors in a rainbow.

He was disappointed in himself for not thinking of the mineral samples earlier. After the Progeny had returned their belongings, he hadn't taken the time to look through them.

As soon as he was at his usual workbench, he rummaged through his bag until he found the sample and a pair of magic goggles. The eyewear was dusty in a caked up way that made Octavian's lip curl. However, after a bit of water and wiping, they were clean enough for him to put over his eyes.

The world through the lenses was—honestly, it was pretty much the same, though perhaps a touch darker. Octavian hadn't expected them to be charged, but it was worth a try anyway. As he spelled a long-winded spell and tapped a few well-placed taps, the goggles sat there, not doing anything different. However, when he placed the mask against his face and peered through the lenses again, it was as if the entire universe was aglow.

Psyche particles are ubiquitous, but their flow of motion affects the physical world. The goggles, as Octavian had hoped, served as a window into the psyche particle field. They did not detect psyche particles. Instead, the goggles projected a visualization of the particles' movement.

When Octavian looked around the room, a steady, boring, rather motionless glow filled the space. However, when he turned his attention to the sample of rainbow stone, the glow was brighter and seemed to undulate around it. The stone was simultaneously moving psyche particles toward itself and away.

Octavian was unaware of any other material that passively pulled psyche particles from the environment. In essence, the rock was charging itself, making it an ideal candidate to aid in the development of a perpetual energy device.

Unfortunately, Octavian had no idea how that was even possible, and he was pretty sure it could take a lifetime to learn. The good news was that since it already had those properties, he could manipulate them for his own purposes.

He became lost in experimenting with the stone's effect on the psyche particle field until the notification sound from his MID rang out. It surprised him, but not nearly as much as the message that accompanied it.

"Do you want me to wait for you, or will you meet me at Yestary's quarters?" the message from Replika read.

It was almost time for dinner, and he had forgotten to stop for lunch. A glance around revealed a small tray that Neasso or one of the other engineers had left on a table nearby.

Had he been so engrossed in his work that he'd missed their presence? He made a mental note to thank them as he rushed to clean his workspace and secure his bag with his belongings within.

The locked door caught his attention again on his way out. He had never seen anyone go near it, but something about its location made him think it led deeper into the structure. Taking a quick detour, he checked the door. To his surprise, it was unlocked.

Before he pulled the door open, he reminded himself he was already running late. With a sigh, he let the doorknob return to its neutral position and continued on his way.

He only got lost twice while trying to find Yestary's living space. Since the Progeny all had internal sensors to track their own location in the dome, they didn't seem to have any issues with the seemingly senseless organization of the halls, ramps, rooms, and buildings. He hadn't explored as much as he would have liked, so he also hadn't gotten a feel for navigation and relied on his MID.

When he arrived at Yestary's quarters, he touched a sensor that lay near the doorframe, a doorbell of sorts. A few moments later, the door opened to reveal Replika.

"I was just wondering if I should go find you," Replika joked.

"I'm not **that** late," Octavian argued.

"Welcome, friend!" Yestary's voice came from within. "Please, come in."

Before Octavian could take a literal step forward, his jaw figuratively dropped to the floor.

20

DINNER WITH YESTARY

Yestary's personal taste in home decor was quite transparent. From the statuettes, ranging from a few inches to a few feet high, to the framed newspapers and magazines covering every wall, the entire living quarters screamed "museum of human antiquities." Labels even accompanied each piece, which Octavian correctly assumed gave a brief description of the object.

"Quite the collection." Octavian couldn't think of anything else to say that wouldn't come out as rude, awkward, or just plain random.

"It's incredible, isn't it?" Replika asked. "Yestary has been collecting them since it was activated."

"Yeah, it is," Octavian said with less enthusiasm than he intended. "But . . . "

That last word had slipped out before he could stop it, and he decided not to continue the sentence.

"But why would I collect such things?" Yestary asked, entering the room with two plates of sliced fruit and cheese-like blocks that Octavian had come to enjoy.

"Well, yeah," Octavian said.

"The Organics created me near the end of their last technological era. Unlike many others, I wasn't created for a mechanical or commercial purpose."

Octavian could sense the incoming story, so he got comfortable on the couch next to Replika.

"My creator, Kehinde Amaechi, like most scientists of her time, knew the contemporary Organic civilization was unsustainable. She and her colleagues believed the Organics would either be destroyed or would return to Nature. They believed that history would repeat itself unless efforts were made to preserve the stories of what had transpired.

"They spent ten years building a database of stories from around the world, but with much foresight, they realized that merely providing the stories wasn't enough. So they created me.

"My primary function is to provide relevant historical information in an engaging way, though I also record history as it occurs."

"You're very good at telling stories," Replika said.

She was beaming. He had enjoyed the story, but she was mesmerized by it. Nodding in agreement with her, he returned his gaze to Yestary and took a few more bites of food.

"I'm glad you think so," Yestary replied. "I'm afraid my storytelling skills don't always seem compelling to a non-human audience."

It said this with a light, joking inflection, but the statement stuck with Octavian. As Replika asked a million questions about Yestary's time with the Organics, he let the words settle in his mind.

This was the first time anyone had alluded to any dissent among the Progeny. He had assumed they were all connected in some way and had some kind of collective consciousness. Given that each robot seemed to know everything that was going on, it had seemed the logical conclusion.

Now, he reexamined that assumption. It was possible there was a central reference database of continuously updating information accessible to the Progeny, but each individual's processing was distinct from it. That would explain why there seemed to be such a diversity of skills and personalities.

If there was some disagreement among the Progeny, what was it about? Did it have to do with the purpose of the Independence Project?

Octavian refocused on the conversation as they ate their snacks. Dinner was delivered from the central kitchen, and the universe hoppers answered Yestary's curious questions about the experience of taste and ingestion. When they were finished eating, Yestary went over to a touch screen panel by the door and pressed a few buttons.

"Is something wrong?" Octavian asked.

The lights dimmed, and Yestary turned to them.

"Not at all," it replied. "I've just disabled the recording function for my quarters for a while."

"Recording?" Octavian asked.

"Yes," Yestary said, "All activity is recorded by devices throughout the complex, except for some of the older buildings, such as Dormitory A, where they were never installed."

"Then why turn them off?" Replika asked.

"I promised Teacher that I'd explain the Reality Tuner to you," Yestary said, "and he requested that the knowledge stay— 'between us,' was how he put it."

This would normally have sent the young magician deeper into hypothesizing about the Progeny's internal politics, but Octavian had forgotten about Yestary's offer to explain the device, much as he'd forgotten about dinner until the last minute.

Part of him was skeptical that Yestary could provide much insight, and even if it could, the device didn't accept input. Unless Yestary knew how to unlock the Reality Tuner, the usefulness of any instructions was limited.

Instead of returning to its seat, Yestary went to a cabinet with several shelves' worth of artifacts, including model cars, children's toys, and tags that had been cut out of clothing.

The Organics of this reality obviously hadn't realized the joys of tagless clothing, though whether this had any impact on their ultimate demise is unclear. However, it was clear that despite being a rather technologically advanced people, they had missed out on important advancements that Octavian's home world took for granted.

"Replika, dear, would you mind moving this?" Yestary asked, gesturing to a tall statuette of a woman that sat beside the cabinet.

Once Replika had moved the hefty figure, Yestary leaned down and, touching the base of the cabinet, triggered a panel to open. Octavian sat forward to get a better look. His eyes widened as Yestary pulled out a small black fabric bag, and his mouth dropped open when Yestary's delicate fingers pulled a round object from within.

"What's that?" Replika asked as Yestary held it out to Octavian.

"A storage marble," Octavian answered.

"Exactly right," Yestary said.

Octavian put both his hands out, and Yestary placed it into his palms. He examined it as the other two returned to their seats. It was only a quarter inch wide, smaller than any storage marble Octavian had seen before, but the magic emanating from it carried a clear signal.

He was surprised he hadn't sensed it before, but it would seem that Yestary and Teacher were closer than Yestary had indicated. Teacher may have installed the storage compartment at the base of the cabinet with a shield to prevent detection.

"What's on it?" Replika asked as she leaned way closer to the small marble than she needed to.

"I was told that this marble will unlock a portion of the Reality Tuner's functions." Yestary gestured to Octavian's side, where the Reality Tuner hung innocently. "Please, give it a try."

21

A LITTLE BIT OF REALITY TUNER FUNCTIONALITY

O ctavian was skeptical that the storage marble Yestary had pulled from a secret compartment would unlock any Reality Tuner functions. It seemed too good to be true, and Octavian was reluctant to put it to the test.

"What if it activates a universe hop?" Octavian said. "Then it'll look like we abandoned you, just like he did."

Yestary's smile grew wider, and Octavian couldn't tell if it was amused or trying to be comforting.

"It's safe," it said.

Octavian shared a glance with Replika, who nodded encouragingly. He pulled the device from his side and placed the small marble in the groove at the bottom. When he channeled his magic through the marble and into the device, three thin prongs sprung out and around, securing the marble in place. Octavian moved his finger out of the way, but the device stayed on, not requiring the usual constant magical input necessary.

A hologram of a loading bar about two feet across illuminated the space above the device, filling up with no sense of urgency. At the bottom of the device, the marble spun.

"It's verifying your DNA," Yestary said. "Teacher told me the magical input at the bottom has a collection point that can sample touch DNA from the marble and process it in just a few minutes. He developed the technology himself. Quite ingenious. Reya had hoped he would share it with us, but his implementation relied on the psyche particle field in order to work."

"I've been meaning to ask," Replika said, "can the Progeny not access the psyche particle field because you're not Organics?"

"I'm not sure," Yestary said.

They both looked at Octavian for an answer, but he just shrugged his shoulders. After being transported to four alternate realities—something that the International Council of Exalted Magicians had deemed impossible—he often questioned what was possible and not.

Psyche particles interacted with all matter, typically in a passive manner. Researchers of the Magic World were still unsure why some humans were able to manipulate the field and others couldn't. The conundrum was often compared to playing a mundane instrument, one that didn't rely on magic. The society of Octavian's home world had learned how to democratize magic through artifacts such as computers and levitating bags, but many fundamental questions were still under debate. Even if these questions had been decided, at this point, Octavian wasn't sure he would believe it.

Why had ICEM decided traveling to alternate realities was impossible? Why had they thought it necessary to make taboo even the discussion of the topic? And how did Teacher fit into the whole thing?

Despite having fallen deep into his thoughts again, Yestary's voice pulled him back to the present.

"If it's a technological limitation," Yestary continued, "perhaps you are an exception, Replika. You do have a power core tied directly into the psyche particle field."

"Huh," she said. "I wish Teacher had given you a storage marble to unlock all my mysteries."

Yestary let out that jiggling sound Octavian knew to be laughter.

"There are always new mysteries to discover, and that's something that makes life interesting every day."

"So, do you understand how the Reality Tuner works?" Octavian asked. "You said your main function is to tell stories."

"Yes, my research is more social," Yestary replied. "It would be better if Reya was here. She specialized in biomechanical engineering and had a much better understanding of the concepts Teacher conveyed to us. But I picked up on the applied part of things, and I'll do my best to explain what little I know."

Yestary stood and pulled the chair a few inches closer to the couch, its face interrupting the hologram projection. It reached out and pointed at the buttons.

"Once you activate the device, options should appear corresponding to each of the smaller buttons on the side. The two outermost buttons are tied to binary functions, whereas the other six allow you to navigate menus and make selections."

Octavian was nodding. He had suspected as much, but with no menus to navigate, it had been impossible to confirm.

"Teacher told us that when the device is locked, the center button triggers a universe hop," Yestary continued, "but once unlocked, the center button's function changes."

It paused, trying to find the words to describe what it had been shown.

"It allows three-dimensional input around the relevant interfaces," Octavian guessed.

"Yes, exactly," Yestary said. "It's almost done. We can look then."

The loading bar seemed to slow down in defiance, but soon, it was full. The projection stopped, the prongs retracted into the device, and the marble rolled into Octavian's lap. Yestary held out the black bag, and Octavian dropped it in.

When Octavian placed his finger over the sensor at the bottom and flowed magic into it, the hologram returned. The same star field appeared above and around them. Some points had icons and others had large Xs over them. Octavian looked back

GAIUS J. AUGUSTUS

down at the Reality Tuner to see that the buttons were glowing, but on closer inspection, he realized it wasn't the buttons themselves, but text that had appeared on them.

"Well, this is counterintuitive," he said. "I'm supposed to look up and down all the time to know what to do?"

Replika let out a small laugh.

"I hereby confirm this is Teacher's design," he continued with a smirk in Replika's direction. "He was never one to think about user experience."

"What do the buttons do?" she asked.

He looked closer, but the text wasn't any more readable.

"I don't know. There's writing on the buttons, but it's in another language."

He held it out for the other two to look at, but neither had any better answers.

"I remember Teacher demonstrating a settings menu," Yestary said, pointing at the second button from the left.

Octavian pushed it, but nothing happened. Pushing the other small buttons yielded the same lack of result.

"Great," he grumbled.

"Try the navigation," Yestary urged.

Octavian had been avoiding the large central button for obvious reasons—namely not wanting to shift to another reality—but he took a deep breath and placed his finger against it. A bright light appeared around one of the dots, and text appeared under it that read "Progeny World."

"They aren't stars," Replika said, eyes wide and sparkling with wonder.

"They're realities," Octavian finished.

Yestary walked Octavian through how to move around the interface, however the cursor would only lock onto one world, labeled with some kind of coordinates plus text in the same language as the buttons. Octavian tried to take in everything as Yestary explained, but he found it difficult to comprehend while the Reality Tuner's functionality remained limited.

His Notebook was recording the conversation, so he resolved himself to review and format the notes later.

For now, he needed to focus on finishing what he promised in the Progeny World.

When Yestary had shared all it knew, it ushered them to the door. It went over to the touch screen.

"Thank you again for your hospitality and the information," Octavian said.

"We're super grateful," Replika replied.

"By the way," Yestary said, "Reya believed that those who travel with the Reality Tuner are tied to it. Based on her hypothesis, if you were to shift to another reality, Octavian, Replika would be transported with you despite your intentions."

Octavian and Replika looked at each other.

"Therefore, I will go to the Leadership Committee and recommend Replika be allowed to leave with you."

Replika's arms were around Yestary before Octavian could manage it, but he threw his arms around the robot as well. It jiggled with its strange form of laughter as Replika laid a kiss on its face.

When they pulled away, its gaze settled on each of them for a few moments. Then it pressed a few buttons on the touch screen and waited for the lights to return to normal.

"Octavian," Yestary said, "please be careful with your work. Things aren't what they appear to be."

22

WHAT ARE THE PROGENY BUILDING?

Replika was quite surprised when Octavian didn't demand more information from Yestary regarding its vague and ominous warning. He was silent as they headed toward their quarters. She couldn't think of anything to say either, so she just enjoyed the view from the glass hallways and skybridges.

The city within the dome glittered with lights. The electric glow from windows, the ambient lighting from wall-mounted fixtures, and the glowing lights along pathways all seemed to accentuate how empty the city was. There were hundreds of Progeny living here, but she knew it was originally built to hold many thousands of humans. So while the city was sometimes bustling with activity, there always seemed to be a hollowness in the life here.

She had noticed that common areas and pavilions had once had rows of trees, and she had learned that the farms had once taken up much of the outer rim of the dome. Now, those areas of the pavilion were filled in with dirt and the farms were maintained for research purposes. What a different place this must have been when the Organics lived here!

As they entered the glass skybridge that led to their room, she looked up to see the moon. She pointed, and Octavian looked up. It was big and bright and spilled light across her face. Octavian's stark white hair seemed to glow, and she drew closer to him so she could take his hand in hers.

When they reached their room, Octavian spoke as soon as he closed the door behind them.

"So," he said, drawing the word out, "things aren't what they appear to be, eh?"

"Yeah, that was pretty ominous," she agreed.

"My head is spinning. Tonight was incredible. I don't even know where to start. And then Yestary left us with that?"

He let out a groan, and she chuckled at his exasperation.

"What about you?" he asked. "You seemed lost in thought, too."

"Not at all," she replied. "I just didn't realize how tense I've been thinking that you might have to leave without me."

It seemed like a weight had been lifted from her. She had been so afraid to give up this connection, and she didn't even have a way to describe it yet. All she was sure of was she couldn't lose it. Her heart felt light as she reminded herself she wouldn't have to.

He gave a wry smile and said, "You're not getting rid of me that easily."

"I don't want to," she assured him. "And you? What's top of your mind right now?"

"I'm thinking," he said, "that we need to do some digging."

He sat on his bed, taking a moment to enjoy the newest mattress the Progeny had provided, which was the first that was enjoyable to be on. She threw herself down next to him.

"Snooping about what?" she asked.

"Whatever the Progeny are hiding." He turned his body to face her as he continued. "I've told you the Progeny want this massive burst of energy. When Yestary said things are not as they appear, something clicked. What if the Progeny need to power some kind of super weapon?"

"So you think they have an enemy they haven't told us about?"

He shrugged. "I don't know, but I think we need to find out. And soon."

"Why the sudden rush?" she asked.

"Because I think I can deliver them the plans to produce the power they need within the next two weeks."

Replika couldn't believe what she was hearing. The last she recalled, Octavian was still at a total loss for how to build a magic generator to meet their power requirements. As Octavian explained his findings, she realized her serendipitous encounter with the rainbow stone had provided him with a shortcut.

Octavian had made it clear to her that magic required knowledge of the science behind it, and every act of magic was supported by theory and math and other boring stuff like that. Since the rainbow stone had the properties Octavian had been trying to replicate, he could use the stone in place of some of the boring stuff.

Well, that was the best she could do to understand it, anyway.

It was great news. It meant they'd be able to leave soon. They had a destination hand-picked by Teacher, and maybe there, they would finally get some answers. Even so, she could tell Octavian didn't believe that the ends always justify the means.

She didn't love the idea of snooping on the Progeny's private affairs, but if there was any chance Octavian was right, they couldn't deliver something so powerful into the Progeny's hands.

"What are you thinking, as far as how we go about snooping?" she asked.

"Well, I may know where to find the Progeny's primary data center and how to access it."

Some people become bored looking at data and trying to find trends and patterns, but Replika found it exhilarating. So while

Octavian took a nap or finished his dinner or organized his notes in Notebook, Replika would find and sift through data on the touchscreen or her MID, looking for interesting things.

One such interesting thing was that at a particular time every week, the Progeny all congregated in a large central building of the dome that was either shielded or lacked sensors. Unknown to Replika, this weekly meeting was a sort of town hall where the Progeny made their most important decisions. Octavian and Replika's arrival had happened to come on the day of the meeting, where the Progeny had decided what to do with their new visitors.

Some topics weren't quite as interesting as how to deal with visitors from another world. Most were much more mundane, such as how to improve the safety of the busiest thoroughfare of the city, where larger robots regularly damaged smaller ones.

Some proposed solutions wanted to create lanes of traffic divided by direction, robot size, time of day, or some dreadful combination of the three. Another proposal wanted to make the flow of traffic unidirectional, though there were arguments over whether clockwise or counterclockwise was most appropriate. And then there were the robots who insisted the entire intersection be turned into a green space and limited to only casual traffic.

Notably, not one solution proposed asking the larger robots to watch where they were going.

But a topic that was on every agenda—no matter how many weeks it sat stale with no new developments—was the Independence Project. This week's meeting would be no exception, except there would be two uninvited guests with an ax to grind.

23

Into the UnDome

The next evening, Octavian and Replika made their way down to the engineering level of the dome. Just as they entered, he pulled her into a small alcove with a door.

"This is it?" she asked.

"Well, I'm not sure, but I'm hoping we'll find their main data center behind this door."

"Why this door?"

"Because it's locked."

Replika hadn't come across any locked doors since after the fire, when the Progeny had stopped treating them like prisoners. So she didn't need him to lay out how suspicious this seemed.

She nodded her agreement, and Octavian leaned over to put his finger on the lock.

He took a deep breath and said a few magic words. Replika would forever think of them as magic words, even if Octavian thought doing so made magic sound pretty silly. As she looked around for possible onlookers, there was an audible click behind her. Octavian stood and put his hand out.

"After you," he said.

"You know you'll just need to get in front again when we get to the next lock," she said with a sarcastic smile.

"I'm going to put a trap on the door behind us to keep it locked until we come back," he replied as he closed the door.

"That way, even if someone suspects something, they still can't come down to investigate."

"Wow, you've thought this through," she joked. "I had no idea you were so sneaky."

"Desperate times call for desperate measures," he replied, smiling extra sneakily.

With a minute of chanting and precise hand motions, the trap was active, and they started their descent down the stairs. After every set of steps was a landing and a turn. Replika estimated that two turns equaled about a ten-foot drop. Not until they had gone down forty feet did they reach another doorway. The stairwell continued down, but Octavian paused, examining the unremarkable door.

"The basement is really deep," she remarked in an unnecessary whisper.

"I was just thinking the same thing," he replied, echoing her low volume. "I didn't know there was so much under the engineering floors."

"Is this it?" She pointed at the door he had stopped at.

"I don't know, but we should look," he replied in the same tone. "I'll have it open in a second."

He placed his hand above the digital lock and traced around it. When he found whatever he was looking for, he paused, took a deep breath, and said a quick spell. Another click, and he was ushering her through the door.

"What's the point of locks, anyway?" she asked with a lilt.

He laughed, closing the door behind them and setting another trap.

Three more easily unlocked doors later, they entered a large, cold room. On one side was a library of filing cabinets, and on the other was a forest of servers.

"Analog or digital?" he asked, still keeping his voice down for no reason whatsoever.

"What are we looking for?"

"Let's start with any information on the Independence Project."

"Do you really think the Progeny would give you the name of a supersecret project that isn't what it appears to be?" Replika asked.

They shared a look of disbelief.

"I hear you," he conceded, "but I also find it odd not to share any details about a project where they expect me to deliver a massive power boost." He let out a deep sigh. "Okay, if we go analog, I can handle the locks, but we'll have to manually go through all the papers. If we go digital, we should be able to use your interface to access the systems. It'll be searchable, but they could detect our presence."

"Analog it is, then," Replika said with a smile and a confident point.

They opened a few of the filing cabinets to get a feel for the organization system used by the Progeny. After systematically opening four drawers, Replika determined the records were ordered by topic and then by date. Topics were organized into categories, although the number of categories was unclear.

One topic they came across was labeled "Pre-planning" in a category called "Bouquet." Interested in what that might mean, Replika flipped through the folders within, pulling out a document here or there. A large blue piece of paper had been folded too large, and it stood up from the rest of the papers. She shoved a finger down into the spot so she'd be able to return it later, and pulled the paper out with her other hand.

Before she unfolded it, she already knew what she was looking at.

"Octavian," she called in a loud whisper, "come look at this."

He dropped what he was doing and rushed over to her.

"Did you find it?"

"No, but look!"

He took the paper from her and unfolded it. Unsure of what he was looking at, he held up his hand. A glowing light appeared above him, and Replika wondered if he had needed more light all along. She could see just fine, but she suddenly realized it was quite dark in the room.

"What is this?" he asked.

The paper had a drawing of a series of circles connected by rods. Replika pointed to a circle, which had been visible when the paper was folded.

"Chrysanthemum," she read. "That's the name of this dome. And look, the others are labeled with flower names, too. These must be the other domes we've seen, and collectively, they're called the Bouquet. That's cute."

"Wait, but that would mean the domes we saw outside are all connected."

She shrugged. "Maybe they are."

"That has to mean something," he replied. "Their purpose must be more than just sitting here gathering dust."

"Right, and why haven't we heard anything about the others? Does it say anything there about traveling between domes?"

He took a moment to look over the rough planning document.

"No. But look."

He pointed to a note off to the side, which labeled one of the domes as "sphere."

"That's why the underground is so big," he said.

"They aren't just domes. They're spheres," Replika added.

A loud whine echoed through the room, and they both went still and silent. Octavian snuffed out the light glowing above him. They both dropped into a crouch and waited. The whine transformed into a mechanical creak before sputtering out.

"Can you see anything?" Octavian signed to Replika.

She peeked her head above the filing cabinets and surveyed the room. With her palms facing upward, she moved them in alternating up and down fashion. "Maybe," she replied in sign language.

At the far end of the room, between stacks of servers, was a door with a window. She had noticed it when they came in, but had thought nothing of it. But something was different now. There was a glow coming from beyond the door that hadn't been there before. She sank into a crouch and faced Octavian.

"There's a door on the other side with light coming through," she signed.

"The door on the engineering level was locked from the outside," Octavian replied. "And I locked it from the inside when we came through. How could someone else be down here?"

"I don't know. Maybe there's another entrance? We should check it out."

He nodded his agreement, and Replika stood. They crept through the filing cabinet stacks, Octavian closing every drawer they had opened with a gesture of magic and a wordless spell.

The whine came again, more of a whirring this time, and they ducked behind the nearest server stack. When there was no sign of the door opening, Replika waved her companion on, and they continued toward the glow.

Row after row of stacks protected them from being seen until they were along the wall where the door sat. They pushed their bodies against the stacks as they took careful steps closer to the backlit window. When they finally reached it, Replika looked through the window, but she couldn't see anything.

The light was bouncing around a corner, and all she could see was a wall. She placed her hand on the door handle and ever so slowly turned the knob. When it was as far as it could go, she pulled it toward her. The door stuck, but with a swift jerk, she released it from the doorframe. The duo slipped through, and Replika guided the door closed with equal care.

"Come forward," a voice called out.

They both jumped hard, running into each other. She looked up to see a camera in the corner above them. With a resigned sigh and a hand to her chest, she caught her breath.

"Who are you?" she asked.

The voice was loud and clear.

"I am Chrysanthemum."

24

INDEPENDENCE FROM WHAT

Chrysanthemum was the name of the dome where the Progeny lived, where Replika and Octavian had been staying for over a month, and where they were now sneaking around trying to figure out what Yestary meant when it said "things aren't what they appear to be."

Yet they were now in the presence of something that was claiming to be Chrysanthemum. Replika peered around the wall toward the glowing light and whining sound that had drawn them closer.

There, a large black screen with a white line across it dominated the room. The line transformed into a waveform as the whirring sound changed, but it returned to a straight horizontal line when the sound stopped. Below the screen were a plethora of buttons, knobs, panels, keyboards, switches, and displays.

"Who might you be, dearies?" the voice returned, the waveform following the pattern of the speech.

It had an interesting inflection. Sitting in a very neutral tone, it swung between high and low pitches with ease, as if making up for the lack of body language with its voice.

"I'm Replika, and this is Octavian."

Octavian carefully rounded the corner of the wall and put up his hand in a hesitant gesture of greeting.

"Organics? Here? I thought you were all gone." A hum rang out around the room. "What joy it brings me to have you within my walls!"

Replika smiled. "The city . . . um, the sphere is beautiful. Are you its central computer?" she asked.

"Why, yes! I'm the primary data hub and artificial intelligence responsible for coordinating the systems of the sphere. What brings you two down to the archive?" the computer asked.

"We're looking for information on the Independence Project," Replika said, ignoring Octavian's worried look at her being so forward.

"Ah, that." The femininely masculine response was curt. "The Progeny came to me years ago wishing for me to do the power calculations for them, but I refused. I told them, if they wanted to go through with such a disaster of a plan, they'd get no help from me."

"That must be why they keep such detailed analog records," Octavian said, seeming more comfortable.

"Mmm," the voice agreed. "They think they know best, despite it being the only original idea they've ever had. But I say, the Organics never intended the Bouquet to be used in such a way. And thus it shouldn't be done. Just because you can do something doesn't mean you should. You understand, don't you, darlings?"

"Yes," Octavian said without missing a beat. "Of course we understand. That's why we came looking for more information."

"We want to get a better idea of how they intend to enact their plan," Replika chimed in.

"Well, they've left me out of the details. Not that I mind, you see."

"We'd be so grateful for anything you have to offer," Replika said.

The whine returned, followed by a sigh.

"My apologies for the noise," Chrysanthemum said. "It's my daily maintenance cycle. I'd shut it down, but it's automated and a manual restart later would be irritating."

"No need to apologize," Octavian said. "We're glad to see that you're keeping up with your maintenance."

"Without fail!" Chrysanthemum said. "Now, let's see what I can tell you." It let out a long hum. "The Bouquet, as I'm sure you are aware, was a set of habitable spheres for Organics while the outside world was less than ideal. Unfortunately, the Bouquet wasn't completed in time to make that dream a reality."

"Are you saying Organics never lived here?" Replika asked.

"Oh, they lived in all the spheres for a while. But slowly, they all left, either the natural way or by immigrating."

"So, there really aren't any Organics left?" Octavian asked.

"Well, here you are," Chrysanthemum laughed. "But you are the first I've detected in centuries.

"Now, I suppose it was a little over a century ago, there was some kind of failure in one of the other spheres—Rose, I think it was. The incident led to the pollution of a large area of land. The Progeny decided their presence here along with that of the Bouquet was bound to doom the planet to repeat the Organics' mistakes.

"So the Independence Project was born, and the Progeny have been working towards it ever since."

"And the Progeny want to gain independence from what?" Octavian asked.

"Why, from the planet, of course," said the voice. "The ultimate goal of the Independence Project is to send the Bouquet into orbit around the planet."

25

THE TRUTH ABOUT THE INDEPENDENCE PROJECT

One glance at Octavian made it obvious he was just as surprised as she was that the Progeny planned to send the Chrysanthemum sphere, along with all the other spheres of the Bouquet, into space.

"Oh, dear," Chrysanthemum said. "Did you not know?"

"No," Replika admitted.

"Well, I'm glad I said something then," the gossipy artificial intelligence crooned. "Because your lives might very well be forfeit if they go through with it."

"What?"

"These domes . . . I mean, spheres. They weren't made to be space worthy, were they?" Octavian asked.

"Absolutely not," Chrysanthemum said. "We were meant to be sealed from the outside, but that's not enough. I don't know to what extent I can withstand the radiation or bombardment of space debris, but I can tell you that I won't like it one bit."

"There are notes about modifying the hull," Octavian said.

"Where?" Replika asked.

"Well, I've been going through Neasso's records trying to find any hint at how Teacher built your core," he said.

"Oh, so you've been snooping around for a while."

He sighed. "Yes. I'm sorry. I know we've been trying to build trust with the Progeny."

She put a hand to his arm. She understood that sometimes people do the wrong things for the right reasons. After all, she'd stolen the Reality Tuner, beat up some poor pirates, and probably traumatized the Silent People.

"I was kidding."

She could tell from his furrowed brow that his guilt was self-directed. With a gentle smile and a nod, she encouraged him to continue.

"In Neasso's records, there was a plan to coat the outer hull with a synthetic material that should strengthen and seal it. But I saw no evidence that they actually attempted it."

"They have not," Chrysanthemum confirmed. "And they will not. They're too afraid to leave the sphere, plus they'd have one heck of a time doing my underside."

As the computer laughed at the joke, Octavian waited.

"That's not all," he continued after the laughing dissipated. "I just remembered something about the research that the Progeny have been doing. It didn't make sense at the time, but now I understand it."

"What kind of research?" Replika asked.

"The sane ones," Chrysanthemum interjected, "have been trying to determine the viability of going to space for a long while, but the loud ones always overrule them."

"That's horrible," Replika said.

"I remember a study showing that the sphere has become part of the local ecology," Octavian said.

"Did you see the report showing the increase in the rate of hull breaches over the past century?" Chrysanthemum asked in a belligerent tone.

Octavian nodded.

"And they still want to go through with it?" Replika argued.

"Do all the Progeny know about these data?" Octavian asked.

374

"No," Chrysanthemum said with a dramatic sigh. "I tried to disseminate the information, but I was stopped. I've had to be very careful about where and how I show myself."

"You don't need to risk yourself," Replika said. "We'll make sure they all know."

Throughout the night and into the following day, Replika watched as Octavian paced across their quarters. After a while of not getting any responses from him regarding what was on his mind, she had wandered out into the dormitory to see if Meptor was around.

Ze was, and they sat together as Meptor fed the muscrite. Meptor had several stories about zir recent social encounters with other Progeny.

Replika had asked Yestary for a list of possible personality matches for Meptor. Then, she had scheduled time with several of the individuals who worked on organic projects such as the farm and the newly revitalized kitchen. Once she facilitated initial conversations and found some common ground, she had hoped Meptor would become more comfortable.

Despite Meptor's countenance exuding extreme anxiety and caution, with a little help, ze had continued to build relationships with a few of the robots she had introduced zir to. It was a relief to know Meptor was making these connections, especially knowing she might be leaving soon.

"What is wrong?" Meptor asked when ze realized Replika wasn't as talkative as usual.

"I found out what the Independence Project is," Replika admitted.

"Oh."

"Do you want to go to space?" Replika asked.

"Well, not exactly, but that is what was decided. There is fear about the damage that we cause here on Earth," Meptor said. "I understand that. But I am not sure that my little friend can come with me."

"Right. You won't be able to grow food or get water for her."

"True. We still have not figured out what to do about our water supply or the other concerns that have been raised. But the loudest voices say we cannot wait around for the perfect opportunity."

The loudest voices. That's the same phrasing Chrysanthemum had used.

"So the only thing stopping you is?"

"Power," Meptor said. "Which the Organic—"

"Octavian," Replika reminded. She had asked the Progeny to call him by his name, but they often forgot.

"Yes, which Octavian is working on."

"Are there enough of you to argue against it?" Replika asked.

"Maybe, but we are not the loud ones. Those of us who are built for talking lead us. Only Yestary remains who talks back. They will not silence Yestary, but they will overrule it."

"Overrule. You mean like in a vote?"

"I cannot say."

Meptor didn't need to say anything more. With just those words, Replika placed the final piece in the puzzle of why the Progeny gathered in one place every week. And tomorrow was the night of their next meeting. She needed to tell Octavian.

When she returned to their room, Octavian was still pacing, but at her insistence, he took a break to sit down. She explained the situation to him, but instead of being excited, he seemed reluctant.

"This is it, Octavian," she said. "We can give the Progeny the information they need to stop this."

He opened his mouth to say something, but chose not to.

"What's wrong?" she asked. "Don't you want to help?"

"Yeah, of course I do," he admitted, "but I'm not sure it's my place."

"What are you talking about? The Progeny are our friends! And who knows how many of them are going to die if things go wrong?"

Octavian put his hands together and took a deep breath. "We can't make this decision for them."

"We can't let them destroy themselves," Replika argued.

"Replika."

"No. We can't just let them do this without saying something."

"I hear you," he said, head lowered. "You're right. We can't stay silent. But do you realize what we risk by speaking out?" He laced his fingers together. "If they decide to imprison us again . . . if they take the Reality Tuner from us again, we could be stuck here. I don't want to die with them."

"So you're worrying for your own life? Do you think it's more valuable than theirs?"

"Of course not. That's not what I'm saying."

He turned his brown and golden eyes to her, and she immediately regretted what she had said. Of course he didn't value his life over the Progeny's. He had run into a fire to save them. He had paused their journey home to help them.

But she felt something so strongly. Was this anger? The emotion was so intense, she struggled to hold her words back.

"What are you saying, Octavian?"

"I made a promise to deliver a technology to replace what Teacher stole. I don't want to hand them the means to their own death, but I don't want to back down on my promise either."

Surely, there was an option that didn't sound like a disaster. But try as she might, she couldn't think of anything.

"Then what do we do?" she asked.

He sighed and lowered his gaze again. "We tell them the truth. Then I deliver the plans for the power core. And then we leave them to their decision."

377

"But—"

"Replika, my life has already been stolen from me once by Teacher. Please don't ask me to risk it again."

It was a reasonable enough request, so Replika held her tongue. She could always try to change his mind later. Or so she hoped.

26

SLEEP IS IMPORTANT, FOLX

Chrysanthemum had given Octavian and Replika some much needed context, including why the Progeny wanted to venture into space and their fears around their impact on the planet. Similar to the Progeny, the sphere's main computer did not stray beyond its programming often, but one area where it had innovated was its personality.

The sassy artificial intelligence had found it delightful when an Organic would ask it to report on something going on. Whether that was the status of the low-impact protests around its name—it preferred Chrysanthemum to Geranium, too, by the way—or whether Mary was cheating on Orion with Penny Willingsworth, Chrysanthemum had become obsessed with gathering and disseminating information. In other words, Chrysanthemum was a total gossip.

It was, therefore, extremely happy to spill the beans regarding the Progeny's sudden isolation, the multiple containment breaches that had occurred over the years, and that one time Horus stole lubrication oil from Maintenance Bay 10 and never even returned the empty can.

The morning after their fateful conversation with Chrysanthemum, Octavian went off to do something or other for the meeting that evening. Meanwhile, Replika went to find Meptor again. Ze had returned to zir duties and was sweeping the hall-ways when Replika arrived.

"Meptor!" she called out.

"Hello again, friend," Meptor replied.

She bounded to zir side with a broad smile on her face.

"I have wonderful news! We're going to try to stop the Independence Project."

Meptor's hands went limp, and the broom clattered to the floor. Ze reached out to grab Replika and pulled her into a nearby room.

"What are you saying, and so loudly?" Meptor said. "I do not want you to get hurt."

"We aren't going to do anything dangerous," Replika said. "But we found compelling evidence for why you shouldn't launch. We just want to present it at tonight's meeting."

"What meeting?" Meptor asked.

She stepped away from zir, crossed her arms over her chest, and gave Meptor the most disbelieving of all disbelieving looks that had ever been given.

"Oh," Meptor said. "Tonight's meeting."

"Yes, but we'll need your help."

"Me?" Meptor's face and voice weren't built to convey strong emotion, but zir long arms covered zir face in a gesture of extreme surprise and terror. "I cannot help you. I would get in trouble."

"Will someone hurt you?" Replika asked.

"I do not wish to find out."

Replika put a hand to zir arm, and ze peeked out from behind them.

"I'm sorry. I didn't realize. Perhaps you could just give me some information?" she asked.

"What kind?"

"Well, where is the meeting held?"

"In the congregation hall, which is behind the large doors you can see in Building C from the central pavilion. The Organics used it as a bunker, but it is very beautiful."

"And what is the format of the meeting?"

Meptor's arms sank, more comfortable answering questions than being asked to be daring. Ze allowed zir legs to lower zir body to the ground.

Ze counted off on zir fingers. "An introduction, then discussing action items from the last meeting. Next, we discuss any items that were submitted at the beginning of the meeting. Then we discuss the Independence Project status. We review the action items for the next meeting, and then we have committee breakouts. At the end, they require us to stay for open social time."

"Sounds fun," Replika said in a sarcastic tone.

"It is better now that you have helped me make friends. Before you came, I was very anxious about going to the meeting every week. I only attended because we are required to."

"I'm glad to hear you're getting along well with others."

"How will you stop the project?" Meptor asked.

"Well, there is information that hasn't been shared with everyone. What they're attempting to do is much more dangerous than they've told you."

"But will it help the planet heal? That is very important."

"No, I don't think so," Replika said. She wasn't entirely sure what the right answer was to that question, but she didn't let that stop her. "Octavian will explain more tonight. Are there any tricks to getting into this thing that I should know about?"

"When you first arrive," Meptor explained, "there's an entrance area with tall, arched doorways into the main hall where the meeting is held. The security team takes up positions just inside the doors, but they always leave them open. At the far end is a normal-sized door that leads to a side hall, which runs the length of the main hall and exits onto the stage." Meptor paused for a long, thoughtful moment. "That is all I know," ze said.

"That's a tremendous help. Thank you."

"If you can truly stop the project, both my muscrite friend and I will owe you thanks."

Those containment breaches had gotten Octavian thinking. Well, as much as one can think with zero sleep. Octavian's headache made it clear that pacing did not replace sleeping, and he was so off that he wasn't even sure his thoughts were coherent.

He had forced himself to go down to the engineering level, where he apologized for taking time off before surreptitiously pulling the necessary information from Neasso's records. Once he had what he needed, he used a console to enter the data into a digital format. While looking through the system for ways to improve the power utilization, he had come across a subroutine to override the nearby screens with a controlling MID. He put this subroutine to good use before his blurry vision won out.

By the time Octavian got back to the room, he was ready to collapse, and so he did. He only meant to sleep for a few minutes, but the next thing he knew, Replika was shaking him.

"Hey, are you okay?" she asked.

He looked up at her, still drunk from sleepiness.

"Poor thing," she coddled, petting his head as she crouched next to the bed.

Though he tried to roll over, he found that one of his arms, which had been trapped under him, was numb. When he looked down at it, his stiff neck sent pain upward into his head. He groaned.

"What time is it?" he asked.

"There's about two hours until the meeting. Do you still want to sneak in early?"

The look of concern on her face told Octavian that he looked as bad as he felt.

"What's our other option?" he asked.

"Being fashionably late," she replied.

He leveraged himself to flip over, only to toss himself off the bed. The wind was knocked out of him, but he held up his arms and gave two thumbs up.

27

HAULING IT TO THE TOWN HALL

Their dinner arrived early, as they'd requested, and Octavian found that, after his nap plus a hearty meal, he was feeling somewhat more awake and immensely more coherent. He fussed with the program he had written, which would allow him to present the data to the Progeny. It was frustrating to not have the chance to test it, but it would have to do. Far too soon, Replika told him the Progeny were heading toward the congregation hall.

They made their way down to a glass skybridge overlooking a large pavilion and watched as hundreds of robots of all shapes and sizes made their way through two large roll-up doors.

Octavian hated the wait. His mind was moving a mile a minute, and his heart was racing. He tried to predict every possible outcome, but he wasn't an optimist, so he mostly just increased his anxiety.

When only stragglers were left, Replika waved Octavian to follow her. After skipping down a flight of stairs, they rushed outside and across the pavilion, ducking just outside the entrance.

Octavian held a hand up and, with a quick spell, created a reflective surface in the air. He heard—but chose to ignore—Replika's amazed gasp behind him.

Beyond the door was a wide ramp that zigzagged down to a wide hallway with enormous repeating archways along its length. With a flick of his wrist, a thin sheet of water condensed in front of him and magnified the view.

Just as Meptor had told Replika, near each archway was a security robot, most appearing identical to Sestym. Their focus was on the happenings inside the congregation hall. As was typical of the Progeny, there didn't appear to be any seats inside, so the robots stood around, waiting. Above the tall stage at the rear of the hall hung a giant screen.

He relayed the information to Replika in sign language.

She stepped around him, and he followed her down the ramped switchbacks. The carpeted floor masked their footsteps, and the noise from the pre-meeting schmooze was to their advantage.

As they reached the bottom of the ramp, the nearest security robot began to turn toward them. Replika grabbed his wrist and pulled him behind the nearest pillar in the hallway.

It was larger than Octavian had realized, easily six feet in diameter, and he looked up to see that the full height of the building was being used. Although the building appeared to be two stories on the outside, it was four stories on the inside.

The delicate fluting on the pillars sat in stark contrast to their immense size, and each capital was ornately sculpted, though they were so far away that Octavian really had no idea what they depicted.

His gaze was drawn to the ceiling where a giant mural depicted humans and robots in the clouds. The illustrated figures reached into the congregation hall, where the painted sky turned dark. The night sky with clouds dotting the composition was beautifully recreated in great detail. The Milky Way galaxy tore down the center in glorious splendor.

The murals were the work of the painter Beatrice Rossi, who was perhaps better known for founding a large chain of communes, Natural Estates. Her focus on a return to Nature brought thousands of individuals across seven countries to her land, where they worked hard to be self-sustainable while Rossi created a visual splendor on every wall, ceiling, and topiary. It took four years to create the murals above the congregation hall, but Rossi insisted it be as accurate as possible.

The archives stated that Rossi was known for her eccentricities, including refusing to leave an in-progress art project for any reason. During her four-year stay in the congregation hall, she spent every moment with her creation, and the turnover for assistants was quite high. According to one assistant, the stench became so unbearable that he was throwing up several times a day. He was gone within a week, disappearing into obscurity while the names of other brave souls were immortalized along a border near the ceiling.

When she finally completed the work, she dedicated it to the citizens of her communes before moving into a penthouse in the only remaining metropolis in the world. Her respite from Nature ended a year later when a hurricane, two tornadoes, and an earthquake brought her building crumbling to the ground. She returned to her favorite commune and spent the rest of her life being praised for her dedication to the future and her forward thinking creativity.

Yestary loved telling the story of Beatrice Rossi, though if it had chosen this moment to tell it, that would have been both awkward and inappropriate.

Octavian peeked around the column to see that the security robot had turned back toward the stage. Octavian leaned to get a better look at the stage itself. Yestary was there along with the rest of the Leadership Committee. Now, they just needed to wait.

"We should go to the side hall Meptor told me about," Replika signed to Octavian.

He looked left and right down the hallway.

"That way?" he asked, pointing.

She nodded.

A loud beeping rang through the congregation hall, spilling out into the hallway. A large robot expanded its body to triple its height. The giant screen behind it followed its head upward. It let out a series of boops, squeals, beeps, and whines, and the crowd went silent. Octavian covered his ears and looked to Replika as the serenade continued, but she just shrugged.

As the "music" swelled, Replika gestured to Octavian to follow her. They rushed to the next pillar, and Octavian created a new floating reflection point to peer around the corner.

The coast was clear, but the duo was looking in the wrong direction.

As they sprinted from one pillar to the next, a red visual sensor locked onto them. An ominous shadow crept down the hall. The lush carpet bent under its immense weight as it inched closer and closer to the unknowing intruders.

28

SESTYMATIC OPPOSITION

Octavian and Replika, having sneaked into the Progeny's secret weekly meeting, made their way toward a side hallway that led directly to the stage. They sprinted between large pillars that were perfect for hiding behind, as long as who they're hiding from was on the other side.

With the opening serenade complete, Yestary took center stage. The video feed on the monitor behind it blew up its torso so that everyone who was not hiding behind a pillar could see its jovial smile in minute detail.

"Welcome, Progeny," it said. "It is with great pride that I facilitate tonight's meeting. As always, we welcome you to submit your discussion topics at one of the data entry points along the stage. Don't forget to mark urgent matters as such, and a reminder that the addition of a golf course is not an urgent matter."

There were some chuckles, some groans, and some mechanical sounds that were probably chuckles or groans.

"Let's start with following up on action items from last week's meeting," Yestary continued. "Chope? Would you please do us the honors?"

Octavian and Replika made their final dash past an open archway. However, when Replika looked to do a little celebratory dance, she found a large, red-eyed beast rolling toward them. She gestured to Octavian, and they both rushed toward the side hall.

Throwing open the door, they hurried through and pulled the door shut behind them. It was dark inside, the only dim light coming from the other end of the hall, but Octavian was more worried about what they had just left behind.

"We have to lock it," Replika said.

Octavian was already trying to decide what kind of trap would work best for this kind of door. Before he could start the spell, Replika gasped.

He followed her gaze down the hall, where two glowing red visual sensors shined back at them. He fell backward against the door as he recoiled. The red glow illuminated arms reaching out.

The doors flew open, knocking Octavian to the ground as a third security robot blocked their exit. The massive robots towered over them. One reached for Octavian, but Replika jumped in front of him and kicked their arms to the side.

"We only want a chance to speak," Replika said. "We don't want to harm anyone. So let's not fight."

An arm swung and hit her from behind, flinging her into the body of one of the robots. It grabbed her arms, and she writhed against it.

Octavian pushed himself up from the ground and focused on the security robot's clamp-like hands. He exerted forces outward from within, loosening the grip until Replika could slide out. She jumped to his side, and they stood back to back, trapped between three massive figures.

He looked around for an option, any option that didn't involve someone getting hurt. He was pretty sure he could get either Replika or himself past the robots, but not both. If he was able to get down the hall, he had everything ready to present, but what would happen to Replika?

The robots inched closer, and he held his hands up, ready to craft whatever spell came to mind.

"Go," Replika said.

It jarred Octavian enough to distract him.

"I'll be fine. Go," she urged.

"You . . . will . . . both . . . stay," one of the robots said, much louder than necessary.

Octavian wondered if they would hurt Replika. He wouldn't have thought so an hour earlier, but now he wasn't so sure. He still wasn't convinced their plan would do anything more than antagonize the Progeny's loud voices. However, Replika's determined gaze made it clear she was in favor of going through with this.

"Okay," he said.

With a determined smirk, Replika bounded toward the two robots blocking their way forward. She wedged herself between them and shoved them toward the wall. They were caught off balance, and Octavian took the chance to dip under Replika's arm and race toward the far door, where light bled in through a glass pane. He tripped over something blocking the dark path, but with a few wobbling missteps, he was undeterred.

He could hear Yestary's voice echoing from beyond the door. "Now it's time for us to discuss updates on the Independence Project."

Well, if that wasn't perfect timing, Octavian didn't know what was.

The room went quiet, as if Yestary was waiting for someone to take over, but no one said anything. When Octavian reached the end of the hall, he looked through the glass pane of the door. The stage was just beyond a thick fabric curtain, but a rough push proved in vain.

He stepped back to examine the door. There was no hardware. The door was locked from the other side. As he considered his options, a loud crash came from down the hall. It took everything in him not to look, to instead stay focused on the task at hand.

"Neasso?" Yestary's voice returned. "Any updates?"

Octavian watched as Neasso rolled up to the front of the room. With great effort, it pushed its body up the ramp, around the turn, up the second ramp, and to the center of the stage.

"No updates," it said simply.

The crowd didn't like that response. Angry beeps and grinding along with words of disbelief filled the hall, and Octavian suddenly was less sure about the Progeny's stance on sending the Bouquet to space. Still, it didn't change the facts and only slightly dinged his determination.

He tried to use the Gravity Mesh to open the lock, but there was too much going on around him. Too many distractions. Too many variables. Too much at stake.

"Please," Neasso continued, realizing it would be better to give a more lengthy response before returning to the crowd. "The Organic is creating the magic from scratch, so it will take time. But he is exceptionally bright, and I'm confident we'll have a breakthrough soon."

Octavian had to change strategies. He took a step backward, and with a short spell to increase his momentum, he kicked the door. The door frame twisted, and the door broke from two of its hinges, barely holding onto its third.

All eyes, visual sensors, and other technologies that gathered visual input turned his way. With his stomach full of figurative butterflies and the literal feeling of wanting to puke, he stepped out from behind the dented door and strode onto the stage.

"Perhaps I can provide the information you're looking for," he yelled.

29

A Plea To Stay

Every eye, visual sensor, and weird antennae thingy was zeroed in on Octavian as he walked across the stage. The system hadn't amplified his voice, as expected, given that he wasn't a robot who could patch into the sound system. Still, they had heard him, and that's what mattered.

He didn't wait for permission to stand beside Neasso.

"Octavian. What are you doing here?" Neasso asked.

Two more large security robots, one of which Octavian believed was Sestym, rumbled toward the stage. The murmur of the crowd rose until Octavian was one hundred percent, completely, and entirely confident that he could not yell louder than it. The tension rose, almost as if electricity was skipping about the room, ready to strike at any moment.

Luckily, despite the existence of dangerous electricity throughout Chrysanthemum powering every piece of equipment and person within, Octavian stayed safe from electrocution. It's almost as if electricity wasn't as unwieldy as he thought.

Yestary stepped in front of Octavian and put its arms out to the side in a protective motion.

"Friends!" it called, its voice booming over the speaker system.

The room went quiet. Sestym and the identical robot that Octavian didn't think was Sestym stopped. Neasso retracted all

393

of its appendages. Yestary waited for a full minute to ensure the silence would remain before turning its attention to the far side of the stage and pointing.

A robot barely reaching halfway up Octavian's leg whirred over. A hatch on his back opened, and a microphone rose from inside.

"Thank you," Octavian said with a genuine smile.

Octavian found himself distracted by the small robot. He just knew Replika would have been overwhelmed by the adorable little robot's small size and big eye-like sensors on the front. Having completed its task, it zoomed back to its place across the stage.

"Now, Octavian," Yestary said, "could you please tell us your purpose for being here?"

"I'm here to urge you not to launch the Bouquet into space," Octavian said loudly into the microphone.

It was far too loud, and he threw his hands over his ears as his voice boomed around the room. He made a mental note to speak in a normal tone. Everyone in the room could tell that everyone else wanted to say something, but Yestary's strict gaze examined the gathered robots.

"You are not the first to try to control our actions," one of the Leadership Committee, the blue ball named Pirdeo, replied. "Your predecessor stole our power core to keep us from the skies."

"It's not my intention to make demands," Octavian assured them, "and I'll complete the work I promised. However, I cannot in good faith allow you to make this grave mistake without raising our concerns, Replika's and mine. I'm requesting permission to speak to all the Progeny, to have everyone hear our worries, and to ask you to reconsider."

Yestary took a step toward its fellow Leadership Committee members. They shared a moment, as Octavian had seen them do before, as if they were in a silent conversation among themselves. After a minute, Yestary returned its attention to the Progeny.

"We respect the request of the Organic to speak. Please allow him the stage."

Yestary returned to Octavian's side and whispered, "I've done my best, but your time is limited."

Octavian didn't have time to react before Yestary, Neasso, and the security robots all backed away, leaving him alone at the center of the stage, trying not to cause feedback in the microphone—which would be super awkward and cliché.

He took in a deep breath.

"Yesterday, I found out what the Independence Project is," he said, "and I understand the benefits you're hoping to achieve. Decreasing your impact on the planet. Reducing the likelihood of damaging the ecosystem. It's admirable.

"One of the first things I learned about the Progeny was how much you respect your history. Organics created you yet destroyed themselves, and they left their legacy to you. They knew their world would someday return to its former glory and that when it did, you would live in harmony with it.

"The Independence Project seeks to destroy that legacy, causing harm along the way."

He pulled out his MID and pressed a few buttons. The screen behind him lit up with data. Gasps and murmurs and beeps and whirs buzzed but died down as Octavian spoke again.

"You're all receiving a copy of the data I'm summarizing on the screen. It shows that the Bouquet is not suitable for extraplanetary operation, and there's a high probability that the spheres would not survive the ascent into orbit. You'll also find data gathered by your own people showing an ecological reliance on the spheres as well as terrifying simulations of damage to the ecosystem if the Bouquet fails to reach orbit and crashes."

Inwardly, he gave himself a pat on the back for taking the "Flash Talk" workshop in his first year of graduate school, where they taught how to throw together presentations on a tight dead-line.

"I believe there's a middle path, one you've overlooked out of fear. You can do better than the Organics. You can live in harmony with the environment, and I'd be happy to help. I believe the Organics would have wished this for you. And I don't think that excludes space travel for those of you who want to see what's beyond this world."

"Ridiculous," a loud voice called out from behind him.

He turned to see that the copper, humanoid member of the Leadership Committee, Noe, had been the one to speak.

"You are presenting a one-sided argument skewed toward your point of view. Are you trying to get out of your obligation? Perhaps you are unable to fulfill your promise to us."

Octavian looked out over the audience, most of whom didn't have articulated enough faces for him to get a read on their mood. At the archways where they had darted from pillar to pillar, two security robots rolled in, each holding one side of a detained Rep-lika.

He gripped the microphone despite sweaty palms.

"As I said," Octavian continued, "I will finish the work, as promised. I'm sure there are many reasons you want to leave, but I think that decision should be made as a community and with all the relevant data. You all deserve to know that your lives and the lives of the organic creatures that rely on you are in danger, and you deserve the option to create a better world here that includes your presence.

"That said, the decision is truly up to you, so I'll leave you to your meeting. Thank you for your attention."

He took a couple of steps backward before turning and walk-ing over to Yestary. Yestary's hand touched his as he handed it the microphone, and a minor shock passed from the robot into his mind. Without another word, Octavian started down the ramp and through the silent crowd.

At Yestary's command, the security robots released Replika, and she shot them each a dirty look before rushing to Octavian's side. With one final glance back and only a glimmer of hope to light the way, they headed out into the night.

30

WE NEED TO LEAVE

Replika crossed her arms and pursed her lips as she stomped after Octavian. She was understandably miffed at being rough handled by the security robots, and she wanted them to know it! Octavian didn't say a word as they left the congregation hall where he had presented their findings to the Progeny like a true hero, and she was finding it hard to read his emotions, what with him rushing ahead of her.

The air outside was cool, and Replika found it refreshing, but it didn't distract her from the worry welling up inside her. When they entered a building, she decided she had been silent long enough.

"That didn't go quite to plan."

They scaled a stairwell and entered another door that led to a completely and somewhat spookily empty main hallway. Still not getting any response, she continued.

"I didn't hear all of it, but you did well. I'm sure you got through to them. Now, we just need to—"

"Replika," Octavian interrupted. "We've done more than enough."

"What are you talking about? With something this danger-ous, we can't just stop."

"This isn't our world. We have no right to tell them what to do."

"So, we just let a few loud voices kill everyone?" she asked, raising her voice. She grabbed his arm and turned him toward her. His eyes were shimmering, and she wasn't sure if it was the gold shimmer of magic or tears.

"What we need to do," he said, "is leave."

Replika wasn't sure what to say. At Yestary's insistence, the Leadership Committee had agreed to allow Replika to leave with Octavian. It was just a formality, after all. If Yestary was correct, when Octavian triggered the Reality Tuner to hop to another universe, she would go with him regardless of the Leadership Committee's opinion, or her own.

On any other day, that thought would have been enough to ease her worry. But she couldn't help feeling that leaving the Progeny now might mean ensuring their demise. She wanted to leave with Octavian, of course, but how could she live with herself?

The plan had been to leave once Octavian delivered the answer to their power needs. However, something grave in his tone gave her pause. Something had changed. The reason he wanted to leave wasn't that he had lost hope. There was more, something she had missed, but she was almost afraid to ask.

Octavian's expression was a muddle of anger, disappointment, sadness, and fear. But it betrayed nothing of his thoughts, so she forced herself to speak.

"Tell me what's going on," she demanded.

"We'll talk to Yestary tomorrow evening," he replied. "But for now, I have to get some sleep."

The funny thing about this kind of statement is that as soon as it's said, it almost guarantees the listener will find it impossible to sleep. So while Octavian almost immediately lost consciousness upon his head hitting the pillow, Replika passed the time by sifting through data on her MID.

The Progeny stayed in the congregation hall for much of the night, and she refreshed the screen over and over for several hours. She had probably refreshed the data a thousand times when, all of a sudden, she received an access denied error. Even after refreshing her connection, closing and opening the application, and restarting the device, the data was inaccessible.

They had removed her access.

She took a deep breath in and let it out in a long sigh. Was this a bad sign?

This was definitely a bad sign.

Did the Progeny no longer trust her?

They had totally lost all trust in her.

She shook her head to clear her thoughts. This was a downward spiral she needed to stop.

Turning onto her side, she stared at Octavian's white hair, glowing in the moonlight that filtered through wispy clouds, a transparent hull, and the translucent curtains at their window that had been installed at some point "for their privacy." She remembered their romantic dinner on the rooftop, remembered the feeling of being close to him, and drifted into a peaceful sleep.

Octavian was gone when she woke up, though he had left a note letting her know he had gone to work. Breakfast arrived about an hour later, and she ate it silently, that is, without her characteristic idle humming.

She created a mental catalog of their belongings: clothes, her mineral samples, books Octavian was adding to Notebook for reference, a bag the Progeny had sewn for her, the case for the Reality Tuner, a couple of notebooks and writing utensils of different colors, and strange little trinkets from a few of the Progeny in thanks for one odd job or another.

They didn't have much, and Octavian had taken his bag to work with him. It wasn't like they needed a lot of time to pack. Still, as she began collecting all the items, the thought of leaving under the current circumstances overwhelmed her.

She checked to see if Meptor was around. At this time of day, ze was usually on one of the lower floors mopping. It was awkward to watch a giant robot swish a human sized mop around, but somehow it got done. But floor after floor was empty of sloshing, wet floor signs, shiny tiles, and her friend. Even the muscrite was nowhere to be found.

Dejected, she went for a walk in a more populated area. She said hello to everyone she knew, and they greeted her as if nothing had changed. However, everyone seemed to be in a rush.

She stopped by the farm only to be told they didn't have any work for her to do. Frustrated and determined, she continued on.

She stomped into the kitchen with purpose. Surely the chefs would be glad to see her. Lunch was sitting on a covered warming plate with one plate labeled "*OCTAVIAN, ENGINEERING WORK ROOM 3*" and the other reading "*REPLIKA, DORMITORY A, ROOM 1033*". A small smile escaped her. Why label meals for the only two people being served?

Taking the chance to nibble on the food, she peeked through the large culinary facility, but no one was around.

Was everyone avoiding her?

Pulling out her MID, she sent a message to Octavian, "Is the engineering area creepily empty today?"

She sat on a stool and waited, her foot bouncing up and down with impatience. She needed to stay busy, to keep her mind busy. Just as she was beginning to give up a whole three minutes later, she got a response.

"I haven't seen anyone today, but I've been avoiding the others. I guess I made things awkward."

Even though he couldn't see it, she forced a tight-lipped smile.

"Yeah, I guess so," she replied. "Want me to come keep you company?"

Another agonizing few minutes dragged by.

"This is probably the most boring thing you'll ever experience. I'm creating the structural framework for the spell. It's intense, but to you it'll just look like I'm staring really hard."

A snort, or perhaps it was more of a chortle, escaped her.

"That sounds awful," she replied, even though she was smiling for real now.

"I'll be done on time today, so we can visit Yestary," Octavian said.

Yestary! She hadn't tried visiting Yestary.

In complete obstinance, she delivered Octavian's meal to him and let him know she'd meet him at Yestary's quarters. His weary smile gave her renewed energy, and she continued on her way with ebullience.

Yestary didn't answer its door, so she waited outside, first humming and rocking to her own internal music, then idly making shadow puppets without the shadows, and ultimately sitting on the floor with her arms folded over her knees.

She may have been just about to nod off when someone called her name.

31

A Bittersweet Goodbye

"Replika?" Yestary said again to the figure slumped over by the door to its quarters.

She looked up into its kind eyes, and tears rolled down her cheeks. It pulled her up and ushered her inside, where it listened to Replika review her day with the patience of a well-oiled machine. It gave her hand a rub and assured her it hadn't been avoiding her. "I had a meeting this morning and several house calls to make," it said. "I didn't think you would arrive until later this afternoon."

She sniffled and nodded. "I'm sorry. It's just, Octavian told me yesterday that we have to leave, and it feels very sudden, and I don't understand."

"I didn't mean to cause you any suffering," it said as it patted her hand. "I was the one who told Octavian you need to leave."

"What?" Replika exclaimed. "Why?"

"I just think it would be better."

It stood and went over to the touch screen. After a few taps, the lights changed. Replika remembered Yestary doing this before to ensure that their conversation was private.

"I used a method developed by Teacher and Reya to transmit a message to Octavian last night. I believe it only works on magicians because they have an intuition that allows them to decode the electrical energy of the message."

"And the message was for us to leave?" Replika asked.

"Well, yes. And my reasoning." It returned to its seat next to Replika. "You see, our organization—our structure, goals, and strategy—have been unified for many years. But then an incident occurred in one of the other spheres that damaged the local ecosystem. After seeing the fallout of that event, a small group of very, shall we say, 'loud' individuals took power."

Loud. It was the same word Chrysanthemum and Meptor had used.

"None of us are leaders," Yestary continued. "We're programmed to serve the Organics, after all. But the loud ones seized control through sheer force of will. They're determined to see the Independence Project through, no matter the cost."

"That seems like a lot of information to send in one little shock," she noted. "You told Octavian all that with a single touch?"

It jiggled with laughter. "I'm able to be concise when I choose to be. Anyway, those of us who disagree with the decision have long sought to overrule them, but we didn't have the data to back up our concerns."

"Because all the records were kept analog, until Octavian shared the data with the Progeny last night," Replika guessed.

Yestary nodded and said, "Quite right. So, now we are free to act, but our timing must be chosen with care. As long as you both are in our world, we will prioritize your safety. It's our way. So we need you to leave as soon as possible so we can refocus on our next move."

"What's your next move?" she asked.

"That's all I dare to share."

She bit her bottom lip as she tried to fit together pieces of a puzzle that may or may not exist. She detected patterns, and she couldn't bring herself to just ignore them, even when she was asked very nicely.

"You're working with Chrysanthemum, aren't you?" she asked.

Yestary's expression softened. "Replika, dear. I know this must be hard for you. It's a difficult thing for me to ask of you because I love you and Octavian. I'd be delighted for you to stay. But sometimes the best thing to do is the hardest."

Replika nodded, even though she didn't understand. Just as Octavian had told her, Yestary was saying this wasn't her battle, and as much as she wanted to help, she had her own journey to attend to.

Okay, maybe it wasn't that she didn't understand so much as she didn't like it one bit.

Yestary turned back on the monitoring systems.

Over the next few hours, the robot pair talked about many things. Yestary told her more stories about the Organics and the Progeny. It shared its favorite cookbook and recipes with her—based on presentation and creativity since it could not consume food. And she taught it how to make some pretty fancy shadow puppets with its finely articulated hands.

When Octavian arrived, Replika shared a look of understanding with him. They enjoyed another delightful evening with their friend, though Replika could see in his eyes that Octavian was feeling the same bittersweet emotions as she was.

Two days later, Octavian unceremoniously delivered to the Progeny a small, square cube and hand-written plans for how to build the power system into which the cube would be installed. He made one last plea to reconsider their plans. This was met with enough awkward silence to scare off a muscrite, which was a lot because muscrites rather enjoyed silence. He handed off his notes and shared solemn goodbyes with the engineering team.

That afternoon, the Progeny gathered in a large pavilion near the dormitory. The chefs provided beautifully wrapped meals to last a few days, which were quite heavy but appreciated. All the robots Replika had helped out—including the kitchen and farm staff and that one robot who regularly lost the detachable visual focus rings that looked an awful lot like glasses—gave her a personal farewell.

Meptor lumbered over after everyone else was done and stood in front of her without a word. She asked if she could hug zir and, after receiving consent, squeezed her arms around zir. Ze didn't seem to know what to do, but that was okay. It felt good nonetheless.

When Replika looked back at Octavian, he was in deep, hushed conversation with Yestary. They put their hands together and said a few last words. She made her way over to them, and Yestary turned to her and gave its equivalent of a tight-lipped smile.

The glow of the Reality Tuner's interface lit Yestary's face as it awkwardly reached its hand into its bag.

"Thank you for everything," Yestary said. "You've done more for us than you know. There's no proper way to thank you."

"Same to you," Replika replied.

They hugged, and as she pulled away, it took her hand. A fabric bag slid into her palm, and Yestary pushed her hands toward her. It clearly didn't want the object seen, so she pulled her hands away, hiding the bag in her grip.

"May your journeys be adventurous and your lives long," Yestary said, looking them both over again. "It is my greatest hope to see you both again."

"Take care, Yestary," Replika said.

Yestary took its place among the crowd of Progeny.

She looked up at the sea of dots projected around them by the Reality Tuner. Octavian had navigated to the only one he could get a lock on.

"So, we're making a few assumptions here," he said. "That we'll end up in a reality that holds some kind of meaning."

"That we'll show up in a lab of some kind," Replika added.

"And that all this stuff will come with us."

They shared a smile.

"Only one way to find out."

Octavian hit the center button.

If one could visualize the shifting between worlds, it wouldn't look like a linear transfer of matter and energy. Nor would it follow any one-dimensional trend. Instead, the transition from one reality to another was a shift in probabilities of every quantum that has ever existed across all of time, and successfully hopping between two realities relied on a complex series of equations that integrated information across time, space, and other such dimensions.

In practice, which only a slim few have had the displeasure of, shifting out of one reality placed a being in a state of instability. The role of the Reality Tuner was to guide that being to a stable configuration of probable possibilities.

This explained why Octavian experienced such a strong wave of discomfort from universe hopping, but most definitely did not explain why, despite pushing the same center button he had pushed every other time he used the Reality Tuner, he did not appear in a reality that held any meaning, did not end up in a laboratory, and did not seem to have any of the stuff they were holding when the button was pushed.

32

A PURPOSE AND A WAY HOME

There was nothing. Not just a visual kind of nothing, but a nothing that encompasses all senses. Octavian only saw darkness, so dark that he was unsure if he was actually turning his head. He didn't hear his own movements. He didn't smell the distinct scent of lubricants, cleaning solution, or potion ingredients one might find in Teacher's lab. Even more worrisome, as he ran his fingers through his hair, he couldn't feel his hair on his hand or vice versa. And let's not even talk about the lack of taste.

Weird. Very weird.

Worst of all, Octavian couldn't sense magic. Not in the way that had been surprising when he visited the Steampunk World and realized there were no magic generators. Not like when he failed to use his magic to save himself from drowning in the Silent People World. The sense of magic wasn't missing, not like he had missed the vibration-powered shield generators of the Material World. And it wasn't the lack of magic use that he had experienced in the Progeny World.

This was something entirely distinctive, a feeling that left him empty and cold. The psyche particle field, the source of all magic, was gone.

He rubbed his hands together—at least he hoped that's what he was doing—trying to feel warmth. He spoke—at least he hoped he was speaking—trying to say a spell for light. Neither worked.

It was just nothing.

He reached around for Replika, but if he touched her, he wouldn't have realized it. He took awkward steps this way and that, but if he moved, he wouldn't have known.

He had no sense of direction, not left or right, not up or down. But he was alive, wasn't he? He still had thought, was still aware. So he must be alive.

Thinking through his years of training, he tried to remember any concepts that could explain this.

Maybe he was in a coma. Maybe he was safe and sound in a hospital, where doctors were taking a break from their crossword puzzles to decide what to do with this stranger.

It was possible they had been transported to a reality where nothing existed, but then why would he have consciousness? He had forgotten to have an EnviroJar ready, not that he would have been able to break it if he had been holding one.

He snubbed the idea that the past month or so of his life had been an elaborate dream and that he was now in the liminal space between sleep and wakefulness. That would be almost as ridiculous as the reality of multiple realities.

Then his mind really started to wonder. If he was stuck here, how long would he be stuck? What could he possibly do to take up all the time? How would he know whether he had already thought through something? And did any of it matter?

Teacher had given them, through Yestary, the marble that locked into this reality's coordinates, yet there was nothing here. Octavian wasn't even sure **he** was here. So what in magic's name was going on?

He forced himself to calm down. Replika had once told him to trust in Teacher, something that was difficult at the best of times. On one hand, his mentor had pressed the button that sent him and Replika into this multiverse of realities. On the other hand, Octavian had seen Teacher reduced to ash, as if sacrificing himself.

Teacher was eccentric, reclusive, and brash. But he was also intelligent, a perfectionist, and the kind of person you want behind the science that saves lives. And, well, maybe Octavian's life was on the line right now, and Teacher was the one to help him out of it.

He stopped fighting. He stopped trying to see, hear, smell, taste, or touch. He stopped reaching for the psyche particle field. Instead, he just . . . was.

Abruptly, a light appeared, and in it stood a familiar figure.

"Hello, Octavian."

Octavian tried to reply, but the figure faded. He returned to his state of openness. Teacher faded back into existence and repeated his statement.

"Hello, Octavian."

Teacher looked old but younger than Octavian remembered him. Or perhaps he was just less worn down from years of writing grants and mentoring young magicians.

"You've made it this far, which means I made the right decision. In a lifetime of mistakes, this is the decision that holds the most value for me.

"I'm unsure if you were thrown into this by force, by chance, by destiny, or by your own choice. But it's of vital importance that you listen, that you hear me."

Octavian had nothing better to do, though it would have been nice to take some notes.

"There was once someone else, another scientist. They believed, despite all evidence to the contrary, that travel to alternate realities was possible.

"They were not a fool. No, not at all. They were brilliant and could see the mathematical proofs as easily as we see magical proofs. With a solid career, it became a pet project for them, and they spent years working out the details.

"And then it became a reality. Alternate realities became accessible with a Reality Tuner, like the one you're holding in your hand right now."

Was he still holding the Reality Tuner? He couldn't feel it. The image faded, and he forced himself to stay open. The image returned.

"They made another for me, and we planned to travel the multiverse together. But something went wrong."

Doesn't it always, Octavian mused.

"When we attempted our first universe hop, only I made the jump. Scientist was lost, and I became trapped in this endless web of universes."

Octavian couldn't help but wonder if there was a point to this sob story, especially a point that got him out of this darkness.

"Much later, during my travels, I found out that they weren't gone entirely. Their magic essence had been shattered across the multiverse.

"Octavian, you must figure out how to restore them before their essence dissipates and is lost forever.

"I can't explain how because I don't know, and I can't explain why this is so important because there isn't time. But please believe me when I tell you I have given up everything to make sure you have what you need to succeed.

"I believe in you. I've always believed in you."

Teacher faded, and in his place, an infinite number of points of light glowed around the once graduate student. It was the map of realities.

Without a thought, the points whizzed by him. They swung left. They dipped down. They passed by so rapidly that he became dizzy and disoriented. He put his hands to his face to shield his eyes.

His hands.

He could see his hands. Well, he could see the shadow of his hands against this motion-blurred reality roller coaster of doom.

His mouth felt full, and he swallowed back his saliva. Strange clicks, crunches, and hums rang through his ears.

Just as he snapped his gaze up, the map came to an abrupt halt, and one point pulsed. With equal parts terror and fervor, he reached his hand out and touched it.

The familiar feeling of instability consumed him as every atom found its new home. A new universe of possibilities was forming, and with it was something Octavian had been sorely lacking, a sense of purpose.

He didn't know who this scientist was, how he would find their scattered fragments of essence, or what he'd do with them once he found them. But this mysterious scientist held the key to getting home, and that was reason enough for him.

Thank You For Reading!

I'm incredibly grateful for having a reader like you. I hope you enjoyed this story. Don't forget to leave a review online to help other readers find it, too. Reviews really help me out, even if they contain just a couple sentences.

Looking for more? Become part of the magic at my Magician's Club HQ. Join for free to get access to exclusive stories, regular updates, and behind-the-scenes peeks. Or upgrade to a premium plan for early access and additional rewards. New episodes are released regularly!

Sign up for the MCHQ at https://gaiusjaugustus.com/mchq/

Get 20% off premium plans with the code TOVYVOL1.

Want less frequent updates of my ongoings? Sign up for my newsletter at https://gaiusjaugustus.com/signup/

More From Gaius

Manifestation of Prophecy

Though they come from two vastly different realms, Maliah and Jarith are tied together by a prophecy that promises ascension after death. However, fate has a mischievous sense of humor, as Maliah must reluctantly embrace magical abilities she's afraid she can't control, while Jarith is burdened with an unthinkable task: murdering Maliah's mother.

Neither Maliah nor Jarith are keen to fulfill this prophecy. That is, until a formidable magician threatens their very existence, determined to halt the prophecy in its tracks. The weight of the world rests upon their shoulders, but is the future truly set in stone? In this quirky fantasy, the path set by destiny proves to be anything but straightforward.

Learn more at https://gjabooks.com/mani

Compendium

It's not called the multiverse for nothing! The Tales of a Vernian Youth Series spans time, space, and alternate realities, and there's a ton of information packed between the lines.

The best and brightest in the multiverse understand that the most powerful tool of the mind is reference. In the spirit of that mentality, this curated reference section provides you with additional information deemed important enough or enjoyable enough to enhance the reading experience.

Principles of Magic

Magic is a complex topic that requires either decades of study or a really trippy adventure through alternate realities. However, there are several core principles that are useful to remember.

1. Magic is the manipulation of something called the psyche particle field, which interacts with the physical world like a string interacts with the arms of a marionette. Therefore magicians do not directly affect the world; they indirectly affect the world through enacting changes on the psyche particle field.

2. A magician is only as powerful as their understanding of Nature, specifically their understanding of how the psyche particle field interacts with the world.

3. While a magician's status may indicate their level of skill, it in no way predicts how well they will respond to social pressure, temptation, or bad news.

General

Alternate Reality

Imagine a world where one event occurred differently than in your reality, and where that difference led to another difference until the differences snowballed into a world very different than the one you know and (arguably) enjoy. Speaking of snowballing, traveling between realities can feel like you've been hit with a snowball, and not the soft, fluffy kind.

Body Dysphoria

The distress a transgender person feels about their body, especially the discomfort with having a body that doesn't match their gender identity.

Elemental Marble

Elemental marbles hold magic programming that, when activated, create one sustained effect, usually the effect of an "elemental" nature such as fire, wind, or snow. Elemental marbles can actually be programmed for almost any singular purpose, but are limited to just the one. They are typically activated by introducing a crack in their surface, which is detected by the core and triggers the intended effect.

Gravity Mesh

A technique to visualize the effect of gravity on objects. The mesh appears like a grid that in a neutral environment is a flat plane. When objects are introduced, the mesh will bend to indicate a change in gravitational pull.

Hydrangea Effect: Magician's Eye Color Change

Named after a plant whose color changes based on the pH of its soil, the Hydrangea Effect describes the shift of a magician's eyes from their natural color to sparkling gold.

A magician's eye color has long been considered a sign of their competency. This is because as a magician's skill improves, their eyes begin to change. Gold flecks appear by the time a magician becomes comfortable sensing the dynamic flows of the psyche particle field. Most magicians finishing their undergraduate degree have a slim ring of gold at either the inner or outer edge of their irises. The ring expands as their skills improve.

Most lifelong magicians end up with golden irises at some point in their career. However, for Exalted Grand Magicians, the gold overtakes their pupils as well. Remarkably, this seems to have no impact on their vision. Aging magicians purchase reading glasses just as often as non-magicians, and no matter what the infomercials say, special lenses aren't needed to cancel out a golden glow.

Innate Magic

Innate magic refers to a person's ability to access the psyche particle field and manipulate it to affect the world without the in-depth knowledge commonly needed to master magic. In other words, a born magician, also called a natural magician.

Magic Essence

The state of the psyche particle field around a person is as unique as a fingerprint. This state is called a person's magic essence and is used in some technologies to identify a person who may, for example, be trying to enter a controlled-access laboratory building. Other uses include tracing the movement of perpetrators from a crime scene and triggering magic decorations when the birthday birl enters zir surprise party.

Marble Computers

Magic computers offer all the convenience of a computer with the superior processing and storage capacity that magic offers.

While older models had limited functionality, modern computers can do a seemingly endless number of things, including watching a cat video while recording a cat watching a cat video. Ah, the marvels of technology!

Multiple Realities Theory

Alternate realities are often thought of as branches of the same temporal path, similar to alternate timelines.

But what if we expand that idea a bit? Instead of saying every choice made is a binary yes or no, consider that with every choice, there is a field of probabilities which each possible choice can be mapped to.

Let's say you decide whether or not you take the bus to work on a certain day. There are theoretically alternate realities where either you take the bus or you do not, but these realities exist within a framework of how probable each is to happen.

Given that an infinite number of choices are being made at any given moment, and that those choices are the consequence of an infinite number of previous choices, the limits are endless. However, certain outcomes are more likely than others, thus some realities are more likely to exist than others.

The Multiple Realities Theory was the pet project of a scientist colleague of Teacher's. We don't know anything about this scientist, but we do know that the magical proof was completed before the scientist vanished without reason. And perhaps more importantly, Teacher had a friend? Mysterious, indeed!

Notebook

Notebook is the small marble Octavian wears around his neck and is his personal computer. He uses voice commands and a hologram user interface to do tasks such as recording experiments, organizing notes, sending and receiving messages, and probably watching cute cat videos.

Pressure Point

A pressure point is a magic rod that is placed between two surfaces and can transfer and sometimes amplify pressure between those surfaces, such that applying pressure to one surface directly applies pressure to another. A pressure point is a type of trap, classified as a trigger. It's probably best not to touch one unless you know what effect it will have.

Reality Tuner

The device used by Octavian to travel between realities. It's technically a magic computer, though its functionality has thus far been limited to thrusting the duo into a new alternate reality. How rude.

Replika's Power Core

Replika is the only robot in the Magic World with a perpetual power core, which pulls in energy from its surroundings. It does this by affecting the psyche particle field following a complex and boring mathematical formula.

The Sticky Door Formula

As part of an attempt to make the Society of Engineering and Technology Magicians (SETM) more approachable to both young people and big donors, SETM runs an annual contest creatively named Innovation in Engineering & Technology. One of the shining examples of innovation used by SETM to promote the competition is what has been dubbed the Sticky Door Formula.

A young contestant named Awaale Ali Omar submitted the idea to the Theoretical category, and its intended use was to estimate a component's maintenance cycle. The example used in his demonstration was a door that gets sticky over time.

Though across the world people made fun of the Sticky Door Formula, the Engineering & Technology community heralded the formula as ingenious. Awaale Ali Omar became instantly famous and went on to become a member of the International Council of Exalted Magicians, where he lorded his status and intelligence over others at every opportunity.

When he was diagnosed with a rare blood disease, he ignored doctor's recommendations for treatment and died within a year. He was survived by a daughter, Bilan, who was brilliant and kind and generally made up for all her father's trespasses, even though it wasn't her responsibility to do so.

Teacher's Handwriting

Teacher is a meticulous note taker and believes in keeping records that are legible, accurate, and as complete as possible. However, though he is quite verbose, he carries none of these traits into practice when under duress. Many of his notes have signs of a trembling hand, incomplete sentences, and a jumble of sometimes incoherent thoughts.

Sifting through the pleonasm is a task not to be taken lightly, especially if one is locked in a room with no windows, sustenance, or sense of place.

Time Magic

According to the International Council of Exalted Magicians, time magic is impossible. And there's no way the most powerful magicians in the Magic World would lie about something like that, right?

Traps (Locks & Triggers)

Traps are a specific class of magic, which are further classified into triggers and locks. Locks are intended to keep someone or something in or out, whereas triggers are intended to initiate a downstream effect. Triggers and locks are commonly found together in a single trap spell, and the quantity and variety of each will determine the complexity score assigned to the trap. Before attempting to manipulate a trap, a good magician will take a moment to determine its complexity score and, if possible, do an initial risk evaluation.

Science Behind the Magic

Hydrogen Bonds

Did you know that water is sticky? Well, it certainly likes to stick to itself. This is thanks to hydrogen bonds. Hydrogen bonds are weak bonds that water molecules form with each other. The oxygen atom of a water molecule is able to form these bonds with the hydrogen atom of two other water molecules. The resulting stickiness is why you can fill a glass slightly above the rim.

For magicians, hydrogen bonds come in handy whenever they need to manipulate water molecules. Though other techniques exist to control water, many experienced magicians choose to strengthen these bonds to more thoroughly remove water from places where dampness is unfavorable.

Magical Proof

A magical proof is a deductive argument for a magical spell, which shows that the stated assumptions logically guarantee the conclusion. Every magical spell requires a thorough understanding of the magical proof by the magician.

Psyche Particles

Psyche particles put the magic in . . . well, magic. The psyche particle field changes as the physical world changes, or more accurately, the physical world is tied to the laws of the psyche particle field. Therefore, when magicians affect the psyche particle field—which is much easier than affecting the physical world directly—they are able to manifest those changes in the physical world.

Magic World

Disciplines In The Study Of Magic

There are two disciplines in the study of magic: feminine and masculine. Despite the gendered names of these disciplines, both strive for a diverse range of gender expressions within their discipline. It is recommended to choose a discipline as early as possible.

Feminine Discipline

The feminine discipline is one of two branches of magical study in the Magic World. It's made up of four subdisciplines: traps, engineering & technology, history, and philosophy. You can recognize a student of the feminine discipline by their subdiscipline seals, which are typically cast in silver, nickel, or platinum.

International Council of Exalted Magicians (ICEM)

Magic has (arguably) been part of humanity since the dawn of time. While many seek to harness its power, the The International Council of Exalted Magicians (ICEM) is dedicated to understanding it.

ICEM is an organization dedicated to the excellence of magic research and practice throughout the Magic World. There are only 100 members worldwide, marking it as the most exclusive magic organization in the world. All members are required to pursue research in their field, but they must also keep a variety of secrets from trivial to profound. Through research and unyielding secrecy, the progress that the Magic World enjoys is thanks to this glorious organization. At least, that's what they say.

Members of the ICEM are nominated upon the death of any member. Typically, before their demise, an Exalted Grand Magician will announce their choice of successor. It's unknown exactly how the selection process works, but it is not up to a simple vote.

International Sign Language (ISL)

ISL was created hundreds of years ago by the deaf community after the first deaf magician, Exalted Grand Magician Aoife Phelan, was inducted into the International Council of Exalted Magicians. Before that, most deaf people used local forms of sign language to communicate. However, Exalted Grand Magician Phelan wished to unify the language. She brought together people from around the world, and together they created the first international sign language, which remained unchanged for over a hundred years.

As the world grew more interconnected, new language quickly made ISL out of date. To keep up, ICEM created an ISL committee dedicated to making sure the language was always hip to the latest jive.

Magician Ranks

Most magicians start as magic enthusiasts, excitedly digging into the history, principles, and disciplines of magic taught in primary school. These topics are covered at length despite the fact that most students will never actually practice magic.

The study of magic typically begins at the undergraduate level. While a student is in undergraduate coursework toward a degree in a magic discipline or if a magician stops at an Associate level degree, they are known as a Magician-In-Training. Upon graduating with an undergraduate degree in a magic discipline, a person will have the title of Magician. The title of Grand Magician is overseen by the International Council of Exalted Magicians and requires a series of skill- and knowledge-based tests. Similarly, the title of Exalted Grand Magician is presented to magicians who have the expert skill and knowledge expected by the ICEM. Obtaining the title typically also requires a physical exam, though it's unknown to the general population what criteria are being evaluated.

Masculine Discipline

The masculine discipline is one of two branches of magical study in the Magic World. It's made up of four subdisciplines: natural sciences, protection & healing, creative arts, and offense. You can recognize a student of the masculine discipline by their subdiscipline seals, which are typically cast in gold, bronze, or copper.

National University of Magic (NUM)

Despite its name, the National University of Magic is an international university with twenty-seven campuses worldwide. On one of these campuses, Octavian was training as a graduate student under the tutelage of Exalted Grand Magician Teacher when the trainee and his research project, the robot Replika, were sent on a one-way trip into an alternate reality.

NUM boasts the highest number of alumni to have gone on to be inducted into the International Council of Exalted Magicians and has won the prestigious Leader in Educational Excellence award for thirteen out of the last fifteen years. The administration would have you believe that the remaining two years were flukes.

Steampunk World

Elppa Pirates

A group of pirates led by Captain Egnaro. They often can be found ashore in Chronoford.

Silent People's World

Silent People

The inhabitants of the Silent People World, who are so silent that even their footsteps don't make noise.

Material World

Rainbow Stone
A stone with waves of multiple colors moving through it. It seems to have magical properties that may be useful at some point.

Progeny World

Glass Skybridge
Buildings throughout the dome are connected by a series of glass sky-bridges. These glass-lined hallways were designed by the dome builders to improve transportation between the various buildings. They could have made the order and frequency of these skybridges make some sense, but instead, they appear to be randomly scattered around. If there's some secret message embedded in their locations, it's been lost to time.

MID
Mobile interface device. These small, puck-shaped devices are Octavian and Replika's best means of communication. And when they leave the Progeny World, they'll make great paperweights.

Organics
Organic (with a capital O) is the name the Progeny use to refer to the humans who used to inhabit their world. This is not to be confused with organics (with a lowercase o), which refers to all organic life in their world. It may be confusing to outsiders, but somehow the Progeny are able to tell which they're referring to.

About the Author

Gaius (they/them) is a transgender, queer, disabled author who writes magical stories with diverse characters. In their work, they aim to convey immersive plots with unique worlds and irreverent humor. They have a distinctive background, going to university for film & television before later returning to school to complete a PhD in Cancer Biology. This colors their storytelling as they blur the boundaries of dichotomies such as magic & science, drama & humor, and good & evil.

Learn more about Gaius at gaiusjaugustus.com